Praise for John M. Green's novels:

'Australian thriller writing at its best.'
– ABC

'The twists hurtle in too fast for the reader to duck.'
– Jack Heath, award-winning author

'… moves at a cracking pace and is impossible to put down
… a compelling writer of master thrillers.'
– *The Australian Financial Review*

'… as good as John Grisham, Robert Ludlum, Lee Child
or Johnathan Kellerman … knife-edge plot, sophisticated
themes and empathetic characters put Green in the front
rank of Australian thriller writers.'
– *The Australian*

'It's no exaggeration to say John M. Green shines
as a very bright antipodean star in the international
firmament of thriller writers.'
– *The West Australian*

'An edge-of-your-seat action thriller that will keep you
guessing until the very last page.'
– *Good Reading*

FRAMED

Also by John M. Green

Nowhere Man
Born to Run
The Trusted
The Tao Deception
Double Deal

JOHN M. GREEN

FRAMED

PANTERA
PRESS

PANTERA
PRESS

This is a work of fiction. Names, characters, organisations, dialogue and incidents are either products of the author's imagination or are used fictitiously. Any resemblance to actual people, living or dead, animals, organisations, events or locales is coincidental, except for the dogs Biscotti Pippen (Scottie) and Winston Jr.

First published in 2022 by Pantera Press Pty Limited.
www. PanteraPress.com

A Cataloguing-in-Publication entry for this book is available from the National Library of Australia.

ISBN 978-0-6453508-1-4 (Paperback)
ISBN 978-0-6453508-2-1 (eBook)

Cover Design: Luke Causby, Blue Cork
Publisher: Katherine Hassett
Project Editor: Kirsty van der Veer
Editor: Sarina Rowell
Proofreader: Pam Dunne
Typesetting: Kirby Jones
Author Photo: Erica Murray
Printed and bound in Australia by McPherson's Printing Group

MIX
Paper from
responsible sources
FSC
www.fsc.org   FSC® C001695

The paper this book is printed on is certified against the Forest Stewardship Council® Standards. McPherson's Printing Group holds FSC® chain of custody certification SA-COC-005379. FSC® promotes environmentally responsible, socially beneficial and economically viable management of the world's forests.

To Scottie and Winston Jr,
and their owners

This is based on a true story …
… but most of it is yet to happen …

'Art is the lie that enables us to realise the truth.'
Pablo Picasso

THE GARDNER MUSEUM HEIST

From start to finish, the biggest art heist in modern history lasted just 81 minutes.

At 1.24 am on 18 March 1990, two men dressed as police officers walked into Boston's Isabella Stewart Gardner Museum. They overpowered two unsuspecting night security guards, then duct-taped their victims to a pipe and a workbench in the museum basement.

'Gentlemen, this is a robbery,' the criminals announced.

The pair proceeded to remove 13 treasured artworks on display in the lavishly decorated gallery, smashing the protective glass of two Rembrandt paintings and cutting the canvases from their gilded frames. Just over an hour later, the thieves made off with a staggering collection of art that's valued today at $500 million.

Despite a flurry of press attention – and the $10 million reward offered by the museum for the items' safe return – the stolen works have never been recovered.

Smithsonian Magazine, 9 April 2021

1

The Farrellys
Belfast, Northern Ireland
2015

C onor Farrelly hoisted both hands to hush the crowd, ignoring the wash of black Guinness he was sloshing over the top of his glass. Standing on top of the long bar, the nuggety entrepreneur surveyed the jam-packed pub, which overflowed with guests and an endless supply of beer. It was a perfect brew for the double celebration – his birthday and the twenty-fifth anniversary of the CCNN Group.

At sixty-six years old – one crucial six short of the devil's number – Conor had made himself into one of the wealthiest men in Northern Ireland. He started CCNN as a small freight operation, but his hard-scrabble drive

1

had grown it into a massive conglomerate that spanned international shipping, pharmaceutical production in India, and clothing manufacturing in Bangladesh. Despite this, Conor remained a man of the people, which was why the festivities were in a pub and not the ballroom of a five-star hotel.

'Niall!' he shouted over the heads of his guests. 'Git your arse up here, boyo.'

As the bald, muscled Goliath pushed his way through the crowd, Conor took a swig of Guinness to hoots and cheers. Niall got up on the bar and, towering over his father, was greeted with a hug, and another cheer. He had a shaved, oiled head and, like his father, his face had what the charitable would call *character*. This was mostly due to his large and flattened nose – a trophy from his teenage years, a brawl with the paramilitaries where a loyalist crushed it with a rifle butt.

'Nessa. You too!' roared Conor. For Nessa, the shouts and applause were deafening. As Niall sneered, the barkeep gave her some unnecessary help onto the countertop. She stood on the other side of her proud father, who downed the rest of his Guinness, put the glass on the countertop, and wrapped his arms around his children.

Nessa was the same height as her Terminator of a brother, but the similarity ended there. Apart from his pug nose and moustache, Niall's dark, round face was the spitting image of their late mother Ciara's, with the same brown eyes and pointy ears, and a cleft chin that on her was charming but which he was notorious for jabbing at people with 'Go on … Hit me, ya shite, and see what happens to ya.' Niall had his father's brawn but lacked his parents' and his sister's brains. He was a ticking time bomb with an explosive temper, no matter how much money Conor threw at anger management and every other kind of counselling.

Nessa was a taller, more willowy version of her stocky father, with fair skin and penetrating blue eyes. Her disarming heart-shaped face – capped with a mop of black hair so wild it made her seem easygoing – meant that most people severely underestimated her the first time they met.

Only Conor could read Nessa. It infuriated Niall that his father was more like his twin than he was, not only in looks but in temperament and intellect. He fumed when they finished each other's sentences or supported each other's ideas, but rarely his. Unlike Niall, who would blurt the first thought that popped into his head, Nessa took her time answering questions, often causing him to slam a fist on a table, or stamp his foot and charge out of a room. But Nessa could be as volatile as her brother when it suited her. It made for torrid family gatherings as well as board meetings since the three, after Ciara's death, were CCNN's only directors.

Conor could sense the tension mounting in Niall, so he pulled him closer, in a warning to behave, and pushed on with a shout, 'If you're enough lucky to be Irish … you're lucky enough.' The crowd erupted in roars of 'Dead on' and 'Too right'. Then Conor called out, 'Who ever thought the Farrellys would come this far?' Applause, shouts and stomping filled the pub.

Conor had come a long way indeed, but most of those present knew only a small part of it. The legal part.

Until the Good Friday Agreement in 1998 ended the Northern Ireland conflict, Conor was the Provisional Irish Republican Army's secret head of 'Transport', effectively in charge of its arms smuggling operations. Fundraising was also part of his job, although he wasn't collecting cheques at parties in tony New York City brownstones or Chicago town houses. Conor was an ambitious, small-time, down and dirty *gombeen*, who branched out into running drugs in London. That line of business, a sure-fire money-spinner, came with a handy sweetener … the corruption of British youth.

Only a few of those present were aware of the fraught circumstances of the twins' birth in Lisburn, a little southwest of Belfast. How Ciara's waters broke while she was driving getaway in a stolen Ford Escort van, just after Conor shot a British soldier in the face. She pulled over into a bombed factory and hopped into the back of the van, where Conor pushed aside the guns, Molotov cocktails and cans of petrol, and delivered their babies himself.

Scuttlebutt had raged for years that CCNN was involved in more than was publicly disclosed. Nothing was ever proved and it wasn't likely to be. Every time an allegation was printed in a media outlet, Conor would instantly swing out with a fierce right-hook libel suit that sent the proprietor and the offending journalist reeling. If it didn't, some of his 'boys' would pay a visit. As time wore on, the stories stopped. No one inclined to follow any leads was left standing. For good measure, Conor also maintained a close and cordial relationship with the local constabulary. Bygones, it seemed, were easily bought.

'Friends,' said Conor, holding up his glass again. 'A smart man goes before he loses it, so tonight I'm announcin' my retirement.'

The crowd, including Nessa and Niall, took in a sudden deep breath, like a single organism.

'My successor to take the reins as chief executive of CCNN is ...' and he turned briefly to Niall, who pasted an enormous smile on his enormous face, '... my daughter Nessa, and Niall here will be her deputy.'

Nessa flushed a deep red, and if Niall was a keg, he would have exploded. If it wasn't at first obvious to the audience that Conor hadn't discussed the plan with his family, it became crystal clear when the son threw off his father's arm, leapt off the bar, and shouldered his way through the crowd and out into the night.

2

My parents – Lauren and Hugh Jego – only had one clash in their twenty-seven years together, one that lasted their entire marriage.

After putting up with Hugh's ... well, Hugh's everything ... Lauren finally walked out on him. It was on 1 January 2014. *A new year and a new life*, I heard through her sobs when she phoned to tell me.

Yet, so soon after her 'liberation', as she called it, here we are in a hospital though, in her case, she's barely here.

Hugh, her husband – they never got divorced – isn't here.

Of course he's not.

6

Tears cascade down my cheeks, filling the dimple in my chin and dripping onto her pillow, grey splotches spreading across the white cotton. It's less than two years after they separated, and four months after she got the diagnosis … stage four pancreatic cancer.

Did Hugh come running, like any decent human being would? No. He didn't even contact her. Not even a measly text.

For twenty-seven years she'd been devoted to the prickly narcissist, giving up her career in fashion to pander to his every want. She cooked for him, cleaned up for him, cleaned up after him, and apologised for him when he offended people – which was most of the time. Yet, because *she* had the audacity to leave *him*, he snapped his fingers and magicked her into a nothing, a footnote in his history.

I can almost hear his thoughts. *How could she walk out on me, a genius who knows better than everybody else, God's gift to the police force?*

The truth is that Lauren was an angel to have stayed with Hugh so long. Some people would blame her for not leaving him earlier, but they hadn't spent decades as a victim of his vainglory and Machiavellian flair for manipulation. We both kidded ourselves that we went along with Hugh's wishes – a euphemism for 'demands' – out of love. There was some love, for sure, but mostly there was fear … a Mount Everest of fear, and we had no Sherpas to help us navigate it. There was no physical abuse. But if we'd known today's language for what Hugh put us through – coercive control, psychological trauma – both our lives might have been different. Better.

7

In my eighteen years under their roof, I struggled with what Hugh did to us. When mean kids at school found out he was a cop, they'd say, 'My dad can still beat up your dad,' and I'd clasp my hands and politely say, 'Please.'

To people who lived outside our suffocating four walls, Hugh was sweet and charming, kind of like Prince Harry before he met Meghan Markle. Eventually, though, if they committed the crime of laughing at the wrong time or daring to disagree with him over something – no matter how trivial – they'd watch his Mr Nice Guy mask drip away to reveal the trademark sneer my mother and I wished we'd never seen.

One time, a fellow detective came over for high tea, a speciality of Lauren's. She presented it on the faux Limoges china she'd bought at the op shop, and Hugh had made her pipe her famous cupcakes with icing that spelled our surname, *Jego*. When Hugh went to the bathroom and Lauren was in the kitchen, the detective, with a cheeky look, held up one of the cakes and told me my father's nickname at work, 'Huge Ego'. I laughed so much I got a stitch, though I made sure it wasn't loud enough for Hugh to hear me through the door.

In my last year at high school, Hugh went undercover and we didn't see him for months. Frankly, it was bliss at home, and probably the reason I blitzed the HSC and won a scholarship to art school. But when the operation was over, we found out he'd almost single-handedly broken up a notorious drug ring, which included senior police. The trials of Mr Big and Detective Inspector Bigger made front-page news for weeks. Hugh, referred to only as Witness G6, gave the crucial evidence that sent them all down but he had to do it from behind a screen, and Lauren and I were forbidden from telling a soul it was him. It was the first and only time I was actually proud of my father, and I had to bottle it up.

During the sting, he'd got hooked on crystal meth, and after the criminals were sent down, the force put him on extended leave and sent him to rehab. Hugh came home 'cured', but was even more insufferable than before, not least because he was denied the celebrity he so obviously craved.

The sad thing is that all that drama gave Lauren yet another reason to stay, even when I told her I was going. 'You go,' she said, meaning it. 'But how can I leave him after what the poor man's put himself through?'

Me, though, I slammed the door on Hugh as soon as I finished my final exams and, apart from a chance run-in – at the National Gallery in Canberra in 2010 – I haven't seen him since.

*

'We've just landed in Sydney,' I whispered to the nurse an hour ago, surreptitiously, under my sweater. It was before the cabin crew announced we were free to use our phones.

Being sneaky while crammed in economy – or coach or tourist, or whatever the back of the plane is called these days – isn't easy. Especially when you're in the centre seat of three, with a hulk of a man on one side, so well upholstered I couldn't see the window past him even if I leaned forward. On my other side, a tall, gawky teenager who was so sprawly that 'shared armrest' clearly meant 'his'.

Because of my mother's decline, I'd actually said no to this work trip, a four-day Van Gogh conference in

Amsterdam – all expenses paid by my employer, the Art Gallery of New South Wales – but she'd insisted. 'It's good for your career and, besides, you'll only be gone a week.' The hospital staff had told me she was stable, that it was safe to go, and promised to call me if anything changed.

That happened yesterday, on day two of the conference, right in the middle of an eye-opening talk by an Italian expert, Francesca Rossi, on 'The Degradation Process of Chrome Yellow in Paintings by Vincent van Gogh Studied by Means of Synchrotron X-ray Spectromicroscopy'. After quietly apologising to everyone around me, I ran out of the conference room, grabbed my bag from the hotel, leapt into a cab and changed my return flight as we sped to Schiphol Airport.

'Thank heavens you've made it home,' said the nurse. 'Come straight to the hospital. No detours. Do you understand what I'm telling you, JJ?'

*

Everyone calls me JJ. It's short for Justine Jego, pronounced Jaygo. This is because, four generations ago, it was Jégo when our people lived in Arles, in the south of France. Hugh bestowed my full name on me, in all its toe-curling glory. Needless to say, he put it on my birth certificate without asking Mum.

The only times I'd be willing to give my full name to anyone is if I was being waterboarded or if I've got to comply with some government requirement, which can be much the same thing. I got more than a lifetime's ribbing in Year 3 after my teacher, Miss Fox, asked about it in front of the whole class. 'Justine Vincent van Gogh Jego. That's a fascinating name, JJ. Can you tell us about it?'

I shrank into my seat, making myself even smaller than I was.

It's why I've gone with JJ my whole life. Even – or especially – in my career as an art conservator, I've concealed my full name better than Caravaggio's miniature self-portrait in his painting *Bacchus*. That's the one he camouflaged in a carafe that virtually every art teacher makes a big song and dance about revealing to newbies in Art History 101.

I raced off the plane, and charged through the airport to the taxi rank as fast as my short legs, cabin-sized wheelie bag, ever-present camera flying on its strap behind me, and border control protocols allowed.

Carrying an almost empty Australian passport helped. No stamps from Syria, Somalia or any hotspots and just the two for Amsterdam, three years apart. From my passport photo, or even in real life, people would probably say I'm pretty average looking. That's if you ignore my flaming red hair and my lack of height. I come in at five foot, child inches. Kind of like Lady Gaga in a red wig, but without her heels, looks or talent.

Hugh used to tell me I was so small that if I'd been born in winter I wouldn't have made it through. He frequently saddled me with reminders like 'Tiny silhouette, tiny brain,' even before I knew what a silhouette was. Poring through a dictionary to find out was no easy feat for a dyslexic, making it even easier for Hugh to enjoy 'proving' his put-downs.

Dyslexia did have a good side. While reading is tough for me, even today – thank heavens for audiobooks and text-to-speech buttons – images have always come easily. Hence, art became my refuge. Initially, my passion was for photography. Ultimately, it led to my job as a conservator.

Unsurprisingly, given our family's Van Gogh connection, my love of art was the one thing about me that Hugh was happy about. His full name is similar to mine – Hugh Vincent van Gogh Jego – but, unlike me, he boasts about it. *Yes*, I can still hear him intoning on automatic pilot, *I am indeed related to the great artist. I'm his great-grandson, actually.*

Sometimes he'd add, *And see my red hair, and my daughter's? Just like Vincent's.*

As if our hair colour proves a thing, especially when a cousin on my mother's side has red hair too.

Hugh's greatest frustration is that his – our – lineage is unacknowledged. There's not a single mention of any Jego, or Jégo, in the official Van Gogh family history, and the recognised relatives, all descendants of Vincent's brother Theo, won't engage on it.

Hugh used to write to them, initially via the Van Gogh Museum in Amsterdam which houses the works the family transferred to the state-sponsored Vincent van Gogh Foundation. It's where I did a secondment four years ago, and where I went for the conference and, no, I didn't reveal my full name on either occasion.

Hugh wrote to them every year on the anniversary of Vincent's death. Always the same letter. *If you really want to honour Vincent, you'll arrange for one of his brother Theo's descendants to join me in a DNA test. That will prove we're related.*

They did respond once, years ago, offering to take the test but on the strict condition that Hugh first sign away any claims we had on the Van Gogh estate. He was incensed and, when I got old enough to understand, it was one of the few times I was on his side. Given our Jego family folklore, why should we give up our rights?

Over the years, there's been all sorts of speculation as to why, on 23 December 1888, Vincent went nuts and sliced off the lower part of his left ear with a razor. There's a book about it called *Van Gogh's Ear: The True Story*, except it isn't the true story.

The *real* true story – so says our family – is that he only did it after my great-great-grandmother, Madame Marie Claire Jégo, a married and generally respectable woman in Arles, popped by the Yellow House, where Vincent lived, and revealed that she was pregnant.

To him.

A child was the last thing the penniless artist with a precarious mental condition wanted. Hence the ear, and the stint in the asylum that came soon afterwards.

Eighteen months later, in July 1890, when Vincent got a letter from Marie Claire telling him about their little boy, he shot himself. He died two days later.

Vincent is renowned not only as a brilliant artist but also a prolific letter writer. So, when Hugh told people our story, they'd often ask how it was possible that not a single one of the hundreds of letters Vincent wrote to Theo made even a fleeting reference to Marie Claire Jégo or their baby. And it's true … they don't. I'm so sure of it because when I did my Amsterdam secondment, I had access to the digitised files – before the letters were posted on the website – and I did a Google search trawling for even the barest mention.

According to Hugh, and his father before him, there were indeed letters between the Van Gogh brothers that referred to the pregnancy and the baby, and also letters between Vincent and Marie Claire. But after Vincent's death, and Theo's own death six months later, from syphilis, Theo's widow began to champion Vincent's work. The idea that Vincent had an heir, let alone one who might make a claim on his estate, did not suit the narrative she spent the rest of her life spinning. She got Marie Claire to sign, in today's parlance, a blatant gag agreement. She paid her off, buying both her silence *and* her letters. She then burned every letter, Marie Claire's, Vincent's and Theo's, that referred to the affair or to the baby.

Hugh gets enraged every time he tells the story. Me, while I understand how he feels, I'm relaxed about it. History is messy.

*

What I'm not okay with – and never will be – is how Hugh treated my mother.

Lauren's hand stirs inside mine, and I squeeze it gingerly. 'JJ,' she croaks, 'Promise me one thing.'

I move in closer, my forehead lightly kissing hers.

'Anything,' I tell her.

'Promise me you won't let your father come to my funeral.'

3

Claude Fontaine
Monte Carlo, Monaco
2020

The penthouse-floor boardroom at the law offices of Fontaine & Fontaine was big enough to house two squash courts and, once, it did. That was before the firm's founder, Jacques Fontaine, bought the whole building, gutted it and, on this floor, tore down the exterior wall to install a metres-long floor-to-ceiling window.

Jacques had a good eye for value. He knew back then that opening up his main conference room to this postcard-perfect view over the famous Port Hercules marina and the Monaco Grand Prix finish line meant he would more easily get away with whacking big premiums on top of his firm's already stratospheric fees. The squash courts' hardwood floor became plush beige carpet, and he made the new boardroom grand enough to house a huge single-slab table of pink Italian marble and thirty capacious black-leather-backed armchairs spread around it.

Despite the steep outlay, the office had barely been used in the past few months. Even today only a skeleton staff were in, the majority teleworking from wherever. One partner, for example, picked up sticks as soon as Covid-19 struck and moved his family to their holiday house in Malta. He hadn't left the island since. Whenever Claude Fontaine, Jacques' only child and his successor as senior partner, asked the émigré how he was doing, he'd say, 'Time simply Zooms by.' Claude was growing to despise him.

The good news was that Monaco's lockdowns and curfews had ended, at least for now, though the principality was still cautious, mandating masks in public and social distancing in private.

Claude, the newly minted senior partner, the '& Fontaine' in the logo screwed into the wall, was one of the handful who still came into the office every day. This practice felt crucial now that Jacques, until recently a towering presence, could no longer manage it.

It was the tail end of Claude's first week as senior partner. Jacques' incipient dementia and his increasingly frequent episodes of forgetfulness and awkward, random spouting of client business had reached the point where the other partners gave Claude an ultimatum … either step into Jacques' shoes, and sit at his desk, take over his clients and send him where he could do no harm, or they'd quit. Claude had no choice, so Jacques was now at home, cared for by the same round-the-clock team who had looked after his late wife Gisèle during her own decline.

It was a sad ending for Jacques. Under his leadership and with Claude's support, Fontaine & Fontaine had grown into a full-service firm that quietly boasted a client list of some of the world's super-rich … tech magnates, private equity tycoons, and two famously competitive global media moguls, who, to Claude's surprise, were as chummy as a pair of Speedos when they'd once sat together in this boardroom. While the firm's clients were a veritable *Who's Who* of the rich and famous, Jacques had drawn the line at Russian oligarchs. Not one had ever darkened the firm's doors.

Jacques had started the firm in a shoebox of an office, doing 'international tax planning and corporate administration' for his very first client, Conor Farrelly. In the more freewheeling 1990s, tax planning and administration were code for plain and simple tax avoidance or, without the sugar-coating, tax fraud. Today, Fontaines still did tax law – what firm in Monaco didn't? – but the work also spanned contracts, construction, finance, corporate law, intellectual property and more.

The Fontaine and Farrelly families had risen together, though Jacques always kept CCNN's work close to his chest, and the Farrellys themselves even closer. Jacques had never introduced Claude – or any other partner – to Conor before he died. He also hadn't introduced anyone from Fontaines to Conor's successors, not that Claude minded. There were plenty of other clients to look after and, besides, with the Farrellys regularly delivering twenty per cent of the firm's billings via Jacques, Claude and the other partners felt he could do what he liked.

Now, though, Nessa and Niall, the thirty-five-year-old Farrelly heirs, had flown in from Belfast with no warning. Given the Jacques situation, Claude was intent on giving full attention to the twins whether they had an appointment or not.

Nessa's suit, the lawyer observed, didn't scream money like the clothes of some of their other clients, who wanted everyone to see how rich they were, even from a distance. It was a no-nonsense elegant trouser suit, grey compared to Claude's black though with no collared shirt, instead with a white silk blouse. Nessa's outfit plus her hair, black and shiny but unkempt, suggested a woman who was practical and direct.

The receptionist indicated for the Farrellys to take their seats on the 'good' side of the boardroom table, where clients always sat opposite their lawyers. Ostensibly, it was so they'd enjoy the panoramic view, but it was also to bring the light streaming into their eyes so the lawyers would have the advantage. As Nessa brushed past, a head taller than the lawyer and literally looking down her nose, Claude could almost smell the woman's disdain.

Niall came across as a rough, nasty piece of work, equally tall but a muscled skinhead. A pumper of steroids as much as iron, Claude thought and, without knowing much Irish, the word *gobshite* came to mind. Niall swaggered to his seat in his *I don't give a crap* clothing, a pair of ripped-knee blue jeans, and a loose-fitting, distressed black leather jacket over a too-tight white T-shirt, with loud fluoro-green Nikes on his feet.

Claude intuited that while Niall was trouble, it was super-cool Nessa who was the one to watch out for. Niall might throw the punches but she'd be the one to land them.

As soon as Niall sat down, he put his Ray-Bans on and, before Claude could utter a word, said, 'You could start off by thankin' us Farrellys for payin' for a fair whack of your feckin' view.'

Claude knew not to respond. Niall looked down at his hands, picked dirt from under his fingernails and flicked it onto the table. Nessa reached over to push her brother's hands into his lap, where Claude couldn't see them.

'Claude,' Niall said, looking up again. 'What kind of name is that?'

'Huh?' the lawyer blurted.

'Enough, Niall,' said Nessa. To Claude, she said, 'Your father knows everythin' about our business affairs … feckin' everythin'. What we conduct through CCNN and the stuff we do, you know, outside of it.'

'And?' said Claude, ambiguously but with a smile the lawyer hoped covered up a total ignorance of what they were talking about. Over the years, there had been rumours of underworld connections, but Jacques swore he knew nothing about them and only did legit work for legit clients.

'*And?* you say,' Niall shot back. 'Nice one, Claude. We Farrellys have done a lot of business with your old man Jacko, and that "retirement" bullshit you wrote us about in your "Dear Sir/Madam" form letter – when you shoulda picked up the feckin' phone – that don't cut it with us.'

A word like feck – let alone fuck – was a rarity in the hallowed halls of Fontaine & Fontaine, yet in their first minute there Niall and Nessa were brandishing it like a fist. Claude wanted to give them a disgusted stare but was smart enough to blink it away.

'Way we hear it,' Niall continued, 'your Jacko's eejit mouth been spoutin' stuff it shouldna to people who shouldna be hearin' it.'

19

Sadly, Claude knew what he was saying was true. Jacques' decay had accelerated rapidly. Only yesterday, when Jacques was speaking to his chief nurse at home, he called her by the first name of another significant client — a household-name tech multibillionaire — and started revealing details of how they'd shifted profits tax-free through Nevis in the Caribbean, back through Bermuda and, finally, through Lichtenstein to Ireland. It was all perfectly legal but if it got into the public domain or leaked like the Panama Papers did, the anti-corporate activists would have a field day.

'Old Jacko's loose lips worry the shite out of us, and the Farrellys don't like worryin'.'

Nessa cut in. 'You don't have a clue what Niall's talkin' about, do you? Jacques never tell you about our, em, shadow business?'

'For sure he didn't, Nessie,' said Niall. 'He weren't meant to tell no one.'

The 5000-euro ergonomic leather chair Claude was sitting on suddenly felt like it was embedded with razor blades. *This 'shadow' business? Is that a euphemism for shady or criminal?*

If, as Claude suspected, the Farrellys were embroiled in truly nefarious activities and Jacques knew about them, or worse, facilitated them, it could destroy the firm. Claude knew to remain in a state of ignorance, not a totally foreign situation for a lawyer. That way, a dose of plausible deniability mixed with a timely shot of shock might just save the day.

Claude's doomsday thoughts got interrupted when Niall, clearly sick of waiting for a response to Nessa's question, said, 'We got lawyer–client privilege here, don't we? You know … like, what happens in Vegas stays in Vegas?'

Claude nodded, even though the proposition was only partially correct. Client privilege did not protect communications when they facilitated the commission of a crime or, as the lawyer was starting to suspect, crimes. Claude knew Niall would not want to hear that, so stayed silent.

Nessa stood up and strutted around the table, almost pressing herself up to the glass and looking out at the panorama, forcing Claude to swing around in the chair. The Mediterranean's languid late afternoon sun was spilling into the room low and long, yet strongly enough to light up the sparkles scattered through Nessa's wild black hair. Claude hadn't noticed them before. Ms Farrelly wasn't as understated a woman as Fontaine had first thought.

'Those yachts out there,' said Nessa, looking out over the harbour. 'One of them yours?'

No was the strictly correct but misleading answer. Claude didn't own a yacht anywhere. But Jacques' pride and joy — redefining ostentation as an understatement — was indeed berthed at the exclusive Yacht Club de Monaco nearby. It was a forty-five-metre super yacht that when Jacques wasn't using her for client entertainment, was chartered out at 170,000 euros a week in the high season. Instead of answering, Claude stared at the back of Nessa's head and said, 'You didn't travel all the way here to discuss boats.'

Nessa swivelled around on her heels and held Claude's gaze, sizing up the firm's senior partner for what seemed an hour but was less than a minute. 'So the lawyer *can* speak. How about that, Niall?' she said eventually. 'And wow! Froggie's got a big plummy English accent. Daddy sent you to boarding school in Old Blighty, did he?' It was true. 'But who gives a shite about that,' Nessa continued, sitting back in her seat. 'You're right. We didn't come here to talk boats. We're here to talk about art.'

4

Monaco's Freeport – a tax-free storage facility – was where numerous Fontaines clients stored valuables or papers for safekeeping. Some did it to protect big-ticket artworks, jewellery or secret documents from the grabby clutches of disgruntled ex-wives or husbands, tax authorities or foreign governments. For them, the Freeport was a highly effective Harry Potter invisibility cloak.

The value of the artworks the Farrellys stored in the Monaco Freeport was eye-watering. According to Nessa, it was easily 600 million US dollars. According to Niall, it was closer to a billion.

If that news wasn't enough to throw Claude as they sat in the boardroom, there was the twins' startling revelation about Jacques. For decades, he'd been operating as both a custodian of the Farrellys' artworks and their trusted middleman in what Nessa brazenly called 'our more unorthodox transactions'.

'These deals can be extremely lucrative, Claude,' she said. 'But making money costs money and findin' the readies to pay our suppliers upfront for their, em, product isn't always a viable option … You know, cash flow an' all that.'

'What products do you—?'

Nessa stopped the lawyer short. 'First our *dadaí* and now us have built up a big bank of trust with our suppliers, which means that all our deals are BNPL. You know, buy now, pay later. They sell us a shipment of product wholesale, and we go on and sell it retail. We only need to pay what we owe 'em once we've sold it through our network.'

'How big are these deals?' asked Claude, not really wanting to know.

'Our last deal? What was it, Niall?'

'Wholesale price, fifty. Street value, two hundred. After expenses, a net to us of seventy.'

'That's millions? Millions of dollars?'

'Right,' said Nessa. 'But because we're not tradin' in fridges, our suppliers take a temporary mortgage over our art … It's to guarantee that we'll pay 'em.'

'How does that work?'

'How do we feckin' know?' said Niall. 'Your Jacko set up all the paperwork, so go ask 'im. Oh, I forgot, he's gone a bit gaga, right?'

Nessa put her hand on her brother's arm. 'Jacques writes up a bill of sale over our stash – the art, I mean – and he holds it in trust for our supplier. When we pay 'em out of our profits, he tears it up and the art's all ours again, free and clear to pledge for the next deal.'

'It's like that song the little kids sing,' said Niall. '*The wheels on the bus go round an' round, round an' round, round an' round.* A feckin' beautiful arrangement.'

'Jacques stands between the parties?' Claude asked.

'Exactly. He's made hisself quite the trusted intermediary in our circles.'

'And if you don't pay your supplier?' Claude was getting paranoid.

'Don't worry. The Farrellys always pay,' said Nessa. 'In our world, renegin' on one of our suppliers would be a life-changin' event, if you catch my drift. Life-changin' for us, probably not for Jacques … or you.'

Probably. Claude's mind was screaming the f-word over and over. The Farrellys' art was stolen – it had to be – and they were using it to finance what …? Drugs? Arms? People smuggling? All the above?

Worse – way, way worse – Jacques was more than aware of it, he was the key to making it happen.

The Farrellys were undoubtedly revealing all this because they wanted something, and it – whatever it was – was scaring the hell out of Claude.

5

To buy time, Claude pressed the host's call button that was screwed into the underside of the marble, a handy device Jacques had installed during the office fit-out.

Seconds later, a waiter in a black tux and white gloves knocked and entered. 'Tea? Coffee? Cakes?' he asked, the words slightly muffled behind his white face mask with a black F&F logo. '*Monsieur et mademoiselle*, our chef bakes the best *galapian* in the whole of Monaco.'

While the attendant had the clients' attention, Claude shot Madame Pasquier a quick text message. *TEXT ME WHAT I NEED TO KNOW ABOUT JACQUES' FREEPORT VAULT DEALS FOR THESE CLIENTS.*

The elderly woman, whose desk was not far from the

boardroom, was always Madame Pasquier to Claude, though when she was out of earshot the associates called her 'Blingette'. Widely regarded as the firm's good luck charm, she had so much jewellery clanking on her wrists and off her earlobes that she was a waddling carillon, though she carried it off with panache. That she could manage to type a letter or bring in a file seemed an impossible feat, let alone raising her hand to touch up her lipstick, which she seemed to be doing every time Claude walked past her desk.

'I know you frogs eat horse,' Niall told the waiter, 'but what the feck's a *gallopin'*? Horse hoof on toast?'

'M. Farrelly,' said the waiter, 'it is a sweet tart. Cantaloupe, cherry and almond glazed with honey. They really are to die for,' he added, words Claude would have preferred he hadn't used in this company.

The phone vibrated. Claude looked down to read a reply, of sorts, from Madame Pasquier. *JACQUES NEVER PUTS ANYTHING ABOUT THE VAULT IN WRITING.*

The phrase *perverting the course of justice* flew into Claude's head and couldn't be shaken out. What had the Farrellys done to Jacques? Claude had always known him to be principled, ethical, incorruptible. Was that not the case, or was there an explanation for why Jacques might have crossed a line he'd always told every member of the firm to stay on the right side of?

Claude deleted both messages, and decided to get Madame Pasquier to do likewise on her phone once the Farrellys had left. It was a deceit the goody-two-shoes lawyer would never have contemplated until now.

The waiter took the clients' orders and left. Claude's was always the same … a double-strength macchiato with

27

a dollop of extra froth on top, and a side of iced water with a zest of lemon, although right now the double shot Claude really needed was scotch or vodka.

'So,' said Niall, 'about those text messages of yours with old Blingette out there—'

'What?' said Claude, so stunned that the phone slipped and fell to the floor. 'How did—'

Niall raised an eyebrow behind his Ray-Bans at the same time he lifted up his own phone. Even from across the table, Claude could see Niall's screen. Both the initial message and Madame Pasquier's reply were embarrassingly visible, neither text having been deleted.

Nessa tossed back her shock of hair and sneered. 'Silly thing to do when you're in the presence of the world master of man-in-the-middle.'

Niall took off his sunglasses, placed them on the boardroom table and stared creepily into Claude's eyes. 'There's nothin' I love more than bein' the man in the middle, if you get my drift.'

'*Niall!* Just show the fecker.'

He shrugged off his sister's words and pulled a small device out of his jacket, a black box with three short, thick antennas sticking up from the sides. 'This little baby squeezes Nessa and me into the airspace between your phone and the local cell tower. Whatever you type on your phone goes through us, so we can read it on our phones. What you receive, we get to read too. What you speak, we hear. It's pretty dope, eh?'

'That's ... that's illegal. You can't ... I'm going to call—'

'We can, we are and you won't,' Niall laughed.

'Niall's a thousand per cent right about that, counsellor. You're callin' nobody no time. Sure this is illegal, but what's a felony or two between friends, eh? Especially when your precious *dadaí*'s been committin' lots of them for us all these years. You're dyin' to know why we're here, right? Because, dear Claude, today's your lucky day. Today's the day that you really step into your *dadaí*'s shoes. You, my friend, you are our new Jacques.'

Claude was momentarily stuck for words. 'You can't just burst in here and—'

Niall slammed his hand on the table. 'Are you feckin' listenin'? We feckin' well can and we feckin' well did.'

'Claude. It's simple, really,' said Nessa, her voice low and purposeful, her eyes locking onto their lawyer's. 'We Farrellys have owned your father and his firm for years, he just couldn't tell you. Now he's passed the firm on to you, we own you too. So, Claude Fontaine, senior partner, from this moment on you will do exactly what we tell you when we tell you, no questions asked. Just like your good father did before he … you know.'

'If I don't?'

'A great question that gets you the same answer our late *dadaí* gave your *dadaí* when he asked it,' said Niall, 'except for swappin' the names around. If you do what the Farrellys want, you and your firm continue to make lots of dosh and, on top of that, you and your *dadaí* get to live long and fruitful lives. Maybe not so much Jacko anymore. But if you screw with us …'

'Claude, you're askin' yourself why your dear old *dadaí* did all of this for us,' said Nessa. 'It's simple, really. He wanted to save his wife and, with her gone – the light of God on her dear departed soul – he wanted to save you, his heir. So now it's your turn to return the favour, if you get our drift. Niall, I believe we're done here,' she finished and started walking to the door. 'We have a plane to catch.'

'I'm the pilot,' said Niall, winking at Claude as he pocketed the hacking device and his sunglasses, got up and followed his sister out.

6

JJ
Sydney
2020

How long is this Covid thing going to last? The state government's just extended Greater Sydney's lockdown, again, so we're all still working from home. WFH is 2020's new buzzword, not that it's a word and, in my opinion, it shouldn't be a thing either, not for people in my line of work anyway.

It might be fine for people in admin, like Goldberg, my friend at work … people whose job is to spend their whole day tapping away at their computers. But how's an art conservator supposed to repair a tear in a Sidney Nolan or clean off the varnish on a Grace Cossington Smith when those works can't leave the gallery, and I'm stuck inside my

31

poky studio apartment twiddling my thumbs, too scared to go out because some mad jogger will breathe all over me, or someone will attack me in the supermarket because I nabbed the last roll of toilet paper?

And what about these virtual video meetings, where we're all little squares, waving at each other and trying to talk at the same time with the wi-fi cutting in and out? How long are we going to be doing that? It's four months so far.

My phone rings where I left it, over on the kitchen counter. It's probably work calling to tell me I'm being furloughed, a word I'd only ever heard in American war movies until now. Not being a big reader – dyslexia! – and with less experience of life than other people my age, movies and TV shows are a bit of a thing with me, a crutch. If I'm nervous, that's where I'll often turn – the older, the more comforting.

I let the phone ring out, to delay the inevitable. Maybe I'll pretend I never got the call.

I hear a beep, so it must have gone to voicemail. I get up to listen to the bad news, and even before I press *play* I know it's worse than I thought.

It *wasn't* work calling.

It was Hugh. His number is still in my contacts.

We haven't spoken since Mum died. The man hasn't even sent me a single birthday or Christmas card. In truth, I haven't sent him any either.

I haven't sent him any Father's Day cards either. I mean, what would they say?

Dear Dad, thanks for all your support. No way.

You were there with me when I needed you the most. Not that either.

I wouldn't be who I am without you, which is true but in this case it's not a compliment.

Ours is a love that leaves nothing unsaid because there's nothing to say.

Yet, out of the blue, Hugh decides on a whim that he's going to crash back into my life.

At first, I don't listen to the message. I'm fuming over him invading my space – what little I have.

Ignoring him – which makes me feel marginally better – I make myself a cup of coffee. It's coffee in name only, since it's instant, just like Hugh's not really a father. I sit back down with my mug and log in to Netflix, deciding I better get as much of it in as I can before I lose my job and can't afford the subscription.

But later, as the end credits roll on *Schitt's Creek*, I pick up the phone, grit my teeth and play the message.

Ah, JJ … hey … hello. Hi. It's me. Hugh, I mean. Your father. But you know that. Obviously. I'm, ah, ringing because … well … I want to apologise. Need to apologise, really. Since we last … you know … saw each other, a lot's happened. I've changed. I've really changed. I'm sure you won't believe that but … Anyway, if you're willing to meet me, I'd like to try and clean our slate …

I hear a woman's voice in the background. *Go on, tell her. Explain.*

I throw the phone at the sofa, pick up the remote and settle down to watch the next episode of *Schitt's Creek*. It's called 'Rebound'.

7

JJ
The present day

The pandemic is now a tragic, lingering memory. We've all got stories, but my mother's great-aunt Felicia … I still can't talk about her story.

For a while now, for most of us, life has got pretty much back to normal, though a different normal, to be sure. My current normal is a lot different from my old normal, hence my smile stretching ear to ear. For starters, it's because I'm in command of this swanky motor yacht … I'm sitting on it right now. And I'm living in the ritzy apartment that comes with it. Or is it the other way round?

In command is a bit of an overstatement. It doesn't mean I'm actually at the helm and steering the boat. Truth be told, my captaincy hasn't moved us an inch off the marina berth. This is the first time I've been on a boat that isn't a ferry, and the only thing I'm really in command of is the vodka and tonic I'm drinking while I'm sitting up on the flybridge and taking photos of the sunset, so I can post the best one on my Instagram later. I'm pretty good at Instagram. While I don't have a zillion followers – not even close – my numbers are slowly building. Same with my views on TikTok.

Taking shots while my bare toes are being licked and tickled is a weird new experience. But that's Biscotti Pippen, or Scottie, for you. He's named after some American basketballer who played with Michael Jordan, apparently. Him I've heard of. Scottie's the third of my short-term charges. Like the boat, he comes with the apartment I'm house-sitting. Scottie's a black-haired two-year-old lurcher, a term for a greyhound–whippet–collie cross I'd never heard of until a week ago.

The final rays of the summer sun are raking down over the hillside onto my face from Mrs Macquarie's Point, the peninsula across the other side of the narrow slip of Woolloomooloo Bay that's right in front of me. With my second V&T slipping me into chill mode, I gently place my camera beside me on the soft white leather captain's chair I'm slowly sinking into. My camera is Sony's latest digital powerhouse – an Alpha. With all the lenses a budding camera queen would ever need, it was my early Christmas present to myself. I saved for years to buy it.

Saving isn't so hard if you kept your job during Covid, like I did, with my everlasting thanks to the Art Gallery of New South Wales. For two years, I had pretty much nothing to spend my money on. Even if I was big on socialising, which I'm not, there were no concerts, shows, restaurants, vacations. Pretty much just Netflix and books though, in my case, audiobooks.

Still, shelling out thousands for a camera was not a big leap for me. Most people don't get it, thinking photography is game over because the lenses on their smartphone are a zillion times better than the one on the box that used to swing off their wrists for taking holiday snaps. *Who needs a real camera?* they say.

Photographers, I reply. People like me.

Of course this isn't my first camera. That one was second-hand. My mother put money aside out of her housekeeping allowance to buy me a used Pentax MZ-5 single lens reflex 35mm film camera for my thirteenth birthday. I loved that camera but we had to keep it hidden from Hugh, or he would've gone ballistic – at her for buying it, and at me for taking my focus off all things Van Gogh.

My new baby is by far my best. It comes with a 50-megapixel sensor. *Fifty!* It can capture bursts of images at thirty frames per second and record 8K video. The autofocus – a feature that previously I scoffed at – does stuff I don't pretend to understand. Its machine-learning algorithms – whatever they are – can pick out faces and eyes over a huge distance, *and* in the dark. Watch out, David Attenborough, I'm coming for you.

As well as 35mm, 50mm and 85mm lenses, I splashed out on a 70-300mm zoom, though what the camera store called *lightweight* doesn't reflect how my triceps experience it. After taking as many shots as I have, I reckon I'll never need to lift weights again.

I'm pretty sure that carrying the gear around so often has given me a shoulder lean. But that's a price worth paying. *You've got to be ready at all times*, say the super-famous photographers. I've listened to all the audiobooks of their memoirs and biographies. *You never know when the frame that'll make your reputation is going to pop up in front of you.* Imagine Max Dupain walking along the sand at Culburra Beach and the *Sunbaker* guy is laying there, but Max didn't have his camera. A disaster!

That said, even photographers need some shut-eye. I close my lids and lean back, letting the leather embrace me as the incoming tide rocks the boat with a motion that normally would be pacifying but is making me a little woozy. It's probably the vodka.

It's been a hot Sydney summer evening so far. It's just me and Scottie on the upper deck of this gleaming white fifty-foot cruiser. I can feel the sun that's slipping behind the trees on the hill opposite, and the sky – when I last looked – was going out in a blaze of oranges and pinks and reds that I got about a hundred shots of. *Where would you rather be?*

After three evenings of this bliss, and with three or four more weeks of it coming, I've begun to live with the cringeworthy name that's slapped on the boat's sides and stern, where everyone can gawk at it.

Seaduction.

Imagine painting that on the hull of your two-million-dollar boat. Picture the guy who owns her, arm-in-arm with a woman he's met on a dating app. *You've got to be kidding,* she says when she sees the name. *Aw, come on,* he says, giving her a cheeky smile and a nudge. *It's just a joke, and your profile says you've got a sense of humour, right?* Hopefully, she turns on her heels and leaves.

This being my third time on the boat, I've allayed my paranoia about what boardwalk strollers think when they spot me basking on the flybridge of *Sea*-bloody-*duction*.

I'm in my best white Kmart shorts, and a new T-shirt, also white, though I'm sweating through it from too much sun and alcohol. Even though I was told I can, I haven't touched the boat's bar cabinet. My vodka comes from Clint Eastwood's older brother – the grumpy codger at the bottle-o down the road.

I'm intent on keeping the vow I made to myself … to come aboard every evening after work, weather permitting, take photographs and luxuriously sip a V&T – or two – as the sun goes down. Being surrounded by paintings and sculptures all day inspires my photography and, despite my misgivings, it's given me pretty grand ambitions. Not that I've told anyone. Well, I've told Goldberg. He's in admin at the gallery. He asked *Why photography?* given my career involves fixing up scratches, dings and rips in famous paintings. But me as a painter? No way. Even though I love my career, wielding a brush is too much like being at work, whereas photography is an escape.

Goldberg often reminds me how I'm somewhat famous, albeit inside the tiny circumference of art circles. I'd made a momentous discovery, bringing to light a long-lost Arthur Streeton painting, *Gloucester Buckets (grey)*, one that in 1894 the *Sydney Morning Herald* described as 'symphonic' and their 'picture of the year', which made its disappearance soon after even more extraordinary. But 125 years later, through X-ray detective work and lateral thinking, I and my bosses, Simon Ives and Paula Dredge – I can't take all the credit – discovered that Streeton had painted a still life, *Lilium Auratum*, on top of the missing work. The *Herald* called what we did 'brilliant sleuthing'.

The following week, I got another call from Hugh. He probably saw my name in the paper. He's rung me a few times these past few years, but I never take the calls. His voicemails are always the same. He's babbling on about changing, about wanting to reach out to those he's hurt – which must mean he's got a massive phone bill – followed with lots of other kumbaya feel-good hooey he probably picked up from an Egomaniacs Anonymous support group.

In terms of my photography, I'm not a Nan Goldin type, with her disturbing peeks into the seamy intimate lives of her friends and lovers. She went much further into the wild side than I could ever venture. No, my photographic hero is Annie Leibovitz. How amazing it would be if, some day, just one of my portraits got compared, in a good way, with hers. Like her shot of Sting when he was my age, where he's lying so exposed, naked and face down, on the cracked, dry lakebed of a Mojave, California desert, an image that really speaks to me. And not just because he's naked. Or maybe because he's naked.

One day, if I'm lucky, it might be me who's taken an iconic shot. Until then, I'll carry on avoiding being noticed, under the comfy, safe blanket of my Miss Ordinary persona.

8

Throughout my school years, I was constantly on tenterhooks that the mean girls would toss off yet another crack about my mortifying middle names. I'd get catcalls … 'Jay Jay cut her ear off, Jay Jay cut her ear off.' *Jay Jay* was what they scrawled on the toilet-block wall. That was when I started pushing my fire-truck-red hair behind my ears to prove them wrong – and started spelling my name 'JJ'.

With the bullies going for me at school and Hugh doing much the same at home, I spent a lot of my life just trying to fit in, to be as unremarkable as grey paint on a greyer day. Despite that, I've been hitting some strides at the gallery. They promoted me to full conservator last year. It was my biggest buzz since they sent me on my four-month secondment in Amsterdam, and, yes, the party they threw to celebrate our Streeton discovery. And only a couple of weeks ago, right out of the blue, Brandy Edmunds, our new director, asked me to look after her to-die-for apartment, her boat and Scottie. The apartment and boat are not actually hers. She's looking after them for an old, and obviously rich and generous friend who's off on a three-year Italian sabbatical.

The apartment is on Woolloomooloo's Finger Wharf, a delightful – when it's not raining – ten-minute walk from the gallery, through the foreshore gardens on Mrs Macquarie's Point and down the steps. The truly killer feature, though, is not its proximity to work, and not even the amazing views of Sydney Harbour. Nor is it the kitchen with its four-door fridge that talks to you and orders milk when you're running out. It's the boat that comes with the place. The marina berth is so close by that a couple of times I've been tempted to leap onto the flybridge from the balcony.

Why I got to escape from my tiny bedsit in Redfern and enjoy all this, I have no idea. For no reason I can fathom, Brandy waltzed over to me in the lunchroom – in front of everybody – and asked me to house-sit, boat-sit and dog-sit while she jetted off to Paris and Boston for three, maybe four, weeks. She's negotiating to bring the biggest collection of Claude Monets that Australia's ever seen. What a coup that would be.

Last July, when the gallery's head honchos, the trustees, announced they'd coaxed Brandy away from her post in New York City as deputy director of the illustrious MOMA – the Museum of Modern Art – the news was plastered over all the media. A coup before the coup. Even with all the coverage, the announcement got the staff gossip mill going – how, with a striking first name like Brandy, our new boss would come striding in like Lynn Yaeger from *Vogue*. She, too, would have a startling orange bob, a face with white geisha make-up, a cupid's bow and dots of rouge, and an artfully frayed vintage Comme des Garçons coat over voluminous layers of multicoloured tutus, a pair of ugg boots on her feet. She would pronounce that *I'm here to kick ass, so deal with it*, the kind of intimidating hello we all feared a loud-mouthed, sharp-elbowed, pushy New Yorker would give.

But Brandy Edmunds turned out to be a silver-haired sweetie who was as warm as a grandma's hug. Almost as old, too. She doesn't wear ugg boots, or any boots. Instead, it's sober, safe pumps, except when she kicks them off under the table and massages her toes, which are so crooked I'm guessing it's arthritis. Her accent isn't harsh and angular, it's soft and pleasant – more Bostonian than Bronx – with a smooth dollop of Australian that comes from growing up in Melbourne. After she left at twenty-one to study in the US, she spent the next thirty-five years climbing her way up to the second-highest step on the international art world ladder. Rather than waiting to become MOMA's next director, she came home. Not that Sydney is Melbourne, but it's close enough, if you ignore Melbournians' incessant bragging about their brilliant coffees. As if they invented baristas.

In humour and shape, Brandy's a squishy ball of energy. She started her first town hall briefing with, 'Please call me Brandy. If anyone says *Dr Edmunds*, you'll have me looking around for my mom.' One of my colleagues, who'd had a long stint in the corporate world, whispered to me that this was an old line a lot of CEOs used. *It's to make them seem human, so keep your guard up 'cos it's probably total bullshit.*

Even if it was just a line, I liked it. The same way I like how Brandy's huge, warm smile stretches her face wider than a rose-tinted dinner plate. She reminds me of my late mother, though that's not something I've shared with anyone.

I still can't work out why she picked me to house-sit, dog-sit and boat-sit, though. I was shocked she even knew I existed. I've wondered about it through three or four V&Ts so far. Was this a rise before the fall, like maybe she's planning staff cuts and I'll be the first to go after she gets back? Or is it leading up to one of those workplace harassment situations where I'll feel pressured into saying *yes* because I'll be thinking, *But she's been so generous.* Or is Brandy just the really, really nice person she seems to be, and I was just in the right place at the right time?

9

A gunshot? Shattering glass?

Scottie, who's been snoozing at my feet, got an even bigger fright than I did and almost leapt off the side of the boat. I pat him as I squint in the direction of the noise, the low sun ahead making it difficult to see.

My best guess is that the *crack* came from across the narrow strip of water that separates me from the foreshore opposite. No one's on the boardwalk over there, or on the boats at that marina, the one that belongs to the town houses in the long terrace facing me.

A movement on one of the upper-level terraces catches my eye. Dark curtains – I can't make out the colour in the failing light – are billowing out through the sliding doors, a slit of internal light coming through the middle.

A scream? I strain my ears. Is it a woman? I pick up my phone to call 'emergency', as a woman sticks her head out through the curtains. 'Get the fuck away from—' she shouts. Her head withdraws – or is it yanked back? – behind the curtains before she finishes the sentence. I start dialling but hear a man yelling, 'Police!'

He's standing on the foredeck of the boat two berths to the right of me and, thank heavens, already shouting into his phone. I put mine down to take up my camera, and start shooting the crime scene to get evidence for the police. The images I'm getting are incredibly sharp and well exposed, even in the fast-fading light.

I switch to burst mode, a rapid-fire continuous shooting of stills at thirty frames per second. When the shouting starts again, I switch to video, scanning from left to right across the front of the town house, keeping the focus on the terrace doors for a good minute. I'm not capturing much movement – mainly the curtains catching the breeze – but hope I'm getting the voices … two voices, I think, though with the drapes muffling the words, I can't tell if the second one is male or female.

There's movement off to the right – and lights coming on – so I shift my camera to catch it. The terrace doors of the next-door town house are sliding open. A woman in her late thirties, a bit older than me, comes out. Her eyes! My lens catches them perfectly, just as Sony promised. She has incredibly intense brown eyes and something about her reminds me of Vermeer's mesmerising *Girl with a Pearl Earring*. If the headscarf in the Vermeer was ruby and emerald, not blue and yellow, this girl would be the spitting image. On a scale of one to Beyoncé, she's Bella Hadid.

'Girl' – as I decide to call her – steps out onto her terrace, her face quizzical. She tilts her head towards the street, as do I when I hear the sirens. The police have come fast, probably because Kings Cross is so close.

Two blue-and-whites screech to a stop at the end of the terrace. Four uniformed police leap out, two by two, leaving their car doors open as they race to the main entrance. I stop filming and wave to the guy on his foredeck. I give him a thumbs up and a nod. He did good.

He shrugs at me and looks back over to the other side, waiting for developments. But I keep looking at him. He's straight out of the Cape Cod issue of *Town & Country* magazine I flicked through in my dentist's waiting room last month … shorts in crayon pink, pastel blue polo, pale yellow sweater slung over his shoulders and down his back, its arms tied loosely below his neck. I can imagine him eating lobster rolls at his country club. Mid-to-late thirties. He's not a young Sting, not even close, but I would definitely take a shot of him if it wouldn't be so obvious.

10

What a turnaround. It's the woman I saw sticking her head out through the curtains. The police are hustling her into one of their vehicles, with her hands cuffed behind her. They're exposing way more of her body than I would like to see or, I suppose, she'd like to show. She's shrieking, which I would be too if I was being shoved through the street wearing no more than a thong, and I don't mean the kind on your feet.

The man running after them is only marginally more clothed. His crew-neck shirt is soaked in blood and his arms are waving wildly. Thankfully his T-shirt is a long one. He's yelling, goading the police. 'Send the fucking bitch down forever.'

I lock up *Seaduction*, and Scottie and I walk back to Brandy's apartment. It's just across the boardwalk, on the upper level of the long Finger Wharf complex. I've been into the hotel part of the wharf a few times but it's not my scene. I'd need heels taller than a skyscraper just to reach the price bracket of the cocktails. Brandy's apartment is at the harbour end. She's got great views but not as good as the apartments at the very tip, like Russell Crowe's. According to the gossip magazines, he's got eleven bedrooms, seven car spaces and an even huger marina berth than Brandy's. His balcony's so big, he's got a Finnish barrel sauna on it and there's still room for entertaining.

After I moved in, I started following him on Instagram. Me and a million other people. He doesn't post much, and there's no chance he'll follow me back, even if I am a neighbour. He's only following thirty-five people, all famous.

But still, a girl can dream. What if he's my first celebrity subject? Maybe a shot of him walking away from the camera – stopping, then turning back? A subtle nod to his scene in *Gladiator*, where Emperor Commodus says, 'How dare you show your back to me?'

Not that I'd have the backbone to even ask him.

If he stepped into the same elevator as me, I'd probably freeze.

11

Brandy's living room's got one of those giant wall-mounted smart TVs that's wider than I am tall. I'm screening my 'incident report' videos and shots, to check if I've got anything useful to send to the police for their investigation wall – like the ones in cop shows, where they pin up photos and maps and Post-it notes, and connect them with strands of pink ribbon or red string.

I've always imagined Hugh solving his cases like that, but I wouldn't know. He never brought his work home with him and, after I left, we only communicated once. It was in 2010, well before Lauren walked out on him.

*

Goldberg had driven me to the National Gallery of Australia in his RAV4. We went to see Van Gogh's brilliant *Starry Night* – a print of it is on the ceiling above my bed – as well as five of his other works. The NGA was exhibiting those six, plus a hundred or so masterpieces it had borrowed from Paris's Musée d'Orsay. This wasn't the *Starry Night* that prompted Don McLean's song 'Vincent (Starry, Starry Night)'. VvG painted *that* one while he was in the asylum at Saint-Rémy, *after* he cut off his earlobe. He painted the Musée d'Orsay's original – my print – in Arles, while he still had both ears.

'Hey, Jego,' said Goldberg, 'that guy over there … the one with the red hair.' It's our little joke that we call each other by our surnames, like we went to one of those snooty private schools. And calling Vincent 'VvG' is our private shorthand.

He was pointing to a man standing in front of a VvG self-portrait. 'You'd be that guy's spitting image if you were a man. And taller.'

'And if I was a total bastard,' I added, a shudder quaking through me. 'We've got to leave. Now. Let's g—'

Before I finished speaking, Hugh turned and saw me. I froze.

He strode over to us, smiling as if all the years we'd been estranged counted for zip. 'Are you going to introduce your dear old dad to your friend?' he asked, with his hand outstretched, and showing so many teeth he looked like a wolf, and without the sheep's clothing.

I couldn't speak.

But 'dear old dad' could, and did. 'I'm Hugh … Hugh Jego,' he told Goldberg. 'And you are?'

'Goldberg. I work with JJ. She's … ah … she's told me so much about you,' he added, which was not just a lie but landed as a total loss of face for me. The last thing I wanted was Hugh deluding himself that his disaffected daughter thought about him fondly, or that I thought about him at all.

'Then you've heard all the good stuff, I'm sure,' said Hugh, winking at me, with a chaser of an icy stare that I knew far too well. 'So, JJ, that self-portrait I was looking at over there … what page?'

What I wanted to answer with was a rather crude form of 'get out of my face', but what I actually said was 'Two hundred and ninety-one.' Worse, I didn't just say it, I blurted it out, like a little kid desperate for validation. Despite everything, the rat bastard still controlled me.

And he actually clapped. 'Wow, Goldberg,' he said, grinning like Ash Barty's dad did after watching her win her last Grand Slam, 'my girl's still got it.' But, unlike the tennis ace, I hadn't done anything extraordinary. The page number just flew into my head and out of my mouth.

I never aimed to be a walking Van Gogh encyclopedia, nor do I advertise it, but it's hardly a surprising outcome, given the combination of our family folklore and Hugh's bedtime ritual with me when I was a kid.

My friends' dads would sit on their beds at night and read them funny or scary stories. But Little JJ never got *Goosebumps* or *James and the Giant Peach*, no *Harry Potter and the Philosopher's Stone*. Hugh's routine – and by routine, I mean what he made me do every night he wasn't out busting criminals – was to wait until I was in my sparkly pink and purple My Little Pony PJs, and pound me with every image in his Walther and Metzger's *Vincent van Gogh: The Complete Paintings*, the 1993 two-volume hardcover edition published by Taschen in a slip case. He'd test me on them – five or six works a night – for each of the 871 paintings printed in the gorgeously produced 700 pages. Because of my dyslexia, I focused on the images, and he'd read me the words, repeating them so many times that I can probably still recite most of that book.

Virtually every night of my childhood it was Van Gogh this and Van Gogh that. But don't get me wrong. Despite Hugh, I grew to love those two volumes. I still do. Turning their pages is a visceral experience – my eyes squint at the repeated and blinding shocks of brilliant colour, and my fingers feel like they're caking over with Vincent's thick and oozy oils. In my studio apartment in Redfern, I've got my own Walther and Metzger – the same edition I grew up with, bought second-hand. It's in pride of place on my shelf, the slip case cover – another VvG self-portrait – facing outwards to greet me when I get home. No one but me has actually seen it there, since I'm not big on entertaining. Okay, Goldberg's seen it, but that's not what you're thinking. We're just friends.

So, yes, that self-portrait that Hugh was looking at on the NGA's wall is on page 291 of my Walther and Metzger. And, once again, Hugh did what he'd spent my whole childhood making a fine art of ... getting me to jump through hoops at his whim, for no purpose except to prove he was in control of me. The rat bastard, like I said.

Thankfully, Goldberg and I had already seen the rest of the exhibition, including *Starry Night*, so without saying another word – or number! – I grabbed Goldberg's hand and pulled him out of the NGA behind me.

'What was that about?' he asked me in the car. 'Is two hundred and ninety-one code for something?'

It was, but I didn't tell him what because I don't like to swear.

*

Given how useless my Woolloomooloo crime scene photos turned out to be, I wouldn't be showing them to the police, or to anyone. There are heaps of shots, mostly showing no more than an asthmatic curtain wheezing in and out while this mini-World War III is being fought, uncaptured, behind it. My videos aren't much better and, given the distance, the sound is little more than a whoosh of the wind blowing across the bay.

On the other hand, and it's an unexpected bonus, my shots of *Girl with No Pearl Earring* are something else entirely. They look good – or, rather, *she* looks good – and somehow I seem to have captured what I think is her essence without even trying. Is it possible that the Annie Leibovitz trapped within me all these years is finally starting to show herself?

I rename the unwieldy original camera file names, changing *DSC7041–DSC7093* to *Girl #1–Girl #53*. Of those images, *Girl #16* is the knockout.

With a bit of cropping, boosting the saturation, turning up the contrast and increasing the colour temperature, it might get even better but, sadly, not so good it would win me a Lucie Award. You've got to be an Annie to win one or, in her case, two. Maybe I could sell it as a non-fungible token? That would be something, if I had a clue about selling NFTs.

Fiddling with the image – *working with it* is the more professional description – should be step two, not one.

Amateurs fiddle. Professionals refine, but only *after* they've got behind their subject's veil. If I'm truly going to make anything out of *Girl #16*, I need to find out what makes her tick. That's what Annie would do.

Except I'm no Annie. Popping over and introducing myself, inviting Girl back for a coffee and a viewing ... really? No way. Not even with Brandy's whizz-bang automatic espresso machine, of which I'm a huge fan, as a lure ... no, even with that as bait, inviting a stranger over would be quite the stretch for me.

I need to be more like David Attenborough when he's stalking a lion ... crouching downwind in the long grass, patient, quiet. Though what I'd do when Girl eventually showed up is anyone's guess. Talking to randoms is not my strong suit at any time. It's why I avoid parties. When I do go to them, I mostly end up in a corner, studying the wallpaper. At the gallery's big donor events – which staff are expected to attend – there's always Goldberg to talk to, thank heavens. He's a lifesaver. But the last event was a debacle because he was away, looking after his sick mother. The ninety minutes of being stuck, smiling and nodding at patrons and hangers-on, was so stressful and exhausting I felt like I'd run myself ragged on a treadmill.

I make myself a double espresso with a twist of lemon rind, and a glass of water on the side – because Annie does, or so I've read – and sit back in front of the big screen, pondering my next steps.

Tomorrow's Saturday. I'll spend the morning walking Scottie and taking photos up and down the boardwalk out the front of Girl's building. I'll be casual and any contact with her will be accidental. She'll come over to pat him – surely she loves dogs – we'll chat about how bizarre the 'incident' next door was, and maybe when we go to part ways she'll make the move – I certainly won't. She'll turn back and say, *Hey, let's have a coffee,* and I'll say, *Sure, that would be nice.* But would I really? Yes, I would. I'd have to! Then she'll say, *Are you a photographer? Yes,* I'll say, which is a stretch if ever there was one. *Really,* she'll say. *I'd love to see your work.*

If only. I'm the queen of *if onlys.* In this case, if only she would ask … if only I'd have the backbone to say yes. When I go home from parties – mostly alone and in the back of an Uber – I'm barraged with *if onlys.* If the driver knew, he'd rate me five stars just on my *if onlys.*

Saturday comes and goes, and Girl doesn't leave her apartment. She doesn't even venture out onto her terrace. The curtains stay closed.

Scottie is happy because I've never walked him so much in one day. I'm also happy, in a way, since I didn't have to force myself out of my shell. But I'm also sullen about the missed opportunity which, this time, wasn't my fault. And I'm a little sunburned on my arms and legs. In my enthusiasm, I forgot to slap on enough sunscreen, a redhead's best friend. Fortunately, my floppy sunhat and the aviator sunglasses I got from Specsavers in a two-pairs-for-one deal protected my face and shoulders. It wouldn't be a good look at work if I was hunched over the Brett Whiteley I'm restoring and bits of nose peel were dropping all over it.

Sunday is just Saturday on repeat, except this time I do slather on the lotion. I keep glancing up to Girl's terrace but, like yesterday, her curtains stay drawn and the sliding doors shut.

After work on Monday, Scottie and I, and V&Ts, are back on the boat. Girl is still nowhere to be seen.

Tuesday, the same. Maybe she's gone on a trip.

I return to Brandy's apartment frustrated, my mood saturnine, which is a word I got from Goldberg. He learned it doing a crossword. It means gloomy, with a brooding ill humour. And with Russell Crowe being the Invisible Man, the absence of sightings – of Girl and of him – my spirits are weighed down even more.

For three more days, Scottie and I head off at sunrise for a brisk walk.

When we get to Mrs Macquaries Chair, the point on the peninsula opposite the Finger Wharf, and I can see the Opera House, the warm golden light is washing over its sails. According to the big official sign, *Macquaries* has no apostrophe, which is confusing. Scottie doesn't care either way. Apostrophes aren't his thing. I walk him along the road past the Art Gallery, where he insists on stopping – Brandy's brought him to work a couple of times – then on to St Mary's Cathedral. That's followed by a run, when we scoot across the park at The Domain and back to the apartment.

After I return home from work each of those evenings, we don't do V&Ts on the boat. Instead, I stay in to work on *Girl #16*. The first night, I spend a couple of hours on saturation, brightness and contrast. The next one, I play with temperature, tone curves and sharpness. The third, I reset back to the original settings.

Nothing I'm doing is making *Girl #16* what she needs to be.

Is it me, or is it her?

Needing a breather, I take Scottie down to Harry's Café de Wheels, the neighbourhood pie cart that Brandy calls a food truck. She raves about Harry's hotdogs. 'You've got to try them,' she told me. I didn't have the heart to tell her that frankfurts and me end as badly as Khloé Kardashian and Tristan Thompson.

I go for their Tiger pie. Thankfully, the vendor says there's no actual tiger in it – the original Harry was a boxer and Tiger was his name in the ring. I choose the chicken one, topped with classic mashed potato, mushy peas and gravy, and take it back to the apartment on an open cardboard tray that, unfortunately, attracts a small squadron of summertime flies, and Scottie too. He's jumping up to get some of it, but I'm pretty sure some of the ingredients in pies are bad for dogs. Probably for people too, the more I think about it.

Back in the apartment, while I'm wolfing down my dinner, me on the couch and Scottie on the floor, his nose deep in a dish of air-dried blue mackerel and lamb – which sounds disgusting but he's finding delicious – I'm debating with him what approach to take now I've accepted that reworking *Girl #16* will get me nowhere.

I don't know if it's his idea or mine but I throw a mosaic of *Girls #1* through *#30* onto the big TV screen from my laptop and let my eyes cycle through them. Four images pull me in and, to my surprise, *Girl #16* isn't one of them. Don't get me wrong, I still love *Girl #16,* but these four give me something she doesn't.

In each of them, there are a couple of blurry objects in the background, at each side of her. They might be motion blur, something moving beside her, or could be due to the shallow depth of field and long focal length of my 70-300mm lens. I'm hoping I can sharpen them up, so I can see a thin slice of her apartment and get a hint of her lifestyle.

I pick the third of my four favourites, *Girl #23,* zoom in and dial up the brightness, and, yes, it's already starting to invite me inside her place. With a touch more brightness and contrast, I'm starting to see what might be … on the wall behind her … is that a painting? Two, it seems. One is a pretty forbidding dark, big blur. Based on the wall spaces and her height, I'm guessing it's two metres high and a bit less across. The second work is brighter, happier and smaller, about a metre high and two-thirds that width.

With a bit more definition, I might find the inspiration I've been longing for.

I keep making adjustments – principally, High Pass sharpening – and, eventually, some detail of the smaller work starts to emerge, like its budding flowers about to break into bloom. That's because they *are* flowers.

It's a VvG *Sunflowers* … But whoa!

That's not just *any* of his *Sunflowers* paintings. It's *Six Sunflowers*, a work that, in the dying days of World War II, went up in flames when the Allies bombed Kobe in Japan.

12

I know pretty much everything about *Six Sunflowers* because … you know … Hugh.

Up till 2013, a high-quality colour image of *Six Sunflowers* like Girl's didn't really exist. Most of the picture books – including mine, at page 411, in case you're wondering – displayed it in black and white, often framed in a grotesquely ornate, gold-encrusted monstrosity that, in my opinion, was one of the world's biggest art crimes. It's true there were weakly coloured reproductions in a couple of Japanese publications from the 1920s and 1930s – one of which was reproduced in a copy of *LIFE* magazine – but, try as he might, Hugh could never track down a copy of any of them.

In 2013 – a long 125 years after Vincent painted it and 68 years after it was destroyed – renowned Van Gogh expert Martin Bailey was rummaging in the archive drawers of a small Japanese museum, doing research for his next book, *The Sunflowers are Mine: The Story of Van Gogh's Masterpiece*. He stumbled over a colour print made in 1921 that was not only rich and vibrant, this was the first time he – or, for almost a century, anyone outside of Japan – had seen *Six Sunflowers* in its original brilliant-orange frame.

Bailey finding the 'orange-frame' print is carved into my memory because, for our family, it's one of those *Do you remember where you were when you heard about the planes crashing into the Twin Towers?* moments. I was Thursday-night shopping in the camera store at Westfield Bondi Junction. I wasn't buying, just salivating over the latest line of lenses, when my mother phoned me. I could hear Hugh whooping it up. They were watching the story breaking on the nightly news.

The *Sunflowers* series are probably Vincent's most popular works and his most highly prized. The last auction of one, in 1987, smashed the record for the most expensive painting ever sold. If a *Sunflowers* was sold today, it could sell for well over US$250 million, experts reckon. If it was the original of the print that Girl's got on her wall, it would most likely, given its backstory, go for way more.

When Vincent was living in the Yellow House in Arles, he painted four original *Sunflower* works, and some replicas, using different colours, different numbers of flowers and different frames. *Six Sunflowers* was his second original. Paul Gauguin, by then an already famous artist, was coming to stay, and Vincent planned to brighten up the bedroom he was preparing for him by hanging all four *Sunflowers* originals on its walls.

Initially, Vincent called this work *Still Life: Vase with Five Sunflowers*. It was later, when he extended the canvas and added an extra bloom, that he changed it to *Six Sunflowers* and gave it the simple, yet extraordinary, frame of four thin wooden strips painted with orange lead, to set off the blues, lilacs and yellows, and make them sing.

Just seeing that print for the first time, on my screen in 2013, gave me the shivers. This wasn't just because of the vibrancy of the colours – the vivid royal blue sky, in particular – but because the thin orange frame was so obviously an integral part of the work.

I'd read Vincent's letters to Theo about the various *Sunflowers* and, for the first time, I could actually see the effect he'd been driving at with *Six*. He was mimicking the stained-glass windows of a Gothic church … the big swathe of the brilliant blue backdrop … the startling yellows of the ray florets – the petals – the oranges of the seed heads at the flowers' centres … the thin orange lines of the frame haloing the greens of the stems, the leaves and the vase … and the lilac tablecloth that two of the blooms and a bud had dropped onto.

For the first time, the work looked to me exactly how Vincent said it would.

I spy a bottle of absinthe in Brandy's bar and pour myself a glass of the green spirit, just like Vincent would have, back in his day. It's supposed to be hallucinogenic, which is presumably why they used to call it *la fée verte*, the green fairy. The liquor's warmth runs down my throat.

So, Girl's got a print of *Six Sunflowers*! I'm liking her already.

I take another sip. My mind wanders, and a wild and crazy, if not completely improbable, thought explodes in my head – *What if this isn't a print?* – and I start to laugh.

Which came first, the dumb thought or the absinthe?

It's clearly the absinthe, but I let myself enjoy the moment.

13

I'm on TV. I'm hallucinating, obviously, because it's *me* who's being interviewed, and it's me *allowing* myself to be interviewed. If only they'd ask me. If only I was someone who'd ever go through that torture.

'Ms Jego, please tell our viewers what happened to the original *Six Sunflowers*?'

My answer slides off my tongue. No ums, no ahs, no stuttering. If only. But I do know the story backwards, even in my dreams.

That's because Hugh forced me to research it for my Year 8 free-choice school project. I did amazing work, even crafting a beautiful imitation of *Six Sunflowers* for the cover of my project book. I used the colour scheme Vincent wrote about in his letters because, at that stage,

I hadn't seen the orange-frame print, or any colour print. But I never actually handed it in because … *Jay Jay cut her ear off.*

What I did hand in had a photography angle, a rewrite of the free-choice assignment I'd got an A+ for in Year 7, about Alfred Hitchcock's 1954 film *Rear Window*. What's plain, if you blow up some of the individual movie frames, is that Hitchcock's got a strip of black tape hiding the make and model – Exacta Ihagee – of the camera James Stewart uses to spy on the apartment opposite. The question camera and movie buffs asked for years was *Why did the famous filmmaker hide those details?* Well, I got my A+ for tracking down the answer. It was all because he made the film during America's fraught anti-Communist, McCarthyist 1950s. He knew that if he revealed those particulars – flagging that the camera was made in Dresden, East Germany – he ran a serious risk of being blacklisted for promoting a product made behind the Iron Curtain.

I couldn't show that assignment to Hugh, so I slaved over my never-to-be-handed-in *Six Sunflowers* project for an additional week.

But there I am in my dream, on TV and confident. If only.

I look directly into the camera's red light to connect with the viewers. I ask them to picture Kobe in Japan on 5 August 1945.

Japan's sixth largest city, I say, *one of the country's most densely populated, and such a major industrial centre that the Allies bombed it repeatedly.*

A cotton textiles entrepreneur, Koyata Yamamoto, lives in Ashiya. That's a wealthy district on Kobe's south coast. Inside his mansion, he's got Six Sunflowers *hanging on his living room wall. He'd bought it in 1920 from a Swiss art dealer, and shipped it to Japan on a mail steamer, the* Binna.

Just before midnight, the Kobe air-raid sirens startle the city, and people run to the shelters. For the next ninety minutes, American bombers blitz Kobe.

Yamamoto tries to save his beloved Van Gogh painting but its frame makes it far too heavy to lift off the wall and carry. He flees to safety.

Days later, he returns to the smoking wreckage of his home. The room where he'd hung the Van Gogh is completely destroyed.

This raid on Kobe, I tell them, *was only a few hours before Hiroshima was wiped out. That was also the day the US president, Harry Truman, announced that, unless Emperor Hirohito surrendered, Japan's industrial facilities and transportation networks would suffer 'a rain of ruin from the air, the like of which has never been seen on this earth'.*

For Kyoto Yamamoto and for the art world, I tell the camera, *ruin had already rained on* Six Sunflowers.

The interviewer then asks me:

How did Girl get her hands on the original if it went up in flames?

I look at him like he's just grown an extra head, and, after having impressed him with how knowledgeable I sound, I'm now totally umm-ing and ahh-ing … because Girl having the original is simply not possible. The whole world knows that.

14

The Farrellys
Monaco
14 May 2021

The second time Nessa Farrelly visited Fontaine & Fontaine, she was expected – not that her one hour's notice was remotely adequate in the doleful circumstances. What the firm's receptionist didn't expect was Nessa's stare of cold indifference to the pain that he and the entire firm were suffering. Now in its second year, Covid was taking a toll on everyone, everywhere, but the tragedy that befell Fontaine & Fontaine was different.

Nessa stood so tall in her heels that she towered menacingly over the top of the front desk's acrylic safety screen. 'Dr Matthieu. He's expecting me,' she said from behind her face mask, voice clipped, hands on her narrow hips, and foot tapping on the beige carpet.

'*Bien sûr, madame*,' the receptionist said, trying to keep disdain out of his voice. Then, with a barely French accent, he added, 'Dr Matthieu will be no more than a moment. Please, take a seat over there,' indicating the rich leather wingback chairs over by the window.

Nessa didn't move, merely glanced at her watch, and then back to the lift lobby, as if she was expecting somebody.

*

Dr Félix Matthieu, the firm's new senior partner, was the third in two years. He knew the Farrelly family's CCNN empire anchored the firm, always top of the top-five biller list, yet he'd never met a single Farrelly. Only the Fontaines – Jacques, then Claude – had dealt with them personally.

Félix, a pale, thin man of sixty, adjusted his black armband and matching face mask, and gave Nessa a slight bow. No one was doing the French two-cheek *bise*. No handshakes either. 'It's an honour to meet you,' he said, standing back, 'especially in these difficult times.'

He led her to the conference room and she took a seat with the view behind *her*, ensuring that this time it would be the lawyer who would be squinting into the light. Nessa eyed him up and down like a breeder checking out a stallion at a horse sale, then said, 'Sorry for your loss. Now that's out of the way, tell me what happened to the two Fontaines.'

'Of course.' A sob caught in Félix's throat. He was shaking. He ran his trembling fingers through the few wisps of grey hair he had left, and dropped his eyes to the table, trying to steady his hands as he removed his wire-framed glasses and rested them on the pink marble. A tear formed at the corner of one eye and—

'Dr Matthieu,' said Nessa, drawing his eyes back to her, 'I understand your pain but, please, get on and answer my question.'

Matthieu bit his lip and, though it pained him to relive the events, started with Jacques, keeping it short, so he could cope. 'Ten weeks ago, our esteemed founder ... the one saving grace was that Jacques got to die at home in his own bed. We gave him a wonderful funeral, the last Monaco allowed before the new restrictions. A month later, Claude had urgent client business in Mumbai. We said, "Don't go! Do it by video."'

'So, why go there? India's feckin' teemin' with Covid.'

'Precisely. We tried ... *I* tried, believe me ... the lack of oxygen supplies ... the hospitals not coping ... the thousands and thousands of bodies piling up ... so many that half are unidentified and the authorities can't keep up ... funeral pyres everywhere ...' His voice cracking, Matthieu reached for a glass of water, briefly undid his mask and took a sip. 'But Claude is Claude ... *was*, I mean. Headstrong, independent, a force to be reckoned with—'

'I don't want a eulogy. Just the facts.'

Matthieu was in a fluster. 'The facts. Of course. Claude went there, caught Covid and died. *Voilà.*'

'Vaccinated, right?'

Matthieu nodded.

'And young ... like, what ... thirty-five?'

'Thirty-three. It was the Delta variant.' The lawyer took another sip.

Suddenly, a blinding flash burst through the door. Nessa's brother Niall clanked into the room, wearing almost as much bling as the firm's old mainstay, Madame Pasquier, but it made him look like a Miami pimp. Even his Covid face mask was bright red with gold sequins. Gold chains dangled from his neck, with more of them looped through his leather jacket, chunky rings on his fingers and an outlandish watch on his wrist.

Nessa was shaking her head. 'You're late,' she told Niall. 'Again.'

'Feck off, sis,' was what Matthieu believed he heard the oaf say behind his garish mask as he sat himself on the edge of the board table, not caring if his metal accoutrements scratched the expensive stone.

'I apologise for my brother's manners,' Nessa said to Matthieu and turned back to Niall. 'Git your arse in a chair, you tool. You got no feckin' respect?'

Niall did as he was told. 'What are you a doctor of?' he said to Matthieu as he pointed to his groin. 'I got this itch and—'

'Jesus, Niall. Stop actin' the feckin' maggot.' Looking back at Matthieu, she said, 'Claude's funeral. When's that?'

'Tomorrow, as it happens, though it will be mainly via Zoom. Would you and Mr Farrelly like to attend in person? The numbers in the chapel will be somewhat limited because of the pandemic but—'

'We want to see the body,' said Nessa.

'Another tragedy, madame. We lost contact with Claude three weeks ago.'

'That's got to be bollocks,' said Niall. 'What about pickin' up the phone, sendin' a text or an email?'

'We did all that, repeatedly. We checked with the hotel and our client in Mumbai. No one had seen Claude for days. We got an investigator on the case, but still nothing. Was it Covid? Was it a kidnapping? We didn't know anything but feared the worst. Eventually, they found the paperwork certifying Claude had died and been cremated. I am so, so sorry to tell you this, but there is no body. We were not even permitted to ship the remains back here.' He put his glasses on and stood up. His eyes were welling with tears. 'Please excuse me,' he blubbered. 'I will only be a moment.'

'Before you go, take a gander at this,' Niall told Matthieu. He took a small computer tablet out of his jacket pocket and slid it across the boardroom table.

'What is it?' the lawyer asked.

'Tap the screen.'

Matthieu did as he was asked. The screen lit up and, instantly, his cheeks turned a shade of red that rivalled that of Niall's face mask. He slumped back in his chair. 'This is a video of my house. What—'

'Not a video. It's live.'

'I don't follow.'

'Watch and learn.'

A crosshair grid appeared, like Matthieu had seen in movies, representing a sniper rifle's sights. The image began to zoom. He watched the crosshairs zero in on his wife, Monique, at the easel in her studio.

15

For Félix Matthieu, listening to the Farrellys was like reliving a nightmare he often had, where he was behind the wheel of a car careening out of control round the treacherous Grande Corniche cliff face. He would always wake up, startled and in a cold sweat, his fastidious legal brain finally conjuring up the tiny but crucial detail he'd neglected to include in a client's paperwork. This was like that, but far worse.

He was in shock. If he didn't do what the twins were demanding of him – the same things the Fontaines had apparently been doing for this family of Irish thugs for decades – the consequences for Matthieu, his family and the firm would be even more unthinkable than the tasks they wanted him to perform.

'I'm glad we understand each other, Dr Matthieu,' said Nessa, with the sated look of a large cat after it had eaten its prey. 'My brother and I look forward to doin' business with you. Business that, we assure you, will be extremely profitable for your firm, and for you.'

Niall added, 'Yeah, about that chalet your little lady's been naggin' you to buy in Chamonix—'

'What?' said Matthieu, somehow finding his voice. 'How do you know about—'

Niall's laugh was the kind of mocking, throaty taunt that Félix associated with horror movies. 'Listen, boyo, if you know what's good for you, you'll work your new Farrelly gig by assumin' we know everythin' ... about you ... about this firm ... about your family ... Assume that and you'll do mighty fine.'

Matthieu knew that if he went to the police, the Farrellys would find out. If he quit the firm and ran, they'd find him. He visualised these thugs holding his and his wife's heads underwater until they drowned.

Eventually, when he accepted that he had no choice, he got up, forcing a fake smile, even if it was behind his mask. 'You've, ah, given me a lot to absorb but I thank you for your, er, ongoing support of the firm, and I, er, assure you of our ... my ... loyalty. One last thing. The funeral. Will you be attending ... do you want me to send you the link?'

'Sit back down, boyo,' said Niall.

'We have a few more details to iron out,' said Nessa, 'includin' a wee visit to the Freeport.'

16

Monaco
Four months later, September 2021

In previous years, Félix Matthieu loved his *rentrée* back to work from his August *vacances* as much as he'd adored the change of scene – the *dépaysement* – that the break afforded him. He'd stroll back into the office with a spring in his step, hands casually in his pockets, itching to get to work and to welcome everyone else back.

Why wouldn't he after a glorious month on Corsica's northwest, where he always took a villa? Located between L'Île-Rousse and Calvi, he and Monique could look down on the quaint seaside village of Algajola as they lounged by the pool. While Monique painted, he ventured down there every day to buy fresh fish – baby red mullet, *rougets*, his favourite – and when he was driving back, he'd thrill to the sight of Corsica's magnificent jagged mountain range in front of him.

But his *rentrée* this September, his first as senior partner and also as joint executor of Claude Fontaine's will, was different.

Claude's will, at least, was done and dusted. It wasn't because Félix did the work with a light touch – not at all. He'd attended to the probate meticulously, despite the fact he'd been bequeathed the Farrellys. Félix couldn't hate Claude for that. Knowing his predecessor as well as he did, he felt Claude would have endured the same trauma from working with the Irish thugs.

The probate work was completed last week, thanks mostly to Madame Pasquier's co-executorship and her willingness not to take an August break. From the day Félix joined the firm, he'd kept no secrets from Blingette, but it was different now. He could not share with her, or anyone, the horrors of what the Farrellys were demanding of him.

Claude's estate was surprisingly straightforward for someone who'd inherited, then briefly led, a successful law firm in Monaco. On the beneficiary side, there really weren't any. Fontaine wasn't married, had no children, didn't live with anyone, wasn't even in touch with any cousins. The will divided up Fontaine's share in the firm among the remaining partners and, as for the rest of the dead lawyer's assets, Blingette's searches through the mountains of paperwork revealed that Claude had spent the past six months assiduously giving almost all of them away.

Félix remembered a TED talk Claude had told him about, just before Jacques died, on *giving while living*. Claude wasn't just a talker, quite clearly. The estate's financial records showed millions donated, in cash, stocks and bonds, to charities and trusts all over the world. There were so many, and in so many places, that Félix didn't have the time or inclination to check out who they were and what they did. He knew that Claude, always meticulous, would have vetted them already, and that was good enough for him as co-executor.

The Fontaine yacht didn't have to go to auction. A tech CEO from Silicon Valley snapped it up after a week on the market. But because of Covid's initial disruption of real estate markets, Félix decided to hold back on selling Claude's two properties, the tri-level apartment in Monte Carlo and the house – formerly Jacques' – on the chic peninsula of Saint-Jean-Cap-Ferrat, where the firm entertained visiting clients and dignitaries, and hosted its annual Bastille Day and Christmas parties. Instead, he'd leased them out for the summer high season. The apartment went to an American private equity maven, and the house to an Australian fund manager who'd wangled an escape from his country's ban on international travel. Now that local property prices were strengthening, just yesterday Matthieu got the same agent who handled the leasing to put them both up for sale.

Madame Pasquier did the estate's messy stuff, all the legal filings and, worse, the down-and-dirty work of sorting through the drawers, shelves and cupboards in Claude's office and homes. Matthieu hadn't yet caught up with Blingette to thank her for making his August so free of the drudgery of probate and, while he wasn't in the best frame of mind, he was all ready for when she got in. He'd bought her two bottles of the best Corsican wines. An AOC Patrimonio from a vineyard an hour or so from the villa, and an AOC Ajaccio whose grapes were grown very close to Napoleon Bonaparte's birthplace.

He was out of sorts, but not because of the travel hassles getting back. He and Monique were fully vaccinated, recently tested, and carried up-to-date Monaco health passes, so they'd breezed through the airports. Nor was it because the office was an echoing emptiness, since most people were working from home, and that was nothing new. It wasn't the tedium of still wearing a face mask. To him, that was a bonus. His eyes might betray his anxiety but at least no one would know he'd bitten his lips raw.

It was all due to the Farrellys. They'd been weighing on his mind all through the break, like a lost wallet. Twice they'd freaked him out – each time via a text message on his normal cell phone, both from *unknown number*. The first came seconds after he'd taken a photo of the villa the day he and Monique had arrived on the island. *Your grandkids will love that shot*, it said. *Why didn't you bring them? What kind of granddaddy are you?* The second came after he took a photo by the pool the afternoon before he and his wife were leaving to return to Monaco. *Love Monique's blue and gold bikini. Don't forget to bring it home with you tomorrow. Her too!*

The Farrellys had conscripted Matthieu. What particularly terrified him was that someone ... the police? ... would eventually discover his name all over the digital paperwork. Some tech-savvy investigator who would crack the encryption on the custom-made app the Farrellys forced him to conduct their business on.

Félix Matthieu was, after all, the golden key to all the Farrellys' deals, just as, he now understood, Claude had been before him, and Jacques before that.

Matthieu, a high-profile lawyer in a high-profile city, was the Triple-A rating that got the Farrellys the credit they needed as and when they wanted it. Every time they bought 'product' he, under his own name but as their representative, pledged stolen artworks in favour of their suppliers, giving them more than adequate security until they got paid.

At his initial visit to the Freeport with the Farrellys in May, Nessa told him, 'All our art is kosher. We Farrellys are businesspeople, not thieves.' She said it as though running drugs and arms and engaging in human trafficking – and whatever else Matthieu suspected they did, but did not know, or ask – was no worse than pilfering a few pens and packs of Post-its from the office stationery cabinet. Conor, she went on to explain, had accumulated all the artworks 'legitimately' over many years. He even had the works' provenance, their line of ownership as they travelled from the original theft to being traded to him – with codewords for the parties' names, of course.

'Feckin' eejits they all were,' said Niall, leaning back in a chair, as if his father's system was his own creation. 'The mob in Miami, the Yakuza, you name it. Tools, the lot of them.'

Nessa filled in the details. The syndicates who'd actually stolen the works from museums or mansions rarely used it as collateral, unlike the Farrellys who did. Ultimately, they bartered it with Conor, in direct exchange for 'product'.

'We got our art stash valued a few years ago,' said Niall. 'By Sotheby's.'

'It was Christie's,' corrected Nessa. 'They put a value on it of just shy of six hundred million … dollars,' she added.

'But we got a new ballpark number recently – potentially as high as a billion.'

'*Mon dieu*,' said Matthieu. Normally a man whose poker face was legendary, the stratospheric sums being bandied about floored him. That, and the fact that he, and he alone, was to be identified as the custodian of this stolen art.

'Yeah, *dieu*,' said Nessa. 'That's the amount that collectors and museums would pay if the art found its way back into the open market, which it won't. In *our* market—'

The blackest of black markets, thought Matthieu.

'—it would only fetch ten to twenty per cent of that. Not that we ever plan to sell it.'

Niall stuck his oar in again. 'Conor didn't even pay ten per cent. Even better, by keepin' it then mortgagin' it over and over, we keep leveragin' its value. It's like the song I sung for Claude. Remember, Nessie? *The wheels on the bus go round an' round, round an'—*'

Matthieu couldn't help himself. 'Surely, a reputable firm like Christie's would never value artworks they know to be stolen.'

'What they don't know can't hurt 'em. A loyal family friend has a high-powered day job there.'

Now, these months later, Matthieu stood at the front entrance of Fontaine & Fontaine, shaking, as stressed as if that original May meeting with the Farrellys was happening again, right here, right now.

He thought about Corsica.

About his wife, Monique.

He bit his lips again, cricked the ache out of his neck and walked into the office.

17

Monte Carlo
The present day

It's late November. Madame Pasquier hovers at Félix's desk while he feigns the grave contemplation she's demanding as to whether the firm's Christmas party macarons should be chocolate or caramel, and whether the champagne should be Bollinger or Taittinger. It's only the second Covid-free Christmas, so she wants to make it memorable.

Félix is about to say *You choose* when he hears a soft pulse from inside his desk drawer – the locked one where he keeps the burner phone the Farrellys contact him on.

'Patricia, let's go with *both* flavours of macarons and *both* champagnes. Thank you.' He returns his eyes to the computer screen and squints in fake concentration at

79

nothing in particular, waiting for Blingette to get the hint. When he hears her bangles and bracelets and pendants jingling to the door, he unlocks the drawer and rests his hand there in readiness. By now, he knows never to let a Farrelly call ring out. The door clicks closed, he slides open the drawer and sees the call coming through over Niall's proprietary encrypted app.

He hasn't spoken to either of the twins since early October, when they gave him the latest instructions to arrange a deal – one of the many he's been forced to do for them. That last purchase of unnamed 'product' was for an eye-watering $175 million, the largest single transaction so far.

Every minute Matthieu finds himself at the behest of these monsters is one he hates, but the consequences of stopping, or worse, going to the police – which he thinks about almost as often as he thinks about the Farrellys – are spine chilling. He takes the call.

'Meet us at the vault in thirty minutes.'

The Farrellys are in Monaco?

Nessa didn't ask if he was free. But that's not surprising … the Farrellys never make requests, only demands. 'Don't forget to bring your eyes and your thumbs,' she adds.

Félix hopes she is referring to the Freeport's biometric security scans. But is she? He takes it as a threat. 'Is there, er, an issue?' he asks.

'Brand-new supplier. Ain't done business with 'em before,' says Nessa. 'They sent their finance guy over to eyeball the art before they commit.'

Since Félix started doing their work, not one of their counterparties has ever asked to verify the existence of the artworks independently.

He's vouched for it repeatedly – and blindly – but he's never seen the art himself. He wanted to see it, of course, but they refused. 'If we tell you it's there, boyo, it's there,' said Nessa when he raised the subject.

'Don't these new people trust you?' he dares to ask, the muscles in his back tightening like they're in a vice.

Niall speaks. 'Maybe it's you they don't trust.'

18

Getting inside the Farrelly vault is quite a rigmarole. First, Matthieu shows his face to the external scanner and what appears to be a solid steel front door slides open. At the front desk, which is unmanned, he repeats the move into a more sophisticated biometric scanner, which does both the face and eyes. It gives an amber light when he passes that test, and then a green light after he's placed his finger inside the vascular scanner that's read the blood vessels in his fingertip. A metre away, an electronically controlled, and apparently bulletproof, sand-blasted glass door opens just long enough for the party of four to pass through, him and his three 'guests', namely the two Farrellys and their supplier's certifier.

Matthieu knows the security team is watching via

CCTV for anything unusual, such as evidence of duress, and he wonders if he should give them a signal. He decides against it.

The four walk along a wide, sleek corridor, with a floor of polished concrete, and walls of blindingly clean stainless steel, with thick strips of black rubber along each side to protect them from forklift, trolley or scissor-lift damage when goods are carted in or out. A track runs high overhead between two parallel strips of daylight-white light tubes, and carries a mobile hoist that, according to the sign, can move two-tonne crates along the corridors.

The total effect makes Matthieu feel like he is in one of the science fiction movies he's always detested. *If only this were fiction*, he thinks as he walks.

At the end of the first corridor, his face, eyeballs and fingertips give the group access through a second electronically controlled door. This one isn't glass, but thick, bulletproof steel. After that, the corridor splits in two. They follow the left-pointing arrow to Vaults 12 to 30, go through yet another set of scanners and a door, and finally reach Vault 18A. He wonders where 18B is. If it exists, it is nowhere to be seen.

The door to 18A is an enamelled white grille. Another set of Matthieu's scans sends it sliding almost silently upwards into a ceiling pelmet. This reveals a second door, four tonnes of three-inch-thick solid steel with piano hinges that swing it open into the vault as effortlessly as if it was made of balsa wood.

A whoosh of air, drier and slightly cooler than the corridor, exits the vault and brushes Matthieu's cheek. A climate-control meter on the far wall is flashing numbers he can't read. Inside are four rows of plywood crates spaced two metres apart. Matthieu counts the boxes – twenty-three which, thank goodness, is the number they've had him attesting to all along. The crates are of varying dimensions, a couple as tall as three metres and as wide as a metre, but most are smaller.

'So here we are,' says Nessa to their prospective supplier's stooge.

The man, who she introduced to Matthieu as 'John Smith', carries himself like he's from a Big Four accounting firm. Caucasian, clean-shaven, a high and tight haircut, a plain dark blue suit, striped red and blue tie with a matching pocket square, crisp white shirt and the shiniest of black shoes. A living Ken doll, Smith's look is so perfectly soulless that Matthieu wonders if the man might actually work in one of those firms.

'Begin,' says Smith. He's clearly a man of few words.

Nessa opens up the inventory list on her phone, closes her eyes and randomly jabs a finger at the screen. 'Start with Number Twelve. It's in the second row, just over there,' she points. Matthieu sees that it's one of the tallest crates.

'It's Rembrandt's *Christ in the Storm on the Sea of Galilee*,' she says, reading aloud. 'His only painted seascape. Who feckin' knew that?'

'Who feckin' cares?' adds Niall, giving a shrug, as if a painting worth $100 million or more is as trifling as a plastic snow globe in a two-dollar store.

For the first time, John Smith shows emotion, even if only by raising an eyebrow. Matthieu, on the other hand, suddenly finds himself covered in goosebumps. Being this close, in private, to a Rembrandt original is one of those *tell your grandchildren* moments, except he knows that if he was ever so stupid as to do that, neither he nor his grandchildren would see daylight again.

Niall unplugs a portable electric screwdriver sitting in a rack on the side wall. He stands in front of the crate and begins to unscrew the bolts fastening the front. When he's removed all sixteen, he takes a small pry bar, and, more gently and respectfully than Matthieu would have expected, jimmies off the facing sheet of wood, which Matthieu sees is lined with a protective layer of thick black foam.

The suspense is electric. The only thing between Matthieu and the Rembrandt is a white Tyvek wrapping that Niall is already stripping off with a boxcutter that Matthieu notes is monogrammed. With *NF*.

Suddenly, the Irish giant shouts, 'Feckin' shite!' He rips off a chain that's looped through an epaulette on his jacket and, turning on the lawyer, dangles it threateningly in his face. 'Nobody toys with the Farrellys, Matthieu. If you think this is a feckin' joke, *I'll* give you a joke.'

Matthieu has no idea what Niall's going on about but, instead of the hoodlum telling him, he snaps his wrist and flicks the chain at Félix so fast that it whips around his neck twice, the tip almost piercing the lawyer's eye. Niall gives it such a violent yank that Félix falls to the ground, choking, squirming, trying but failing to pull it off, unable to breathe, his eyes rolling back into his head.

'Stop,' Matthieu thinks he hears, unsure if it is Nessa or John Smith. 'Farrelly, stop.' It has to be Smith.

He feels the chain loosen at the same time he hears the kick snap his ribs – strangely, before he feels it. Despite the piercing pain, Félix is gulping air. His eyes crack open and he sees Smith holding Niall back with a full nelson wrestling hold that he couldn't possibly have learned in Accounting 101.

Through the gap between Niall's legs, Félix can now see what sent the thug off the deep end.

There is no Rembrandt in the crate. No painting at all.

Just a scrappy plywood sheet with a movie-poster-sized photograph of the masterpiece crudely stapled to it. And scrawled over it in thick black marker ink is:

Payback is a bitch …
Fuck you, Irish!

19

Sydney

After seeing my first-ever life-sized print of *Six Sunflowers* – via *Girl #23* – I'm working on the second artwork in the photograph. It's the big, dark one. As I zoom in for a closer look, I'm starting to see a wild storm. A sailing boat is tossed by the seas. A giant wave is crashing over the bow, and the crew are desperate, struggling to regain control.

It's a work I've seen before, I'm sure of it. With the contrasts of light and dark, the *chiaroscuro*, it's most likely by one of the Old Masters. Caravaggio? I keep searching through the drawers of my mental filing cabinet. Is it him? Rembrandt, maybe?

It's still not coming to me, so I take a screenshot of the artwork – cropped without Girl or *Six Sunflowers* – and do an internet reverse image search. In less than a second, I see that, yes, it's a Rembrandt. Go, JJ!

It's his *Christ in the Storm on the Sea of Galilee*, but something is bugging me, something I can't put my finger on, until Wikipedia does it for me. The painting was stolen from Boston's Isabella Stewart Gardner Museum in 1990 and has never been recovered.

I'm kicking myself, because the Gardner Museum heist was the biggest and most brazen art theft in modern history. I should have remembered it instantly, as it was only a couple of years ago that the gallery put on a special staff screening of *This Is a Robbery*, a Netflix documentary about the heist and the fruitless search for the stolen works.

It's a crazy story. In the dead of night, two men posing as police officers, claiming they'd come to check out a disturbance, overpowered the security guards, duct-taped them to a pipe and a bench in the basement and, in just over an hour, stole thirteen works that, at the time, were valued at $200 million. Now, the museum reckons they're worth over half a billion. The haul included *three* Rembrandts, not just this one. A stunning Vermeer as well, one of only thirty-four Vermeers in the world. A Manet, too, and five works on paper by Degas. And more.

Is it weird that the two works I've spied on Girl's wall are prints of a stolen work and a destroyed one?

I think about it for a minute and decide it's no weirder than me sticking a print of *Starry Night* on the ceiling above my bed so I can see it when I wake up.

That she's chosen prints of two such magnificent works – stolen, destroyed or not – tells me something I didn't know about her before. That with her taste in art, she's a kindred spirit, less of a stranger than just a few minutes ago. For that reason alone, I'm keen to meet her in person.

20

Monte Carlo

All the crates are empty. All the art is gone.

Félix Matthieu would be gone, too, if Smith – and Nessa – hadn't stopped Niall beating him to death. *There's plenty of time for that anyway*, thinks Nessa.

She's calculating the damage. The plundering of their vault blows the Gardner Museum heist out of the water by hundreds of millions of dollars.

But standing around, waiting for their empire to sink beneath their feet, is not an option. In the Irish twins' dark world, loyalty is transitory. Once the news gets out, there'll be a flood of their lieutenants defecting to rival syndicates.

Dirty water always finds the crack.

If the sharks constantly circling below the surface discover that the art financing the Farrelly operation has vanished, Nessa knows that there will be blood in the water, and this time the Farrellys will be the prey.

Apart from the thief – Félix Matthieu, it seems – the only witness is John Smith. After Nessa whispers to her brother, he says, 'Smith, five million euro and you say nothing … to your employer, to nobody.'

With Matthieu groaning on the concrete floor, blood seeping out of his nose, Smith coolly looks at his fingernails, as if they hold more interest for him than the Farrellys' crisis, the haggling or the lawyer's pain. 'My loyalty to my employer is everything to me, Mr Farrelly. It can't be bought.'

'Six million,' says Niall.

Smith smiles and, ignoring him – a brave move at the best of times, and this is not one of them – bows to Nessa. 'A pleasure to make your acquaintance,' he says. 'I hope we meet again, in better circumstances.' He turns and takes a step towards the door.

'Smith, stop.' Nessa taps his shoulder – a light touch but one that clearly has a heavy intent.

If he gets her message, he doesn't show it. Coolly, he turns back around and checks his watch. 'My employer is expecting me to call in three minutes. No call, no deal, and you can guess the rest.'

'It seems we have an impasse, Mr Smith. Given the situation, I expect you have a suggestion?'

He pinches the edge of his pocket square and pulls it out with a flourish. It's the most animated he's been. He bends down, rubs a blob of Matthieu's blood off the toe of his left shoe, folds the cloth and places it back in position. 'I'm partial to the number fifteen. They call it *la niña bonita* in Spanish. Over the years, I've found it quite a lucky number. You might too.' He knows the Farrellys know that he's got their backs up against the wall. 'All of it paid into my account before I leave the vault.' He reaches into his inside jacket pocket, pulls out a pen and card and writes on it. 'Here … my account details.'

The twins look at each other and nod. 'Done,' says Nessa as Niall pulls out his phone, takes the card and executes the transaction. He shows his phone screen to Smith, who takes out his own phone, taps it, smiles and goes to leave. He turns back, casts his eyes down at Matthieu, and says, 'A pleasure meeting you, *mon bon docteur*. Give my fondest regards to your *belle femme*.'

Smith leaves, and Nessa, furious, kicks Matthieu in the stomach.

Niall looks on, surprised she would risk scuffing her shoes, then takes his phone out again and, this time, uses it to make a call on his app. He watches the lawyer's eyes grow even wider when he hears what the Irishman has ordered one of their local minions to do.

Outside the Freeport, Smith makes the scheduled call to his employer. Despite the deal he'd made with the devils he'd left inside, he spills their secret. Like he'd told the Farrellys, his loyalty can't be bought though, he laughs to himself, that doesn't mean he can't profit from it. His employer – who happens to be his mother – laughs too when Smith tells her.

Half an hour later, Niall is driving Matthieu's car, a Maserati Quattroporte Trofeo. He takes a call on his app from their confederate. He puts him on loudspeaker so Nessa and Matthieu – both in the back, his sister seated and the lawyer hunched – can hear.

'I have *très* sad news, Monsieur Niall,' says the man, in a thick French accent. 'On Monsieur Smith's drive back to Aéroport Nice Côte d'Azur, he swerved on la Grande Corniche to miss an oncoming van. Unfortunately, he crashed through the safety barrier and made a *plongeon* over the side, to his death.'

Niall terminates the call. 'I'll retrieve our fifteen from the bloodsucker's account later,' he says over his shoulder.

'Why stop there, ya gombeen?' asks Nessa. 'Clean him out before anyone goes looking.' She turns to Matthieu. 'So, Félix, are you still stickin' to your feckin' bullshit you don't know where our art is?'

21

Niall begins to roll the black plastic sheet around the body parts he's taken so much pleasure in severing. He hasn't enjoyed a butchery so much since before Covid, when the health-based moratorium on dismemberments took all the fun away. For the Farrellys, life is back to normal, and so is death.

Niall is wearing his favourite kill suit, the head-to-toe DuPont TY125S with extra-grip booties, like the forensics teams wear on TV. It was white when he took it out of the plastic pack, but that didn't last long. He loves these suits. They pack small and play big. Coming in at 100 grams, they're feather-light to wear and breathable so, no matter how hard he's working, the wetwork always stays on the outside.

He lets go of the plastic sheet and stands behind Monique's head, waiting for it to stop rolling. Her eyes are still frozen open from the terror he meted out to her while forcing her husband to watch, with the lawyer losing his fingers, one by one, then his toes and, finally, worse.

'Nessie, it weren't Matthieu,' he says. 'If it were, he woulda fessed up to save his missus. So I'm thinkin' one of the Fontaines betrayed us before he came into the picture. Problem is, the dead don't feckin' talk.' Furious, he gives Monique's head his best football V-pull and kicks it from one side of the Matthieu family basement to the other, her blood spraying in circles like he's just set off a bright red Catherine wheel.

Niall's scalp is aglow with sweat, his cage-fighter body pumping adrenaline. He takes out an asthma inhaler and puffs on it. Only Nessa knows he carries one. *Show no weakness, no time, nowhere* is a Farrelly aphorism their father had beaten into them from an early age.

When it comes to Nessa's shortcomings, she admits only to one … her brother. His hotheadedness has thrown them into deep and murky waters more times than she cares to remember. In her manipulative hands, Niall is a finely honed weapon. Out of her hands, if she isn't keeping close tabs on him, he can be a ticking clusterfuck, itching to explode at any time, wreaking indiscriminate carnage and, worse, risking massive blowback.

Today, he's been in check, so she lets him have his gratuitous Diego Maradona head kick without comment, a reward for trying, even if they didn't find out what happened to their art stash. Nessa coolly watches the head spin through the air and, to her surprise, quite enjoys hearing its wet crunch onto the floor. It lands so that

Monique's eyes are staring directly at her. A normal person would throw up but Nessa and her hair-trigger brother are as close to normal as a category six hurricane and just as unpredictable.

Until now, she's been standing in darkness across the other side of the room. The victims knew she was there. Hearing her clipped, steely voice coming from out of the shadows ramped up their terror. The impact pleased her, though the reason she's been obscuring herself was far more mundane: to avoid their blood and Niall's spit splattering over her shoes.

She steps out into the light and stands quietly, twisting a loop of her wild black hair round a finger. Niall knows not to disturb her, since her tongue has a sharper slice than the tools he's used to carve up their victims.

After a minute, she says, 'You're right, Niall ... the dead *don't* talk, but their tracks might.' Nessa runs her hands down the sides of her dress, a black one that's perfect for the occasion. 'I been thinkin' ...'

She looks down at the notes she's typed into her phone, details extracted from an increasingly willing to talk Félix Matthieu ... usernames, passwords and more. 'Niall, we got some diggin' to do.'

22

Two weeks later

Every news outlet in Europe is reporting that Cannes' police forensics team has finally put a person's name to the lone body part that, for three days, has been the talk of the French Riviera. Armed with that snippet of news, journalists are rushing from Cannes, where the carcass washed up on a beach, to nearby Monte Carlo. In less than an hour, the law offices of Fontaine & Fontaine are under siege.

If it wasn't winter, the bloated bag of bones might have bumped up against a circle of children frolicking in the water and messed up their heads for the rest of their lives. Instead, it was a local municipal council employee who found it, among the bottles, condoms and other debris left by the Cannes midnight zoo of party animals.

The firm's streetfront entrance is bathed by TV spotlights. Jostling reporters shove furry microphones that look like raccoon tails into the faces of everyone exiting the building, hoping they're employees who know something, any scrap, that can be sensationalised into a scoop. There's a raucous barrage of questioning as the lawyers and other staff come out with their heads down, hands in pockets, a few of them wishing Covid was back and they still had masks to hide behind.

Another bevy of journalists is lined up on the other side of the street, talking to camera … 'Who killed Félix Matthieu?' … 'Leading Monaco lawyer Dr Félix Matthieu has been identified as the victim' … 'Christmas will not be the same for the law firm of …'

They're all asking the same questions. How did a solid, respectable professional like Matthieu end up as a headless, limbless torso? Where is his wife, Monique, a popular local artist? The couple have been missing for two weeks. Has she ended up the same way?

Madame Pasquier exits the elevator at the foyer. Just before she left the office, the partners had taken the final step to formalise the appointment of their fourth senior partner, the third since the founder – her mentor and friend Jacques – died in 2021. She's sobbing so much that her bling is clinking loudly. 'Some good luck charm for the firm I turned out to be,' she mumbles. Through the glass doors ahead, she spots the bedlam on the street and makes a decision … she can't go through this again … she won't.

She turns around and takes the next elevator back upstairs, to hand in her resignation.

23

Sydney

It's half-past sparrow, just after dawn's first peep. I'm leaning back against one of the boardwalk security bollards out the front of Girl's building, watching the incredible summer morning break into flares ... lilacs and golds, and yellows and oranges ... all shooting over the roof of the Finger Wharf. It's a cracker of a sunrise.

'Hey, Scottie,' I say, nudging him. He's lying at my feet, his front paws toying with the rubber bone I bought for him yesterday. Because I've grown to love him so much – how could I not? – I got him a wishbone-shaped one, hoping that Brandy will let me come by and take him for walks when she gets back from her trip. 'Look up there, Scottie. Isn't that the most beautiful sunrise you've ever seen?'

I post a couple of shots to my Instagram. A cute one with Scottie chewing his bone, and one of the breathtaking sky. I look back down at Scottie, but he's still chewing, ignoring the lightshow. I wonder, *Can dogs see colour?*

I use my phone to do a quick search. Apparently, a dog's colour spectrum is restricted to greys, browns, yellows and blues. So, it's no wonder Scottie's not as entranced with the sunrise, or art, as I am. It probably also explains why he prefers my bright yellow wishbone to the red one back at the apartment. Or maybe it's just that mine is new, and chewier.

Girl hasn't been around for days, mornings or evenings. Today is probably going to be no different.

*

As well as loitering, before and after work, I've been staying up nights, working on my portraits of Girl. Previously, I was focusing on *Girls #1* through *#30* but now I've moved on to *Girls #31* to *#53*.

It's been such a great summer's day that, even at 9 pm, the balcony tiles are as warm as toast. Scottie's sprawled out there, having a snooze, while I'm inside comparing *Girl #52* with the shot that first revealed her two art prints to me, *Girl #23*. It's the oddest thing – I took both photos from a similar angle, but the two blurs behind Girl in *#52* are considerably brighter and more colourful than they are in *#23*. They're the same size but more luminous. I see it's the same with *Girl #53*. I'm detecting patches of reds, oranges and blues that aren't present in *Girl #23*.

Did she switch on her lights just before I took these later shots and I got some kind of reflection?

Or is it because I've just downed my third V&T and my eyes are a bit wonky?

It's time for a cuppa, definitely, even though I've got Brandy's amazing espresso machine. My mother always drank tea in times of contemplation. She drank so much tea, the family joke was that her blood group was Earl Grey. 'Tea makes everything clearer, and better,' she used to say which, given how long she took to wise up to her wreck of a marriage, was another joke, sadly.

It turns out Brandy's got a great selection of teas too, and I go with green tea, despite the fact that when Goldberg came round the other week, it gave him a migraine. 'Who said herbal teas are good for you?' he moaned, as I gave him two Panadols and an icepack. But tonight, together with a couple of gingersnap cookies, it's perfect.

I sit back on the couch to start working on the photographs – the same routine I used with *#23*. I'm quicker this time, but what I'm coming up with doesn't make sense.

Instead of the Rembrandt print revealing itself, what I'm getting looks like a big Matisse – bright, chirpy swathes of colour, blotches of the reds and oranges and blues I thought I detected before. It's like one of Matisse's cut-outs but, even at this distance, I can see it's lacking his verve and vitality. *Six Sunflowers* isn't there either. In its spot, I see a Banksy-like stencil of a black cat on a white background. I'm thinking Banksy-like, not Banksy, because the cat is Hallmark-card cute, and there's no visual gag, no barbed or political point.

I do reverse image searches of these two works, but neither gets any relevant hits. Lots of similar works, but none the same.

I'm up till midnight repeating the sharpening process on other *Girl* photos, going backwards one by one from *Girl #52* to *#42*. Each one's showing me the Non-Matisse and the Non-Banksy.

Then, from *#41*, it gets weird. From there through *#35*, the two rectangles of bright blurs get thinner and thinner, until at *#34*, and then through to *#30*, they're fattening up again, getting wider and wider. By the time I reach *#30*, they're back to the same sizes and colours they were in *#23* where the big one, the Rembrandt, is dark and forbidding, and the smaller one is brighter and happier, with the yellows, blues and lilac of *Six Sunflowers*.

*

By 4.30 am, I've worked solidly on six of them: *#40, #38, #36, #34, #32* and *#31,* and what they're showing me is blowing my mind. If I printed them out, stapled them together and riffled through them with my finger, I'd get a jerky movie of *Sunflowers* and *Storm* slowly flipping over until they're hidden flush against the wall, simultaneously bringing to the front what's affixed to their backs: the Non-Matisse and the Non-Banksy.

What the hell?

Who hangs prints back-to-back with an elaborate – and expensive – mechanism that does a *now-you-see-'em-now-you-don't* switcheroo? Girl does, obviously. But why?

Who is Girl anyway? Some kind of magician?

I think on it some more, and the best explanation I come up with is that maybe she's a set designer for a theatre, trying out different and fancy mechanisms for fast set changes.

*

For the past two days, I've been pondering my set-designer theory. While it's not bad, the alternative that keeps jumping out at me is far less benign … that she's some kind of master forger. One who creates fake Rembrandts and Van Goghs, hangs them to show her clients, but if someone else turns up … her cleaners, maybe, or the police … she flips them over with a simple flick of a switch, concealing her forgeries from their prying eyes and only showing them the rubbish pictures.

Perhaps that's why she keeps her curtains drawn. If that ruckus hadn't happened the other day and she hadn't opened them, my camera and I would never have got a look-in.

Come on, I tell myself, *I've watched too many movies*. Not that you *can* ever watch too many, but I have watched a hell of a lot, and some of them multiple times.

If she's really a forger and not a set designer, proving it could be extremely risky, given that forgery is a serious criminal offence. And if it involves a Rembrandt and a Van Gogh, the stakes would be pretty high.

Then I remember a line Geena Davis used somewhere. A movie or an interview, I can't remember which. 'If you risk nothing, then you risk everything.' Hence the need to ramp up what I've already been doing … setting out to bump into her accidentally on purpose and, hopefully, befriend her and find out more. I haven't seen her anywhere for over a week. Maybe she's gone on vacation. Or maybe she flew off to Art Basel in Miami, Florida, to check out the next artwork she's going to counterfeit.

Or perhaps she's just working on a set for a theatre company in another city.

Whatever it is, I decide, it can't last forever and she'll be back soon enough. *I just have to stick with my plan and hang around.* So … big move … I decide to take leave from work.

The gallery's HR department doesn't have a leave category for *exposing master forgers* and I don't intend to chuck a pile of sickies, so I organise to take a couple of weeks' annual leave. I've got heaps owing.

That sorted, I refine in my mind the scene I'm hoping for. When we first see each other – *eventually!* – I'll act really cool but I'll do nothing. The next day, we'll catch each other's eye in the distance, and I'll nod and she'll nod back. A day or two later, I'll get up the courage to say something, like a friendly *Beautiful day*, and it'll go from there. Eventually, she'll invite me over and, well, you know.

Obviously, I'll need a cover story. The house-sitting, that's fine. Nothing about me shouts rich and/or successful, and if I lied about that, she'd catch me out in a flash. Like with a possible first question, *Hey, JJ, who's your strata manager?* I'd be screwed straightaway.

But if she does turn out to be a forger and not a set designer, me fessing up to being an art conservator would be a massive no-no. So, I definitely need to pretend I have a different job.

I look at the city's skyscrapers and run my eyes over the neon signs. I could be a mid-ranking insurance claims officer at QBE. *No!* That's as bad as being an art conservator – worse, since they probably insure art and she might suspect I'm an undercover investigator. Then I see an accounting firm. *That's it!* I'll be a box-ticking auditor at EY, a job that fits me and my less-than-sparkling personality down to the ground.

24

I've been on annual leave for three days, and Scottie and I still haven't had a Girl sighting. We've been walking here, there and everywhere – mixing it up at various times of the day – and she's still a ghost. Scottie's over the moon because I've never walked him so much, but I'm on a mission. If I, a fair-skinned redhead, truly wanted to spend three days of my summer holidays in the great outdoors, it wouldn't involve hanging around Woolloomooloo where, if anyone noticed, they might start to think I'm a hooker, or a druggie looking for a fix.

By day four, when I'm thinking of ditching my plan, she finally reappears. It's *Gone Girl* becomes *Now You See Her*. As she swings around the corner, I see an unexpected bonus.

Dog people love other people's dogs.

I pretend I'm checking my watch, then the sky, then lean down to give Scottie a scratch on his muzzle. Out of the corner of my eye, I see her watching, so I give him an extra big cuddle.

Her dog is one of those gorgeous tiny poodle crosses. I'm not an expert on dogs, so I'm unsure if it's a labradoodle or a cavoodle or a schnoodle. Her puppy – *is it a puppy?* I don't have a clue – is the exact colour of the salted caramel gelato I get at the Circular Quay Gelatissimo.

Scottie likes any dog, but little dogs often pull away from him. He's built like a miniature horse but being young – or a dog – he doesn't know it. This whatever-oodle seems to like big dogs, though, and it's actually doing my work for me, dragging Girl towards us.

With what was just the bare bones of a plan – more plan-ish than an actual plan – about to burst into becoming a reality, I break out in a sweat and my mouth dries. I feel a little woozy, like the time I walked into Cargo Bar for my first Tinder date, which was a disaster. The guy kept excusing himself. First to go to the bathroom, then to step outside to make an important work call, then to go to the bathroom again. I didn't know how to take it, until the waiter took pity and said the creep was two-timing me with another date, one he'd seated at an outside table.

Like when I was on that 'date', I'm now worried that JJ's biting off more than she can chew. Yes, I often talk about myself in the third person. Judgement is less confronting that way.

But … *ooph!* Scottie jerks the lead out of my hand and is racing off towards them.

25

Fifty metres ahead of me, Girl is bending down to pat Scottie, who's nuzzling his nose into her oodle-doodle's bum. She's picking up his lead for me – *thank you, Girl* – and giving him a friendly hug that's about as big as my encroaching panic attack.

She stands up and gives me a little wave, one of those *I know we don't know each other, but we're dog people and this is what dog people do* kinds. She smiles. Her teeth – OMG! – glint in the sunlight, whiter than white, all straight and perfect. Like Tom Cruise, apart from that middle tooth of his, which is weird but kind of charming.

Maybe Girl's a movie star and she's in Sydney on a shoot? She sure dresses like one, wearing a loose-fitting kaftan with a swirl of bright, summery colours. And, like the first time I saw her, she's wearing a headscarf. It's not the same ruby and emerald one. This one's much closer to the real *Girl with a Pearl Earring* … solid ultramarine blue piled on top of her head, with tails of yellow silk falling down her back. Classy. And she's so beautiful. Her skin is like honey, and I'm already betting that her accent is a plummy English one you would be force-fed in some finishing school somewhere. She's barefoot, so it's a good thing it's early or the boardwalk would be burning the soles off her feet.

Unless she's spent the last week or so locked inside her apartment making forgeries, Girl being an actor is definitely another possible reason why I haven't seen her. She might have been learning a script, strutting around her apartment and reciting lines to the walls and to her dog. Or maybe she's been away, not to Art Basel but on location somewhere … Broken Hill maybe, to make a new *Mad Max* movie, or the Great Barrier Reef for a climate-change-disaster film.

Hey, what if she knows Russell Crowe? I could get a shot of the two of them together and offer it to one of the gossip columns. Except then I'd be a paparazzo, and that's not how I want to start my climb up the photography ladder. *The paparazzi world shocks me. I always want to know the person. I want to know who I am photographing.* That's not me talking, it's Annie Leibovitz. I've watched that interview so many times I know it by heart.

Girl is heading my way, and Scottie and her dog are bouncing and bounding all over each other like they're old buddies. My body is awash with sweat. I go to step forward, to be friendly, but I can't do it so I do the next best thing. I lift my camera – it's been hanging around my neck – and start taking shots of the boisterous trio as they approach. A camera's often a convenient barrier to my discomfort. It can also be a good conversation starter, so I don't know why I didn't think of it before.

But today it's different. Girl sees me snapping and stops for a split second, like I've taken a liberty … like she doesn't want her photo taken. I lower the camera, and my distress that I might have blown it overtakes my panic and I head towards her, blathering, 'Look, I hope you're not upset that I took the shots just then. I should've asked first, I know, but you all looked so cute together … it was just a reflex. I'll delete them straight away if you prefer.' Then I inhale.

She smiles. *That* smile. Close up, it's even more dazzling, and her eyes … none of my shots from a distance did them justice. A deep chocolate-brown, they're fringed with long lashes, like a portal into some exotic, magical world. Maybe they're fake?

'If you wouldn't mind,' she says. Her voice isn't at all plummy like I expected. It's husky, deep and raspy, like Miley Cyrus after a rough night. And if Cyrus was Scottish. 'I don't want to be mean or anything,' she says, 'but I've recently had a nasty break-up – really nasty – and if you post any of those photos, my ex might see them and work out where I'm staying and start harassing me again. Shots of my dog, Winston Junior, they're fine. I got him *after* the split.'

I raise the camera, show her the photos on the screen … she says nice things about them … I say half a dozen *Sorrys* … then I delete the ones with her in them.

'Thanks,' she says, and holds out her hand. She's got the two leashes in her other one. 'Our dogs seem to be instant friends. Do you live around here? I'm Lesley, by the way.'

Not plummy English at all, but Scottish. And she's a Lesley, which is for sure a cool actor's name. Or maybe a model's ... though her being a set designer is still a possibility. Her Scottish brogue wouldn't be a problem in any of those jobs. Good actors can do any accent, and set designers can be from anywhere. Models never need to open their mouths or, if they do, it's to utter some rubbish line about world peace like Sandra Bullock did in *Miss Congeniality*. While I'm overthinking, as usual, Girl's hand is hovering in the air. I put mine out and give hers a shake.

She's not a forger. A forger wouldn't be a Lesley. She'd be an Ingrid or Adeline or Lavinia. Maybe a Svetlana.

I go to say *I'm JJ*, but my tongue is suddenly stuck. I raise my hand and give a little covered cough. 'I'm JJ. I live just over there, on the Finger Wharf. The apartment with the – oops – embarrassing red towel on the balcony and—'

She winks. 'You don't know Russell Crowe, do you? I read he lives over there. Running into him in the lobby would be amazing. Have you ever?'

She's so starstruck, she's clearly not an actor or a set designer. So, what is she, a model or a forger? 'No, I don't know him,' I say. 'I'm only house-sitting, and I haven't been here very long. From what you said – sorry about the break-up – you must be a local too?'

She points to her place. 'That's me there. Maybe we can wave to each other from our balconies.'

This is the moment I should invite her to come over to Brandy's, to check out how the sunset looks over hers – so that tomorrow she'll be inclined to return the favour – but instead all that comes out is, 'Right. Yes. Exactly.'

The dogs are scrabbling around our feet and she says, 'I'm dying for my morning coffee. There's a cool cafe across the street—'

Despite my tongue sticking to the roof of my brain, this is turning out even better than I imagined.

'—and what's really great is that Bruce over there – the barista – he doesn't mind dogs. Want to join me?'

If I believed in a higher power, I'd be raising my head to the heavens right now and thanking whoever's up there for rescuing me. 'Sure,' I say, 'I'd love to. He's Scottie,' I add, tugging on his leash. 'It's short for Biscotti Pippen.'

'Hey, that's cute. Like the basketball player, right?' Her dog, she tells me, is a cavoodle.

'Why Winston Junior?' I ask her, expecting her to tell me it's something to do with Winston Churchill … or John Howard, whose middle name is Winston. I don't know why I know that, by the way. I was never a big fan.

We're crossing the street towards the cafe. 'I grew up in Edinburgh, and my parents bought me this huge, adorable teddy bear from a toy shop in London when they went there for a trip. He was already called Winston. He was really huge … towered over me until I was about four and started outgrowing him. So, a few weeks ago, after the break-up, I found this adorable little fellow and he's exactly the same colour.' She bends down and gives him a rub. 'Winston seemed the obvious name, but I added the "Junior" out of respect. I know it sounds stupid. I mostly call him Winston, or Winnie. Or Win, if I'm annoyed.'

I make a mental note of the story, it's so sweet. Maybe I'll quote it on Instagram or TikTok when I post some images of the dogs. 'Edinburgh,' I say as we take a table outside on the footpath, the dogs curling up at our feet, pawing each other like the old gay lovers at the table that's three across from us. 'It's pretty bleak there, isn't it? Gosh, sorry,' I say, tapping my wrist in a slight rebuke. 'I guess if you were born there—'

'No, no. It's fine, really. Oh hi,' she says to the waiter. 'I'll have a double espresso in a large cup, with a second cup, same size, but full of milk froth. No milk, just froth. And an iced water on the side, with a slice of lemon zest.'

It's almost the same as Annie Leibovitz drinks.

She turns to me and adds, 'And you? It's my shout by the way, to make up for the pictures you deleted for me.'

Lesley is a delight. 'Oh wow, thank you,' I say and, without thinking, tell the waiter, 'I'll have what she's having,' and then I worry that she'll think I'm being corny because it's a line from *When Harry Met Sally*. So I explain to her I'm a mad movie and TV buff and couldn't help saying it. The last thing I want her to think is that I'm a stalker which, actually, I am.

'Ah,' she says. 'Got it. It'd be a pretty small world if you shared the same coffee fetish as me. I love it strong and I don't like milk, so cappuccinos, lattes and flat whites are out, but I really love the milk froth. If I ask for a long macchiato with extra froth, they *never* make it how I like, so I go DIY. Today's waiter is new but Bruce makes my usual to perfection.'

There's something about Lesley that's … I don't quite know. Whatever it is, it makes her really engaging and pleasant to be around. And her lashes are so long, I kind of want to tug on them.

I owe Scottie big time for making the introduction. I give him a rub, and he looks up at me with his dreamy goggle-eyes and licks my hand.

26

The way Lesley talks to me over our morning coffees for the next two days, it's like she's craving company. I'm an aggressively quiet person – it's the only assertive thing about me – so we make a pretty good pair. She's bubbly and chatty, and I'm bland and unthreatening. I feel like I'm a comfy old sofa that she's nestling into for the evening.

The bubbliness stops, though, when she feels comfortable enough to tell me her story. It's so sad. This Aussie tourist – Paul – he visited Edinburgh. He's handsome and charming, she says, and goes to show me some photos. She's not keeping them because she misses him, she adds, 'It's in case I need to show the police.' For some reason, I'm visualising someone like a Chris Hemsworth. A girl can dream, right?

She holds back on passing her phone over to me. I see a tear in the corner of her eye, and I stay quiet.

Lesley gathers her strength and tells me how, at first, everything was rosy. They date for a few months, he's always bringing her flowers and gifts. Her parents welcome him when he pops into their chippy – the fish and chip shop they run – which he starts to do a lot ... to say hi or to pick up a deep-fried Mars Bar. Then his visa runs out and he's got to return to Melbourne.

He wants to have The Big Discussion, so Paul and Lesley take a slow midnight stroll along the Water of Leith. I'm visualising Emily from *Emily in Paris* hand in hand with Gabriel walking along the banks of the Seine, which is the best imagery I can drum up on short notice.

Lesley's won over and agrees to fly to Australia with Paul ... to get a work permit, maybe apply for residency, go the whole let's-be-together hog. But as soon as they're back on his home turf, her Prince Charming morphs into Lord Voldemort. The flowers and the gifts stop, he's *Out with my mates* a lot, and the second he walks through the door of their Carlton apartment, the mean, controlling behaviour starts up, regardless of whether he's drunk or sober.

He sounds just like Hugh, except that Hugh never had alcohol as an excuse for being a bastard.

Lesley doesn't put up with it for long. She's smarter than my mother. Well, maybe not smarter, but more decisive, and she doesn't have a kid to worry about. Plus, an inheritance from Lesley's uncle – 'a bucketload of money' she says – comes through to her, which was enough to make a fresh start. So, with her new stash of cash, she flits to Sydney, leaving Paul a note saying she's flown back to Edinburgh, which she hasn't and won't because she'd lose too much face with her parents, who'd never wanted her to move to Australia in the first place. They still don't know it hasn't worked out with Paul. All she's told them is that they're in Sydney now, and whenever she and her parents do Zoom calls, she tells them he's at work.

If Paul finds out where she is, and that she's got money … She doesn't finish the sentence. She doesn't need to.

After a respectful lull, and without pressing her to show me Paul's photograph, I change the subject and ask her *What do you do?* Her answer has me in awe. She's not anything I'd guessed. *I'm a writer,* she says. Dampening my awe a bit, she adds, *Or I hope to be.* Then, mistaking my apparently quizzical look, she asks, *Don't you like writers?*

It's not that, of course. It's that I'm wondering why a writer's got that flipover art. I explain it away by telling her about my dyslexia, though I quickly add, *But, hey, if your novel's published as an audiobook, I'll buy it the first day it's out.* Then I say, *What's it about?* to keep the subject off me for as long as I can, since I'm always uncomfortable talking about myself. And that's when it's the real me I'm talking about. It'll be even harder when it's the fake me.

It's the Great Australian Novel, she laughs – she's got a beautiful throaty laugh – *by a Scot who was brought up above a fish and chip shop, who's lived in Australia for five minutes, knows pretty much nothing about the place, has never been to the outback or the Great Barrier Reef, still finds it weird that it's hot at Christmas and that people put beetroot on burgers, and, oh, has never written anything before.*

She does that little laugh with the tossing-back-hair thing, but it doesn't work because of the scarf wrapped around her head. Today it's an orange one, which really sets off her eyes, and those incredible lashes.

But I'm a woman and foreign – foreign-ish – so I hope the publishers will be all over me. If I was a lesbian, that would seal it. The more diversity the better, right? She laughs again.

Is that code? Is she sending out feelers? I don't ask, of course, but I start wondering if that's why she's so friendly.

I've never tried sex with a woman. But then, I haven't tried a lot of things in that department.

My questions are running out and I can't keep probing Lesley or she'll get suspicious. I've got my 'boring old auditor' line ready except that, by now, with her being so candid, I feel rotten about lying to her.

I lie just the same. What choice have I got? I *could* go with the truth but that's not the plan and I'm already mentally screening that *You can't handle the truth!* scene from *A Few Good Men*, with me as Jack Nicholson and her as Tom Cruise. She does have his teeth.

For the past two days, back at Brandy's apartment, I've been staring into the mirror a lot, practising how to convincingly look boring, like an auditor. I found – unsurprisingly, I guess – that it comes quite naturally to me.

Despite all my prep, I'm starting to sweat again as I talk because Lesley is leaning forward resting her head on her hands, her elbows on the table, looking at me and listening so intently, like auditing is the most fascinating job on the planet. The only people in the world who could possibly think so are lawyers and proctologists, and Lesley is neither of those. But writers, I remind myself, are always interested in character.

And then I get a brainwave: if I'm lying about what I do and who I am, maybe she is too, which is exactly what she'd be doing if she really is a master forger.

She lets me babble on about ticking boxes and random sampling, and green pencils and debits and credits and such. Her first question throws me. *But you're dyslexic?*

I hadn't seen it coming, so I'm thankful I had the smarts to pick a black shirt today, so the burst of perspiration isn't as obvious. I pick up my napkin and cover a cough, then surreptitiously wipe my face and collect my thoughts.

It's not that I don't have a good answer. I've got a great one … because it's the truth. But I'm dripping because I haven't rehearsed it.

I set the words in my mind and go for it, explaining that there are different types of dyslexia, and mine is about trouble with reading and spelling. If a person's difficulty is with numbers, it's often called *math dyslexia* but it's more accurate to call it *dyscalculia* and, fortunately, I tell her, I don't have that. This is also true.

She nods and gives me one of her disarming Tom Cruise smiles, and I step down from the witness stand, relieved.

Immediately, I start back on her, to see if I can find any cracks in her story, and to delay any other difficult questions she might have up her sleeve. *What's your book really about?* It's the obvious question a person would ask a writer. I pick up my coffee to take a sip, but by now it's empty and I probably look like an idiot. If she notices, she doesn't say. She looks at her watch and starts to get up. *An author never tells*, she says. *It's bad luck. Besides, the story might change ten times before I finish it.*

That makes sense, I suppose. She pulls on Winston's leash and says, *Tomorrow?*

She seems so genuine, I'm now thinking she's not a forger. I've been checking out her hands every morning. No paint. None. Nothing under her nails. Not a skerrick in her knuckle wrinkles, the spot where my own scrubbing after work usually misses.

As Lesley wanders off with Winston, I wonder about her writing ritual. They always ask authors about that at writers' festivals. Does she wake at 4 am, plump her pillows and sit up in bed with Winston curled beside her, then flip open her laptop and start working on her grand opus? Or does she wait till after our coffee, go home to make herself a big brekkie, then head to her desk and get stuck into her manuscript where she left off yesterday?

Maybe she'll make me one of her characters. *That* would be so cool. Perhaps that's why she's so friendly, and I totally misread the girl-to-girl thing.

> Midnight. Mousy redhead wannabe photographer moonlighting as auditor for scratch found dead on Finger Wharf, her inkjet lurcher Scottie howling into the cloudless night sky. Her camera lies beside her, the viewfinder casting a dim light across the spreading pool of blood, a mirror reflecting the image of a man who's looming towards her with a knife held high and a snarl on his stubbled face.

I walk back to Brandy's with a spring in my step. I really don't want Lesley to be a forger. What we've got between us is so incredibly comfortable, I feel that we could *actually* become friends, except for the fact true friends don't lie to each other.

I stop in my tracks.

What if she wears gloves when she paints?

27

Belfast

As far as the Farrellys know, no one alive apart from the art thief – whoever that is – is aware that their treasure trove is missing. John Smith is gone, disposed of by Angel, a towering man originally from Algeria, who works for them when he's not moonlighting as a mixologist at the Casino de Monte-Carlo. What the Farrellys ask, Angel does. He never asks why.

Nessa and Niall are back in Belfast. They're watching Angel via the CCTV camera image they are projecting onto the wall screen in Nessa's office at the docks, recording it so they can review it later if they need to.

Angel swishes into the storage unit at Monaco Self-Stockage, wearing a *Luther*-inspired greatcoat. 'The guy really does fancy himself as Idris Elba,' says Nessa to her brother. The unit is one that Félix Matthieu and his co-executor rented to stack and store the personal items of Claude's they couldn't bring themselves to dispose of.

Before Angel begins his rummage through the dead lawyer's things, Nessa spies a stack of paintings leaning against the far wall. Hopeful, she nudges Niall. 'Angel,' she says using the talk feature on her brother's app, 'hold up each of those paintings on the back wall so we can see them.' Listening through an earpiece, Angel goes to do as he is told. Nessa holds her breath and mentally crosses her fingers as Angel pulls up the first work and turns it around to show the camera.

It's a photograph, not a painting. Nessa slams her fist on the desk. 'Damn.' It's a shot of a man extracting himself from what she guesses is a Formula One racing car. He's wearing a red suit, and an orange-and-black-striped helmet.

'Ayrton Senna's crash of 1988,' says Niall right off the bat, letting her know he knows stuff about stuff. 'Monaco Grand Prix, team McLaren–Honda.'

'The sponsor was Marlboro, I see,' Nessa adds unnecessarily. 'When did they ban tobacco ads?' she asks. She doesn't care but is giving her brother an opportunity to brag when it can't do any harm.

'It was 2006, but it wasn't exactly a ban. What happened was that—'

She stops listening.

Angel shows them the other 'paintings'. They're all photos of iconic moments in Monaco's history. Three more are Grand Prix shots, the details of which Niall rattles off, and a few are of weddings. The only one Nessa picks is Grace Kelly marrying Prince Rainier. The others are just 'another feckin' prince marryin' another feckin' pauper'. She wonders why Claude gave a shit about crap like this and then notices one of the photos has thick handwriting at the bottom, just above the frame. 'Hey, Angel, hold that writin' up to the camera.'

To my dear Jacques Fontaine, she translates for Niall. Her brother isn't great with languages. Not even English. The words are clear enough to her, though the signature below them is illegible. Presumably, it's the photographer's. 'Claude kept these because they belonged to Jacques,' she says, talking more to herself than Niall.

Niall wears melancholy like he wears a tie – namely, he doesn't. 'Angel,' he says, 'shove that giant teddy bear aside. I want to see what's in the box behind it. What's with that?' he says to Nessa. 'A fully grown adult keepin' a feckin' toy bear …'

She could remind him of his precious collection of *Star Wars* action figures, but doesn't.

Angel shifts the caramel-coloured bear aside but knocks the latch on its collar so it drops from around his thick neck and falls to the floor. He goes to pick it up, but Niall says, 'Eejit, the box. Show us what's in the box.'

Fifteen minutes later, Angel is done. He leaves the storage unit, the hem of his *Luther* coat sweeping behind him.

He's shown them everything, and they got nothing.

28

Sydney

I'm gaping at today's cloudless evening sky the way I imagine Titian did when he daubed a splotch of ultramarine blue on his canvas for the first time. That mixed feeling of awe and chutzpah and Catholic guilt I'm sure he experienced when he dared to dip a brush into his first little pyramid of powdered lapis lazuli. Mined in Afghanistan and costing five times more than gold, that blue tint was an almost forbidden treasure back then. And in this Sydney sky, it's still a treasure but we're getting it for free. The truth is, I'm going all lyrical because it's a hook to reality. Constantly practising in front of the bathroom mirror how to pretend to be an auditor means I also need to keep reminding myself I'm really an art conservator.

The sun is still high and the wind is so low that the water in Woolloomooloo Bay is a glittery mirror. I'm sitting cross-legged on *Seaduction*'s foredeck, right up at the pointy tip of the bow, close to the anchor well. I lean slightly to my right – starboard – and look over the side of the hull into the water. Reflected back at me is my practical, though hardly elegant, headwear, that floppy, wide brim bucket of a hat. I'm wearing it because my new cap hasn't been delivered yet. That's a baseball cap, basic black but with a white rabbit on the front panel. I ordered it last week, off the website for the South Sydney Rabbitohs, the rugby league club Russell Crowe owns part of. You can never be too prepared, right?

I push my glass – plastic on the outside and V&T and ice on the inside – into the safety of one of the drink holders conveniently set in the lid of the anchor well. I resume taking casual snaps of the scene, desperately hoping that Lesley will pull open her curtains again so I can get more shots of the Rembrandt and Van Gogh. We haven't got to the *invite me over* stage yet.

I hear a *Hey* come from behind me. A man, on the marina.

'Can I come aboard?'

I freeze. His voice is earthy and guttural, and warm. Could it be … Russell? If only I had my Rabbitohs cap on. I'm afraid to look behind me – in part, because I'm not only wearing the wrong hat, it's *this* hat.

If it's him, what do I say?

'*Hello*,' the it-might-be-Russell voice repeats. I slowly turn around, and force-curl the ends of my lips into a smile.

Oh.

I only barely recognise him. It's Nantucket Norm, the guy from two boats down, but he's ditched his country club outfit for a monkey suit. He's got to be a banker in the city, I decide. Probably like the clown I met on Hinge who kept asking me inane questions about interest rates and then answered them for me, and who laughed at his own jokes while touching or, worse, jabbing my arm.

I get all of that from Boat Guy's *Hello*, and from his grey pinstripe suit, crisp white shirt and sharp maroon tie.

Is that a green pen I see in his breast pocket? What if he's an auditor, like I'm supposed to be? That would be a total disaster. Or, being positive about it, and leaning into the opportunity, I could pepper him with questions, to give me the nuances I need to keep building my cover story for Lesley.

'Hey there.' I smile and nod but he's already taking off his shoes like he was going to come aboard regardless.

'Are you a photographer?' he asks, leaving his shoes on the jetty and picking up the longneck of Great Northern pale malt he'd put down. It's a Queensland beer, so I'm wondering if he's from up there.

If I had more self-confidence, I would've said *Sure, I'm a photographer*, the same way Lesley told me she's a writer, even though she hasn't published a single word. Instead I say, 'Kind of.'

He's padding across the deck in his socks, black ones, no holes – I hope he doesn't slip on the gelcoat surface – and gives me a *Cheers* by saluting with his bottle before he takes a swig. 'Do you mind?' he says, and goes to sit down.

'Watch that there.' I point to a dried-out dollop of bird poop on the deck.

He says thanks and sits. He chooses my side of the mess, which brings him a bit closer to me than I find comfortable. I squidge my bum a bit further over to the left where I can get a better look at him and, boy, is he handsome! He tips his head to the side and stares across to the other side of the bay. He has mysterious deep-lidded bedroom eyes and salt and pepper hair, like George Clooney in, well, every movie he's ever been in. Swoon.

'I'm Paul,' he says. *Paul!* Panic instantly rises from my stomach. I'm almost throwing up. *Calm down*, I tell myself. *It's a common name, goes back to the apostles – before that, even. True*, I argue back, *but it's also the name of the bastard who Lesley's escaped from.*

Or who she believes she escaped from.

29

'Where's your dog?' he asks when I don't tell him my name.

'Scottie's curled up down below,' I say. The last time I saw him, he was snuggled up on his faux fur bed.

Paul nods, telling me he's seen the two of us on the boat most evenings, or walking in the mornings. 'It's not my boat … that one there.' He points to the one I've seen him on. 'I'm boat-sitting for a friend. Have you been a photographer for long?'

He's asking a lot of questions. A lot. My mind is racing, imagining the horrible things he wants to do to Lesley and how it's up to me to stop him. 'When did you get here from Melbourne?' I just blurt it out, like a kid high on the sugar from three bowls of Froot Loops without milk.

He looks at me like I'm that TV psychic you phone who's correctly divined that your mother died last week, that her name was Mary and she always burned the chops. 'How'd you know I'm from Melbourne?'

OMG! He *is* Paul … Lesley's Paul. He says it with a little shrug, as if he's embarrassed to admit it, which means he is definitely hiding something.

'I can pick a Melbourne accent a mile off,' I lie. 'How long are you in Sydney for? Is it work? Pleasure?'

He's been here six years for work, he tells me. If that's true, he can't be Lesley's Paul – but is it? He goes on about how he's a leasing agent. He rents out a few of the properties across the bay, he says, pointing over to Lesley's, and he's just signed the paperwork to lease three floors of one of the towers at Barangaroo, after a five-month negotiation. All of which, if it's true, makes his job as big a yawn as an auditor's, except with better views.

I remind myself that Lesley's Paul is manipulative and clever, so I must keep my guard up. If he's seen me walking these past few mornings, he's probably seen me having coffee with her.

If he's Lesley's Paul, I know why he's come aboard. If not, what's he doing here?

'I'm JJ,' I finally tell him, since I can't think of anything else to say other than *Are you here to harass or kidnap Lesley?* 'I'm an auditor,' I add.

He starts babbling on about the new accounting standard for leases, like it's as thrilling as Jeff Bezos or Richard Branson walking on the moon, and I start to freak. I barely know what a lease is, and all I know about the accounting for them is how my landlord hit me with $360 for melting the kitchen laminate when the oil in my deep-fryer caught fire last year.

'Enough work talk,' I say, sounding bolder than usual. Hearing myself taking charge is a funny feeling, like putting on a coat you never thought would suit you but finding it fits pretty well and looks quite good on you.

Just then, my stupid hat nearly blows off but I rescue it, unfortunately. Wanting to keep my new self-confident pose, I smile and hand it to him. 'It's a family heirloom.'

Paul puts down the beer, wipes his hands on his pants – but would a professional man really do that? – then takes the hat and looks at it intently, like he's thinking of bidding on it in an auction. 'The logo says, "Since 2022",' he notes. 'How's that an heirloom?'

I think more quickly than normal. 'What's a collectible before it's a collectible? It's that thing you love and keep in your top drawer, right?' It's probably the adrenaline from panic that's giving me a buzz, but maybe it's something else. Maybe I'm beginning to like this Paul.

So long as he isn't Lesley's Paul.

30

It's becoming a morning ritual with Lesley and me. I walk for a bit, then it's *Hey!* when we see each other, a pat and cuddle of the dogs, then coffee – her regular times two – a chat, and *Bye!*

Today, Lesley does pass over her phone to show me a photo of Paul. This is a big moment, at least for me. I'm holding the phone but I'm not looking. Not yet. I'm not really sure that I want to find out if her Paul is my Paul.

Did I actually say *my* Paul? I'm getting way ahead of myself, even if we have had sunset drinks three times now, and a lot of laughs. Paul and I have something in common, too, apart from 'both' of us having boring jobs. He's a movie buff. He even knew about the Hitchcock *Rear Window* camera thingy, and I thought nobody knew about that.

I was tossing and turning all last night, worrying about the 'Paul' situation. Should I tell her that a guy with that name just turned up on my boat with a beer? That he's from Melbourne? That he's kind of cute, especially for someone with a job in leasing? That I might be seeing him, as in *seeing* him? That he says he's hanging around the area because he's looking after a mate's boat and is also the leasing agent for her building? That he likes haggis? I tried to ask him in a way that he wouldn't know why I wanted to know. The poor guy was raving about the northeasterly views from the twenty-fifth floor of Tower Something-Or-Other, one of the floors he's leased at Barangaroo, and I just come out with *Do you like haggis?* He didn't seem to notice anything was up, though. He just said, *Um, sure* and kept on about the views, but didn't say if he'd ever lived in Edinburgh.

I pull Lesley's phone close and take a deep breath, momentarily closing my eyes. I open them and see that her Paul is not my Pau— not Leasing Paul. Thank heavens! Her Paul is way hunkier than Leasing Paul, though he's not so much the Chris Hemsworth type I pictured. He's more of a luscious white-chocolate version of Regé-Jean Page, the dreamboat Duke of Hastings in *Bridgerton*.

Lesley sees my reaction, and jabbers on about how her Paul completed two triathlons a week – is that a sexathlon? – and did daily workouts in the gym where he's a personal trainer. The guy apparently burned off fuel like he was a Brazilian rainforest.

After we've done the Paul thing to death, I go for it. 'Hey, Lesley, how about you and Winston pop by for sunset drinks tonight?' I lean down and give her cavoodle a rub on his muzzle to seal the deal. Winston looks up for a second, then drops his head back down to nestle into Scottie's neck.

'On your boat?' asks Lesley.

To create the *my turn, your turn* quid pro quo I'm trying for, this drinks session can't be on the boat, plus Leasing Paul might horn in on us, which would sidetrack my plan. 'No, at the apartment,' I smile. 'The vantage point is higher up. All the better to see the glow the sunset casts over your rooftop,' though I regret those words when they come out as they sound a bit Big Bad Wolfish, as in *Little Red Riding Hood*. But I press on, 'It'll be spectacular – especially if we get clouds.' I look up at the sky. This isn't just some puffery to suck her in. I'm picturing Claude Monet's *Twilight, Venice*, one of my faves. It's the painting that Pierce Brosnan steals from the Met in *The Thomas Crown Affair* – the 1999 remake – even though the real Met never owned it. Dramatic licence, I guess, and if Pierce Brosnan is the one doing it, who cares?

Lesley's coming over at seven o'clock. Sunset is at eight.

31

I spend all day preparing … plumping up the cushions, cleaning the sliding doors with Windex, putting out little biscuits I got at Coles Express. I set my tripod up on the terrace for taking shots later. None, of course, will be invasive zooms through Lesley's curtains into her place, or anyone's place. I can't risk her twigging to what I've been doing.

I check Brandy's ice maker four times. I pop across to the bottle-o three times for the right array of drinks, since I don't want to abuse my bar privileges at the apartment. I get four beers, two Tennent's Lagers – because geriatric Counter Guy says it's the most popular beer in Scotland – and two 4 Pines Pale Ales, because it's from Sydney and won't carry any bad vibes for Lesley. I also get a bottle of upmarket vodka, not the plonk I normally drink. I go for an Archie Rose because Goldberg bought me a tour of the distillery for my last birthday, and a bottle of their gin, plus plenty of tonic.

Even though I'm still on annual leave, I've been fussing around so much all day that it's ten before six when I realise I haven't eaten or showered or dressed. While I'm pulling a black T-shirt over my head, hair still damp, I start worrying that, with my empty stomach, I risk getting so light-headed with my first drink I might blurt out my real intentions. While I'm zipping up the fly on my jeans, I raid the fridge and gobble down a slice of carrot cake that's been on the shelf since last Saturday. It's so dry and stale I'm washing it down with water from the kitchen tap when the doorbell rings.

OMG. Scottie pounds to the door before I can, wagging his tail and pawing with all my anticipation but none of my trepidation.

I look at my teeth in Brandy's mirrored kitchen backsplash … bits of carrot and cake crumbs stuck in the gaps. I fill my mouth with water and give my teeth a big rinse, and spit into the sink. My hair is a total mess, but I have to go with it. I join Scottie at the door and open it. Winston bounds in and, before either of us humans can say a word, our fur babies are already out on the balcony and Winston's knocked over my tripod. Luckily, I hadn't attached the camera to it.

'JJ, I'm so sorry,' says Lesley, horrified at the havoc. 'Winston! … Winnie! … *Hey, Win … come back here!* Naughty—'

I interrupt with, 'No harm done. Come in, Lesley, great to see you.'

She is a blazing wall of colour, a shimmering fold of gold and vermilion kaftan sweeping down from her shoulders over her hips and a matching headscarf. Gold strappy sandals. She obviously likes kaftans. And scarves. I pretty much haven't seen her in anything else. What's with that? Camouflage, maybe … in case Melbourne Paul comes snooping? I dare not ask.

Lesley's carrying some flowers and a bottle. She hands me the dozen perfect daffodils, their yellow so intense it makes their blue wrapping paper seem iridescent. She's got a great eye for colour.

Then again, I tell myself, so would a forger.

From the bag slung over her shoulder she produces a packet of chips, Mackie's of Scotland, flame-grilled Aberdeen Angus potato crisps. 'They're dripping with fat but remind me of home,' she says. 'They sell them in Old Grumpy's across the road.'

If I'd seen them there, I would've bought a packet myself.

I can't help but look at her. She's incredibly beautiful. Perhaps that's how her Paul saw her – at first, anyway.

She holds up the bottle. San Pellegrino mineral water. I'm about to make a crack that I didn't know it was a Scottish brand but she gets in first, 'I don't drink alcohol.' She hands it to me. 'I hope you don't mind.'

Actually, I do mind given my three trips to the bottle-o and the $198.46 I've spent on booze, but that's my bad, since I never checked with her.

I'll take my purchases back to the old codger tomorrow and smile sweetly, and maybe he'll give me a refund. A girl can dream.

I take the flowers and the bottle to the kitchen, find a vase, add water and place the daffodils on the dining table, which is a twelve-seater, believe it or not – a huge glass sheet balanced on three rough-cut logs. I've already got the glasses out, so I add ice cubes and twists of lemon, and pour in the mineral water. I open her munchies and dump them into a bowl. 'Here,' I say as I hand over a glass, 'Cheers!'

She gives me a 'Cheers' back, I take the bowl and we step out onto the balcony. Lesley picks up the tripod and resets it. We don't yet need sunglasses or caps, but it won't be long before the sun starts dropping and its rays stream into our eyes.

God! Those eyes of hers!

32

Apart from the unnecessary booze and the uneaten food I left in the fridge, last night's plan worked a treat. We didn't talk about my auditing – to my relief – or about her writing, which was a shame. Most of the time we were talking about the dogs, given the two cuties were jumping all over us most of the time. The key point is that my quid got pro'd and I'm invited over to Lesley's tonight ... to see the paintings, although she doesn't know that.

She's buzzed me into the shared back garden and now I'm standing at her door, my heart thumping in my chest like a trapped budgie. I'm holding tight onto Scottie's leash because I don't want a repeat of last night's tripod incident – especially where it's a priceless artwork and not a tripod that gets knocked over.

Scottie and Winston are scratching at the door from opposite sides, saying *Hi!* to each other. I'm wondering what Lesley will be wearing. Last night, it was like she'd walked straight out of a movie screen. No matter what I wore from my wardrobe I'd be underdressed compared with Lesley's extravaganza. I'd thought of going shopping today, to up my fashion ante, but after my bottle-o debacle – he did take them back, by the way – I decided I'd just be me. Auditor me, not conservator me.

So it's black T-shirt, black jeans and newish black ASICs on my feet. I'd ordered a jokey T-shirt I found on the internet, which says *Auditor (noun): A person who does precision guesswork based on unreliable data provided by those of questionable knowledge. See also: wizard, sorcerer.* But, like my Rabbitohs cap, it won't get to me for a week. So, here I am, black, black and black, with windswept red hair sticking up at the top, like I'm a flaming pork chop at a Sunday barbecue.

My one concession to style is my earrings, the Ceylon blue sapphires my mother is wearing in all her wedding photos. They were her *something blue* item, and they are definitely something. I don't know if they're real gems or costume jewellery, and I never want to find out. They were Lauren's and that's all that matters. She pressed them into my hand one of the last times I visited her in hospital. 'The blue sets off your coiffure,' she said. She had this thing about French words, I don't know why. Maybe it was another of her attempts to pander to impossible-to-please Hugh, with his obsession about Arles and VvG's time in France.

I touch both stones to make sure the wind didn't blow them off me on my way over – a southerly buster is gusting up – then push my fingers through my hair to settle it down. There's one good thing about the wind, though. We won't be spending the evening out on Lesley's balcony.

I'll have more opportunity to snoop.

33

I'm Boy Scout-prepared for seeing The Art. I popped into work today and borrowed a few tools of the trade that, if I can sneak the chance, will let me surreptitiously do some quick and dirty on-site forensic checks of Lesley's VvG and Rembrandt, assuming they're not just prints. The equipment's weighing down the tote bag slung over my back, but it's not so heavy I'm forced to lean backwards, like a gumtree in a gale.

The door opens. Scottie charges right in, of course, but after that nothing is what I expected, and I don't mean Lesley's outfit which, yes, is her uniform of kaftan and headscarf.

As she leads me into the living space – huge, by the way – I'm instantly disappointed. The Rembrandt and

VvG aren't on display. They're somehow hidden behind that Non-Matisse – which I see is signed Boris Zac – and that unsigned Non-Banksy.

Close up, both those works are what Goldberg would call *schlock*. The Non-Banksy, a cheesy graffiti stencil of a black cat, is the kind of thing you'd buy in a flea market to get your four-year-old up off the ground, where she's lying on her back, arms and legs flailing, and shrieking *Susie want pussy cat!* The Non-Matisse looks like the artist has torn up random bits of coloured paper and stuck them on an unprimed canvas. There's no mood, no emotion. All these works are saying to me is that the artists snort a lot of cocaine and, if they don't, they probably should.

What I can't work out – because the two schlock works are jutting out of the wall only about as much as any normal paintings would – is how Lesley's fixed *Storm* and *Six Sunflowers* to their backs.

When she goes off to get us drinks, I try to pull the Non-Banksy away from the wall a bit, to check if I can see the VvG behind it, but it won't budge. Neither will the Non-Matisse.

As I move further into her place, I pass a virtual art gallery of schlock. In some spots, she's got twos and threes hung one below the other. While she's in the kitchen, I try tugging on a few but, like the first two, they're all fixed solidly.

Surprisingly, not least because Lesley's got a great eye for clothes, nothing in here is to my taste. I don't recognise any of the works, and none seems to be by an artist whose name I know. Her walls are covered in so much of this dross, you can hardly see the wallpaper – and I'm not being an art snob here but, frankly, I'd rather see the wallpaper.

Ah, relief. Finally. I see a familiar work over her fireplace. It's one of those Torana paintings by Ben Quilty. I wouldn't lie to Lesley's face about the junk works, but for a moment I do imagine complimenting her on her Quilty – how it *oozes with paint and metaphor* – until I realise I'd be falling into a trap I made myself. There wouldn't be an auditor on Planet Earth capable of uttering those words, or even thinking them. By the way, that quote's not a JJ invention. I read it in an auction catalogue once. I liked how it sounded but also thought it might come in useful one day because, at the time, Quilty was one of the trustees where I work, and storing up a few good lines so I'd be ready to schmooze up to him was good workplace politics. Or it might have been if I ever ran into Quilty. Getting to meet celebrities doesn't seem to be my thing.

I'm concentrating so hard I don't hear Lesley coming up behind me, and do a little jump when she asks, 'So, what are you thinking?'

What I'm actually thinking at that precise moment is *I want to see your Rembrandt and VvG.*

She hands me my drink – she got me a V&T and herself a mineral water – and leads me to the sofa. I'm positioned so I can see back down the corridor to the front door, where my bag is lying on the console table, crammed with my work equipment, with as close to a hangdog look as a tote bag can have.

After a while, we do take a few photos outside, though not many, because of the wind. It's all friendly enough but my subtle attempts at cross-examination get me nowhere. Artwise, the evening is a total bust. She gave me nothing about her collection other than, 'It came with the town house. When they said "furnished", I didn't realise I'd be living in the Louvre.' She laughed. A good joke, just not the way she meant it.

After that dead end, we spoke for, I reckon, a good hour about her writing ... what it's like to be a writer ... why she's working on a novel at all ... what's her daily routine ... who are her writing idols ... what does she think of audiobooks ... what's the best book she's read in the past year. The usual kind of chitchat.

But later, when I was walking home with Scottie, I couldn't remember a single piece of detail that was remotely helpful, and got to wondering if there'd actually been any.

34

Belfast

Nessa hangs up on her stockbroker. She's finally feeling good about herself again, a sentiment that's especially welcome with the more nefarious side of the Farrellys' business empire having turned to shit. She's spent the past three days hunting for answers about where the art has gone, and the one she's got from the Freeport's CCTV security video files is conclusive only in its inconclusiveness.

She's gone through the CCTV records for every single occasion the door to Vault 18A was opened in the past five years. Félix Matthieu had only been there twice. The first time was with the Farrellys when they registered his scans. The second and last time was when he went with them and John Smith. Claude Fontaine had visited eight times, once every month over the period of their 'relationship'.

Fontaine's visits were pretty much indistinguishable. Apart from Claude's different clothes, Nessa would have sworn she was watching the same video on a loop … Claude scans in, walks the hallways and rescans at every security door until arriving at the Farrellys' vault … scans in again … stands in the corridor as the roller door opens, then the inner vault door … head pokes inside, nods up and down, like someone counting the crates for a stocktake … then the doors close and that's it.

Nessa watched Fontaine's mind-numbing routine eight times, the meticulous lawyer checking and rechecking that the Farrellys' art was, indeed, where it was supposed to be – confirming it was there whenever they set up a new deal that demanded fresh transaction papers.

Nessa's big conundrum is what the CCTV files are *not* showing. A whole day of entry logs and videos is missing. It was a day when the Freeport suffered a power cut, a little over eight weeks before Claude flew to India. The blackout happened late at night and it was short – only for a few seconds, according to the power company records – but it apparently fried the entire day's data, which meant that when the offsite backup process kicked in at midnight, there was nothing to copy and store. No visit logs, no CCTV files.

Nessa discussed this with Niall yesterday, and they decided that the art must have been nicked during that missing twenty-four-hour period. What's still unknown is who stole it.

It was clearly a sophisticated, well-planned operation. Whoever did it replaced all the crates with decoys that looked so good they fooled the Farrellys when they turned up with Matthieu and Smith. And they fooled Claude Fontaine, who kept turning up for those punctual monthly stocktaking rituals, the last of which was a day before flying off to India.

Unless, pondered the Farrellys, Claude Fontaine was the thief and those ongoing visits were clever decoys.

Niall was working hard on the case, using the considerable tech skills of him and his 'friends' to see if there was some way to recover the files or find some other method to attack the problem. Meanwhile, Nessa had been boring herself crazy trawling through both Claude's and Félix's personal records.

Félix Matthieu had handed over all his logins when he naively believed Niall's promise that his wife's life depended on it. That way the Farrellys got access to his and Claude's emails, their files on the cloud, bank records, credit card statements, phone records, airline and hotel memberships and more.

Nessa focused especially on the two lawyers' records for the weeks either side of the power cut, to see if she could track down anything remotely suspicious, but they both came up as cleanskins. From what she could see, the two of them had incredibly dull lives. Matthieu, at least, was a car nut but Fontaine seemed to have no interests whatsoever. For Claude, it was all work, work, work and when it wasn't work, it was tossing money at charities like it was confetti.

The one saving grace Nessa got from all this boredom, and it was unrelated to the missing art, was a juicy snippet of inside information about an imminent takeover on the London Stock Exchange. A takeover that Matthieu was working on. Hence the quick and satisfying call to her stockbroker – part of a little side hustle that she's decided not to tell Niall about.

35

The next day, Niall slides his iPad across Nessa's desk. 'The dead lawyers' records don't talk ... but what if the art does?' She sees he's got a video set up ready to play. She recognises the opening image ... it's the Monaco Freeport's loading dock. She's about to speak when Niall, with a smirk, says, 'You said you checked it all out, Nessie, but *did* you ... did you *really*?'

She can feel her brother's dagger of accusation like a cold blade against her throat, but she *did* check ... she checked *everything*.

Niall presses *play*.

'This isn't from the Freeport,' Nessa says, more to herself than to her brother.

'You don't say,' he says. 'Watch and learn, sis.' It's footage from across the street, looking into the loading dock. The camera must be on a lamp pole or the side of a building.

Damn it, Nessa thinks, furious at herself for missing something so obvious that even Niall found it. *He's the one who fucks up, not me!*

Wondering how she'll live down her blunder, she watches in silence. A truck pulls up at the loading dock, and two men in black coveralls get out, pulling their baseball caps so low she can't see their faces. They open up the roller door at the back of the van and begin to unload packing crates – boxes of various sizes that look very similar to those stolen from the Farrellys.

'It's twenty-three crates exactly,' says Niall. 'That number ring a bell?' He presses *fast forward*. She watches the men speak into a monitor and show some ID to a camera. The dock gates slide open and a hand waves them in.

Niall spreads his fingers on the screen to zoom in on the hand before Nessa can ask him to. 'We can't see who it is,' he says. 'Man, woman, Fontaine, Matthieu, some other geezer … no feckin' idea.'

The moving men roll the crates inside on trolleys. Thirty-five minutes later, according to the tape, but fifteen seconds on fast forward, they wheel twenty-three identical-looking crates back outside, load them onto the truck and drive off.

Nessa picks up her pen to write down the truck's licence plate.

Niall pushes her hand down. 'Angel's already workin' on it,' he says. 'An' before you ask – yes, there are CCTV cameras across from the Freeport's *front* entrance and on the approaches to the place, but they got disconnected years ago. Apparently, allowin' the cops to monitor the Freeport's clientele comin' and goin' weren't much good for the place's business. But they musta missed this camera out back, or it got put there later.'

'That hand we saw,' says Nessa.

'It could be anyone's,' says Niall. 'Yours, maybe?' He laughs.

You manky tool! She stands up, walks over to the window and looks out over Belfast Harbour, watching the seagulls shitting on the tugboats and ferries as they ply the waters. She grits her teeth and turns back to her brother, but her eyes catch the portrait of their father hanging on the wall behind her chair. She'd hung it there to give herself more authority but now it's more of a reminder of the legacy that she and her brother have blown.

'Good work, Niall,' she barely manages to say, but she's thinking, *Fuck you!*

Nessa checks her watch and adds, 'Let me know what Angel finds out. I've got a lunch.' She struts out, slamming the door behind her, remembering only when she gets to the elevator that it was her own office she'd just left.

36

Hours later, Nessa returns and is standing at the door to Niall's office. His secretary Meabh is bent over his desk and Niall, pants crumpled at his feet and the tail of his shirt barely covering his arse, is pounding her from behind, seemingly to the rhythm of the Bee Gees' 'Stayin' Alive', which is playing in Nessa's head as she watches.

'Oh, Niall,' Meabh's calling out, one hand sweeping the papers off her boss's desk, the other moving frantically between her legs. 'Don't stop, keep going ... please ... oh, oh, yes, yes.'

Niall pumps into her even faster. He's throwing his head back, eyes to the ceiling like he's thanking God and not Meabh for his pleasure.

'Meabh,' Nessa says out loud, 'that's quite the prick you've got in you.' She laughs and relishes the horror that flies over Meabh's face – how she stands up so quickly that Nessa hopes she might have broken Niall's penis. But apparently not. He's bending down and pulling up his pants.

'*Bitch!*' is all he says.

Meabh pats down her skirt and runs out of the room.

'Hope you enjoyed that, sis.' He looks up at Nessa, not a skerrick of embarrassment on his sweaty face.

'Not as much as you.' Nessa sees her reflection in the glass door as she passes through – how she's pulled her hair back into such a taut ponytail it looks as if she's squinting. She's now in sportswear, rather than the black pantsuit she had on earlier. Her stomach is grumbling because, despite what she'd told him, she hasn't been out to lunch. She hasn't eaten a thing. Instead, she's spent the past three hours working out in the nearby boxing gym to blow off steam. She sits in Niall's visitor chair, feeling no better than before.

Her brother is picking up his papers from the floor and tidying the desk. 'While you've been out stuffin' your face at lunch—'

'*You're* talkin' about stuffin', dear brother?'

'Quit your gurnin',' he says, sitting in his chair. 'An' what the hell have you done to your hair? Anyhow, sis, I got us some damn good intel, so I'm feckin' entitled to celebrate.' He shifts in his seat like he's mentally changing gear. 'The gobshites we're dealing with … If I didn't hate their guts so much, I'd have to respect 'em for how well they covered their tracks. It goes like this, Nessie. The removalists' HQ in Lyon takes a call from a company in

Amsterdam that's hirin' them for a three-step operation. Pick up twenty-three wooden crates from a warehouse in Rotterdam, take 'em to the Monaco Freeport ... that's a thirteen-hour drive ... swap 'em there with twenty-three similar crates from inside vault 18A and deliver those crates to a warehouse in Genoa ... a two-and-a-half-hour trip.'

'And?' she prompts, noticing a pinprick of blood beside Niall's latest ear stud.

'Amsterdam company's a fake, don't exist,' he says. 'An' the funds to pay for the transport got wired from a bank in the Caymans, an' we know how that's a dead end. The Rotterdam pickup warehouse is rented out to a company with a Moscow address, but that don't exist either, and the dosh for the warehouse rent came from the same Caymans account. The bullshit Moscow company is also on the lease for the Genoa warehouse, an' yeah, you guessed it, the money for that came from—'

'The Caymans account.'

'Right. In short, sis, this whole sting was done by Mr Feckin' Nobody.'

'The crates in the Genoa wareh—'

'Place is as empty as a dead man's eyes. While you've been lunchin', or whatever, Angel's been and gone.'

'No CCTV?'

He shakes his head and the blood dribbles down his earlobe. 'This took some pretty high-end mastermindin', sis.'

She nods this time. To be as clean and tight as this operation was, it's got to be an underworld rival aiming to take over the Farrellys' network. 'You say the bullshit company had a Moscow address?'

'Yeah, but the street don't exist on Google Maps, an' the company name don't appear in Russia's corporate registry. The lovely Meabh did a search, bless her.'

Nessa freezes, her body suddenly as cold as a Siberian winter. She plants her palms on Niall's desk, but not anywhere close to where he and Meabh had been fucking. She leans forward. 'It's got to be the Bratva boys.' She whispers it, not that anyone but Niall is listening.

He lets out a long, loud moan as the colour drains out of him, his face suddenly looking as white and sickly as a stinkhorn mushroom egg.

The Farrellys have done business with the *Solntsevskaya Bratva*, the Russian mob, for years, and it's always been cordial, and always mutually profitable. It's reputed that with cells all over the globe, the Bratva bring in over ten billion dollars a year. 'If it *is* the Bratva,' says Nessa, 'why us, and why now?'

'The past ain't a guide to the future, sis, everyone says that. For a sting as tricky an' gutsy as this,' says Niall, 'they got the brains, the bollocks an', if it means they get to gobble up our entire organisation for free, that there is the feckin' motivation.'

Nessa shifts in her seat with an uncomfortable mix of respect and dread – admiration that anyone could do this right under their noses, and alarm about the consequences.

Normally, the Farrellys would respond to any threat to their enterprise with sledgehammer retribution but whoever has done this to them has cut them off from their illicit funding resources. If it is, indeed, the Bratva, retaliation is not just unthinkable, given the Farrellys' strained circumstances, it's a death wish. 'We gotta think this through, Niall. It's like that Chinese fella says, *Every battle is won or lost before it is fought.*'

'Subaru, right?'

'Sun Tzu,' she says, muttering *eejit* under her breath. 'Either way, we ain't lost it yet.'

'What if it's not the Russkis,' says Niall, knocking his knuckles against his desk. He stands up and this time it's him who goes to the window. 'If the Bratva did it, they wouldn't stay shtum about separatin' us from our art. Goin' public is what they'd do – it's what we'd do – creatin' a stampede of our people to defect right into their welcomin' Cossack arms.'

He spies a woman down below, on the docks. She's leaning over, her pert backside pointing up at him. 'Before we jump to conclusions, sis, shouldn't we reach out to 'em?'

'An' say what? *Hey, Vlad, are you the fecker who cut off our bollocks?*' She's looking at the back of Niall's head like she's just seen his brain fly out the window. 'If they did it, then the gobshites will spit in our faces. If they *didn't* do it, we'll be handin' 'em an intel goldmine and *then* they'll spit in our faces. Niall, reachin' out to 'em in any way means we're fucked.'

Niall keeps his eyes on the woman below until she stands up. She's cradling a small poodle. He turns back to his sister. 'A dodgy Moscow address doesn't automatically mean it's them.'

'If it's *not* them, then who … Claude Fontaine? What, our starchy lawyer nicked our art to screw us over, except the fecker went to India, got Covid and ended up bein' the one who got screwed?'

'That'd explain why no one's blabbed. Not yet, anyhow.'

Nessa didn't want to admit it but her brother had a point. 'If it was Fontaine, where's the art … in some feckin' ashram? We got nothin' on Fontaine – nothin'. Not a single lead.'

Niall tugs his earlobe, then sees the blood on his fingers. He licks it off. 'Look again.'

37

Sydney

It's as gorgeous an evening as any since I've been staying at Brandy's, but this time I'm inside – reliving part of my barely misspent teenage years by bingeing on *Buffy the Vampire Slayer*. Scottie is asleep at my feet. He's not a *Buffy* fan.

Before streaming was even a glint in Netflix's eye, I used to sneak into the living room after my parents went to bed to watch the reruns on TV. It wasn't just the show that grabbed me, as I'm reminding myself now, it was Angel. Who wouldn't fantasise about a steamy-looking vampire with a soul, one constantly troubled by his past victims?

Out of the corner of my eye, and across the bay, a light snaps on. I swivel my head towards it and see it's coming from Lesley's. She's pulling her curtains open. I'm guessing what I see will be as eye-opening as last night – in other words, zilch. *But … what*? I rub my eyes and look again.

I grab my camera from the couch next to me, and use Brandy's iPad app to turn off the TV and the room lights. I step over Scottie so as not to wake him, and go out onto the balcony to see what I can get through my lens. Sure enough, VvG and Rembrandt are back on her wall.

The curtains are also open on another couple of her windows. She's in her living room, pouring a glass of wine … My camera tells me it's a … Tyrell's Vat 47 chardonnay … a 2014 vintage. I start musing whether 2014 was a good year, before I start laughing, because what would I know, or care. The only chardie I drink comes out of a bag inside a box or it's whatever brand the gallery serves at openings.

But hang on …

Lesley. Does. Not. Drink.

If she's got a guest she's pouring for, I can't see them. Or was she lying about not drinking?

Her house clothes are different too. No kaftan, no headscarf – just a black zip-up top, matching shorts and bare feet, and her hair in a cute beer-bottle-brown mussed-up pixie cut, like Halle Berry in *Die Another Day*.

And *wait … what?* Is that a Vermeer above her fireplace, in the same spot where the Ben Quilty should be? The composition … it's Vermeer's typical chiaroscuro of light and shadow, much more light than shadow …

It's got me asking the same unanswered questions as before. Print? Forgery? To see yet another masterpiece on Lesley's walls is making me feel crazier than a sprayed cockroach.

Taking a few deep breaths doesn't help so I go back inside, get my V&T and down it in one slug. The cold liquid felt good running down my throat but it's not doing much to slow down my heart rate. I go to the bar and make another, take it outside on the balcony with me, and pick up my camera again.

I focus on the new painting like I would at work when I'm giving an assessment, which is an intensive process I always find calming. The work's central figure, the girl, is playing a keyboard instrument. A harpsichord, I suppose, since pianofortes and pianos weren't around in the mid-1600s, Vermeer's time in the sun. The hue of her blouson is as vivid and appealing as the lemon curd tart I had last week from Bourke Street Bakery, and the fabric's so rich and voluptuous I want to caress it. If it was a real Vermeer, people like me – conservator JJ, not auditor JJ – would know that colour as lead-tin yellow, a highly toxic paint that was all the rage in Vermeer's time but completely out of fashion by the 1750s. That's when Naples yellow came into vogue.

If I had access to the work – assuming it's a painting, not a print – the first thing I'd probably test for is whether it's got the 1600s yellow that Vermeer used. The XRF spectrometer, still in my tote bag after last night's abortive covert operation, would give me a pretty good indication of that in a flash.

The girl's white skirt is wow too! It falls from her waist to the black and white marble tiles on the floor like it's got a life of its own. It's as good as any silk that Vermeer ever painted, and he painted some sensuous silks.

After taking shots of the 'Vermeer', I upload the best one, like I did with the Rembrandt, into a reverse image search. In what should be a shock but isn't, the top hits take me straight back to the Gardner Museum website.

What I'm seeing on Lesley's wall is not only a Vermeer – warranting a big round of applause in itself – it's *The Concert* which, it turns out, is another work stolen in that 1990 heist and, like the others, never recovered.

And while my imagination is flying off in all directions, I see a tab on the Gardner website labelled *Museum Theft – an active and ongoing investigation*. I click on it.

The Museum is offering a $10 million reward for information leading directly to the safe return of the stolen works.

Ten million. That's a hell of a lot, and even more in Aussie dollars.

Should I go to the police and let them check all this out?

That would be a pretty extreme step. For starters, it would ruin what's shaping up to be a beautiful friendship, even if it's built on lies, at least from me if not both of us.

Even more, if the cops did get around to raiding Lesley's place and found that her paintings were simply prints or cheap fakes that weren't for sale – which has got to be the most probable situation – it would end my career. I would become a laughing stock in the art world and, with an exposé like that, they'd be sure to use my cringeworthy full name.

Imagine the headlines … *Art expert cries wolf* … *Doesn't know a Klimt from a print* – not that Lesley's got a Klimt. At least, I assume not.

I'm picking up my glass for another slurp when my eye catches some more movement over at Lesley's. Camera up,

I peek through her third uncurtained window, the one opposite her front door, where Winston is pawing and scratching like he's expecting a guest. I move my lens back through another window and see that Lesley's wineglass is only half full. Is that how high she filled it or has that supposed non-drinker guzzled some? She's cocking her ear and looking up quizzically. She checks her watch. I check mine. It's 8.30 pm, give or take. She picks her phone up off the coffee table, swipes it and rubs her chin, then raises her eyebrow.

Putting two and two together, I'm deducing that Winston heard someone outside, they buzzed the doorbell, and an alert popped up on Lesley's phone with an image of their face.

She walks towards the door, then stops short. She calls out … I can't hear what she says, obviously, but her head tilts towards the door and her mouth opens. *I'm coming* is what I imagine she's saying. She briefly rests her palm on the wall just above the console table, the one where I left my tote bag last time, then pulls it away, and a small panel, no bigger than her hand, slides open, revealing a small recess. She presses a previously hidden green button.

She waits. I wait. Winston keeps scratching at the door.

And … Holy Mary, Mother of God!

The VvG and the Rembrandt … and the Vermeer … all of them are like dancers in a ballet who, as one, do a 180-degree-spin via her hinge setup. And as they flip over, I start to see the other works on their backs appearing … the Quilty, the Non-Matisse and the Non-Banksy, pretty much what I captured before in my *Girl* photos. I'm photographing on burst. I don't want to miss capturing any of this.

Lesley goes out of view and, a couple of minutes later – when the schlock and the Quilty reappear – she returns, wearing one of her kaftans, a scarlet red one, and no scarf, but a pearl blonde wig cut in a shag with choppy bangs, her pixie cut consigned to history.

I don't wear wigs, but lots of women do. Whether it's for fashion, for fun, or because they're Moira Rose in *Schitt's Creek*, or because of cancer therapy. Does Lesley have cancer?

She's checking herself out in the hallway mirror, adjusting the hairpiece, poking a few stray locks of brown beneath the blonde fringe. She goes back into the living room and, after picking up the wine bottle and glass and taking them into the kitchen, comes back out and, leaving the chain latch on, opens the door and speaks.

I guess it's *What are you doing here?* since her phone already told her who it is. She listens to the answer, pushes the door shut, undoes the latch and reopens it. A man steps inside.

It's Paul.

My Paul. Not her Paul.

Unless my Paul is truly her Paul.

Which he can't be since I've seen a photograph. I'm being paranoid, right?

Wait. He did tell me he was the leasing agent for her building. Maybe he's come to see her on business?

But at eight-thirty at night?

He hands her a big buff-coloured manila envelope, so maybe he's there to hand-deliver some important paperwork to do with her lease. An insurance policy cover note for the paintings, maybe?

But at eight-thirty at night? Really?

She leads Paul out onto the terrace, goes back inside briefly, then brings out two glasses and a bottle of San

Pellegrino. She pours them both a glass. They clink them and say 'Cheers'. It's a still night, and the sound travels across the bay.

So, the Lesley I'm seeing now doesn't drink alcohol – except when she's alone – and the Paul I'm seeing might not be the Paul I think he is.

I step back but knock over my glass. It smashes on the tiles and wakes up Scottie, who bounds out and starts barking, and it's all I can do to keep him away from the shards.

I look over to Lesley's and … damn! The two of them are looking towards me.

38

I snap my curtains closed, then decide that was the worst thing I could possibly have done. If they've actually seen me, I must look as guilty as hell.

I've never been in a pickle as bad as this, so for the first time – apart from the one with the absinthe – I raid Brandy's bar and pour myself a double shot of eighteen-year-old single malt scotch.

After I slug it down, the edge is still there, so I pour myself a triple this time. Then another double.

If I exclude my very recent habit of one or two V&Ts a night, I've just downed more spirits in fifteen minutes than I've consumed in months, and maybe a year.

The scotch has an effect, but not how I expect it to.

I flake on the couch.

Aargh! Next morning, with a throb in my bulging head and a gurgle rising in my stomach, I feel as bad as the three buddies in *The Hangover.* Worse! *Oh no!*

If I'd got to the bathroom a second faster, I would have made it to the toilet. I wipe my face on a towel and then use it to clean up the limestone tiles. I crawl my way up to the sink and lean on it to support myself. At the best of times my legs are not firm and steady, but this morning it's like I'm suffering the Jelly-Legs Curse from *Harry Potter.*

I hang tightly onto the sides of the sink. I study the brand name staring up at me ... Kohler ... then I check myself out in the mirror. I don't like what I see. This is not a totally novel sentiment but today it's worse. I look up to the heavens, except the view is interrupted by a too-bright white ceiling with a giant ant crawling across it. *How do ants walk upside down?*

I drop my clothes on the floor and go to put my head under the tap, which isn't easy in a bathroom where the taps are squidgy little things and the sinks are shallow. All I get out of it is a bruise on my forehead. I step warily over to the shower, turn it on, and get in without waiting for the water to reach the right temperature.

I spy a blurry Scottie looking at me through the shower screen. His eyes seem bulbous and his tongue is lolling out of his mouth.

He tips his head to the side, like he's asking if I'm okay, and I just blow like a bomb – I scream at the top of my voice, 'No, I'm not fucking okay!' I scare the bejesus out of myself as much as I do Scottie, who jumps backwards.

The shower is pounding down on me like I'm under Niagara Falls. With water smashing into my scalp and pouring down my face, I drop to my knees, head in hands, and I can't tell what's tears and what's shower.

39

I curl up on the couch. Scottie's at my feet, with a bowl of water I poured at the sink, and I'm nursing a triple shot of espresso from Brandy's machine. I made it so strong that one drop on my tongue is as bitter as the old witch who lived in the flat upstairs when I was growing up.

Virtually everything I know about Lesley, and Paul, is open to question.

Do I believe *anything* Lesley has told me? Is she a writer? Is she truly a refugee from Scotland via Melbourne? If the story about her rich but dead uncle isn't true, how did this otherwise unemployed woman get enough of the folding stuff to set herself up in a fancy town house, with all her amazing clothes? Maybe he's not a *dead* rich uncle. Maybe he's the kind of 'uncle' who visits once a week when his wife is out playing bridge or golf or going to the hairdresser or entertaining the pool boy?

And maybe Paul isn't a leasing guy. Maybe *he's* the 'uncle'?

No, that can't be it. While she knows Paul well enough to let him into her place at night, the trust clearly wasn't there. She hid the famous paintings from him – the booze too. And her pixie cut.

Paul – who I kind of had hopes for – could well be the Leasing Paul who's boat-sitting for a mate, the guy who schmoozes me and everyone he meets. But one thing's for sure – he's not Melbourne Bastard Paul, or Lesley wouldn't have put on a wig and kaftan and asked him inside when she saw his image on the doorbell app. Plus, I've seen the photo.

Or have I? Who's to say she didn't show me a fake?

And ... is Lesley even her name?

What if she's someone else from Scotland, like a ... I don't know ... a woman who's in witness protection with a new name and identity because she's grassed on some Glaswegian crime lord? Or what if she's a crime lord herself, and that's why she might be sitting on a bunch of stolen or missing artworks?

If any of that's right, I've put myself ... no, she's put me ... in grave danger every time we've met in the open, when we're gabbing at a table on the footpath, in full view of whoever might want to drive by and shoot her. *Fuck!*

Everything about 'Lesley' has to be up for question.

Given her impressive and, I imagine, hugely expensive efforts at artwork concealment – like Geoffrey Rush when he was playing a sleazy art dealer in *The Best Offer* – the notion that she's a writer living off an inheritance is about as likely as a kangaroo hopping over the Harbour Bridge. Yes, okay, that happened in 2018, though it was a wallaby not a kangaroo, but it *was* just that once, which is my point.

Suddenly I'm picturing myself as Veronica Mars, the TV girl-detective played by Kristen Bell. I shake my hair out and stand up ... big mistake ... splitting headache. I quickly sit back down and ask myself, *What would Veronica do?* Apparently I say it out loud because Scottie looks up at me with dreamy eyes, wagging his tail expectantly.

'You're right,' I tell him. 'We'll go for our morning walk, and we'll catch up with Winston and whoever-Lesley-really-is, but we'll keep our eyes peeled for drive-bys.'

40

'Hi, JJ. Hi, Lesley.' This morning's barista is our regular, Bruce. He saw us heading across the street, so he's already standing at his machine steaming Lesley's extra froth. She's wearing a kaftan and headscarf as usual, but in a spray of oranges this time, which is a combo I haven't seen before. I get that kaftans are loose and comfy, especially in summer, but why wear a headscarf… or a wig, for that matter? Why not let the breeze tousle your hair, however short it is?

Before we sit at our usual table on the footpath, I pop my head inside and, given the delicate state of it and my stomach, ask Bruce to make my espresso a 'double-double'. I have no clue if such a thing exists, but he nods, so either it does or he'll simply charge me double for nothing.

I take the chair facing the roadway, like a spy or a mercenary on high alert would do, or Elizabeth in *The Thursday Murder Club*. Scottie and Winston are nuzzling each other at our feet, and Bruce comes over and puts two water bowls in front of them – no share plate for dogs at this cafe. Despite this, the pups go for the same bowl and, in their dash for it, tip over the second one, which spills over my ASICs. But I don't care, it's only water.

While we're waiting for our orders, Lesley looks across the table, her expression more serious than I've seen it before. 'I heard a ruckus over your way last night,' she says. 'I couldn't see anything, it was too dark, but I thought I heard smashing glass and some barking. I thought it might be Scottie.'

I give her my best *I-don't-have-a-clue-what-you're-talking-about* look, and am wondering what words should come out of my mouth when Bruce turns up, bless him, with our orders.

'I would have phoned you,' she says when he leaves us, 'but we hadn't exchanged numbers. Here,' she continues, pushing her phone across the table. 'Put yours in so I've got it.' After I've done that, she taps it to call mine, then hangs up. We're on first-phone terms at last.

I take a spoon and stir my coffee. I don't know why, since I don't take sugar and I've grown to like the froth as froth, rather than mixed in. After the unintended stirring, I'm staring into what looks more like a slurry of machine oil than a coffee.

A TV program on body language I saw claimed that mirroring another person's actions can create stronger bonding and reinforce the rapport between the two of you. So, since I need Lesley to believe we're simpatico, when she raises her cup to her lips, I do likewise. She takes a sip, I do the same, except – because mine's a double-double – it makes me screw up my face so that I probably look like a puckered prune. She puts her cup down. I do ditto. And so on.

I'm glancing over her shoulder at the cars whizzing by so often that she asks me what I'm looking at, and I realise that if she truly was a hardened criminal, she would've grabbed *my* seat, so *she* could be on the lookout. Or, more likely, she would've got us to sit inside.

I tell her *I thought I saw a friend driving around and looking for a parking spot, but I was wrong.* The Veronica Mars in me returns and manages to steer the conversation to *Why don't we photograph the sunrise from your balcony?* and Lesley agrees. We're on for tomorrow morning. *Go Veronica! Go mirroring!*

I'll have to set my alarm for five, but who cares about sleep deprivation if it's in the cause of Art with a capital A?

As we walk our separate ways, I'm feeling pretty good about my detective work, almost that I'm a natural. Maybe, I think, I've got it in my blood. Then I shudder. Hugh!

41

Scottie is at the foot of my bed, leash dangling from his mouth and tail wagging faster than a metronome, like he's telling me we're late for a date with his new BFF, Winston. I casually check my watch – it's 6.07 am.

Damn it! Sunrise was at 5.37.

Either my alarm didn't go off or I didn't hear it. A glare of daylight is spilling through the slit in my curtain and I jump up, throw open the drapes and look across to Lesley's.

Winston is out on her terrace, bathed in the golden flush of the morning light. Lesley's curtains are closed, even though the sliding doors are open. I guess she's keeping the sunlight off the paintings on the wall behind them. She pokes her head through the drapes to talk to Winston. She looks up towards me so I flick on the lights and wave, and hold my arms out wide to give her an apologetic shrug. She smiles and pokes her hand out to give me a thumbs up, like she's totally okay with me forcing her to get up at the buttcrack of dawn for no reason at all.

I'd phone her to apologise but I feel it's better to do it in person.

It's 6.36. I'm showered and dressed, kind of, and Scottie definitely senses where we're going as he's pulling me there. We're almost at Lesley's. As well as my camera and tripod and, on my back, the bag of tricks from work, I'm carrying two bagels as peace offerings. I got them from Bruce, who was just opening up and pulled them out of the delivery box for me. 'Pay me later,' he said. 'I haven't switched on the EFTPOS thing yet.' I make a note to give him a tip and, given my question mark over Paul, I wonder if he's single but dare not ask.

As I walk up to the entrance gate to the terraces, I'm picturing Bruce – or Paul – bringing me coffee in bed. We're in Brandy's bedroom where, as of yesterday, I found out I get to sleep for another three weeks. She's extended her trip so she can squeeze in a white Christmas in New York with friends.

I'm staring at the intercom, the kind with a number pad and a camera.

If I truly was a Veronica Mars, I'd already know the code and type it in, but I'm not and I can't. So, for the second time, I follow the instructions written on the brass plate above it, and tap in the number of her town house then press the button with a bell icon on it.

Scottie starts growling. I turn my head to see what's bothering him and, across the street, there's a forbidding double-door fridge of a man dressed in black, with big arms, big chest, big everything – except for hair, which he has none of – and a mangled ear, and I don't want to imagine how he got that. He's got a tattoo on his neck but I can't quite make out what it is. It might be a word or the top of a wreath sticking out above his shirt collar. He turns away just as Lesley buzzes me through.

Spooked, I close the gate firmly behind me and hear it click, then pull at it twice to make sure it's locked. I wander down the narrow garden plot running along the back of the town houses. Scottie has already forgotten about Godzilla. He's yanking against the leash, pulling me forward, and his tail is wagging so fast that he'd swat any summer flies stupid enough to go anywhere near him.

We reach Lesley's front door and I'm looking at her own intercom. The detective in me kicks in again and I'm visualising myself sneaking back here some time when she's out. How to get in? Do I dust the numbers to see which ones get more use? What order do I press them in? If there's a facial recognition system, do I make up 3D images of Lesley from my multiple shots of Girl and try to fool it?

She's only half-opened the door when Scottie races right in between her legs, disappearing for a fraction of a second in the folds of her kaftan and then out the other side where he and Winston frolic around and go bounding off.

When I look up, the sight of Lesley is … wow!

A dazzling blaze of pink light is pouring out of her door, like it's the sunlit-sea taking you to Narnia in Disney's *The Lion, the Witch and the Wardrobe*. The pink outfit she's wearing is in a different class from her others. It's heart-stopping – evoking the same fabulous frivolous pink that

Fragonard used for the girl's racy, flouncy silk dress in his whimsical painting *The Swing*. Lesley's garb is so suggestive of it I almost want to check behind me to see if the pervert hiding in Fragonard's bushes is in her garden, still trying to leer up billowing skirts.

The girl on that swing is so joyous, so untroubled, that I've always felt she represents the carefree adolescence I yearned for but never got, not that I wanted any dirty old men looking up my skirts.

But next to this lustrous Lesley, the ensemble of black T, black shorts and black ASICS I threw on is so pathetic that I'm feeling somewhat dresstitute, a word Goldberg told me he heard on Richard Glover on ABC Radio.

I hold out the bagels and go through the apology ritual, saying how embarrassed I am having put her to the trouble of getting up early and then not turning up on time. She tells me not to worry, because she used the time to play with Winston and to write some great new paragraphs – a lie? – then takes the bagels and invites me in.

My ears and mouth are participating in the conversation while my eyes are checking out her walls as she leads me inside. Unsurprisingly, the art on show is not The Art.

It's why, I realise, she's pulled back the curtains and is drenching the room with light. No one would ever let this amount of sun onto 'real' art, unless … I'm looking at her windows. If she really is loaded, then she might've coated them with a UV-filter film. If she has, that's another pointer to The Art being genuine.

Lesley's got her back to me and is calling out to the dogs as her dazzling outfit swishes us towards the kitchen. Before I go more than a step, I make a point of checking out the panel that I now know is above her entry console.

The square outline on the speckled grey wallpaper is scarcely visible. It's as faint as a pencil mark. If I didn't know it was there, I would have missed it. I touch it lightly and as soon as I do, it presses back against my palm. I remove my hand, and the square silently lifts out of the wall no more than a centimetre, on some kind of well-oiled scissor hinge. Noiselessly – thank heavens – it slides itself to the side, to reveal the niche where the green 'go' button I've seen before is inviting me to press it.

I am sorely tempted. Knowing what I know, I desperately want to hit my hand on it and, as the paintings flip themselves over, scream *Explain yourself!*

But, as usual, I go through the scenarios in my head – for what must be the fiftieth time. If she is a master criminal, how would that go down for me? *Not good* is the answer, as it's always been. It's way too soon, and would be way too stupid, to try anything as risky as that.

Instead, I touch the panel again and it slides closed, the button safely back in its hidey-hole.

I mark this discovery down on my mental notepad as VM Exhibit D. The VM stands for Veronica Mars. I've now christened my original *Girl* photos Exhibits A and B, and my photos of the Vermeer I'm calling Exhibit C. This one is Exhibit D.

42

Even though sunrise came and went an hour ago, the light over the Finger Wharf is still spectacular, so we've agreed we'll do the photo session. I go to a window with my iPhone and pretend to take a shot looking back at Brandy's.

'What's that dongle you've got plugged into your phone?' Lesley asks as she swishes up behind me.

'Ah, it's one of those battery-charger thingies,' I lie, quickly flicking the screen back to the camera so she doesn't see my UV-detector app that the dongle is actually communicating with. What it's told me is that her windows are letting through zero UV rays, which means they've got to be coated with sunlight-protective film.

It's true that anyone with big windows facing due east might use UV-filter film, but hers isn't domestic grade, it's top museum quality. To me, it says she's trying to protect more than her carpet. VM Exhibit E.

She's carrying two glasses of orange juice. 'I thought we'd drink these out on the terrace while you set up.' As I take the glass and follow her, an idea for getting her entry codes comes to me. The dogs are already at each end of the terrace, their paws flicking a fluffy yellow tennis ball between the two of them like they're budding soccer nuts practising for tryouts of Fido Football. Unsurprisingly, the view is glorious, so it's not hard to look like I'm taking it in. I put the juice down and take a few snaps with my Sony, fiddling with the filters and apertures since I'm looking into the sun. I hold the camera towards Lesley and tell her to take a peek through the viewfinder.

Up close to me, the whiff of her perfume slaps me with the freshness of flowers after a spring rain. It makes me a bit light-headed – swoony, if I'm being honest – then I remember why I'm here. I reach down into my tote bag for another lens and she steps back.

'Oh no,' I say, trying to sound surprised. 'I must have dropped a lens cap on my way over.' I hold up the capless lens. The cap is actually in my pocket. 'I'd better go and find it. These lenses cost a bomb. Do you mind?'

She smiles, showing those amazing teeth, and we go to her front door.

'Fingers crossed, it's in your garden,' I tell her.

She opens the door, and I wave her through ahead of me. As I exit, the door closes behind us. 'It's easier if Winston and Scottie stay inside,' Lesley says.

I nod. 'I hope you've got the key,' I say jokingly, but not really joking.

'Not necessary. A keypad,' she adds and points to it.

Veronica Mars would be proud of me. While I'm checking out the path from her door to the front gate – and, thankfully, The Human Fridge is nowhere to be seen – she's looking in the garden beds but standing far enough back from them so she doesn't get dirt on her stunning outfit. After a minute, when she's got her head down, I pull the lens cap out of my pocket, bend to the ground and shout, 'Got it!' then hold it up for her to see. As we head back to the door, I take out my phone and say, like it's been on silent, 'Who's calling me at this ridiculous hour? Hope it's not work. Damn, it *is* work,' I say to her as we get back to her door. 'An auditor's always on the job even when she's on leave,' I add, then wish I hadn't. I fake taking the call … *JJ here … Yes … Yes … That's right … No, you put that in the left column …* Would an auditor really say that? I've got no idea. But the camera's on, and I've started the video. I keep pretending to talk while I'm surreptitiously recording Lesley's finger moving over the numbers on the keypad – *voilà*, the recording will give me the entry code for her front door.

When she's done, I end the 'call' and ask her, 'Doesn't it have facial recognition?'

It's broken, thank goodness, or I'd never be able to get in when she's not here.

43

When I get back to Brandy's, the first thing I do, since Scottie is already scratching at the balcony door, is let him out there so he and Winston can serenade each other across the bay. For a split second, I worry it might annoy the neighbours, and then smile briefly as I picture Russell Crowe coming by to complain. Then I tell myself to get real and check my video of Lesley working her entry keypad. I couldn't see what numbers she was pressing when I was there, but I did count six finger presses. And now I know the actual numbers: 4-3-6-2-8-9.

I type them into the notes field in my contact for 'Lesley Monroe'. Monroe is the surname she gave me when we swapped numbers. If I'd delayed 'finding' the lens cap until we were out on the street, I could have recorded the code to the front gate as well, but I didn't want to chance my luck too much and tailgating was probably the way to crack that one.

Now that I've got access, I'm suddenly freaking out about the idea of breaking in. Channelling Veronica Mars, or any other TV detective, to gather information is one thing. Acting on it is a step I'm not certain I can stretch myself to actually take.

I replay the video to double-check I've got the number right but, this time, I notice Lesley doing something I didn't notice before.

I rewind, then slo-mo that part of the clip, holding my finger on the thumbnail bar below the main screen and sliding it forward frame by frame. There it is … she's putting a small black object into a pocket in her kaftan. Who knew they had pockets? I rewind and spread my fingers on the screen to blow up the image. Damn! It's one of those tokens the gallery used to give us to do two-factor logins before we had apps on our phones that did much the same thing. The kind that generates randomish numbers that match up with a device which, in Lesley's case, is her keypad.

Which means 4-3-6-2-8-9 was a oncer.

Damn, and damn again.

*

At seven o'clock the next morning, I'm about to head out for my morning rendezvous with Lesley when my phone rings. It's her. Our first phone call!

Is she standing us up, me and Scottie? Has she realised that I've been casing her place, and she wants to avoid the questions I've spent all night dreaming up and intend to drop subtly into our conversation?

'JJ, I'm not feeling well. I've got to pass on today.'

Embarrassingly, my first thought isn't compassion, it's *Bugger, I've lost a day.* Scottie yanks on his leash and gives me a look that says *JJ, be nice. Winston's my buddy, remember?* I give him a reassuring pat. 'What's up?' I say into the phone. 'Can I do anything?'

'Actually, yes. It's an imposition, I know, but could you possibly pop by and take Winston for his walk with you and Scottie?'

Five minutes later, the two dogs and I are taking a new route. We're walking past Harry's Café de Wheels and on to Garden Island, then up the winding hill to Macleay Street, and we keep going till we get to the El Alamein Fountain in Fitzroy Gardens. It's spraying water today, so looks like a huge dandelion. I sit on the dry edge while the dogs jump in, frolic around and drink.

Out of the corner of my eye, I spy two men across the street who seem to be glaring at me. They're garbed in black. I avert my gaze, wondering if it's really me or the fountain they're looking at. Or maybe it's the dogs. What if they're council rangers about to stride across Macleay Street and write me a ticket?

When I look directly over at them, I see one of them is the same colossus I saw yesterday but this time he's with a mate, and together they're like clones of Arnold Schwarzenegger and Danny DeVito in *Twins.* They both turn away – not something rangers would do.

Danny looks shorter than me, but it could be parallax error or the fact he's standing next to Arnie. His circle of hair is like a monk's tonsure, and he's got huge black, bushy eyebrows. His arms may be short but they're like curved slabs of chiselled marble.

Twice in two days I catch the Schwarzenegger eyeing me up and now there's the DeVito too. It could be a coincidence. Kings Cross has supposedly been gentrifying forever – the posh people call it Potts Point – but there's still a hell of a lot of seedy types around. Before I have a chance to think any more about it, the dogs bound out of the pool, leaving sprays of water behind them, and shake themselves off right between me and a bag lady wheeling a banged-up supermarket trolley overflowing with her worldly possessions.

Instead of yelling at the dogs, she digs her hand into a Macca's paper bag that's teetering on top of her hoard, pulls out a half-eaten hamburger – which I doubt was originally hers – and tosses it to them.

When I check back across the street, the goons have vanished but my heart is thumping in my chest like a broken-winged bird trying to get out of a cage.

44

Taking photos and being a general snoop is one thing. But catching Dr Evil and Mini-Me spying on me, if that's what they were doing, is right up there in the too-close-for-comfort department.

Has Lesley hired bodyguards to watch over her? Is that why she's so relaxed about sitting out on the footpath when we're at the cafe? Or, are the goons watching her as well as me, though I can't imagine why?

Of course, there's the coincidence theory ... that they're just minding their own business and I happened to be there.

Yeah, right. Twice? I don't think I buy that.

One thing is 100 per cent for sure ... I'm fast getting out of my depth. Which means that my role as citizen detective isn't really working for me right now.

I'd go to the cops, except what are they going to say? *They glanced at you from across the street? Is that all, lady? Twice? It was just a glance, right? No harm, no foul.*

I'd hear them laughing as they hung up on me.

*

The doormat says *Hello* in a chirpy, welcoming script. I doubt it's meant for me and, frankly, the feeling is mutual.

It's outside a door I haven't passed through for years. Back then it was my parents' door, to the Surry Hills apartment I grew up in.

It's Hugh's door now. When Lauren moved out, he stayed. When she died. He stayed.

After so many years of him burning in the fiery hell I've consigned him to, I like to imagine he's bald and pallid with a spiderweb of craggy wrinkles, and so fat he'll have man boobs down to his ballooning waist. That's when I think of him at all.

I'm running the lines he'll probably use when he opens the door. He freezes for a second with a WTF pause. Then he says, *Perfect, you fell for my little ruse … all my fake calls about how I wanted to apologise. Ha! Beautiful! I reeled you right in, hook line and sinker, stinker!* Then *slam!*

Or, if he's struck it lucky with a new bit on the side, it'll be *Hey, honey, there's a young woman out here who looks just like my wife of twenty-something years* – he wouldn't even remember how long – *the devoted partner I abandoned to die alone from cancer, who I didn't give any moral support to whatsoever.*

Do I really want to be doing this?

I turn around and leave.

45

At seven o'clock the next day, my phone rings for the second morning in a row and, again, it's Lesley.

This time she sounds like she's holding back tears. 'Ah, JJ ... I'm, ah, at St Vincent's Hospital ... Had a thing this morning ... nothing too dramatic ... Well, I suppose it *was* a wee bit or I wouldn't be here.' I almost sense a forced *haha* coming, intended to lighten the burden she's placing on me, but it doesn't. 'They want to keep me all day for observation and most probably overnight.'

'My God,' I say, shocked and distressed that whatever ailed her yesterday has landed her in hospital. I'm not thinking about the goons. I'm thinking about the days she wasn't around just after I took my *Girl* photos, and wondering if that was also because of a visit to hospital. I'm also thinking about the wig and the headscarves.

I don't ask what the problem is. I know that you're not supposed to pry, and that if she wants to tell me, she will. So I go with, 'How are you feeling?'

'I've been better, obviously, but the staff here are great, and they tell me they've got this … but the reason I'm—'

'Winston?'

'Exactly.'

'I can look after him for as long as you need. Don't worry about it for a split second.'

'It's a big imposit …'

As Lesley goes on with the sorts of things people say when they really want you to do something for them, an awkward image pops into my head, an angry Brandy standing at her front door and tapping her foot, hands on hips. I mull over whether it's such a smart thing to do, bringing someone else's dog into my boss's apartment for an overnight playdate. Will Winston chew on the furniture? Will he knock over Brandy's *Aphrodite* sculpture – a genuine Jenny Green bronze, by the way! – which, in turn, would gouge a chunk out of her hallway parquetry floor? I decide on the spot that, with Brandy being away, what she doesn't know, blah, blah, and I continue, 'Scottie will be on cloud nine, or whatever cloud dogs are on. Where's Win—'

'At home. He'll be fine by himself for a few hours but,' she chokes up a little, 'not if I'm gone all day *and* all night.'

'I'll go get—'

'The thing is, JJ, if he stays at your place, he might get overexcited or disoriented and misbehave – you know, unfamiliar territory – and I'd never forgive myself if he—'

'Don't worry about—'

'—and you're already house-sitting over there, so ... it's not right if I ask you to ... Look, I know this is an even more massive imposition but I'll ask you straight out and if you say no, I'll completely understand. But do you think you might stay over at *my* place tonight and bring Scottie with you? I can walk you through all the security ...'

The expression *music to my ears* suddenly found true meaning.

Then I think, *Oh shit! How callous am I when Lesley could be ... you know ... dying?*

Am I really such a bad person?

46

Lesley's front gate has a code that all the residents use. She's just texted me the number, 6-9-8-3-7-5. It works perfectly, letting me into the garden. When I'm right outside her front door, it's my turn to text her. I hear Winston, scratching the other side of the door and barking hello to me – well, to Scottie, who's looking up at me with his big, dreamy eyes like he's asking *You're not really going to betray Lesley's trust and snoop around in there, are you?* I give him a calming pat on the head.

After I punch in the second number that she texts me, which she gets off her randomiser thingy, Scottie and I go inside. Lesley's internal security alarm is off, of course, since she's left Winston at home. She offered to give me the code for it, for when we go out, but I told her I hate alarms, which is the truth. I've only turned on Brandy's once and it was a disaster. When I came back, I forgot all about it and the noise was so ear-shattering I had to spend ten minutes calming Scottie, and myself, down.

All the curtains are closed but she's got the lights on in every room … for Winston, I guess. And, no surprises, but the art inside I'm seeing today is not The Art. In the living room, I slide open the terrace door, so Scottie and Winston can run through the curtains and play their version of the World Cup with the yellow tennis ball outside.

Then, before going 'full green button', I check out the rest of her house. *Surveil your environment* … that's what a true detective would do, not that I'm close to being one.

Surprisingly, her kitchen is a bit of a mess. It's not dinner-party-for-twelve kind of mess but more like her breakfast got interrupted suddenly. A bowl filled with muesli – honey and almond, according to the packet – is plonked on the counter next to an opened two-litre plastic container of lite milk, its blue lid on the floor. I pick it up, rinse it in the sink, sniff the bottle – it smells fine – screw the lid on and put the milk in the fridge. I tip the cereal into the bin and put the empty bowl in her dishwasher.

I'm not sure what I'm looking for, but walk around the apartment. When I'm standing in the doorway to her study, I see it doesn't look quite right. It's a super-neat room. It looks like no one's ever been inside it, let alone a wannabe novelist who supposedly spends night after night torturing herself over whether Marsha ever hooks up with John, or whether the lake in Provence that her fifty-six-year-old divorced heroine's room overlooks is a canvas of deep-blue crystals or is a swamp of dead grey reeds that remind her of her shit of a husband.

The study furnishings are so sparse you'd think Lesley had been burgled. It's just the bare essentials … a desk of light-coloured wood, beech or oak, with a laptop computer and a photo frame on top, a chair, and a bookshelf with no books. Not one. A writer without books around her is like me with no art in my tiny studio apartment, even if they're only prints. Unimaginable. On the wall opposite the desk, there's a framed photo of the Sydney Opera House lit up by an explosion of green fireworks in the night sky. New Year's Eve, I guess.

That's all.

I pick the photo frame up off her desk. It's a stylised portrait shot of an older couple on a beach promenade in front of a grand old building, one that looks like it's from early last century. The sixty-ish couple are elegance personified. The woman looks like an older version of Lesley, though her dark brown hair is swept back into a bun. She's wearing a stunning slim-silhouette jacket and skirt crafted from black and gold brocade. The man is a Jeff Goldblum look-alike, with salt and pepper hair and a tan that I could only dream of. He's impeccable in a blue check herringbone jacket with a gold pocket square, and a white shirt, blue tie and camel trousers.

Ordinarily, I'd think that if Lesley kept a shot like this on the barren expanse she calls a desk, it'd most likely be of her parents. I may be stereotyping but these don't look like people running a local chippy who've spent years sweating day and night in front of a deep-fryer. They don't look like people who make *dinners*. These are people who make *reservations*.

Maybe they're friends of Lesley's?

There's something else about the photo … but I can't put my finger on it. Their pose? Like it evokes a painting that's stuck in the recesses of my mind? That kind of thing is always happening to me. I try to force it but get nothing.

Scottie appears at the study door, whining, with the tennis ball in his mouth. Winston slides into view, coming across the parquetry hall floor like Tom Cruise in *Risky Business* and tries to snatch it from him. They have a tussle, then disappear. I put the frame back on Lesley's desk and reach underneath to find the spot where she told me she's Blu-Tacked her spare randomiser token for the front door. I locate it and slip the token into my pocket. I don't want to forget it when I take the dogs out for a walk later.

I check out Lesley's bedroom. Her bed is so big it could fit her, me and three more people. She's left it unmade, which is no surprise. Her doona, folded back, is turquoise silk with golden sprays of daffodils, and her bed linen is beige with a wide white stripe going through it.

I go over to make the bed for her, and while I'm pulling back the sheet, I do a visual of the thread count. It's a thing I've been doing ever since I was taught the technique for canvases. It can be a key decider for determining if an old painting is genuine. From the look and feel, I'm guessing it's at least 300. That's 150 threads in the length (warp) and 150 in the width (weft) per square inch. In metric, per square centimetre, the count is 120. I know my stuff.

In prep for coming over, I logged in to the gallery's archive to check what canvases VvG used for his other *Sunflowers* and noted their warp and weft. I found three excellent articles on it by a Dutch professor, Louis van Tilborgh, who I met when I did my secondment at the Van Gogh Museum. He knows his stuff better than I do.

When I've made the bed, I notice another photograph of Sydney Harbour. This one, on the wall opposite next to a TV, is an aerial shot at sunset. I could go to town over the photographer's skill, the composition, the light, all of that, but I'm on a tight mission, a compressed one-day and one-night timeframe.

For thoroughness, I check out her ensuite and walk-in closet. Apart from what you'd normally find, there's about thirty kaftans hanging in there, one for every day of the month, it seems. Freakishly, she's hung them to array the colours like the rainbow – reds at the left, heading though the oranges, yellows, greens and, finally, the blues and violets to the right. And she's got four shelves with nothing but scarves on them, similarly colour-coded. Not only is Lesley kaftan crazy, she seems pretty obsessive-compulsive about colour.

Next, I head for the second bedroom, where she's told me I should sleep. In there, I'm welcomed by a cheery topaz doona and orange throw pillows on a queen-size bed. There's a wall TV here too, and next to it a photograph of a huge yacht. I can't see its name but I'm sure it would be classy, not like *Seaduction*.

Scottie comes in with a flat, rectangular object between his teeth. It's the photo frame from Lesley's desk and I scold him as I try to wrest it from his mouth. It's got his drool all over it. I manage to pry it loose but it slips out of my hand, and I can't catch it before the glass smashes on the parquetry.

I grab Scottie and carry him away from the shards and out onto the terrace. Winston is curled up asleep on the rug in the living room, out like a light in front of what he probably is dreaming is a raging fireplace. He'd be hopeless as a guard dog. I lift the little fur ball gingerly, put him outside too, and close the sliding door. With a broom and a shopping bag I take from the kitchen, I sweep up the glass and dump it in the trash.

Replacing the glass – so Lesley is none the wiser – isn't really an option, not today. The hour or two it would take me is time I can't afford to waste, so I'll have to go with the truth, and blame Scottie.

As I wipe off his saliva with a rag – yuk – I gently lift the photo out of the frame to check it for stains or teeth marks. Thankfully, it's undamaged. There's a scrawl on the back, mostly illegible, but I can make out the last few words … *ta maman et ton papa*.

So, they *are* her parents. And now I'm focusing on the elegant woman's features, I'm pretty sure I'm seeing Lesley's nose and eyes.

47

With my phone, I take snaps of the photo, front and back – VM Exhibit F – then, as I'm sliding it back into the glassless frame, I think of the thing that's been bugging me. It's the grand building they're posing in front of – the belle époque Hotel Carlton in Cannes. I haven't been there but I've seen it heaps of times, like pretty much every year when I'm ogling the movie stars as they walk out of it to head for the red carpet at the Palme d'Or awards.

So, here's Lesley's parents, very classy-looking if not dripping in money, and they're striking poses outside one of the most expensive, elite locations on the French Riviera as if it's their natural habitat. So … what about her Scottish accent? Is that a put-on? And her writing …

a *real* fiction, if you get my drift? How about Melbourne Paul, fact or fake? Where does Leasing Paul fit in? And the hospital. Is she really there?

I dial it to find out and first I hear, *If this is an emergency, dial blah, blah.* Well, it is an emergency, kind of, but not that kind. Then it's *If you want admissions, press 1 … If you want radiology, press 2 …* and finally, after I *don't* press 1 to 6, a real person, a man with a warm and friendly radio voice says, 'How may I help you?'

'I'd like to speak to a patient, please. Lesley Monroe? She's my sister,' I add, because on *Grey's Anatomy* there's always some officious clerk roadblocking enquiries with *Sorry, we can only put next of kin through.* After I've said it, I wonder if I should have put on a Scottish accent.

'Can you spell the surname?'

I do it.

'Thank you. And your name?'

'Skye.' It's the first Scottish name that pops into my head, probably from the island mentioned on Brandy's whisky bottle. 'Skye Monroe.'

'Putting you through to her room now.'

I hang up before the first ring. Okay, she's there, but what about all the rest? Lesley's told me more lies than a married man in a wine bar.

The green button is really calling out to me now. I go to the wall panel, touch it and watch it open. My hand hovers over the button.

I dearly want to press it. It's like that moment when I was at Hugh's door. That moment when if I take the next step, I can't go back.

I retract my hand and go to the kitchen for a glass of water. With each sip, I count out the four possible scenarios.

One, The Artworks are simply prints. No biggie, but Lesley and I can be friends.

Two, they're high-quality fakes that she's either collected or commissioned to enjoy in the privacy of her own home. Also no biggie, and still friends.

Three, they're forgeries and Lesley's planning to sell them to unsuspecting buyers. That one is quite a biggie. Bye-bye to our morning coffees.

Four, the works are the real McCoys. That's the scenario that's really terrifying me — that Lesley might be a big-time criminal, sitting on hundreds and hundreds of millions of dollars' worth of stolen art. The implications are more than sinking in. They're driving nails into my brain.

I go back to the green button.

It's make-or-break time.

48

Most people would've pressed the green button without a second thought, but I'm not really one of those 'just do it' Nike types. I'm intrinsically more of a 'don't do today what you can put off till tomorrow' type – though without any real sense of urgency – especially if the words *criminal, millions of dollars* and *prison* are all trying to cram themselves into the one sentence.

I remove myself from the green button and make myself a cup of lemongrass and ginger tea. I'm about to take it out onto the terrace but I see through the glass that the dogs are sprawled out on the tiles. The sun is a tangerine disc hovering over the top of the Finger Wharf. The sky is still pink, and a kookaburra is cackling outside, later than usual. It's probably laughing at me.

As I sip the tea, I decide that before I green-button my life away, I need to do another reverse-image search, one I should have done long before now … using my *Girl* photo series to find out if Lesley is really Lesley.

After that, I'll do the same thing with the photo of her parents, or whoever they are.

I scrunch down into her sofa, open the *Girl* photos on my laptop, choose the absolute sharpest one where she's looking to camera, and start the search. All it gets me is hundreds of thumbnails of random stylised images of women in headscarves, and none of them look much like Lesley at all.

I AirDrop my shot of the desk photo to my laptop, and that too generates lots of junk … couple after couple looking front on, including the grim-faced farmer and his daughter in *American Gothic*.

Hopeful as ever, I keep scrolling and, eventually, one thumbnail stands out. I click to enlarge it and … *boom!* … It's the couple in Lesley's photo. They're in a similar pose but it's a different scene.

It's like they've just walked out of a *Vogue* magazine spread aboard a yacht – and when I say yacht, it could easily be an ocean liner. Both are wearing sunglasses. The man's hair is windblown, while the woman's is protected by a headscarf. She looks like Marilyn Monroe in one of those retro 1950s glamour shots. Something about the man now reminds me of Dante, the naked guy who lived next door to Samantha in the first *Sex and the City* movie, but older and greyer.

They're definitely the same people. I click the link – it's to a newspaper article – and according to the caption, they're Jacques and Gisèle Fontaine. Or they *were*, because the first article sends me to an obituary notice a few years later in the same paper.

Jacques, it tells me, was the founder of a major law firm in Monaco and he died in March 2021, two years after his wife, Gisèle. The only family mentioned is a child, Claude, who became the firm's senior partner after Jacques' death.

I'm thinking about this Claude. He must be someone who's pretty special to Lesley if she keeps a portrait of his parents on her desk. Maybe she was married to the guy … I know Claude's supposed to be a lawyer, but – and I don't know why – I'm imagining him as some Jeffrey Epstein paedophile monster who Lesley walked in on and then, in disgust, ran for her life.

I need to know more about this beast, so I do a Google search for *Claude Fontaine +Monaco*. I get two hits. One is from *Monaco Life* and the other is from *Monaco-Matin*. I go with *Monaco Life*. The images are slow to load, so I press the text-to-speech icon and hear a woman speaking in quite a soft English voice.

Covid tragedy strikes elite Monaco law firm

15 May 2021: Wealth and influence made no difference when India's second Covid wave condemned leading Monaco lawyer Claude Fontaine, 33, to a grim and miserable death.

Fontaine, like the 2000 other patients crowded into the same makeshift hospital, fell victim to a health system at breaking point, with a drastic shortage of doctors, drugs, oxygen and ventilators.

Only last year, Fontaine was named senior partner of one of Monaco's most prestigious law firms, Fontaine & Fontaine.

In April, the lawyer had flown to Mumbai on business and soon after contracted Covid.

Sources in Mumbai report that Fontaine, frantically trying to keep breathing, went from one overcrowded hospital to another in the city's oppressive summer heat.

Eventually Fontaine was admitted to the BGM Jumbo Hospital on the city's outskirts, a pandemic facility that is basically a huge metal tent. It's not only Covid they're fighting there but Mumbai's stifling humidity and excruciating heat.

Desperate patients crowd the entrances to the hospital, their numbers increasing every day, but with insufficient beds, doctors and ventilators to deal with the crisis, most are turned away.

Fontaine was one of the lucky ones, but not lucky enough.

I press *pause* on the reading aloud. My Epstein speculation seems to have been way off. The poor man died horribly, tragically. If Lesley was married to him, she'd be a complete mess. So was that the reason she ran off to Australia?

I press *play*.

Within three days, Fontaine died a lonely death. She was immediately cremated on a funeral pyre in the local manner.

It was two weeks before anyone in Monaco knew their friend and colleague had died.

She? Did I hear right … that Claude Fontaine is a *she*? I look closely at what's on my screen and that's what the words seem to say. I replay the paragraph aloud again, just to make sure, and yes, it's telling me that Claude was … is … a she.

The French have lots of unisex names – like Jules and Simone and Gabriel – but I never knew that Claude was one of them.

So … was Lesley married to a woman?

Is that why I think I picked up some vibes?

Before I can ponder that question further, the *speech function* continues, like it's got a mind of its own.

For Fontaine's partners at the law firm, her death is a double tragedy.

Only 10 months ago, Ms Fontaine assumed the firm's leadership after her father, Jacques Fontaine, a well-known philanthropist and a stalwart of the Monaco business community, retired for health reasons.

Sadly, Jacques Fontaine died only four weeks before his daughter's fatal trip to India …

Finally, the newspaper photograph loads and … *What!* … The face beaming up at me is Lesley's.

Lesley is standing right next to Jacques Fontaine, but the caption doesn't say *Claude Fontaine's wife, Lesley Monroe*. It says *Claude Fontaine (left) and her father Jacques Fontaine*.

I feel like screaming.

Everything … every single thing I know about Lesley is a lie. Not just Melbourne Paul, but her job … *she's a lawyer* … her name … *Claude Fontaine* … her background … *she comes from Monaco, not Edinburgh* … her family … *wealthy A-listers, not working-class chippy owners* … and more than all that, she's supposed to be fucking *dead!*

D-E-A-D!

And she has been since May 2021.

What the holy fuck have I got myself into? That single online article – Exhibit G – has got me asking another barrage of questions.

If she's fucking dead, what the hell is she doing in hospital right now?

If I'd just discovered that Lesley had a false name and accent – even a false backstory, given her supposed Melbourne Paul situation – I could cope.

But that she's a millionaire Monaco lawyer who died a pauper's death from Covid in India, back in 2021, and then turned up alive in post-Covid Sydney under another name?

My normal reticence about swearing has, it seems, flown right out of the fucking window.

If what I've just found out is true, this is almost definitely a scenario-four situation. Meaning that The Art is real, and Lesley … or Claude, or whatever the fuck her name is … is not just some lawyer but an international art criminal who's hiding hundreds of millions of dollars' worth of stolen paintings and I've stumbled my way into *The Godfather IV.*

And how the hell does someone like her manage to turn up in Australia with a fake identity?

Surely she didn't just google *Riviera lawyer faking death in India needs fake Aussie passport so she can pretend to be a Scottish writer.* That said, I do actually google those words on my phone and find several websites that claim to sell counterfeit passports online, including Australian ones for anywhere between $600 and $4500.

There's got to be more. I race back into Lesley/Claude's office to see what I can find in her papers. Sitting in her chair, I yank out the desk drawers but they're as empty as my bank account the day before payday. Not even a pen and pad. Not a single trace of her past, except for the one trip-up. Putting that photo on display was clearly a blunder in an otherwise meticulously executed plan.

Apart from that, she'd been so careful, even that day we met, when she got me to delete the snaps I took of her and Winston.

What I suddenly realise, though, is that I don't want her to be Claude. And the very, very last thing I want is to find out she's a master criminal.

49

I'm hanging on by a thread ... but what's one more rummage around the internet? Maybe she's an identical twin – wishful thinking, I know – but it's got me searching for *Claude Fontaine +sister*. Of course, I get no sister ... no Lesley ... no anyone.

I find myself typing *Fontaine & Fontaine +scandal* into my search engine. I've hardly had time to take my finger off *enter* when I see the headline. My body freezes, though somehow I manage to catalogue this mentally as Exhibit H.

Police identify mutilated torso washed up on Cannes beach as Monaco lawyer – 'organised crime involved'

Dr Félix Matthieu, respected senior partner in the beleaguered Monte Carlo law firm of Fontaine & Fontaine ...

For once, my dyslexia is an advantage because I'm only catching every second or third word. Given what they are ... *body parts* ... *murder* ... *missing wife* ... I don't switch on text-to-speech.

The report is recent, from less than two weeks ago ... thirteen days in fact.

Suddenly I'm visualising Tom Cruise – again – this time in *The Firm* but with a sex change. He's Claude, faking her death as the only way to escape her own corrupt firm. The way I'm imagining it, Claude 'died' and became Lesley so the killers – whoever they are – would stop looking for her.

But given those two goons I've seen checking me out, have they actually stopped looking?

That's one version for sure. But what if it's Claude who's the puppeteer – the mystery woman who's pulled the long-distance strings on her successor's murder – with the two thugs being her bodyguards?

Fuck!

I go to stand up but am lightheaded, so sit back down at the edge of Lesley's chair and lean forward, head in hands, elbows on her desk. Where are the paper bags when you really need them?

Breathe, I tell myself and close my eyes. But I instantly feel claustrophobic and quickly open them. I feel like I'm getting trapped inside an invisible spiderweb, a situation made worse because I've been spinning it myself. If I hadn't been a snoop, if I hadn't orchestrated meeting Lesley, etc., etc., I wouldn't be here, freaking out inside the home of someone who's on the run from killers … or is a killer herself.

So, fuck the green button. I grab Scottie and run out of there as fast as I can.

50

I step onto Hugh's doormat. I look down and my right foot is partially obscuring the tail end of the welcome greeting, so all I can see is *Hell*.

The door opens, as if Hugh, lurking inside, has detected my presence, even though I haven't knocked or even called ahead.

A cute little boy no more than four years old, a ginger-coloured fringe flopping over his forehead, looks up at me and says what the doormat's supposed to say.

I drop to my knees so our eyes are level. His are blue like mine, but they're as deep and untroubled as Sydney Harbour on a windless, sunny day. 'Hello back,' I say. 'My name is JJ. What's yours?'

'Vini,' he says, cheeks flushing to match his hair as he rocks from side to side, hands behind his back.

Vini! Of course he's a Vini. Either he's a half-brother Hugh never bothered to enlighten me about, or he belongs to Hugh's lady friend, and his name, hair and eyes are a total coincidence. As if!

New wife, new life?

If I'd known, I would've sent a set of steak knives for the wedding he didn't invite me to, the blades extra sharp and engraved with *To Huge Ego from JJ*.

I'm gazing into Vini's blue eyes and conjure up a sad image of an old, fat and crotchety Hugh struggling to get down on the floor with this beautiful little boy so he can shove some VvG history down his throat, but instead he falls backwards and rolls around like a tenpin at the bowling alley.

Once Vini and I are inside, he produces a paintbrush and waves it at me. 'I'm going to be a famous nartist when I gwow up.'

'You mean *artist*, don't you?'

'No,' he stamps his foot. 'A *nartist*.'

Did I say he was cute? 'Sweetie,' I say, kneeling again and hoping to get the boy with his guard down, 'have you heard about me. About JJ?'

Before he can answer, a man enters the front room. He has echoes of Hugh but looks ten years younger than when I last saw him – like a svelte Colin Firth in *Girl with a Pearl Earring*, though without the long, scraggy hair or, thankfully, the sexual innuendo.

This version of Hugh's got a quiet, brooding, almost reserved demeanour I don't ever recall seeing on him. The red hair is still there, though it's thinner and possibly boosted with product, and he seems taller than I remember. I hate to say it but Hugh actually looks terrific – as if cutting my mother and me out of his life has turned out to be the best thing he ever did for himself.

Bastard!

He pauses at a bright yellow toy truck on the floor and stoops down to pick it up. Getting back up does look a bit difficult, and I understand why when he places the toy on a sideboard and limps further into the room.

It's 9.30 am, and he's wearing a loose black bathrobe over striped pyjamas. Is that because it's Saturday? Because he's retired?

I stand up as he shuffles across the living room. Facing him instantly brings back scars from the cut glass I constantly had to dance around as a child to steer clear of his volcanic, nitpicking temper. *Poor Vini*, I think, and get an urge to hug the little boy tightly to my chest. I resist it, of course.

'How can I help you?' Hugh asks. He stops midstep, and his eyes go wide.

Vini turns around to him and says, 'Papa, this is JJ. Is she a stwanger danger? Can I play with her? She's nice.'

Vini clearly has no idea he has a half-sister. That said, he's also clearly smart, with an instinct for people, a quality he did not inherit from his ... our ... father.

Hugh is halfway across the room and looking at me like he has just seen a ghost, which isn't far from the truth because the mere sight of him is sucking the soul out of me. Coming here was definitely a huge mistake.

Before either of us can speak, a willowy blonde appears in the room. She's forty if she's a day, barely older than me. She's Scarlett Johansson to Hugh's Colin Firth, with the same turned-up nose and full red mouth. She also looks to be in way better shape than me, which is not exactly difficult.

Like her son, Vini's mother is gorgeous. Fingers crossed the poor woman doesn't get cancer or she'll really find out who she's got into bed with.

She's doing up the buttons on a dark blue cardigan – cashmere? – which she wears with a gold crewneck top and light blue slacks. I see a wedding ring on her finger, whereas Hugh's is bare. He's still the same narcissistic bastard.

All three of them are barefoot, which I was never allowed at home. Under them is a thick mauve carpet with tiny white splodges that, no doubt, help hide the detritus of daily life. Either Hugh's doing pretty well for himself lately or he married for money, because when I was growing up in this apartment, the floor was cold, peeling vinyl that mocked parquetry and loved to collect grit. From when I was Vini's age, it was my job to sweep the flat out twice a day, after breakfast and when I got home from kindie or, later, school. I can still see my mother looking on, helpless, as I try my hardest to sweep with a broom that towers over me. She's wincing but saying nothing, having learned the hard way that silent resignation was best for both of us.

I feel weak at the memory, and I'm already dreading whatever other toxic flashbacks this place is going to throw up at me.

The woman, who has a concerned and kind face, asks, 'Are you okay?' like in those mental health ads. 'Would you like to come in and sit down?' she adds. It is both comforting and surprising, since she has no idea who I am and probably would never invite me in if she did.

51

Hugh turns his head away from me as he introduces his wife. I'm sure it's not only because he's embarrassed that he's a cradle-snatcher, it's because of her name ... Kate. It's my mother's middle name. I don't know whether to slap him and stomp out, or snigger, but my arms and feet won't move and my mouth is gaping.

I'm shocked when Kate comes over and embraces me, with the biggest, warmest hug I've had since before Lauren got cancer. 'JJ,' she says, 'I've wanted to meet you for years. Hugh's told me so much about you.'

I don't know what to say and, even though I don't want to, I'm enjoying the warmth of her welcome, feeling it radiating from her body into mine.

She finally steps back, arms outstretched and still holding me, looking at me like we're old friends who haven't seen each other for a very long time. 'Hugh would struggle to say this to you …' She pauses and looks at him as if for permission.

I look at him too, and instead of his face I see a beetroot burning with embarrassment on top of shoulders slumped in shame. He says nothing but nods to her.

Kate continues, 'What he'd like to say to you, JJ … what you deserve to hear …' She turns her head back to him, ever so briefly. 'JJ, he's so sorry … for what he did … and for what he didn't do.'

She pulls me close again and, I can't help it, I burst into uncontrollable laughter. I laugh so much that we're both shaking.

Kate pulls away sharply and looks at me as if I'm the only sociopath in this room. After all these years of radio silence, that pathetic excuse for a husband and father tells *her*, not me, that he's sorry for ruining my life and my mother's. As always, he's manipulating someone to do his dirty work for him. So much for those calls he kept making to me.

He probably met her on the internet. That way she wouldn't have twigged he was old enough to be her father until it was too late. He would have reeled her in by spinning a slick sob story about his failings, to make her believe that, deep down, he was brimming with so much guilt and remorse that he was worth saving, much like the sleazy bastard Ian McKellen plays in *The Good Liar* when he slithers his miserable way into Helen Mirren's life.

'JJ,' says Hugh, stepping forward. 'I don't expect you to forgive me but—'

'There are *no* buts,' I snap back.

I feel like I'm clamped in a vice, but look down and see it's because Vini has grabbed me around the legs and is hugging me. It's like the kid's worked out that I'm important to him in some way.

I reach down to pick him up. Holding Vini in my arms, I turn to Hugh. 'You … you don't deserve her … or him … or this,' I say, waving my hand around. 'Everything that you've got here. I don't resent it. I salute you for it. You seem to be the luckiest man in the world. But don't expect forgiveness, not from me. You're lucky but not that lucky.'

'So, why did you come here?' he asks me. To be fair, it's an entirely reasonable question.

I can't give the long, complex and gory answer in Vini's presence, so I go with the one that I know will win my father's complete and immediate attention. 'I've found *Six Sunflowers* … in Sydney.'

'What?' Hugh's face drains of so much colour, I'm worried he's going to faint.

Vini pipes up and, waving his paintbrush, says, 'JJ, that pitcher got destwoyed in a whirl war.'

He's only four and he's already been indoctrinated.

'To help me prove it …' I take a deep breath, staring at Hugh, and then I say three words I never expected to leave my mouth, 'I need you.'

52

Vini plonks himself on my lap and does his best to braid my hair, which isn't easy, since it's not much longer than his fingers *and* he's a boy. Still, being fussed over by a relative – even if he is a four-year-old – is a novel experience for me.

Hugh's gone to get dressed, and Kate is also fussing. She's plumping up cushions like I'm royalty, and bringing in a tray with two cups of tea and two muffins. She blows me away when she says that Hugh baked them.

Quick as a flash, Vini disputes it, but not how I expect him to. '*Vini* is the pastwy chef! Papa was my helper.'

It's like I've stepped into the same place I grew up but it's in a parallel universe. Not once in my entire time here did Hugh cook with me. 'It's women's work,' was the answer to any suggestion that he spend more than a minute in the kitchen, even if it was simple stuff like making chocolate crackles with Rice Bubbles or sprinkling fairy bread with hundreds and thousands. The only times Hugh would venture into our kitchen were to get a beer from the fridge, to complain to Lauren that she was taking too long preparing dinner, or to show his manliness when the sink needed unblocking.

There was one other time – one I've tried to, but can't, forget. He was having one of his 'conniptions', as Mum used to call them. Today, I'd call them eruptions of volcanic rage. While Hugh never hit either of us, not once, he'd often raise his hand like he was going to. The slightest lift in his right arm would fill me with dread. I cowered so many times, waiting for it to fall on me, but it never did. Maybe the fear felt worse than if he actually hit me. I'll never know. But that one time, he wasn't just using his hand. He flew into the kitchen, grabbed a carving knife from the drawer and, brandishing it over his head, screamed at Mum until she ran from the room. I was at the door, watching … quivering. I was nine. He looked over to me, saying nothing. Then he replaced the knife and went back into the living room to watch some crap on TV as if nothing had happened. What was my mother's crime? Making arrangements to go to a girlfriend's place for a card night without asking his permission.

Kate places the tray on the coffee table and surprises me again by sitting down on the couch next to me, so close our knees are almost touching. She picks up one of the cups and asks Vini to get off my lap because the tea is hot. He slides off without a murmur and goes to play in the far corner, where he's got an easel, paints and brushes set up on a small blue plastic tarpaulin.

A rubber plant is growing over there too. It has big leaves, shiny like someone's been polishing them. The old Hugh hated indoor plants. 'They suck the oxygen,' he used to say, which I'd learned at school was the complete opposite of the truth, but I knew that arguing with Hugh was a one-way path to a barrage of invective and hours stuck in my room.

She hands me the cup, and asks if I'd like milk, which I would. She then pours some milk in and says, 'I thought I'd take a moment while Hugh's getting dressed. There's something I need to tell you. It won't change how you feel about him, not straight away, but you should at least know about it. After your mother died, Hugh fell into a massive—'

I'm seething. I put my cup down, to make sure I don't throw it, and glare into her eyes. 'I don't care what he went through. Whatever vortex of hell he got sucked into, he got off lightly. I'm not saying that to offend or upset you. It's the way I feel.'

She blinks a couple of times and puts her hand on my knee. It's like an electric shock of intimacy from a woman I really don't want to like.

'The thing is, JJ, not long after your mother died, he was diagnosed as bipolar. I'm sure you know it's a mental illness that's marked by extreme shifts in mood. While it doesn't excuse his behaviour to you and to her – and, from what he's admitted to, it's totally inexcusable – it does go some way to explaining it.'

I point to her ring. 'And you found out about it after you two got married. Typical.'

'Er – no. He told me the first time we met … so I could walk away if I wanted to. JJ, Hugh wears his past with you and your mum like a noose around his neck. He's been on meds for bipolar for years, and he was put on antidepressants for a long while too. So, you coming here today is … well, I don't know what it is yet. But I'm hoping it's a blessing.'

She says it like it's a question. Like she's wanting me to pat *her* knee and tell her *Yes, all is forgiven*, and then she'll see Hugh and me kissing and making up.

Well, that's not happening. 'You're prepared to live under this roof with the constant threat that Hugh will do to you and your beautiful boy what—'

'For as long as I've known him, he's been fastidious about his meds. We've been together for five years, married for four, and he's never once had an episode. He's a different man, JJ, if you could just give him a chance. I'd love you to be in Vini's life. And mine. I know Hugh would love it too.'

'If he's such a saint—'

'No one's saying that. It took him a long time, I know, to reach out to you but he did try. He wanted to do it earlier but the police force's psychologist advised against it, very strongly. He said the risk was twofold … to you and to Hugh. That if you'd managed to get past it all and had moved on, him reaching out would reopen old wounds and cause you even more pain. If you rejected him, which the psychologist said was highly likely, it might have triggered a relapse. And that, JJ, would risk everything he has with Vini and me. Right now,' she indicates the direction of the bathroom, 'he's in there popping a Prozac.'

Hugh walks back into the room, as if the pair had planned her intervention to the microsecond. Either that or he had his ear to the door while he was chewing on a tablet.

Kate seems genuine but I'm not even close to buying the whole *he's a new man* thing. If it's true, that's great for her and Vini – really it is – but it leaves me fuming with resentment and contempt.

What I wish I could say, to his face, is *Why didn't you get yourself fucking diagnosed when you were with us, you bastard?* But I didn't come here to make a scene in front of a four-year-old. Even less to reconcile with a good-for-nothing leech who tossed his wife away like a used Kleenex, and did his best to turn his daughter into a timid husk.

I came here – a giant step for me – not to hear his excuses, not to forgive and forget, but because he has something I need, and he owes me. I don't want love, I don't want apologies. What I want are his detective skills.

Hugh's still barefoot but has changed into blue jeans, and a black T-shirt that throws me when I see it. It has a cartoon poking fun at art – something the Hugh I grew up with would never countenance in his home, let alone parade on his chest. Seeing him in that T-shirt is boiling up my years of repressed fury, even though it simply shows a campervan painted like VvG's *Starry Night* and says *I Have No Monet For Degas To Make The Van Gogh*.

Perhaps I'm the one who needs to pop a Prozac. A T-shirt's just a T-shirt, right?

I clench my hands at my sides and drive my fingernails hard into my palms. Their couch is beige, so I hope my hands don't bleed.

Kate goes to pick up Vini and take him to his bedroom, but the boy runs over to me, throws his arms around my neck and gives me a kiss. Tears start flooding down my cheeks and it's all I can do not to start shaking.

He lets me go and looks up at me. 'Why are you cwying, JJ? Don't you like Vini?'

'Vini, of course I like you.' I would've said *love*, but I couldn't get the word out.

Kate takes a tissue from inside her sleeve and gives it to me. I wipe my eyes. 'Sorry,' I say. 'I don't know what …' I know if I try to finish the sentence, I'll end up even more of a blubbering mess.

'Come on, Vini,' Kate says to him. 'Let's get ready to go to the park. Papa and JJ have to talk.' She takes his hand and Vini skips off with her to the bedrooms.

Hugh sits lightly beside me on the couch. He's not too close, seemingly respectful of the Great Wall of China that's casting a heavy shadow over the space between us. He hands me a plate with one of *his* muffins. 'Vini helped me make these,' he says with a forced lightness in his voice.

I attempt a smile and break off a piece of the cake. If it wasn't Hugh's, I'd be saying *Wow!* Biting into this thing is like going to heaven. The edges have a perfect crispiness that leaves the centre soft and moist. I always love raspberries in a muffin, but these have such an intense flavour!

But I say nothing about his muffins, and instead I notice – silently – how his nose and ear hairs need a trim. Hugh used to be meticulous about his grooming. I remember the hum of his clippers when he locked himself in the bathroom.

Vini and Kate return, shoes on, and go to the front door. Just before they leave, she turns back. 'Hugh, text me when you guys are done, okay?' He nods.

'JJ, it's been a genuine delight to meet you. I hope we get to see more of each other.' She looks down at her son. 'We would both like that, wouldn't we, Vini?'

He starts jumping up and down, which I take as a yes, and she closes the door behind them before I get to say anything I regret.

She's a smart woman.

53

When I decided to come here, I visualised Hugh pinning up all my exhibits on his wall, like they do on the TV cop shows – running different coloured strings from one item to another to show possible connections, tease out the kinks in my theory and plan the next moves. While I could have easily shown him everything on my camera or phone, I used the printer at Brandy's to make copies. Hugh is laying them out on the coffee table, which is fine but not as cop-like as I'd been expecting.

'Your limp?' I ask him.

'A perp had lousy aim. It's nothing.'

I blurt out, 'Nothing?'

'It's just a twinge. But the upside is, they put me on

recovery leave, so I've got more time with Vini ahead of Christmas.'

I bristle.

He leans back in his seat and takes a deep breath. 'You know, when you were his ...' He starts blushing. 'I really would've liked to—'

'Don't.' The last thing I want to hear is Hugh playing a whiny violin about all the things he would've done differently. 'Focus on these,' I say through gritted teeth.

Unexpectedly, he doesn't argue, doesn't shout. There are no *How dare yous*. He just does as I ask. He listens intently and silently to everything I tell him and, as we go through it all, examines each photo as if he's wearing cotton gloves and I've handed him the *Mona Lisa*. Gone are the cheap, sarcastic shots he'd typically batter me with. He raises an eyebrow when I show him the report of Félix Matthieu's murder, but that's about it. It's only after I've taken him through the whole inventory of my exhibits that he starts asking questions. He's got a heap of them, and they're all good.

An hour later, he stands up and leans back to stretch. 'I don't exactly know what you've uncovered, but coming to me, JJ ... that was the right thing to do. It was smart. We don't know why the lawyer's body was cut up, but what we do know is bad people can do terrible things when someone stands between them and a bucket of money, or the equivalent.'

'Like a fortune in stolen art?'

'Right.'

'So, you think they're genuine?' I never expected to be seeking validation from the man who never gave it to me when I really needed it, and I don't like the feeling.

His hand seesaws in a fifty-fifty gesture. 'Let's get some sodas.' As we're walking to the kitchen, he says, '*Six Sunflowers* didn't survive World War II – even Vini knows that – so if *that's* a forgery, the rest probably are too.'

'Why keep them in Australia? Sydney is hardly the bustling centre of the world's black market in fake art.'

'There is that. The one sure thing is that they're not prints.'

'Because ...?'

'Instincts from forty years as a cop.' He takes a bottle of fizzy water out of the fridge and pours it into two glasses. 'Lemon? Lime?' He's got a lemon in one hand and a knife in the other. I tense up, even though he's not holding it over my head.

I force myself to say, 'I'm fine, thanks.'

He cuts a slice of the lemon and pops it into his glass. 'Are you sure?' he asks, waving the knife.

My hands are in fists at my sides. It's all I can do not to scream. He obviously doesn't remember what happened.

He hands me a glass. 'Thank you for coming here, JJ. And thank you for trusting me.'

I recoil. Trust and Hugh are not words I can abide hearing in the same sentence. I almost knock the glass to the floor, except that's what he would have done and I've spent my whole life not being him, not repeating the sins of the father. 'I *don't* trust you. I *need* your skills.'

His shoulders droop and the smile on his face heads the same way. He says he understands, which is definitely bullshit, and leads me into what used to be Mum's favourite room, her sewing room.

The old Singer sewing machine – bought second-hand – and all her other paraphernalia are gone, of course.

Lauren took all of that with her when she left him. Now the room is a his-and-hers home office, with two desks pushed up against opposite walls. They're new and they're from IKEA. I know this because each one's got a screw missing from the identical hole and there's an Allen key in a plastic bag taped to the side of his. Pushed up against the window wall is Vini's desk, one of those red and yellow plastic ones I've seen in Kmart a million times. Hugh rolls his wife's chair over for me, so it's beside his at the computer, and gets comfortable.

I ask him what Kate does for a living, not because I'm interested. I'm just making polite conversation. I expect he's going to tell me she's the new Mother Teresa.

It turns out I'm close.

'She's an educator – early childcare,' he says as he turns on the computer. 'I was leading an investigation into the father of one of the kids – a sordid story – and I interviewed her. After the guy went down – he got four years, should've got twenty – I asked her out.'

'Okay,' I reply.

'She's smart. She's in the running for the top job at her kindie.' He says it proudly, like he really wants her to get it.

What *is* this? The past winner of Male Chauvinist of the Year twenty-seven years running is making out like he's a feminist? Pull the other one. I remember when my mother got offered a job outside the home, running a women's clothing boutique in Darlinghurst, and it was like the world crashed down around our heads. *His* head, really – *No wife of mine is taking a job*, blah, blah. Mum had a degree in design and, before she made the mistake of falling in love with Hugh, a promising career in fashion.

225

I hold my tongue. I'm here for a purpose.

He's logging in to the police network. 'They let you log in from home?' I ask. 'What if some criminal's broken in and they're holding a gun to your head and—'

'We've got that covered. I'd add a special code to my password. I can still log in but that code activates an SOS alert and they know exactly who and where it's coming from.'

'Being on leave … doesn't that make logging in suspicious?'

He keeps tapping, navigating his way into I don't know where yet. 'We're understaffed, as usual, so they've got me doing some desk work from home … Okay, we're in.'

54

After an hour of Hugh leading us down one rabbit hole after another, we come up with nothing. 'This is impossible,' he says. 'Our system's got nothing on a Lesley Monroe or a Claude Fontaine that even gets close to the description of your … er … friend. There's not even a parking fine.'

He logs in to the immigration department database and roots around like a dog sniffing for truffles. I'm surprised he has access to it. 'Doesn't a state cop need a warrant to search a federal department?'

He taps his nose in a conspiratorial way. 'People do people favours. That's all you need to know.'

I hope this will help with my eventual not-guilty plea for aiding and abetting an illegal search.

He keeps on with what he's doing and I hear a lot of *hmm*s. Eventually, he says, 'Again, nothing. No visas, no border entry permits for a Lesley Monroe or a Claude Fontaine.'

He logs out. 'Last thing to try is property. That's where people often let their guard down.' He types her address into a real estate website, and, sure enough, Lesley's place comes up as having been leased a year ago. The letting agent is none other than Paul, so he wasn't lying, which makes one of us. 'I've met him,' I tell Hugh. 'Also, I saw him come by her place the other night. He gave her some papers and they had a drink.'

Hugh puts Paul's details into his phone. 'So, let's recap. All we've got on this Lesley Monroe, or Claude Fontaine, in Australia is a rental through this real estate agent. He'll know what name she used on the lease. She's not known to the police, she's not on any international watchlists, and no one by either of those names is supposed to be in Australia – at least, not officially. Bottom line, the woman knows how to cover her tracks—'

'Which, given what happened to this Félix two weeks ago, isn't a total surprise. So, Hugh, do I go to the police, officially?'

He kicks his chair so it rolls back into the middle of the room and rubs the side of his face. 'Mmm ... Not yet.'

His *not yet* doesn't seem quite right. It's like he's debating something with himself. I'm intrigued as to what it might be but let it go when he asks, 'You say you've got equipment to test the paintings – to see if they're real or not?'

I explain that the gear I've borrowed from the gallery – currently in Brandy's apartment – will go some of the way to telling us if the works are fakes or genuine, but that to be conclusive, I'd need the big-gun machines back in the lab.

'Okay then. Let's go get your stuff and see what we can do with it.' He rolls forward, takes a key from his pocket and unlocks the top drawer of his desk. He scrabbles around inside and pulls out a well-worn khaki leather pouch with a newish black disc stuck on it. 'This is my equipment contribution.' Hugh shakes out a set of lock-pick tools. One slips out and it spears the floor, narrowly missing his toes.

I'm about to tell him I've got the security codes, so we don't need lock-picks, but I decide not to. As he's leaning down to pluck the tool out of the floorboards, I notice a sheet of paper in his drawer. It's glowing with an almost radioactive red all-caps *FINAL NOTICE* stamp from Bitcoin Warehouse International. Dated ten days ago, it says that Hugh owes them $967,800 – and rising – and they're threatening foreclosure on the apartment. '*Whoa!*' I say, without thinking.

'What?' asks Hugh, as he comes back up with the pick.

'Does Kate know about that?' I'm reaching for the paper but he grabs my wrist.

'Leave it be, JJ.' He lets go of me, closes the drawer and turns the key.

No wonder he keeps it locked. 'How do you lose a million dollars? How does a career detective even *get* a million dollars to lose?' Did Hugh turn into one of the bent cops he was so proud of bringing to justice when I was a kid?

'Really bad investment decisions with my superannuation.'

'On cryptocurrency? *Really?*'

He looks away.

'You risked the roof over your family's head … on *Bitcoin*?'

His face goes beetroot again. 'I got greedy, punted on a portfolio of cryptocurrencies. Worse,' and he shrugs, 'I doubled up by borrowing most of the money.'

'I thought you couldn't do that with superannuation?'

His pupils have shrunk to pinpricks, like he's avoiding the light I'm shining on his dark secret. 'Let's get back to why you came here, JJ.'

'You *haven't* changed, not at all.' Words start flowing that once I would have kept inside. 'You're still that same arrogant know-it-all. Punting the roof over Vini's head on some dicey, high-risk speculative bullshit … the old Huge Ego.'

For a microsecond he looks hurt, then glowers at me, 'Kate doesn't know, that's true. But JJ, you will *not* tell her. Do you understand?' He gets up like he's the old Hugh getting ready to whack me.

55

Instead of raising *that* arm and bringing it down on me, Hugh steps over to the filing cabinet in the corner of the room and opens a drawer.

He lifts a tangle of black belts out of the drawer. Thankfully, I see pouches halfway down it, which tells me the apparatus is a shoulder holster and *not* a strap.

On the other hand, it's terrifying for a different reason … *because* it's a shoulder holster. 'You've got a *gun* … in your heavily mortgaged home … where you've got a little kid?' I can't remember if he kept a gun when I was growing up. If he did, he kept it well hidden.

Hugh's shrugging his arms into the straps. 'I'm a cop,' he says, adjusting the fit and takes a blousy black jacket off a hook on the back of the door and puts it on over the top.

'And cops have guns. Did you forget that little detail when you suppressed your loathing and came here to ask for my help?'

'I didn't suppress it. I parked it.'

His eyes flash at me like a cornered rat's and I see a steel in his jaw that's scarily familiar. Then the flash dissipates, and he forces a smile at me. The rat's no longer feeling cornered but he's still a rat.

'The gun's in case Monroe or Fontaine – or those goons you're worried about – make an entrance while we're in her house.'

'She's hardly likely to shoot me.'

'She who? She the writer? She who's either a millionaire lawyer on the run from something or someone? Or who's a killer biding her time? Who, either way, could be hiding a stash of priceless art? JJ, we don't know what's going on there. We don't know who she is, what she's capable of, who might be protecting her, or who might be coming after her.'

He opens the closet beside the cabinet, *pings* the digital combination lock on a small safe inside it and swings open the door. I'm expecting a gun but he removes a small spray can and throws it to me.

'It's OC spray.' Hugh sees the look on my face and apparently mistakes my deep misgivings for ignorance. 'It's capsicum spray,' he adds, as if I didn't know. 'Shove it in your pocket.'

'Isn't that illegal?'

'For you, yes. For me, no,' he says, as if that offers me any defence if I'm caught with it. Before I can protest, he takes a black handgun out of the safe, pulls the slide back to check there's no live cartridge inside the chamber, then holsters it under his left arm. He takes out two bullet clips, which he inserts into the slot under his right arm, and zips up his jacket.

'Let's do this.' Hugh grabs the lock-pick pouch and tosses it to me.

Between dealing with that and the spray can, I fumble and drop them both, panic squeezing the air out of my lungs.

Hugh shocks me. Almost like a gentleman, he bends down and picks them up for me.

56

Hugh's got a midnight blue Toyota Corolla hatchback parked in a residents' permit zone on the street outside the apartment building. As I hop in, I notice the child car seat in the back. 'Shouldn't you let Kate know we're—'

'I texted her while you were in the loo. Told her I'm taking you to lunch so we can talk.'

I *was* in the loo … throwing up.

Our first stop is not Woolloomooloo. It's the brutalist concrete police centre in Goulburn Street, five minutes from Hugh's place.

'Give me that security token for Fontaine's door,' he says. 'I'll go in and clone it,' he adds, in answer to the question I was about to ask. 'In case we need to get back inside after she comes home from hospital.'

I hand it to him, and my whole body shudders with the knowledge that I'm actually doing this.

We park in a metered spot in the street behind Lesley's. Hugh lifts a laminated police card from the gap between his seat and the console, and puts it on my side of the dash so a parking inspector can see it.

'We're not here on official business,' I say.

'So?' He opens his door and gets out and, while I'm doing the same, takes two boxes off the back seat – he got them at the police centre – and puts them in the trunk. He's told me that one's a surveillance camera, the other is a drone. 'Just in case.'

We walk around to Brandy's so I can get my tote bag full of tricks. I leave Hugh at the front entrance downstairs. 'I'll just be a minute,' I tell him as the lift closes, but it turns out to be longer because I needed to open a can of dog food for Scottie and refresh his water bowl.

When I come down, Hugh's got an enormous grin on his face.

'What?' I say.

'You'll never guess who I just met.' He passes me his police-issue notepad and I see, *To Vini, from Russell Crowe.*

I really do hate Hugh.

Soon enough, we're at Lesley's front gate. Hugh steps up to the security pad. 'Entry code?' he asks and I give it to him. He punches in the numbers and the gate starts swinging open. 'Damn,' he says as he pats his pockets, 'must've left my phone in the car. You go ahead and I'll meet you inside.

Remember, I've got *this*.' Hugh holds up the random number generator he's cloned. He repeats the front gate's entry code as if he's asking me to confirm it, which I do, then turns away and goes back to his car.

I put Winston out on the terrace with a bowl of water and some doggie snacks, and close the door behind me, as well as the curtain. I don't want him fretting when I let a stranger in and, equally, don't want any snoops spying on us – Paul, for example, if he turns up to sit on his boat.

The click of the front door startles me. For a second, I'm worried Lesley might be returning home early but, thankfully, it's Hugh. He swings open the door, holding up the cloned token. 'My magic worked.'

I've already opened the panel over the green button and press down on it. '*Hey presto!*' I say.

Nothing happens.

I try again. The same thing.

Hugh comes over. 'See there?' He points to a small keyhole poking out beside it, then holds his hand out. I pass him his lock-picks.

57

'The old boy's still got it.' Hugh wiggles his fingers and puts the picks away.

'Let's find out,' I say, as I tap the green button again. This time it does sink into the wall a little, but for a couple of seconds nothing else happens. Then we hear a *whirr*, the slightest of sounds, and all the works on the walls slowly start to swing open, hinged on their left sides, like mini-doors or casement windows all opening in sync.

'Keep your eye on that one,' I tell Hugh, tilting my head towards the Non-Banksy, the stencilled black cat. '*Six Sunflowers* – print, forgery, whatever – should be behind it.' For some reason I take his wrist, and his pulse is racing at least as fast as mine. Whether it's the thrill of the chase

237

or that this is the first time we've touched in years, I can't be sure.

I move us closer in, so we're only a few centimetres from the right-hand side of Non-Banksy as it yawns away from the wall. Hugh is at least a head taller than me – like most people – which means both of us can comfortably rest our right ears against the wall to catch a glimpse of the work underneath as early as possible. The gap is widening, light sneaking behind it.

The artworks are moving very slowly, with no jerky movements. The engineering that's gone into this is impressive but, more importantly, if these works are genuine, Lesley's mechanism accommodates their likely fragility.

'*Ugh!*' says Hugh.

I take a deep sniff, wondering if he's caught a tell-tale odour, because smells, or the lack of them, can be great indicators of a work's age. What conservators call our smell library. I'm checking for linseed oil. A whiff of that from a 150-year-old painting would be a huge clue it was a forgery, no matter how good it looked, because the volatiles in the oil should have evaporated long ago.

But the painting behind the Non-Banksy is giving me nothing. All I'm getting is Hugh's disgusting aftershave.

When I see the golden monstrosity of a frame coming into view I realise that it's not a smell that Hugh's noticing.

'Give it a few more seconds,' I tell him.

And when the brilliant shock of blue hits our eyes, he steps right back. '*Wow!* It's cobalt blue, like in—'

'*Starry Nights.*'

'And on the orange-frame print,' says Hugh.

By now, all The Art is visible. The schlock works and the Quilty have completely flipped over and Lesley's mechanism is zooshing The Art back towards the right on an invisible track. We watch until they're all positioned in the precise same spots, as if the other works were never there.

Hugh scans the room. 'If this is really *Six Sunflowers* and that one over there is truly a Rembrandt … Hey, is that a *Picasso*? Hell, JJ, if these works are real …' He turns his gaze back to *Six Sunflowers* and starts to cry. 'Whether this *Six Sunflowers* is genuine or not, you've made me the happiest man alive just by bringing me here to see it in all its glory.'

The first and very obvious thing we can tell is that not one of the paintings is a print. Most are oils, some of them incredibly rich and lush, like *Six Sunflowers*. Apart from the Van Gogh, the Rembrandt and the Picasso, there are two more that look like Rembrandts, one that could be a typical long-necked woman by Modigliani, five works that might be by Degas – though they're not oils, they're pencil, inks and watercolours – a Léger look-alike, a Braque, and … whew! … a *real* Matisse. Or at least I think it is. And there's more. All up, we count twenty-one paintings – none of them prints – and two small bronze sculptures – an urn and a fierce-looking eagle.

I take photos of each work on my iPad. I could use my phone but I want to see them on a bigger screen. I'm starting to feel light-headed as I go. The mere prospect that all these works might be real … that *any* of them might be real … that what I've stumbled onto is … frankly, I really have no idea.

I get Hugh to come sit beside me on Lesley's sofa while I start doing reverse image searches. Sitting elbow to elbow with him focused on art is a strange throwback of an experience for me, but the circumstances that have brought us together are proving even stranger.

My searches are telling me that all the works stolen from the Gardner in 1990, all thirteen pieces, are in this room with us. We get up and, as I walk around the walls and pick them out for Hugh, I'm really getting woozy. If these are real ... but I'm getting ahead of myself.

We sit back down and find that Interpol's stolen art database tells us that the originals of four of the other works come from private collections, and five were stolen by a thief called 'Spider-Man' from the Paris Museum of Modern Art in 2010. And there's *Six Sunflowers*, of course.

Unlike the Gardner works, but like *Six Sunflowers*, the Paris five – the Picasso, Matisse, Modigliani, Braque and Léger – were supposedly destroyed.

'Quite a haul,' I say, trying to make light, but feeling very anxious.

Hugh's shaking his head. 'The chance that your mystery girl's walls in Sydney are hanging the real *Six Sunflowers* and every single work stolen from those two museums is ...'

'Remote?'

'As likely as a lotto win, which tells me they've got to be forgeries. And this,' he drags me back to *Six Sunflowers*. 'You're the expert, but the more I look at it, the more I think it *has* to be a fake, even though I'd love it not to be. Just a sec,' and he takes out his phone and starts googling. In hardly any time at all, he's pulled up an image of the orange-frame print and holds it next to the painting. I think I know what he's going to say, and he doesn't disappoint. 'The colours, JJ,' and he's tapping the image on his phone screen. 'The blue's a match. It's stunning, but the other colours are different. See the yellows on the print? Here on the painting, they're brown. And the tablecloth under the vase, it's not the clean, crisp lilac in the old print, it's an insipid—'

'Pale blue, I know.'

'Which means,' he says, 'it's a pretty shitty forgery, right? Hey, why are you smiling?'

'Because you get top marks for picking that up. Except,' I tell him, 'these colour variations tell us that either the forger is brilliant or what we've got here is absolutely the real deal.'

'But they're such different colours.'

'For a forger to paint *Six Sunflowers* using those exact colours – the browns not the original yellows – they'd really have to know their stuff. Take the lilac tablecloth. An expert forger would have read VvG's letters—'

'VvG?' he asks.

'It's shorthand that a work friend and I use for Vincent but, like I was saying, a forger worth their salt would have studied the academic analysis to learn how he mixed his lilac—'

'And how did Vincent … VvG … do that?'

'First,' I tell Hugh, 'he'd make up a pink by mixing geranium lake, a stunning red colour, with zinc white. Then he'd add touches of cobalt blue, dab by dab, until he got the exact shade of lilac he wanted.'

'And?'

'The thing about that red is that it's a notorious "fugitive" colour, meaning it fades with exposure to light. Over time, the red kind of washes out until what's left is just the white mixed with the blue.'

'Okay ...' He says it slowly, and I'm not sure if he's taking in what I've said or he thinks I'm full of crap, so I decide to show him the best way I can think of on the spot.

'Give me a minute,' I say, picking up my iPad. I open up the *Unravel Van Gogh* app on the Van Gogh Museum's website. 'Here,' and I show him VvG's *The Bedroom*. 'He painted this a month after he painted *Six Sunflowers*.'

'My point exactly,' says Hugh. 'The doors and the bedroom walls ... they're lilacs and violets, pretty close to what the tablecloth here on *Six Sunflowers* is supposed to look like, but doesn't. The lilacs on *The Bedroom* haven't faded, so ...' He's looking at me like a mugger who's staring down his mark.

'Hugh,' I tell him, 'what you're looking at is *not* the actual painting. It's effectively an animated colour reconstruction. It's what conservators *believe* that work looked like when VvG painted it. They've based that on his letters and all the other data accumulated over the years on the paints he used.' I hand him the iPad. 'Here, slide your finger across the image.'

He does and, almost like magic, *The Bedroom*'s vivid lilacs fade to pale, greyish blues. 'What you're seeing on the screen now ... they're the actual colours you'll see if you visit the museum in Amsterdam today. Given VvG painted *The Bedroom* and *Six Sunflowers* at around the same time—'

'The two lilacs should have faded pretty much the same way,' he says, shaking his head, but I think it's in wonder. 'I get that, I do,' and he pauses, but he raises a sceptical eyebrow. 'But what about these brown flowers? They were originally yellow, so ...'

'The red *fades*, like I said, but the yellow VvG used for the blooms contains chemicals that *darken* over time.'

'Heck,' says Hugh, lowering his eyebrow and looking at me warmly, not an emotion I'm used to. 'It's not just forgers who have to know their shit, JJ. You do, too. *Wow!*'

It's the first compliment I think he's ever given me and, in other circumstances, I'd be stoked but I can't let a brief buzz of pleasure impair my objectivity. 'Even so, these discolourations don't swing it one way or the other. One thing that might though, is this,' and I point to a horizontal indent that runs under the paint right across the work, about seven or eight centimetres from the top.

'And that is ...?' asks Hugh, then he sucks in his breath and quickly adds, 'Holy shit! You wrote about that in your Year 8 assignment.'

He remembered!

And his smile ... It's the same impression of a proud father I was jealous of when I watched him with Vini.

Luckily, he never found out I didn't hand that assignment in. 'Do you remember what I wrote?' I ask, kind of testing him, wondering if this moment is actually real.

'Do I? I've still got your assignment at home. I've read it to Vini, like, a million times. You wrote that, according to Vincent's ... VvG's ... letters to Theo, he originally painted only five flowers on this canvas, not six, which is why he called it *Five Sunflowers* for a short time. But he was unhappy with the aesthetic, and decided it needed a sixth bloom. To give it room to breathe, he mounted the canvas on wood and—'

'—extended it, enlarging it by around thirteen centimetres, ten at the top and three at the bottom. Spot on.'

'But,' says Hugh, looking a little downcast, 'that line's less than ten—'

'Because of the frame.'

'Ah!' he nodded. 'I guess that's why we can't see a similar line near the base, right? So does that mean it's—'

'Real? Probably ... *most* probably. But it's not guaranteed. If a girl in Year 8 knew about the extension, a master forger would too, and they could—'

'How can we tell for sure?'

'We could test the age of that wooden extension ... not here obviously ... but if we could slip off the frame—'

'That huge chunk of gilded crap?' says Hugh. 'How would that help?'

'For well over a century, the frame's been shielding a few finger-widths of the canvas's outer edges from the light, so—'

'You mean this crummy frame might've done us a favour. We might see *actual* lilac under the frame?'

'Exactly. The lilac under there's been covered over, protected from the light, for yonks, so the geranium lake pigment in it won't have faded anywhere near as much as on the rest of the work. A forger *might* try to mimic that detail, but it's pretty unlikely they'd go to that much trouble.'

'So let's get started.'

I tell him we can't, not here. How removing the frame's a tricky operation that could damage the work, so I'd need to do it back in the lab at the gallery, where we have all the right equipment.

'Can we do *anything* while we're here?' asks Hugh, obviously frustrated.

I nod and, after huffing my tote bag into the middle of Lesley's living room rug, I take out the gear I've brought from the gallery. 'We'll start with this,' I say, and lift up the portable XRF spectrometer. XRF, I tell him, stands for X-ray fluorescence, not that he cares.

'Looks like one of those handheld barcode scanners,' says Hugh. 'Like the shelf-stockers use at the supermarket.'

'Except it's bigger and heavier, and it shoots X-rays.' I let him have a feel of the spectrometer. 'It identifies the atomic elements in the paints,' I tell him. 'When I hold it up close to a specific colour and press this trigger—'

'Whoa. Won't that damage—'

'It's totally non-invasive. The X-rays cause whatever elements we're aiming at to fluoresce and travel back to the detector inside the machine. Say we're shooting into one of the yellowy-brown patches in *Six Sunflowers*. If the detector picks up chrome, we've got a hit. VvG used chrome yellow. It's called that because it's actually got chrome in it. Chrome fluoresces with a certain signature and the machine picks that up. No chrome, no Van Gogh, end of story. Rembrandt, like in that work over there, used an entirely different yellow. In his case, we absolutely do *not* want to find chrome. What we want is lead and tin.'

'That little baby does all that?'

'And it can do it right here and now. Watch and learn.' I'm a bit over-cocky, but I'm talking to the man who thought I'd never amount to anything, so I feel entitled to be. I step in front of *Six Sunflowers*, switch on the XRF gun and wait for the red light to come on, start flashing and go green.

I wait some more but there's no red, and no green.

I press the 'on' button a few times and wait a bit longer.

'*Shit!*' I exclaim and thump a thigh with my free hand. 'Battery's flat.'

Hugh goes to my tote bag but I stop him.

'I didn't bring the spare battery *or* the charger. Dammit. And I was going to bring our new portable FTIR/Raman analyser as backup, but the weight ... *Dammit!*'

'FTIR ... Raman? Sounds Japanese,' says Hugh.

'Where the XRF uses X-rays to identify elements – like chrome, lead or tin – the other gun uses both infra-red and laser, helping to round out the analysis. It can pick out organic compounds and pigments.'

'That might not be Japanese ... but it is all Greek to me. Listen, the gallery's only five minutes away,' he says, clearly trying to be helpful, and jiggling his car keys in his pocket.

'Good idea, but let's try a couple of other tests first.'

I call up an image of the orange-frame print on my iPad so we can see it on the larger screen, and then I place two fingers on it and spread them apart to make the image even bigger. We're looking at the top right sunflower. 'It's not the best-quality image, but look here,' and I point to the bloom's outer edge, where the petals touch the sky. 'See how he's painted the sunflower first, then he's worked over the background with these criss-cross basketwork brushstrokes. So, now let's compare.' We check out the area on the painting. It looks the same. We repeat the exercise with a few other parts of the painting. 'Again, it's not proof but it's a damn good indicator. A meticulous forger would do their best to replicate the artist's brushstrokes – in direction, thickness, style – but you'd expect them to make a mistake somewhere. If this is a forgery, it's a damn brilliant one.'

I've now got us peering into the seed head at the centre of Lesley's painting. Hugh says, 'Hey, is that what I think it is?'

He's found a fingerprint. I take a few photos of it, this time with my Sony. 'The museum in Amsterdam's got a database of VvG fingerprints from other works. We'll be able to compare this one. It could well be a decider.'

Pending us picking up the spare battery for the XRF gun and the gallery's FTIR/Raman analyser, I ask Hugh which work he'd like us to look at next.

He's checking out the Picasso. 'What did you say it was called?'

I check the image from the Paris MAM that I've still got open on my iPad. '*Le Pigeon Aux Petits Pois*. It translates as *Pigeon With Green Peas*.'

'You're kidding me. Where's the pigeon? Or the peas? You know, I never did get Cubism. Leave that one till last. Give the pigeon time to fly back. Let's weave your magic on the big Rembrandt.'

I'm glad he's chosen that one. Before we came here I'd already uploaded a high-quality image of *Storm* I got from Interpol's database. 'See these hairline cracks all over the painting surface?'

'The *craquelure*, you mean?'

I look at him, amazed. 'You know about that?'

'Sure,' he says. 'It's from the different layers drying out at different paces, right? Kate and I watch that BBC show, what's it called … yeah, *Fake or Fortune?* … and one episode gave chapter and verse on it.'

'Right. It's another kind of fingerprint … how every painting dries out and ages is unique to that work. There's drying cracks, like you said. They tend to leave a crazing effect, kind of like alligator skin. Then there's ageing cracks – they're from a canvas expanding and shrinking with changes in humidity. They can be deeper, longer and more irregular. With a Rembrandt, I'd expect to see ageing cracks more than drying cracks. The thing is, *craquelure* is really hard to forge. That said, we've got to allow for extra cracking through post-theft mistreatment, but if the *craquelure* overall differs big-time from what's shown on this pre-theft image,' I show it to him, 'it's definitely a forgery.'

After spending an age together comparing *Storm*'s *craquelure* against the image I've brought with me, I'm almost sure that what Lesley's got on her wall is the actual Rembrandt stolen from the Gardner.

58

So far, this hasn't just been a good session, it's been extraordinary. But it's time, we've decided, to pop back to the gallery to get the battery for the XRF gun and the additional gear.

Just in case Lesley comes back while we're gone, we're tidying up. I'm packing away my equipment and Hugh has flipped all The Art so that all walls are now back to showing the dross. And the Quilty.

Just as Hugh closes the panel to conceal the green button, his phone buzzes. 'It's Kate,' he tells me, beaming. 'Hi,' he says, then his smile vanishes and he suddenly tenses up, the colour draining from his face. '*No!* Where?' It's clearly bad news. 'I'm coming.'

Vini's fallen off a swing at the park, he tells me, and Kate's worried he might have fractured his arm.

'I've got to go to the hospital,' he says. I see tears forming. 'We'll discuss all this ... decide our next steps ... a bit later, okay?'

'Of course. Go!' I say, though I'm wondering if he would've reacted the same way when I was a kid. 'I'll finish up. Give Vini a kiss for me.'

After Hugh's gone, I peek out through the curtain to the terrace to check on Winston. He's sleeping, spread out on the tiles in the sun.

People say *It's a dog's life* as if that's a lousy existence. Why? Lying around all day, getting cuddles – even from strangers – being taken on walks, food and drink handed to you ... most people would kill for a life as rotten as that.

Some light is glinting on the water glasses on Lesley's coffee table, so I take them back to the kitchen, wash them and put them away.

I hear the click of the front door. 'Hey, Hugh,' I say, 'what did you forget?' It's not his phone. I saw him put it back into his pocket. It must be his car keys? I'm wiping my hands on a tea towel as I go to meet him.

It's not him.

59

esley's eyes are fixed on the equipment still scattered on her floor, then they shoot over to me. 'What's going on here, JJ?' She looks behind her, like she's checking that no one is creeping up on her. When she turns back to face me, her kaftan – a black one this time – makes her look like she's standing in the middle of an earthquake, she's shaking so much. Part of her headscarf falls over her face. She swipes it back and the terror I see in her eyes is not what you'd see in the face of a mistress of her own destiny. 'They found me, didn't they?' she exclaims, without a hint of Scottish brogue. In the stress, she's clearly let her defences down.

The petrified woman in the doorway is definitely not a cold, calculating criminal mastermind who's been quietly sitting on millions of dollars of art until the moment is ripe to fence it.

'You're not an auditor, are you? You work for the …' she pauses, gulping, and a car alarm goes off in the street. It's so loud, I can hardly hear her finish her sentence, '… for the galleries?'

She looks as though just saying *galleries* out loud will bring all hell down on her.

'The gallery?' I admit, wondering how she found out, but, making sure to use the singular. 'Yes, I work there. How long have you known?'

She's shaking her head hard. I can't tell if it's due to disgust at my deception or another shudder of panic. She reaches down into the overnight bag she's got at her feet, unzips a side compartment and pulls out a pistol.

'Stop with the games, JJ, if that's really your name.' Waving the gun at me, she takes a step inside.

I know I could retort that the one playing real games is her, but there's the gun in my face and, worse, just as her heel hits the parquetry a black hood descends over her head, a hand swipes that gun, and another jabs her neck with a syringe. She struggles for about a second and slumps to the floor.

It all happens so fast, my mouth is still gaping when the doorway darkens, and the goon I'd named Arnie appears, steps over Lesley's body and comes inside, pointing the gun he's taken from her at me. 'One peep and you're dead.' Close up, the gorilla of a man is even more powerfully built than I thought.

I go to speak, to ask what this is all about, but he waves the gun at me, so I shut up.

The one I was calling Danny – the shorter of the duo – shoves past him and strides over to me. 'It's sleepy time, dog lady.' He's speaking so close to my ear, I can smell his stinky tuna breath. He jabs a syringe into my neck.

I start to say, 'I might be allergic,' but my jaw and all my limbs turn to mush. Everything goes black.

60

Cold concrete is sapping any flicker of heat out of my bones. My head is so heavy, the floor seems like it's a magnet pulling me into it. I flutter my eyes to try to force in some light, but it's useless. I take a deep breath and a thick cowl of fabric presses into my mouth – like I've got a hood over my head. I try to wiggle my fingers. At least they move. So do my toes.

I should be panicking yet, strangely, my heart is *not* hammering, sweat is not streaming out of my pores, I'm not lying in a pool of my own urine, and I don't feel like a caged animal … despite the hood. It's like my brain is on super slo-mo and I'm levitating, viewing myself from above, as though I'm having an out-of-body experience. Is this what death, or near death, is like? I squeeze my eyes, as if it'll make me think better. It doesn't. I lie sprawled on the floor, quietly, breathing slowly.

I'm starting to remember things ... a jab ... my body turning into a blob of Aeroplane Jelly ... which suggests my semi-spiritual sensation is due to drugs and not death. At least, I hope so.

I try licking my lips but they're stuck together with dried spit. I force my tongue to break through, and lick them. I'm cold, yet I'm not shivering ... in a daze, but not freaking out. All of this is amazing in the circumstances which, I'm slowly recalling, are that Lesley pointed a gun at me ... a goon drugged her ... took her gun and pointed it at me ... a second goon drugged me ... then, apparently, they bagged my head and brought me here, wherever here is, and dumped me onto a hard, freezing floor.

Normally, inner strength and I are total strangers, so it's becoming increasingly clear that this airy composure is coming from whatever was in that needle. I wonder what the drug is and if I'll be able to get it over the counter when all this is over.

From the gazillions of action movies I've seen, I know that in any abduction or hostage situation, panic is the absolute worst reaction. Instead, you're supposed to act calm, keeping your breathing regular, slowing everything down. I take in a few deep breaths, staying as quiet as I can. I don't want to alert my captors, in case they're skulking around, waiting for me to wake up. I'd rather stay lying on my side, trying to eavesdrop – hopefully, finding out what they want ... who they are.

I get why Lesley's in trouble, since it looks like her real past has caught up with her. But me? These guys saw me walking the dogs, and maybe they spied Lesley and me having coffee, but that's pretty much it.

I cock my ear. Someone's talking, but I can't make out who it is. Is it Lesley? The woman who pulled a gun on me and had the hide to ask if JJ was my real name! I stifle a laugh. Is this what smoking weed is like?

A second person is speaking. A man, definitely. 'Two hours and you've given us nothing. We're running out of patience.' He's clicking something metallic. A set of pliers, maybe, like Laurence Olivier in the torture scene in *Marathon Man*?

'Do your worst.' The voice *is* Lesley's. 'I'm dying anyway, you bastar—' and she gags, like the man is forcing something into her mouth. '*Aargh!*' Her scream is so loud, long and bloodcurdling that it breaks though my drug haze. Something clatters on the floor. The thought that it might be one of her beautiful teeth sends another shudder through me.

Did I hear her right? That she's dying? If she's telling the truth – and with her, who knows! – whatever she went to the hospital for, whatever she was sick with yesterday, it sounds like it's terminal.

'*Vous n'êtes qu'un tas de merde!*' she shouts in French. I don't know what it means, but it's not good. 'The Farrellys and their criminal empire,' she continues, '*ils sont finis!*'

Ah! It wasn't the *galleries* she thought I worked for, it was the *Farrellys*.

'Tell those *enculés* their glory days are over. Tell them I'd rather die than give them the art back!' Lesley's yelling, though it's muffled. Now she's gagging, like the pliers are grabbing another tooth … '*Aargh!*'

Then nothing.

'Fuck her,' says the man. 'Yeah, fuck her,' says a second man.

I think she's passed out from the pain.

How did the Farrellys find her? Did they find her through *me*? 'Fuck!' I say it out loud, without thinking.

'Ah! Seems like little bloodnut's awake,' says one of the men.

I lie still, not moving, not reacting, hoping they'll forget I'm there.

It doesn't work. 'Get her up,' he says, and I'm dragged to my feet. By the angle of the man's arms I can tell he's short, so it's probably Danny. He dumps me on a chair.

Behind me, I hear the *scritch, scritch, scritch* from a roll of duct tape being unwound. He grabs my left arm. Even though I don't struggle, the other guy whacks me across the cheek … not with his hand, it's something harder and colder … a length of pipe? Two of my teeth come loose and a slick of blood drizzles into my mouth. Even though I'm fully aware of what's going on, the drugs are still weaving some of their dulling magic, thankfully.

I sit still while Danny tapes my wrists tightly to the back posts of the chair. With my shoulders forced backwards, this isn't particularly comfortable but at least it stops me slumping. Who knows, when the cops eventually ask these guys why they didn't kill me – I'm being optimistic – maybe they'll say, *Her posture!*

Without thinking, I blurt out, 'Winston.' I have no idea why I'm suddenly more worried about him than me or Lesley, but I ask anyway. 'What did you do with Winston?'

'The mutt? We ate him for lunch.'

I scream.

'Just fuckin' with you,' says one of them. He leans into me. It's Danny, unless they've both eaten tuna – not dog – for lunch. 'But first things first, lady. Who the fuck is Huge Ego?' Before I can say anything, a massive punch to the stomach forces the air out of my lungs.

61

Belfast

Niall gatecrashes the early-morning meeting in Nessa's office. He thumbs at her visitor to get out. 'Give us the room.' It's a strutting macho line she knows her brother heard on one of the TV crime shows he's addicted to. 'It's research,' he told her when she caught him watching *Line of Duty* in the office.

Nessa says nothing, but waits for their finance director to gather up the spreadsheets and papers scattered over her desk and leave.

Her brother has got even more strut and swagger than normal. He strides forward and sits in the visitor chair, clearly bursting to tell her he's hooked a really big fish. She's seen this look on him before but, apart from the

CCTV he found outside the Freeport, and the work he did about the removalists, he usually lands on his arse.

Due to his recent efforts, however, she's giving him the benefit of the doubt. His smile is cracked so wide, his ridiculously brambly moustache looks like a black weasel is squatting above his lip. He puts his boots up on her desk, surprising her – not so much at the disrespect but because he's had more surgeries on his dodgy football knees than Kim Kardashian has probably had on her bum.

Nessa snaps, 'What have you got?' The two days of freaking out that the Russians might be launching an onslaught against their operations is wearing her thin.

Niall puts his legs down and slides his iPad towards her, like he did only a couple of days ago. 'Look an' learn, sis.' She sees he's chewing gum, like some of the two-bit crims in their employ, a habit she hates.

She eyes the screen for no more than a second and slides it back to him in disgust. 'A TikTok video of a dog? You know I hate the feckers.'

'Look again,' he says, glaring at her until she takes the tablet back.

'Just tell me,' Nessa says, but looks anyway. She sees the dog video was posted by @Dont.Cry.For.Me.Annie. Leibovitz and it's got lines and lines of hashtags beneath it:

#sydneyphotography #photographyislife #photooftheday
#photographyeveryday #photographylover #mysonylife
#ilovemysony #sonyrules #amazingsunsets #amazingsunrises
#eclectic_shotz #day_shooterz #night_shooterz #phototips
#photographytiktok …

and on and on they go.

A caption with hearts and smiley faces runs across the screen. *Today's star ... Winston Jr ... named after his owner's childhood teddy bear ... so gorgeous! Shot on my Sony Alpha...*

'Jesus, Mary and Joseph, tell me you didn't come in here just to show me this mindless shit, Niall.'

He does that sideways neck-crick thing she reckons is an affectation he's picked up from on-screen tough guys, probably from his hero, Bruce Willis. It was ten minutes after Niall came home after seeing *Die Hard 4.0* that he shaved his head.

'Flick to the next image, sis.'

Nessa looks back to the screen, and when she sees the storage unit where Matthieu had housed Claude Fontaine's belongings she lets out a long sigh.

'Be patient, sis. It's the footage we recorded when Angel was there searchin' for us.' He leans over and clicks the *play* icon. The video starts rolling, and he waves his hands like he's conducting an orchestra. 'Hold on to your britches ... wait ... wait ... wait ... *there!*' He reaches over and presses *pause* just as Angel is moving a huge teddy bear out of the way, knocking its collar to the floor. He spreads his fingers out on the screen to zoom in on it. '*There!* Read me the bear's fuckin' name on that collar, sis.' He slams his hand down on Nessa's desk. 'It's feckin' *Winston*. Claude Fontaine's childhood teddy bear was called *Winston*, which is the same name that puke-coloured mutt's owner gave to their bear when they were a kid. Am I wastin' your time now?'

'You're suggestin' that Claude Fontaine didn't get Covid, didn't die from it and didn't get cremated in India? An' that instead she turned herself into the Invisible

Woman, did the same with our art, and we missed the whole feckin' thing?'

If that's really what Niall's suggesting, Nessa realises that she'd made a huge mistake taking Fontaine's charity spree for the six months before she died at face value. What better way to shift money and not get noticed? But she doesn't mention that to Niall. Instead, she says, 'Show me videos of the dog with its owner.'

'@Annie.who.gives.a.fuck don't post vids of people, just dogs an' sunsets an' shit.'

'Where do we find her?'

'At long last, you're askin' the right question, sis. Right there is where we find her,' Niall says, pointing to the hashtag #sydneyphotography. Then he runs the video again and pauses it to show a food truck in the background – its signage says Harry's Café de Wheels. 'See that long wharf behind it? It's on a bay in Sydney called Woolloom— oh, fuck it.' Then he sounds out, 'Wool-loo-moo-loo.'

'We need eyes on this,' says Nessa. 'Just eyes, mind. No goons, no arm-twistin'. That's for later. Agreed?'

'The eyes have it already,' he smirks.

His sister glares at him. 'What have you done?'

'Same as Conor woulda done,' Niall says, running his eyes up to the portrait of their father on the wall behind Nessa. 'Check this out.' He flicks his screen to a photo.

The shot is grainy, taken through bushes with too high a magnification. A red-headed dog walker is handing the small caramel-coloured dog's leash to a woman at her front door. He zooms in on her face.

'You're kiddin' me,' says Nessa, moving closer to the image. 'Fontaine? Wearin' that feckin' kaftan bullshit?'

'*Bingo!*' He turns and starts walking out of her office, but stops at the door. 'Oh, and you're feckin' welcome, sis.'

'Hey,' she says, without even a word acknowledging his sleuthing triumph. 'We've got to talk about next steps.'

'Talk all you want.' And he's gone.

62

Sydney

I don't know what's worse – Danny twisting my nose or his foul breath. He repeats his question, 'Who's Huge Ego?'

The other one, Arnie, says, 'This Huge Ego ... he's left, like, fifteen messages on your phone. Who the fuck is it?' His voice is gruff and raspy, like he's a chain-smoker, 'Is that some kind of code?'

He's kind of right. It is a code, though it's really more of a barb. It's the way I entered Hugh's phone number in my contacts all those years ago. I could answer these thugs with *He's a cop, he's got a gun and I hope he's searching for me* but I don't. In every screen abduction, every Liam Neeson movie I've ever seen, they teach you that the biggest risk is turning up the time pressure on kidnappers, because it escalates the chances they'll blow. Given these two bastards are already going full 'black site', the chance of them blowing is pretty high.

I also know – despite the drugs – that a hostage should try making a connection at the human level. So, here goes. 'Er, he's my fiancé. The name … it's not a code, it's a private joke. He's the sweetest, nicest guy … wouldn't hurt a fly.' Only a few hours ago, saying good things even about an imaginary version of Hugh would have been as nauseating as shoving a finger down my throat, but I wasn't trying to save my life then. 'We were supposed to meet at a jewellery store in Potts Point … See, we're choosing our engagement—' A whack on the ear stops me continuing.

'Keep your life story for *The Bachelor.*'

My head is ringing, though it's oddly pleasant, like the St Mary's Cathedral Sunday bells that chime at breakfast. Not the ones that start clanging earlier and wake me up. I hate those.

Something plasticky clatters on the floor and what sounds like a boot is smashing it into a million pieces.

'Your phone,' he says. 'In case you're wondering. Huge Ego won't be ringing you anymore.'

I suck up the blood that's pooling in my mouth, and pull my lips over my front teeth, pressing down hard on them while I wait for whatever comes next.

I don't have to wait for long.

'Where are the fuckin' paintings?' These people don't beat around the bush.

I'm about to plead ignorance except I realise they'll have seen my equipment on Lesley's floor. If they've gone through my tote bag, they'll also have seen the VM evidence folder I showed Hugh, including my printouts of the Rembrandt, the VvG and the Vermeer.

Then I remember, to my relief, we left those on Hugh's desk. If I could, I'd be wiping my brow right now.

'This bag over my head, it's suffocating,' I say, partly because it is and partly to deflect attention while I'm trying to work out how to answer them about the paintings. 'Instead of this bag, can you maybe blindfold me with your duct tape? And, please, I really need some water.'

'She'll piss herself—' starts Arnie.

Danny interrupts, 'Come on, bro. It's just water.' Is Mr Tuna Breath turning into Mr Nice Guy? I'm not complaining. If one of them is starting to be vaguely human, I'm apparently making progress.

Either that or he owns shares in Perrier. I giggle.

It's the drugs.

63

One of them removes my hood. The other grips my neck from behind, his fingers like a clamp. He's forcing me to look away from them so I can't see their faces. It's probably luck that they don't realise I saw them near the fountain that day I was walking the dogs.

That said, I suspect they won't let me see anything for very long, so I dart my eyes around to take in as much of my surroundings as I can. The building we're in is partly demolished. There are no internal walls. It's all bare grey and dusty concrete, and the view through the glassless windows tells me we're on quite a high floor. I can't see Lesley, so she must be behind me.

About two metres in front of me is a gaping hole in the floor – a three-by-three-metre square cut into the concrete. The men scrape my chair forward so its front legs, and my own legs, are teetering over the edge. They tilt the chair so I'm leaning headfirst into the chasm. Instantly I'm giddy, like that brief weightless moment at the very top of a roller-coaster when you feel like the bottom's about to fall out of your stomach. Below me, similarly sized holes are cut into each of the lower floors, ten or twelve at least. It's like the building's wrecking crew created an internal shaft so they could dump the debris from each floor down to ground level fast and cheap.

'It's a long way down,' says Arnie, who seems to be the talker of the two and a master of speaking the obvious. He pulls the chair back a metre or so and, taking my bait, winds a long strip of duct tape around my head, believing he's covering my eyes.

Here's a little-known fact that I know from being a movie tragic … unless you duct-tape around someone's head very carefully, the tape going over their nose leaves an air gap either side, which the captive can expand if they scrunch their nose a few times. Which I do, and which means that provided I'm looking downwards, I can see quite well.

The first thing I expect to see are my knees knocking together but, weirdly, they're not. My drug-fuelled state of calm deliberation seems like it's in control, at least for now.

Danny's shod in dark brown, steel-capped boots that I suspect are very effective in crunching bones. Arnie's wearing a giant pair of black Dr Martens lace-ups, and the blood on the right one is telling me it's been doing some unpleasant work very recently. The hands of these two knuckle-draggers are also in view. Arnie's are like ham hocks, and one of Danny's is holding a plastic water bottle. I can't see their jackets but, going by the chains hanging from them, Hoodlum Hire is doing a roaring trade.

If I tilted my head back I'd be able to see their faces, but that's a move likely to end one way, by Arnie kicking my chair down the hole, with me still taped to it. Besides, I've already seen their faces.

A phone rings. Arnie's pulling it out of a pocket. 'It's Niall,' he says. 'We better take this out of earshot, Bones.' So Danny isn't Danny, he's Bones. I'm doing my best not to speculate on why. 'Yeah,' says Arnie. 'Gissa minute,' and the pair walk off, with my water. I slowly tilt my head back until I can see they're walking past my hole of death to the other side of the floor. Arnie's talking, but the combination of distance and him keeping his voice down means all I hear is a mumble.

I take the chance to twist my head around until I see Lesley. Like mine, her wrists are taped to a chair, but her head, uncovered and untaped, is slumped over her chest, and that is spattered with blood. '*Psst*. Lesley,' I whisper. 'It's me, JJ. Are you awake?'

She tips her head slightly in my direction. An eye opens. 'I'm so sorry,' she says. 'I accused you …' Blood is dripping out of her mouth. 'I got you into … I'm truly sorry.'

Surprising myself, I get to the point. 'Give me the facts, okay? Who are these people? Who are the Farrellys, and who is this Niall guy? Yeah, and why do you have a priceless stash of looted art on your walls … and last, who the hell are you … Lesley Monroe or Claude Fontaine? Be quick.' And then I add, 'Please.'

'How do you know about the art?' she whispers back.

'You're wasting time. But okay … I'm an art conservator, not an auditor. I saw some of the art through your window, accidentally. So I lied to you because I wanted to find out if it was real. Your turn.'

64

Like me, Lesley talks fast, in a rat-tat-tat of facts. Her Scottish accent is history, all pretence gone. Her English isn't plummy though, it's more international with only a slight French lilt.

As she's racing through the information, my impression is that she's relieved to be telling me, as though she's easing her guilt by unburdening herself of the truth. Either that or she's convinced the goons are going to kill her and she needs somebody left alive ... me, I hope ... to know what she knows.

The Farrellys, she whispers, own a legitimate business called CCNN run out of Belfast, but it's a front for a global criminal empire ... drugs, people trafficking, arms. The Farrelly patriarch was a gun-runner for the IRA during the Troubles, and Niall, the guy talking to Arnie on the phone, is his son. Niall and his twin sister – I don't catch her name – run the show now.

She confesses that she is, in fact, Claude Fontaine, the wealthy and supposedly dead Monaco lawyer. I'd give myself a little clap for my stellar detective work except that my hands are taped behind me.

The Farrellys blackmailed her into facilitating their illegal activities. The art was theirs, stored in a freeport – whatever that is – in Monaco, and they used it to bankroll their evil enterprise.

If she'd reported any of this to the police, she claims, she'd have ended up dead. 'The Farrelly tentacles reach everywhere.'

Which is kind of obvious, since … you know … the situation we're in right now. I don't mention that her successor's body parts were found washed up on a French beach, but I expect she knows that.

The only way she could bring the Farrellys down and stay alive, she tells me, was to steal their art from under their noses and stage her own death, but make the events seem totally unconnected.

'I spent months creating my own personal witness protection program,' she says. She salted away millions of her own money in untraceable offshore accounts to fund her new life, routing it through fake charities so no one – especially the Farrellys – would suspect. 'Yes,' she says, 'there was no rich uncle.' No Melbourne Paul either. 'Sorry about all the lies, JJ.'

As soon as Covid started running riot in India, she saw her big chance and grabbed it. She abracadabra'd the art and, months later, arranged her own 'pseudocide' as she calls it, which I gather is lawyer-speak for faking your own death. She doesn't explain how she got the art and her newly disguised self to Australia, but they're not things I need to know.

If she's telling the truth, then she's no *criminal* mastermind, but she definitely is a mastermind. But one aspect of her narrative seems too convenient. 'Disappearing yourself, that much I get,' I tell her. 'But keeping the art and shipping it to Australia? Not *how* you did … *why* you did it. Surely the innocent victim you claim to be could have got an anonymous tip to the police, so they could've raided the warehouse and got all the works back to their rightful—'

'You might think so but you'd be wron— Shit! They're coming back. Listen quick. I dressed up the theft to make the Farrellys think the Russian mob was moving in on their turf. If I got the cops to raid the art, they'd have known the Russians weren't involved. They'd revisit every detail and eventually link it to me. They'd work out I faked my death and come hunting.'

'As it turns out, they did that anyway,' I say.

'Shh! No more talking.' She drops her head back on her chest.

A minute later, one of the men yanks my head back by my hair. 'Bloodnut, it's your turn to talk.'

Knowing the truth doesn't turn out to be a comfort, since now I'm terrified I won't have the strength to keep my mouth shut. 'My water,' I remind them, hoping to buy time to work out what to say.

'*Here*,' says Bones, but rather than him putting the bottle to my mouth, I feel the liquid pouring down over my head. The two of them laugh like a riot of kookaburras at sunset.

What's so funny? I think.

'What's so funny?' comes a man's voice from somewhere behind me. It's loud and echoes off the concrete.

The kookaburras go silent.

65

Arnie calls back, 'Who the fuck are you?'

'I'm the guy with the gun trained at your heart.'

It's like all the action movie clichés I've ever seen. Except this is no movie, and the man sounds exactly like Hugh.

'JJ, are you okay?' he calls out.

'They drugged us – me and Lesley – but I'm fine.' I call her Lesley so the goons don't know that I know. 'Lesley's in a bad way. She's over there.' I tilt my head in her direction, which this time makes me a little woozy. 'Hugh, these men are arm—' and one of them thwacks me across the ear while the other fires his gun. One bullet and then another whizz past my head. I'm unsure if he got off two shots or if one of them was Hugh firing back.

'*Aargh!*'

I can't tell who was hit. If it's Hugh … Oh my God! … what did I get him into? But no – it's not Hugh. I can hear one of the goons stumbling close by, and now he's yelling, '*You fucking fuck!*'

Arnie screams, 'Bones, watch out!' and '*No-o-o!*'

I slant my head back and see Arnie running towards Danny – or Bones – whose chest is drenched in red. He's staggering, and he's close to the demolition shaft, very close. Arnie goes to reach out to him as one of Bones' boots seesaws over the edge and, just before Arnie can grab him, he falls.

The sound of a man screaming as he plunges to his death is the worst thing I've ever heard – until the wet thud at the bottom … *that's* the worst.

I'm about to throw up, and I want to cry but my tear ducts are dry. I kick the heel of my right foot into the shin of my left leg and it hurts like it's supposed to – like hell, in fact.

'And then there was one,' says Hugh, his tone sounding so incredibly cool, like killing a man is an everyday activity for him. 'Big guy, if you don't put your gun on the ground,' he tells Arnie, 'you'll join your midget mate.'

Hugh's clearly not taken on board any of the police department's sensitivity training, assuming they do that kind of thing. And if he's told them he's a cop, I didn't hear it.

'Put your gun down … *now!*'

Arnie shouts back, 'You put *your* gun down, you fuck. That was my brother you killed.'

So, they *were* like the guys in *Twins*. Minus the comedy.

I hear Arnie's Dr Martens clomping towards me.

'*Stop!*' says Hugh. 'Stay back from her.'

'Not happening, man. If I so much as *think* I hear your trigger pulling back, I'll blow her fucking brains out, and she's way closer to me than I am to you.'

I lift my head again, just a little, and see Arnie's boots getting closer. His gun is also in my field of vision, though I wish it wasn't … I'm looking straight into the barrel.

Everything is slowing down … each of Arnie's steps seems to take forever, and each time he puts his heel down it's like a crack of thunder. Through the fog in my mind I hear Hugh saying, *Police … stay back!* but his words are getting drowned out by the snap of each footfall.

The cold steel of Arnie's gun is pressing into my forehead. I look down my nose to his boots. The blood is fresher than before. This time I do throw up, all over his jeans … and his boots. He kicks my shin so hard I want to scream, but I don't in case it makes him shoot. He's digging the gun deep into my temple. I'm starting to swoon like I'm going to faint, but what flies into my head is the Black Widow torture scene in the first *Avengers* film, where Scarlett Johansson's hands were taped to a chair. I start to raise my right leg, like she did, and …

Hugh calls out to Arnie, '*Oi, you!*' Perhaps he's seen what I'm doing and is trying to distract him.

I brace myself. I close my eyes – not that I can see much anyway – and give Arnie the biggest kick to his balls I'm capable of. Even before he's *oophing* and bending over in pain – and before he can get a bullet off – I lurch my body to the right, tipping over my chair so I'm on my side, out of the way, and he's totally exposed … and *whoosh* … I hear Hugh's bullet whizz by and slam into Arnie with a sickening *sploosh*, just as he fires a shot in return. I brace myself, expecting to die right then and there. I feel the rush of his bullet in my hair, and it's heading in Hugh's direction.

A long '*Fu-u-ck!*' comes from over there.

The bastard's hit Hugh.

Down my nose, I can see Arnie lying on the ground, close to my feet. Blood is starting to pool beside his stomach and mingle with my vomit, but he's raising his gun to take another shot … this time at me. I give another almighty kick and smash my boot into his head, and the gun drops out of his big ham of a hand.

I counterweight the chair with my body to do a 180-degree roll forward and, as the side of the chair hits the ground, the wooden supports crack beneath me. Part of the chair back breaks loose so I can lift my hands away … kind of. I manage to get to my feet, then raise an arm, which has a broken part of the chair still taped to it, and I start to rip the tape off my eyes.

'Let me help you.' It's Hugh.

'Didn't h-he h-hit you?' I stammer.

'I'm going to cut the tape,' he says. 'Okay?'

I feel metal at my right temple – the blunt edge of a blade, not a gun. He slides it under the tape, saws through it and says, 'Brace. I'm going to rip it off.' Before I can, he does it, but leaves a few inches of the duct tape hanging off my hair. 'You can get the rest off later.'

I'm blinking away tears I didn't know were coming. His leg is bleeding, though not badly, some red soaking into his jeans. 'He *did* hit you.'

'A graze. Same bloody leg as last time, too.' He laughs, but I'm sure it's forced. He picks up the roll of duct tape, cuts it and winds it tightly around his wound. 'All good. Happy?'

Now he's cutting the tape off my wrists to free them. That done, he says, 'Hey, Monroe, or Fontaine, or whatever the fuck your name is. You okay?'

Lesley is glaring at him, mouth bloody but gaping open, her tongue running over her teeth as if she's checking how many are left. 'I'll be better when you cut the tape off me too.'

'In time, but what I want from you first—'

'Before we get to what *you* want,' she says, 'like that bastard bleeding out on the floor said, who the fuck are you?'

'He's my father … and a cop. Hugh,' I say, turning to him, 'how did you track us?'

'I had your mobile number and, like you said, I'm a cop.'

66

Hugh's taken Arnie's pulse and is rolling him over, duct-taping his stomach to staunch the bleeding. 'He's in shock but he'll live.' He takes Arnie's wallet and phone out of his jacket. He flips open the wallet. 'JJ, meet …' He laughs as he reads Arnie's name. 'Henry Charles Windsor.' He looks down at Arnie, 'Your schoolmates call you Prince Harry the Huge, by any chance? Were your parents monarchists, or did they have a black sense of humour?' He holds Harry's phone up to his face. 'Nope.' He tries again. 'Second time lucky, and we're unlocked.' He's looking at the screen. 'Well, what have we here? An app that's called *Kneel Before Me*. Have you heard of it?'

'Kneel or Neil?' I spell out the words. 'He … Harry …

Just before you got here, he took a call from someone called Neil.'

Lesley spells out, 'N-i-a-l-l. Niall Farrelly. Irish crime lord. As bad as they come.'

'Just a minute.' Hugh's tapping the phone.

Lesley flips. 'You're not calling him? Don't. *Please* don't.'

'I'm changing his passcode. That way we can explore what's on this device at our leisure. Passcode's your birthday, JJ.' He taps the phone some more, then holds it back in front of Harry's face for a security confirmation.

I'm stunned. 'You remember my birthday?'

'Best day of my life. How could I forget?' He looks at me like my friends' dads looked at their kids – with adoration. Like how I saw him look at Vini. Who is this man?

'Vini!' I say, remembering. 'He's in hospital. Is he—'

'It was just a sprain. He's got a splint to show his mates at kindie, so that's made him as happy as a puppy with two tails.' He puts Harry's phone in his pocket. 'We'll get to the phone later.' He looks down the demolition shaft and turns back to me. 'Bones is gone. I'll have to call this in, but,' he looks back at Lesley, who's still tied to the chair, 'JJ's shown you mine, it's your turn to show us yours. Who the fuck are *you*?'

Before Lesley says anything, I say, 'She's told me everything, but let's step away from Arnie ... Harry ... just in case he can hear.'

After I tell Hugh what Lesley's told me, he scrapes her chair – with her still taped to it – even further away from Harry and cuts her free.

For a few minutes, we're metronoming between calling her Lesley and Claude. Eventually, she says, 'Can we go with Claude? It's kind of refreshing to be me again, despite the circumstances.' After putting a finger in her mouth to check her teeth, she starts pressing Hugh to let her disappear into the wind. 'I can't get put into the system. Now they've found me here, the Farrellys won't give up till they kill me. If I'm here when the police ... the other police ... arrive, I'm done for. They'll take ten seconds to find out I'm in Australia illegally ... that I'm in possession of stolen goods ... that I had an unlicensed weapon until that goon took it from me ... If I'm arrested, even if I'm only on remand, the Farrellys will have someone on the inside ... they'll find a way to get to me. I'll be dead in a day.'

I look at Hugh, and wonder what's going through his mind.

He says, 'What about the art?'

She shrugs. 'Give it back to the rightful owners. It's what I always intended. Now the Irish know I'm alive, there's no point in me hiding it anymore. You guys can return it, collect the reward ... rewards. Pay off your mortgages. But me, I can't be here.'

I'd told Hugh about the Gardner reward, but his eyes are wide. 'The *Sunflowers*,' he says. '*It's* not stolen, it's not supposed to—'

'—exist,' says Claude. 'Yet, amazingly, it does. I asked the Farrellys about it when I was flattering them, trying to stay on their good side. They said they traded it with the Yakuza, that's the Japanese—'

'—mafia,' says Hugh. 'I know.'

Who doesn't, right?

Claude continues, 'The history books say it got destroyed when—'

I can't help myself, '—Kobe got bombed.'

'Except just before the air raid, after the owner abandoned his house with the painting in it, the Yakuza turned up – he owed them money – and they grabbed it, took it in payment, moved it to a shelter.'

'Apart from you and the Farrellys, and now us, who knows it exists?'

'You're asking because?'

I know why Hugh's asking. 'Hugh, no! We *can't* keep it.'

'But, JJ, it's *ours.*'

Claude is open-mouthed, again. And given the state of her teeth, it's not a pretty sight. I tap under her chin with my finger, gently. Before closing her mouth, she says, 'How is *Sunflowers* yours? That's crazy.'

I quickly run through the family connection.

Claude lets out a chuckle. 'So, JJ, you're not only *not* an auditor, you're an art conservator *and* a direct heir of Vincent Van Gogh.' She adds, 'Wow!' except, given her teeth situation, it sounds like *Wargh!* 'Look,' she continues, 'I'm in no position to argue with you one way or the other. What you two do is up to you.'

She might not be able to argue with Hugh but I can. And I will. Just not now and not here.

Hugh starts on about it again but Claude interrupts with a sudden '*Hey!*' She's pointing to the pistol he's got shoved behind his belt. 'That's *my* gun. When I leave, I'm going to need it.'

'*Yours?*' Hugh takes it out, and holds it so she can see. 'Are you sure? I took it from—' and he points it at Harry.

We all look over.

Even up on one knee, Harry is a behemoth, and he's aiming a gun – *his* gun – at us. He fires.

So does Hugh.

67

Before I can scream or leap out of the way, both men go down.

'*No-o-o!*' I shriek.

Hugh's on his back, blood spurting from his chest. His eyes are rolling back in his head, and his face is a yellowish colour. My knees crumple beneath me.

I hear Claude running the other way but I'm focused on Hugh. 'Stay with me,' I tell him. I'm pressing down on the wound, blood spouting through my fingers. 'Please stay with me. Vini and Kate … they need you.'

I'm choking up. 'Hugh, I … I need you.'

Claude returns with the roll of duct tape and Harry's gun. She hands me the weapon, says, 'Harry's dead,' and pushes me aside while she scritches the tape tightly around Hugh, exactly how he did with Harry.

I've never seen a man ... three men ... shot ... let alone seen anyone killed. Not in real life. The adrenaline is pumping through my body. I look at the gun in my hand. I look at Hugh lying there, barely alive.

My entire body is numb ... with shock ... with fear ... with a depth of sadness I never expected to feel. He remembered my birthday. *The best day of my life*, he said, like he meant it. Yet, never once in my whole life did he let me know I was loved. Until now.

Claude is patting Hugh's pockets and pulls out a phone. I can't be sure but I think it's Harry's. She holds it to Hugh's face to unlock it, and that doesn't work. Before I can tell her my birth date, she walks over to Arnie to try it with his face. He might be dead but it works, and she dials 'emergency'.

I hear the words *policeman down ... guns ... shot ... dead ... ambulance ... fast ... dying.* 'Just a sec,' I think I hear her say into the phone. Something about bringing up the maps app and giving them our location. A moment later, she says, 'My name?' but the name I hear is mine and not hers.

She pulls me up off the floor. 'JJ, speak to me.'

I can't.

'JJ.' She slaps my face. 'Listen. We don't have much time. The ambulance ... the police ... they'll be here any minute. When they arrive, I need to be gone. JJ, are you listening to me?'

I'm blubbering like a child, hearing Claude's words but not taking them in.

She shakes me by the shoulders. 'Listen to me. Get your act together. Are you listening?' She slaps me again. 'Do you hear me?'

I take a deep, wet sniff and I nod.

'I've staunched Hugh's wound. The ambulance is on the way ... Listen.'

I can hear the sirens too. 'They're coming,' I say uselessly.

'I've got to go, okay? But first, I need you to promise me something.'

'I've got nothing—'

'When the police get here, give them Harry's phone. Tell them the Farrellys in Belfast are behind all this. Tell them that phone's got what they need to bring the bastards down. Tell them to contact Europol or Scotland Yard, but *not* the Ulster police. The Farrellys own the locals.'

'The galleries.'

'The *Farrellys*. Tell them about the Farrellys.'

'Not Ulster police.'

'Right. But *don't* say anything about me. Not yet. What I need from you is time, JJ. I've got to get back to my house, clean myself up and leave the country. I've got a go-bag ready, travel papers in a new name, but I need time to get on a flight and land so they can't turn me back.'

'Your teeth ... your lovely teeth,' I'm mumbling.

'And Winston,' she says. 'Can you find a home for Winston?'

'Scottie loves Winston.'

She grabs my shoulders again and glares into my eyes. 'Don't tell the police about me until tomorrow. Not my name ... neither of my names ... not where I live ... nothing about the art. Not till tomorrow night. After that, tell them … tell them everything. I'll get a message to you.'

'A message. Not till tomorrow.'

'Tomorrow *night*. Pretend you're in shock.'

I *am* in shock.

68

'How are you feeling?'

I look up. I'm inside a big blue cocoon and an unfamiliar yet attractive woman is inside it with me, handing me a paper cup. She's in blue too, so her head looks like it's floating around, like we're on a movie set, inside a blue-screen room. I peer into the cup. It's water ... or vodka. I smell it. Sadly, it's water. There's an ambient smell – sharp, like bleach, or antiseptic. I take my arm out from a blanket that's weighing down my shoulders. A thingy is sticking out of a vein in the back of my hand. It starts with a C. Or is it a T, for thingy? No, it's a cannula. Yes, that's it. Another term I learned watching *Grey's Anatomy*. I drink from the cup.

She'll piss herself. Arnie ... no, it was Harry ... said that.

I go to feel my jeans, but I'm not wearing any, and my legs are dry and stretched out in front of me, on a bed, under another blanket. I'm wearing a cotton gown. It's white, the same washed-out colour as … *No!* … I'm seeing Hugh's eyes rolling back into his head. I twist around, spilling the water, and see my name on a whiteboard on the wall behind me … but it says Justine, not JJ. No one calls me Justine, not even Hugh when he was angry. *Hugh!*

A new face comes into the blue cocoon … black hair … Cristina Yang? … Yang makes a gap in the blue, then disappears, leaving the blue swaying around my bed, and it's like she's let in a hubbub of noise.

'You're in the emergency department,' says the nurse. 'We'll be moving you to peck shortly.'

'I'm not hungry.'

'Psychological Emergency Care Centre. PECC.'

'I'm not crazy.'

'It's only for assessment … before we send you home.'

I can hear a doctor talking to the man in the next bed. He sounds like he's Indian – the doctor, I mean. 'How many pills did you take, Marco?' Marco answers in a deep, raspy voice with an American accent, 'Fuck off and let me die.'

'Shouldn't *that* guy be in PECC?' I ask the nurse.

'It's a process,' she says.

'Hugh?' I ask.

She puts her hand under my chin, and goes to lift it so I'll be looking into her eyes. That can mean only one thing. I start wailing and tear my head away from her.

'Ms Jego,' she says. 'Your father—'

'No,' is all I can manage, and it's barely a whisper. I've lost my father when I'd just found him.

'Justine, it's not what you think. He's in theatre.'

'He's *not* dea—' Sobs of relief surge through me, saving me from even saying the word. The nurse takes a syringe off a side table, points it upwards into the air and gives it a spurt.

'What's in that?' Syringes no longer seem benign to me, even in a nurse's hands.

'Diazepam. To calm you down.' She takes my hand, pokes the needle into the cannula and presses down on the plunger.

For the first time, I notice the cop sitting in a chair inside the blue curtain. She's in blue too, but it's a dark blue. She's looking at her phone as if the nurse and I aren't here. I blurt out, 'Is it tomorrow night yet?' The moment the question leaves my mouth, I realise I sound like an airhead who doesn't know if she's coming or going.

The nurse – Sarah, according to the ID dangling from her hip, says – 'Justine, you're in shock. You've only been here,' she checks the watch pinned to her shirt, 'an hour. The ambulance brought you and your dad straight here.'

My *dad*. I like the sound of it.

The cop looks up. 'Can we talk? I've got a few quest—'

The nurse cuts her off. 'Officer, I've told you already … no questions until the social worker gets here and okays it. I really can't have you hanging around in here and—'

'She's our only witness. Two men are dead, maybe a—'

'*Stop!* You need to leave now!' Sarah positions herself between the cop and me, and starts to usher her out.

I'm starting to nod off.

I love my cannula.

69

The sound of whimpering wakes me and I blink my eyes open. I'm on my back, still inside the blue curtains. I suppose it's Marco in the next bed. I lean up on one elbow to see if the cop's back. She's not.

It's not Marco who's crying. It's Kate, Hugh's Kate – her head's in her hands, and her body's heaving.

She hears me sniff, and rushes over to my bed so fast her handbag falls to the floor, spilling its contents. She throws herself at me. She's hugging me and repeating my name, my proper name – JJ – over and over, like a good luck incantation, despite the fact that all I've brought her is tragedy.

I reach for a Kleenex. When she hears the *psht* as I pull it out of the box beside me, she looks up. I pat her eyes

291

with the tissue and hand it to her. She blows her nose, and tries to smile but can't.

For I don't know how long, we're gazing into each other's eyes, terrified by the question dangling in the air between us. I ask a different one. 'Vini?'

She blows her nose again. 'He's with our next-door neighbour. She babysits for us sometimes. I couldn't bring him here … he wouldn't understand.'

I nod as if I agree, except I've got no idea what four-year-olds are capable of. Kate's hair's a mess and her clothes are what she was wearing this morning … gold top, slacks the same pastel blue as the curtains here, and a navy cardigan, but its cuffs are now stretched and wet, like she's been twisting them around her fingers and biting them.

'Vini adores Hugh,' Kate says and suddenly she's bawling.

My body shudders with one long sob and we're hugging again. She won't let me go, like I mean something to her.

A cough kills the moment. I crack open an eye, worried it might be the cop, but it's Sarah, the nurse. I nudge Kate, and she gets up. I introduce them as she wipes her eyes on her sleeve.

Sarah's holding the handles of an empty wheelchair. Kate takes my hand and grips it like I'm the only thing holding her up. 'The doctor's waiting for us in the family room,' says the nurse. 'Justine, are you able to get out of bed?'

'It's JJ,' says Kate softly. 'She likes to be called JJ.' She lowers her eyes to the floor, sees her belongings, lets go of me and drops to her knees. 'Sorry,' she says to everyone and no one, and starts to put her lipstick, purse, a toy soldier and an assortment of other items back in her handbag.

Sarah gets down too and assists her. When they've collected everything, she says, 'Come,' and helps Kate up.

Kate follows as Sarah wheels me out of ED, down a corridor and into a room painted muted green with a circle of armchairs in the centre, a box of toys in the corner. A doctor wearing light blue scrubs is standing at the window. He's looking out at a brick wall. He turns. The doctor looks like he's barely out of high school, but with heavy-lidded eyes from, I assume, working double and triple shifts. He's clasping his hands in front of him, his mouth tight. He tells us his name but I don't register it. Kate comes closer to me, biting her bottom lip, pressing her nails into my hand.

The doctor clears his throat. His demeanour is signalling what's coming, but it's the nurse, Sarah, who speaks. She's older than him, and probably been at three times as many telling-the-families. 'Dr Petrellis is our best trauma surgeon. He's been with your husband, your father, in theatre since the ambulance brought him to us. Dr Petrellis?' She nudges him.

'Mr Jego was in a critical condition when he arrived, suffering significant internal bleeding,' says the doctor. 'We did everything we could but I'm so sorry—'

Mashing my hands against my ears and squeezing my eyes shut did nothing to blot out Kate's unearthly wail … or my guilt.

70

I wake to the savoury aroma of Vegemite and the crunch
of teeth biting into toast. I blink my eyes open and see
a cop seated on one of the visitor chairs near the foot
of my bed, eating. I'm no longer curtained off in a bay in
emergency. The room decor is clinical, the furniture minimal.
The door is open, and I see a sign on the corridor wall
saying PECC. I'd slept right through the night. Diazepam,
probably.

'Ms Jego, my condolences,' says the officer, laying the
rest of his toast on a plate on the floor and licking his
fingers. 'I worked with Hugh a year ago. He was one of
the best.' He gets up and slides the box of tissues across the
table to me.

I don't know if it's the drugs, but his mention of Hugh

in the past tense that he '*was* one of the best' doesn't seem to throw me. I pull a tissue out of the box and blow my nose because I sense it's expected of me, not because I need to. It's like all my feelings have been sapped out of me and remote observation is all I have left.

'I've got some good news,' says the cop. 'The Farrellys were arrested in Belfast overnight, and that's all down to you. Here.' He hands me his phone, which shows an article on the *Belfast Telegraph* website. I look for a 'read aloud' button, and press it.

33 arrested in major organised crime rout – crime bosses and top Ulster police charged

Sunday 6 pm Belfast

In what's been hailed as a major breakthrough in the fight against organised crime, police arrested 33 people today in coordinated raids across Belfast, north Antrim and east London.

Among those arrested were alleged crime kingpins 35-year-old twins Niall and Nessa Farrelly, heirs to the Conor Farrelly empire, and eight of the Northern Ireland Police Service's most senior officers.

The raids are the culmination of Operation Oberon, a long-running joint task force of the NIPS's formidable Anti-Corruption Unit and Scotland Yard.

An ACU spokesperson says that police seized electronic equipment, weapons and drugs and, with cooperation from Europol and the FBI, have frozen bank accounts in eight countries.

The task force sprang into action after a Saturday tip-off from Australian police that gave them a crucial missing link ...

'But I didn't do anything.'

'Actually, you did,' he says.

Apparently, my actions in the minutes after the first responders arrived were crucial. The tip-off that led to the arrests came from me, though I don't remember a thing, apart from being a whimpering mess hunched over Hugh's body.

The cop says that when they dragged me off Hugh, I held the goon's phone out to them, saying over and over, *It's the Farrellys … from Belfast … check the app.* When I gave them the phone's passcode, my birthday – which I also don't recall doing – they found enough intel that they knew they had to act fast, before the Sydney media got wind of the shooting and the Farrellys picked up on it.

'Hang on, this article,' I say and hold up his phone, 'it's dateline is Sunday six pm Belfast … what's that in Sydney time?'

'Five am Monday, which was, ah,' he looks at his watch, 'two hours ago. Is that a problem?'

'A problem?' I say. 'The problem is that if I'm in Sydney … and I am in Sydney, right?'

He nods.

'Then it's *Sunday* morning here, *not* Monday.'

'Actually, it *is* Monday. You were zonked out the whole of yesterday.' He presses the call button beside my bed. 'The nurses will be glad you're awake,' he says. 'And I've got to tell HQ.' He takes his phone back and taps it. 'After you've eaten and dressed, and all that, the detectives will be coming over to interview you.'

He leaves the room, and when he closes the door behind him, something happens to me. I feel like the bedding is engulfing me, suffocating me, dragging me down into an abyss of loss – into a world violently blown apart just when I was putting it back together.

71

I'm propped up behind a table in Room A113, with two detectives seated opposite. I'm feeling like Nemo – in deep water, except I don't have a lucky fin.

There's a mobile phone in the middle of the table. 'Do you mind if we record this?' asks the older cop.

I shrug.

During our introductions, the old guy tells me he's worked with Hugh, that he 'greatly admired' him and, while I'm sure he means it kindly, I hear it as code for *great at his job but a total prick*. It rankles even though he didn't say it, and even though a mere forty-eight hours earlier I would've applauded him for a character appraisal I'd spent my life believing was spot on.

The thought brings on a dark cloud of guilt and I drift off into it … I don't know how long for, but I stir to find the other cop shaking my shoulder. I can't hear what he's saying. The front of my gown is wet and now he's wiping my face with a towel. 'It's okay, JJ. It's okay.' A nurse is taking my temperature and blood pressure. 'I think she'll be fine,' she says.

The older cop settles back in his chair and smiles at me. 'If we're going too fast, stop us any time. Okay?'

I nod.

'You're the only witness, JJ. I know this is hard, but we need your help, so we can understand what happened,' he says. I seem to remember his name, but not when he gave it to me. It's Detective Inspector Marshall. George Marshall.

They say you form impressions about people in the first seven seconds. Well, George Marshall doesn't come across like a hard-nosed cop, more like a genial dad – not the one from my childhood, obviously – the kind of dad who ferrets around to find the TV remote so the two of you can sit down and watch the footie grand final together. I'm guessing he'd be a Rabbitohs fan. I don't know why. But if he is, maybe he knows Russell Crowe.

I sit up higher and try to get it together. 'Anything I can do to help,' I say, and mean it. I owe that to Hugh. And because it's after 'tomorrow night' I don't need to stall to make sure Claude is safe. 'But isn't your job done and dusted? The bastard who shot Hugh is dead, his partner too. And I saw a press article just now that says the Farrellys, who I assume are those guys' bosses, got arrested in Belfast and …' and I stop.

With eight senior cops being arrested in Belfast, it dawns on me that these detectives sitting opposite might be probing to find out if *we*, Hugh and me, were corrupt … to investigate whether *we* were in bed with the Farrellys and whether our nefarious operation – whatever they think it was – went belly up. 'Hey,' I say, 'Hugh was an innocent bystander. He was only there because he came looking for me.' I start bawling, I can't help it.

The younger cop, Detective Petty, pulls a bottle of water – one of those pink ones supporting breast cancer research – out of his bag, twists off the top and pours it into a glass on the table. Petty's got a forehead that could host a billboard, a rectangular face with a jutting jaw, and thin, cruel lips. Unlike Marshall, he's not at all likeable. The bad cop to Marshall's good cop. He probably doesn't even follow rugby league.

Marshall pulls a tissue out of a box and hands it to me. After I calm down, he asks why Hugh came looking for me.

'I was investigating a … a neighbour—'

'Would that be a Lesley Monroe?'

I stiffen and hope they don't notice. 'Ah, how did you know?'

'We'll get to that. Keep going.'

'Sure. I'd gathered some evidence—'

'And you took it to Hugh.'

'Right.'

'Is this the evidence?' Petty leans down and pulls a folder out of his bag. I can see it's my VM material. One by one, he spreads the printouts on the table … just like Hugh did … my *Girl* photos … the newspaper articles from France and Monaco … the photos of The Art.

'Where did you get them?'

'Kate. Hugh's wife,' says Marshall. 'She found them on his desk.'

Sounds and images are filling my head … bullets thwacking into bodies … screams … Hugh's eyes rolling back into his head. And though I haven't actually seen it, Kate cuddling Vini and running her fingers through his red hair … telling him he no longer has a father.

And all of it is down to me.

'I need to go to the bathroom.' I get up out of my wheelchair and, despite my wobbly legs, burst through the door and into the corridor, almost knocking down a passing nurse. 'Bathroom,' I say, trying desperately not to cry again. 'Where?'

She points back inside Room A113. 'There's one behind a door in there.'

I feel like an idiot. I slink back in, go into the bathroom and sit on the toilet for ten minutes, mostly with my head in my hands. All of this happened – Claude tortured, Hugh murdered, Vini an orphan, Kate a widow – because I insisted on playing out some stupid fantasy that I was Veronica fucking Mars.

72

The cops are assembling a timeline, using me and my evidence sheets to help them. 'Tell us more about Lesley Monroe.'

'She lives in the Wharf Terraces. We've been walking our dogs and having coffee together most mornings this past little while. Actually, it's not *my* dog. I'm dog-sitting. And house-sitting. Boat-sitting too, if you want the full—'

'What's your precise relationship with her?'

'I wouldn't say we had a relationship – not really.'

'Had? Past tense?'

'She's gone.'

'Where?'

'She didn't tell me.'

'That's all you know about her?'

'I didn't say that.' I give them the full context. What I saw – The Art – which was why I was so desperate to meet her, how I found out she's also Claude Fontaine, everything that Hugh and I discovered when we checked out her town house. 'She'd given me the security code,' I blurt out, to make sure they don't add breaking and entering to my list of crimes. And I tell them what she told me about the Farrellys just before she ran off. 'She only worked for them under duress.'

Saying it out loud like that in a single stream of words has drained me but I can tell Petty's sceptical. He's twirling his pen like he's angling for a gotcha moment. 'What else do you know about this Monroe, or Fontaine?' he demands, glaring.

I glare back at him and let loose. 'What else do I know? If there was a Nobel Prize for contribution to the arts, she would win it hands down.'

'Because?' asks Petty, pressing.

I'm gripping the side of the table. I want to tell him to fuck off but, even in the circumstances, and seeing that Marshall also seems uncomfortable with his partner's attitude, I can't bring myself to do it. *Breathe, JJ, breathe*, I'm telling myself.

'Because?' It's Petty again.

'Because those bastards were ...' I stop and bite my lower lip. Then I start again, trying not to collapse into a blithering heap. 'Because even though they were ... pulling ... out ... her ... teeth ... she wouldn't tell them a thing.'

Marshall pushes over the glass of water to me. I take a drink. 'Do you want a break?' he asks.

I do, but shake my head. I need this to be over with. 'They took us because they wanted to know where the art was, but she point-blank refused. *Do your worst* – her words. And that was after they'd yanked out her second tooth. They were going to kill her whether she talked or not and, anyhow, it doesn't matter because she's dying, so ...'

Marshall leans forward and I can tell what he's about to ask, so I continue, 'I knew she'd been sick, but not that sick. It might be why she'd rushed off to hospital that day. St Vincent's. You can check.'

Petty writes it all down.

'Anyway, she collapsed. If Hugh hadn't turned up when he did ...' I take a sip, 'they'd have turned the pliers on me.' I feel like throwing up, so put my hands on the table and do some more deep breathing.

Marshall coughs and I see him give Petty a flick of the head – the kind that says *Let me handle her.* He asks about the shootout but he's softer, less inquisitorial.

I tell him what I remember. Then Petty puts his hard hat back on and pushes, 'That's all you know?'

I squirm a little in my seat. 'There *is* one more thing. After the ... er ...?'

'Shootout?'

'Right. Lesley ... Claude ... she ran, like I said. No, she called the emergency line first, said it was me calling, *then* she ran. But just before she left, she said she'd send me a message.'

Petty smirks like he's going to relish his next move. He leans down and brings up an iPad, plonks it on the table, unfolds the cover so it stands upright, and turns the screen to me.

It's displaying a document. I squint to read the heading ... *Deed Poll*. The rest of the typing is in a small font. Whatever it is, it looks very formal.

My mind immediately jumps to a place I don't want to go ... figuratively and literally ... a new life under a name that's not mine, in a city I don't know. To live like Claude, always looking over my shoulder, never feeling safe.

And I know how that ended up for her.

Are they really going to offer me witness protection? Are they going to tell me that, despite the arrests in Britain, my life's still in danger?

I push the iPad away. I don't want to read what's on it. I don't even want to try. 'I'm dyslexic,' I tell them.

Marshall removes his glasses, and swivels the iPad back to face him. 'So's my daughter,' he says. 'Now, this Lesley or Claude ... whatever ... she did send you that message. This legal document was attached to it.'

'You mean that's not a witness protection ... That's from her and not from you? *Whoa!* Then how did *you* get it?'

'It was in your email inbox,' says Petty. 'It arrived late last night.'

I'm about to explode when Marshall frowns at his colleague and turns to me, putting on his affable-uncle voice. 'JJ, you were totally out of it ... sedated ... Saturday night, and the whole of Sunday and Sunday night. With what we found on that phone you handed over, we couldn't wait for you to come round. We got a warrant and accessed all your devices.'

'That was fast.'

'We're cops,' he says, channelling Hugh almost verbatim. 'We had no choice. I'm sorry.'

I'm furious, but also relieved because now I know Claude is safe, even if I don't know where she is. 'I didn't give you permission—'

Petty gives me a smarmy put-down smile. 'A warrant means we don't need permission.'

I nod, and Marshall starts to read the document to me.

73

I close my eyes so I can take it all in.

Deed Poll

I am the Lesley Monroe described as lessee in the attached lease of the Woolloomooloo town house I occupy (the 'Lease' and 'my Town House').

JJ Jego is the only person I trust. She and her father risked their lives to save mine.

Petty interrupts. 'You've only gone on a few walks and drunk a few coffees, yet you're the only person she trusts? Why is that?'

Frankly, I'm as surprised as he is, especially because I was lying to her for most of our time together. 'I've got no idea,' I say, then try to make a joke, 'We can email back to ask her?'

He doesn't grant me a laugh.

Instead, Marshall says, 'She must've knocked this up on the plane. She is a lawyer, so …' and he reads on:

> In deep gratitude to Ms Jego, and in consideration of her loss and her sacrifice:
> 1. I unconditionally and absolutely sublet to her and assign to her all my rights and title to, and my interest in the Lease of my Town House for her exclusive use and occupation, noting:
>   a) that the Lease continues for a further four years eleven months,

'What?' I exclaim. 'I can't afford that place! The rent would be … I don't know … five thousand a week? … ten thousand? … I've got no idea. How is sending me bankrupt a sign of gratitude?'

Marshall holds his hand up to stop me carrying on, then keeps reading.

> b) that as a gift to Ms Jego, and for her sole benefit, I have today, in advance, paid all the rent and estimated outgoings for the full period of the Lease, by depositing those amounts in the rental agent's bank account, and

This is definitely an *Oh, fuck!* moment.

I quickly do the calculation. Words can be difficult for me but, like I say, numbers and pictures are where I shine. 'At five thousand a week that's, like, over a million dollars … a million and a quarter,' I say, not realising I'm speaking aloud. 'Lesley's just handed me a fortune! But if it's *ten* grand a week … *Holy Jesus!*'

'That's what we figured. So, enlighten us. Why would Lesley Monroe/Claude Fontaine do all that for you … unless …'

'Unless what?' I'm lost for words. Apart from my parents – mostly my mother, and only now, Hugh – no one has given me anything. Ever.

House-sitting for Brandy for a few weeks doesn't count, even if it's been amazing. *Giving* me the use of a harbourside town house for five years rent-free … that's beyond incredible. 'There's no "unless". I can't explain this,' I tell them. 'I've honestly got no idea.'

'There's more,' says Marshall.

2. I further gift to JJ Jego all the contents, fittings and fixtures of my Town House, including each of the artworks listed in the Schedule. She has full power to deal with them as she decides and at her discretion, noting that the provenance of a number of the artworks is either unknown or is open to dispute.

I'm no lawyer, obviously, but if this means what I think, Lesley's just made me one of the richest women on the planet. Her gift will be subject to any prior claims on the art, of course, but until all those claims are resolved, I can waltz around Woolloomooloo pretending to be a billionaire. I could even get Harry's Café de Wheels to do home delivery.

Marshall taps the table with a pen to bring me back to earth – which it doesn't, not even a bit. 'The thing about this art,' he says. 'We've been into Lesley's town house—'

'Another warrant?'

'Yep. And while there's art all over the walls, we didn't see any of the art in your photos. And the works that *are* there aren't listed in her schedule … apart from a painting of an old Torana—'

'By Ben Quilty, right?'

'Right.'

'So, given what Monroe/Fontaine says in the next para of this Deed Poll—'

'Read it … please.'

3. Ms Jego should feel free to tell the authorities in Sydney that I will separately be providing a sworn written statement – with supporting documentary evidence – to Europol. I will explain how, under extreme duress from Nessa and Niall Farrelly of Belfast, and in acute fear for my life and that of my father, I came into possession of the artworks and how the Farrellys forced me to play a crucial role, using those artworks and my legal skills to finance their criminal activities.

   My aim is, and has always been, to bring the Farrellys to justice. But even if I succeed, given the global reach and influence of their organisation I remain at grave personal risk so I have again taken a new identity and I will never contact Ms Jego again.

'What do you know about that?'

'It confirms everything I told you, including why she faked her death in India. She was terrified they'd kill her.' I rummage through my printouts and push forward the one about her law partner's murder. 'If she needed any justification for heading back on the run, that's it right there.'

'No, what I meant was … what do you know about the *artworks* … *these* ones.' Petty pushes back to me my fuzzy shots of the Rembrandt, Vermeer and Van Gogh. 'Like the boss says, they're not at the town house.'

'Yes, they are. Take me there and I'll show you.' I stand up, but am a bit unsteady on my feet, so get back into the wheelchair. 'Give me time to shower and get dressed.' I go to wheel myself out but swivel back. 'Did Lesley say anything else in the email? Anything at all?'

'Actually, yeah. Will you look after her dog?'

74

Blue-and-white-checked police tape is criss-crossed over Lesley's front entrance, which is flanked by two uniformed cops. 'Please go ahead, JJ,' says Detective Marshall as he nods to the cops and lifts the tape so we can go under.

'Hey, George,' says a woman inside. She's carrying the type of bag a pilot would have and she's clad head to toe in white Tyvek coveralls.

'Hey, Nikki,' Marshall says back to her.

'Pete,' she says to Petty. 'I'm all done, guys. Just leaving.'

Nikki looks at me, ever so briefly, then ducks out under the tape and heads off to her next assignment or to the pub, or wherever forensics people hang out to yak over drinks about cadavers and bullet wounds and such.

'Is her name really Nikki?' I ask Marshall, who I've started thinking of as George.

'*You* watch *Silent Witness* too?'

I nod, but don't tell him I stopped at series twenty-two.

'Crazy fluke,' he says, 'that she's got the first name as a forensic pathologist on a TV show. She's as good as her, too. But her wife's a public defender, so she's got to recuse herself whenever the prosecution's relying on Nikki's evidence.' He leads me to the living room. Black fingerprint dust is everywhere. 'Sorry about that,' he says, as if I'm really going to be living here. 'Not too hard to wipe off, though. A spray of Purell or Nifti … anything, as long as it's got ammonia in it … add a bit of elbow grease and, easy-peasy, it's gone.'

A thoughtful cop has laid out on the glass-top dining table the gear I was packing up when I got attacked. It's on a towel, so it doesn't scratch the surface. My tote bag's there too.

'Where's Winston?' I ask, looking around, worried he's run off somewhere. 'Lesley's dog.' George told me on the way over that an officer here is meant to be looking after him, and similarly with Scottie at Brandy's.

'Winston? The dog that got you into this shit?' says Petty.

'Huh?' I say.

'Not now, Pete,' says George. He turns to me and says, 'We'll explain later. Hey, Nguyen!' he calls out to one of the two cops guarding the door. 'Where's the mutt?'

Nguyen pokes his head in. 'Out on the terrace, Inspector.'

'Do you mind?' I say to George. He doesn't. I go to slide the doors open, but then see I don't need to bother.

Winston is asleep in the far corner, which is why I didn't notice him before. It's the only sunny spot left at this time of day. His tail is slowly swishing the tiles, so he's probably having a pleasant dream, assuming dogs dream. Someone – Nguyen? – has put a bowl of water out for him, and a second bowl with dog biscuits.

'Not much of a guard dog,' says Petty.

I ignore him. So does his boss. 'So,' George says, 'when we came here yesterday, we walked in on this … I don't know … art gallery, I guess. I've never seen so many paintings in one house, but virtually none of these are on her list. We looked around, obviously. Her office was cleaned out – no computer. That photo of her folks, the one you showed us, that's gone too. Wall safe open but empty. Closets … the last time I saw so many kaftans in one place was when I worked security at Bluesfest in the nineties. So, the art?'

I move to close the front door. 'We need the AC to kick in,' I tell him, 'to bring down the temperature.' That having happened, I start closing the curtains. 'If the works are genuine, which I think they are, too much natural light's not good for them.'

Petty helps me, to speed up the process. It's only then that I place my hand over the wall panel. The cops are watching, mouths open, as the panel slides across to expose the green button.

'Well, how about that!' says George.

'Impressive!' says Petty

'If you think that's good, watch this,' I say and press the button. '*Hey presto!*' I add, then nudge George to turn around, so he can see all the art starting to slowly flip over.

While there's a lot of art here, my focus is still on *Six Sunflowers*, and my pulse is racing as it repeats the revelation pirouette that Hugh and I watched. I remember how I'd held his hand.

Six Sunflowers. Lost to the world for eighty years and now, I hope, found. Maybe.

George's eyes are on the biggest work, *Christ in the Storm on the Sea of Galilee*. 'Is that *really* a Rembrandt?' he exclaims. 'The men on the boat?'

He's stepping towards it so fast that I shout, 'No touching!' He stops. 'And, yes, it's a Rembrandt,' I tell him. 'Almost four hundred years old. Over there,' I point across the room to *A Lady and Gentleman in Black*. 'That's another one.'

'Another Rembrandt? And that's real too?'

'Like I told you, there's a lot of testing to be done but, yes, I believe they are.'

'What's the big deal with Rembrandt? Those paintings are both so dismal,' says Petty. 'I wouldn't want either of them on my walls. The list says there's a third Rembrandt. Which one is it?'

I point to the self-portrait – an etching not much bigger than Petty's brain.

George holds up a printout of the list. 'When I read Rembrandt, Van Gogh, Picasso … they're the only names I recognised … they were just names on a page, but standing in front of the *actual* pictures … it's …' He's speechless. Art has had that effect on people all through history.

'That one over the fireplace,' I say. 'It's a Vermeer. *The Concert*. Incredible, don't you think? The girl's satin shirt and her skirt, it's like they're reaching out, asking you to touch them.'

I see Petty stepping forward. 'Which, Detective Petty, you're *not* going to do. No touching, okay?'

'Vermeer?' echoes George. 'Like that Bette Midler song?'

I have no idea which one he's talking about and I've got a pretty extensive Spotify playlist of art-related songs. Aside from 'Vincent (Starry, Starry Night)', I've got Jay-Z's 'Picasso Baby', Kanye's 'Famous', Lady Gaga's 'Applause', Bowie's 'Andy Warhol', Lil Wayne's 'Mona Lisa', but a Vermeer song by Bette Midler? Nope. 'I don't know it,' I tell him.

'I'm humming it in my head,' he says. 'So catchy. Here goes … Don't worry, I won't sing, I'll just give you the words … *Vermeer bits touché, please let me explain … Vermeer bits touché means you're grand* … that's it. You know it?'

I decide to move on. 'Detective, that painting. If it's the genuine Vermeer stolen from the Gardner Museum, it's probably worth more than all three Rembrandts put together.'

'Who'd guess that?' asks George. Now he's looking at another painting, his brow furrowed and mouth pinched. 'That one over there,' he points, 'the one that looks like a cut-and-paste? That's the Picasso?'

'Yep. *Pigeon with Green Peas.*' I could give him the French name but I'm guessing I'd have to translate it.

'Where's the pigeon? And the peas?'

I almost choke. It's like Hugh is standing beside me. I compose myself. 'With Cubism, you've got to use your imagination.'

'And those,' says Petty. 'Those paperweights?'

'The bronze eagle,' I tell him, 'is a finial – an ornament from the top of a flagpole – and I'm pretty sure the Gardner website said it came from Napoleon's Imperial Guard. The trumpet-shaped object, a Gu, is a bronze beaker from an ancient Chinese Dynasty … Shing or Shang, something like that. It's over three thousand years old.'

George continues to check artworks off the list as I walk him around all twenty-three of them … the thirteen stolen from the Gardner in 1990 … the five stolen from the Paris Museum of Modern Art in 2010 … the four stolen from private collectors … and *Six Sunflowers*. I leave my favourite till last.

'JJ, your eyes have been darting back to that one the whole time we've been here, like a kid looking through the window of an ice-cream shop. What's so great about it? Okay, it's …' he glances at the list, 'a Van Gogh, but half the flowers are dying and they've dropped out of the vase. It's bright, that's for sure, but the subject's pretty maudlin.'

To me, it's far from maudlin. It's the most astonishingly beautiful painting I've ever seen, especially if it's come back from the dead and I'm the first person since 1945 to see it, to know it still exists – outside of the Yakuza, of course … and the Farrellys … and Claude.

I'm thrilled that Hugh got to see it too. And even more thrilled I was the one who got to show it to him.

75

The detectives are wrapping up. I've flipped The Art back around to face the walls and opened the curtains. Winston's running up and down the corridor, sliding on the parquetry like a snowboarder on the slopes at a fancy ski resort, and totally oblivious of how his real mistress has abandoned him, leaving him to me.

I don't know how I'm supposed to feel. Half the time, I'm teetering on a cliff edge and staring down into an abyss of loss over Hugh — a man who until Saturday, I never expected, or wanted, to see again. The other half of the time, I'm gazing at a galaxy of stars shimmering on the potential discovery of the greatest haul of lost modern art in human history.

There's been no media to worry about, so far, and I'm petrified about how I'm going to handle the spotlight when it comes. I tell George how I'm feeling. He warns me that the *Belfast Telegraph* article's got the Australian media speculating about who in Sydney gave the tip-off leading to the Farrelly arrests – and what the connection is – but assures me that the police have managed to keep a tight lid on it so far. 'We've put blinders on the whole operation here,' he tells me, 'and that's at the request of Scotland Yard and Europol. As a result, those thirty-three arrests you read about have bumped up to fifty-two, with six more cops among them, including a deputy assistant police commissioner.'

He hands me his phone to show me the latest in the *Sydney Morning Herald*, with 'reliable sources' saying that the tip-off came out of a feud between rival criminal gangs in Sydney's southwest. That's *reliable* for you.

But he's right – there's not a peep about the shootout, or Hugh's death, or Claude Fontaine, or me, or The Art. Not yet, anyway.

I've been sitting on Lesley's lounge and go to stand but George gestures me to stay. He sits beside me, cautiously, respectfully, the same way Hugh came to sit beside me at his apartment. Winston's rubbing himself against my legs. 'JJ,' says George, 'one thing before we go …'

My heart sinks to my stomach. I suspect what's coming … the old one-two kick in the guts. The cops start off making out they're your mates, so you lower your guard. You don't get legal advice – 'Why would you need it?' – you tell them everything, and then they hit you with, *I'm sorry, Ms Jego, I've really got no choice but I'm arresting you for …*

But, in a way, what he says is worse. 'I've just heard from the commissioner … We're going public tomorrow.'

It's to keep control of 'the narrative', as he puts it. There's to be a police press conference – a 'presser' – and they want me there, 'To put a face to the narrative.'

I shift away from him on the sofa. 'I don't want my face anywhere near this. *No way!*' I say it without thinking.

Behind a lens I'm the happiest person on the planet. Fronting a battery of cameras and blazing lights, and reporters shoving at me those long mics on sticks like accusing fingers … I'm not doing it.

I don't tell him I'm scared stiff, but it's obvious when I see my reflection in the glass on one of the faux paintings opposite. My arms are crossed tightly over my chest, and I'm hugging myself like there's no tomorrow.

'JJ?' he presses. 'For Hugh. Will you do it for Hugh?'

I need to buy time. That's what witnesses and crims do on TV. First up, I try by saying, 'I … I need to talk to my director first,' meaning Brandy. 'She's in New York,' I tell him. 'And it's the middle of the night. If I do anything to damage the gallery's reputation, that would be a career-limiting move … a real don't-come-Monday.'

I'm counting on two things. Not being able to contact Brandy quickly, and that when I do manage to get her – with, hopefully, just the two of us on the call – she'll say no.

'Damage? Hell, JJ,' says George, 'what you've done will put the gallery, *and* you, on the map.'

Which only makes me feel worse. I press on and say, 'Also, I don't have her number. It's in my phone – the one the goons smashed? When I get a new one … tomorrow, maybe? … I'll call her then. Okay?'

Petty's standing over at the window, looking out at the bay. 'Which kind of phone?'

'An iPhone something,' I tell him. If it was a camera, I'd know all the model details, but a phone's just a phone. Steve Jobs wouldn't want to hear me say that, but he's dead so it doesn't matter.

Petty's already on *his* phone. He stops talking to the person on the other end to say to me, 'We'll have a loaner here for you shortly.' Before he hangs up, I hear him say, 'And make it asap.' Then he gives Marshall one of those eyebrow raises – the glower that says *Come on, it's time. Tell her.*

Marshall, looking uneasy, points to the Quilty over the fireplace. 'That Torana,' he says. 'My first car was a Torana.'

So, now *he's* the one buying time? It's definitely not old cars that Petty wants him to raise with me, which he makes clear by saying, 'Boss,' and raising *both* eyebrows this time. 'She has to know at some point.'

'Know what?' I ask.

George gives an embarrassed cough, then tells me.

Even before he's finished, I'm sobbing, and I run off to the bathroom. It's becoming a habit, I know. I lock myself in there, crying my eyes out.

It was my stupid fucking *I wannabe Annie Leibovitz* videos … the ones of Winston I posted on TikTok!

From what the police found on the dead goon's phone, it was those videos that led the Farrellys to me and then to Lesley. It's what got her tortured and Hugh killed.

If I'd never posted them, Hugh would still be alive, and Lesley … Claude … wouldn't be on the run. It's all my fucking fault.

The bathroom's echoing with knocks on the door. I don't know how long it's been going on, but judging by how wet the tissue in my hand is, it's been a while.

'JJ, please come out.' It's George. 'I've made you a cup of tea.'

I get up from the toilet seat and go to the sink, splash water over my face, then pick up Lesley's towel and wonder, *Should I or shouldn't I*? Will they send it to the lab and find both of our DNA on it? Will that be a problem?

'JJ?'

I open the door. Winston leaps up at me. I pick him up and he licks my face. It turns out I didn't need the towel.

George has the grace to say nothing further about the videos, and neither do I. He breaks all the rules, and puts his arm gently around both me and Winston, and slowly guides me back to the living room. His embrace is warm and fatherly – or what I imagine that's like – and I fall apart in his arms.

He puts Winston down, holds me close and I blubber into his strong shoulder. He smells of laundry starch.

I find that strangely comforting.

76

George … he's definitely George now … passes me a teacup. I watch him put three teaspoons of sugar in his, and am instantly worrying about his health, like he's a friend not a cop. The three of us drink silently, except for Petty's slurping.

'Apart from the press conference … is there anything else?'

George's eyes look like he's scrolling down a mental checklist. 'In the interests of full disclosure, yes. The internal investigation … given Hugh's role and all—'

'Hugh didn't have a role,' I say quietly, drained. 'I dragged him into this,' I add, almost in a whisper.

'It's a formality, truly. When the desk jockeys back in Goulburn Street read my report, your dad will come up roses.' George's face goes red. I wonder why, then realise it's that I'll think of flowers on a grave, which, obviously, I have. He recovers quickly. 'At the presser, I'll be citing him as a hero.' Then he says, 'That way, the pen-pushers upstairs won't have any wriggle room.' Petty gives him a disapproving glance, but George stares him down and says, 'Petty, can you go get me some more milk from the fridge?'

Like Petty, I can see the milk jug on the coffee table in front of us is full, but he doesn't say anything, just picks it up and heads off to the kitchen.

'JJ, this isn't for Petty's ears, but I want you to know I've got your back. Hugh and I grew pretty close these past few years … after he stopped being such a prick … and I owe him. He saved my life three years ago.'

I don't know what to say, so just sit quietly.

Petty comes back in with the jug, filled to the brim. 'Shall I pour?'

'Changed my mind,' says George. 'Sorry.'

Petty looks at him, then at me, and back at him, like he's trying to suss out what's just happened between us, but all he says is, 'Fine.' He puts the jug down, spilling a slurp of milk on the coffee table glass. He does nothing about wiping it up, but says, 'Boss, the art. Tell her.'

Given the last time Petty pressed George to tell me something, I'm worried. My head's instantly filling up with nightmare scenes … burly constables stripping The Art off the walls, lugging it into the summer heat and tossing it all into the back of a van … the vehicle bumping along Sydney's potholed streets … it all being unloaded inside some dingy evidence locker full of bags of drugs that breathe acid into the air and etch it into the paint.

The FBI, Scotland Yard and Interpol would never do that. They have teams dedicated to art theft. But here? Local cops handling these works would be a debacle.

'Detective Inspector Marshall,' I say, going all formal, 'you and your people are not *moving* those works, let alone *touching* them.' I jump to my feet, congenital hesitancy peeling from me like the skin off a snake. 'It's a job for professionals.' I glare down at him from on high … high-ish.

Marshall and Petty exchange glances. I brace myself for a fight but Marshall takes out his phone again and says, 'What time is it in New York? We'll call your director and yank two weeds with one pull.'

The bastards are going to go over my head. 'You're wasting your time. You won't get her, and if you do, she'll say exactly what I said.'

'Relax. My commissioner doesn't want police hands anywhere near the art. If we damaged any, we'd never hear the end of it. This is what you gallery people do. What we need is a point person – someone we can trust to supervise the operation.'

I sit down again, relieved. 'Good. *Great.* Well, that's obviously Brandy … Brandy Edmunds.'

Then I realise he's laid a trap. He's tricked me into agreeing to call her now, and that way he can also get her to okay tomorrow's press conference.

Fuck!

77

I'm cornered, but since I don't have my phone, I don't have Brandy's mobile number. I tell Marshall to call the gallery and ask for Lily, who is her right hand. That number, I know off by heart, and give it to him.

He puts the phone on speaker and, when Lily answers and he makes his request, she grumbles, 'You do know it's two am in Manhattan?' We do, of course, but since it's the police, she still transfers us.

It's so noisy at Brandy's end – the phone's still on speaker – it's like she's on a float at a Mardi Gras parade, but it turns out it's a closing-night afterparty in a Broadway producer's apartment on Park Avenue. Brandy is obviously well connected, not that I'm surprised.

I mouth to Petty – because I'm sure George wouldn't have a clue – 'Is that Sarah Jessica Parker we can hear in the background?'

'Who?'

Brandy goes into a bedroom for some quiet. After she absorbs the shock of all the news, her immediate focus is on my mental health. I tell her I've already seen the social worker at the hospital.

'Not good enough,' Brandy says and adds she's texting Lily to line me up with a proper grief counsellor.

George interrupts with, 'You're right, Dr Edmunds.' Yes, Brandy has a PhD but I've got no idea how he knows that. 'Please hold off, though. I can get JJ the best help. Leave it to me. Please.'

She agrees, so George moves on to the topic of the transport and authentication process, but not in any way I expect. He says, 'You'll probably think this is a bit unorthodox, since JJ is a witness, but we would like her to be the gallery's point person with the police. Will that be a problem?'

It's a huge problem. For me. I expected him to be asking Brandy to be point person, or at least be asking for someone more senior than me. The only thing I've ever led at work was a tinned food drive for flood victims. 'What about Simon?' I suggest to Brandy. Simon Ives is my immediate boss. He's a decent guy, brilliant at his job and way more experienced than me.

'Simon will be thrilled if you'd do it,' she says, misunderstanding me.

'No,' I say. 'What I mean is, shouldn't *he* or *you* be the point person?'

'JJ, if Detective Inspector Marshall doesn't have an issue with it, neither do I. Heck, you've got the skill. And

Simon will support you. We all will. Plus, it was you who made the discovery. If the works turn out to be genuine, you leading the orchestra on this … it could be huge for your career.'

Yeah, I'm thinking, *if they all turn out to be just really good forgeries, my career will be toast.* But it's obvious that Brandy's not interested in debating it. She's already moved on, telling the detectives about the gallery's giant new vault, which was part of the recent upgrades. Steel walls half-a-metre thick, air conditioning, time locks, CCTV – more bells and whistles than Santa's sleigh. In fact, so many that Goldberg and I stopped listening during the walk-through briefing and started pulling faces at each other in the mirror-finished panels.

Brandy undertakes to call the heads of security and logistics so they can start planning the move and the storage. She'll also call our general counsel, to get her to work on upping our insurance with the State Treasury.

Finally, George gets to what I thought the call was really about – the 'presser'.

'It's your decision,' Brandy tells me, 'and no pressure, JJ, but it'll be a huge boost for the gallery if you'd do it.'

No pressure, indeed. 'I'll fall apart in front of cameras,' I tell them, but all that achieves is Brandy saying she'll text our head of communications to give me some media training. 'Stop,' I say. 'I'll do it, but no training. I won't need it because I won't be speaking.' I turn to George, 'I won't say a word, okay? I'll just stand there. Agreed?'

He does.

I might 'only' be standing there, but I know myself, and that I'll still need something to stop me falling apart.

There's a hack to de-stress before big events that Hillary

Clinton swears by in her audiobook: a few minutes of alternate-nostril breathing before you go in front of the cameras.

It works for her, so …

George hasn't finished, it seems. He wants to run Brandy and me through the security arrangements. Until the move, he's stationing four officers at the town house – the two I've seen at the front door but two more on the boardwalk on the bay side. Plus, he's got a further two officers watching the approaches from a blue-and-white parked on the street. They'll be in position 24/7, on six-hourly shift rotations. He wants to place an additional officer inside Brandy's apartment, to keep the roof garden above Lesley's place under surveillance. She agrees. If it's fine with her, it's fine with me – though I'm wondering if he wants the officer there to watch the roof or to watch over me.

George stands up with the phone, winks at Petty and says, 'I need one more minute with Brandy.' He goes into Lesley's study and closes the door.

'What's that about?' I ask Petty.

'Procedure.' He gives me one of those shrugs that I'm sure means *None of your business*. I don't like Petty but his name is perfect.

It's been way more than a minute when George comes back – enough time that Petty's been making fresh cups of tea.

We spend the next thirty minutes going over minor procedural things, none of which feel at all pressing. Almost the whole time, George and Petty are looking at their watches and at each other, like they're waiting for someone or expecting a call.

Finally, Petty gets up, gathers the crockery and takes it to the kitchen.

'We're off,' says George when he returns. I pick up Winston and we all head for the door.

'I should've asked before,' he says, 'but do you have a friend or relative who can come stay with you, for company?'

Apart from Goldberg, I don't really have any friends. And while he's close, he's not that close. 'I'm fine,' I tell him. 'I'll just go home to Brandy's. Your officer can keep me company.'

His phone lights up as we reach the doorway. He hands it to Petty, who takes it outside. George turns back to me. 'You could stay here, you know. Get used to the place.'

'Here?'

'It's *your* home now … unless we find out that Fontaine paid for it with the proceeds of crime.'

I hadn't forgotten about the sublease. I'm not an Elon Musk-type tycoon who might accept a $1.25-million gift the same way a normal person would a pair of socks. It's just that it hasn't sunk in yet that it's real. 'But,' I say, 'what if she did pay for it, you know, like you said … proceeds of crime?'

'It's possible, which is why I mentioned it, but it's got to be incredibly unlikely,' he says. 'What she did … faking her death and, creating a new identity … yes, that was all illegal, but hell, JJ, she did that to *stop* the Farrellys, not to *help* them. Besides, she was already stinking rich to start with. So my money's on you living here free and clear for the next five years.'

Just then, Petty walks back in.

George prompts, 'And?'

Petty's eyes are ablaze like he's got fireworks bursting behind them. He gives George a quick wink and hands him his phone.

Unlike Petty, his boss keeps a poker face that's really got me guessing. 'We'll need to sit down for this,' says George, and leads me back inside.

78

George places the phone on the coffee table and puts it on speaker. It's Brandy again, and either the afterparty's over or she's gone back to her hotel. She's spoken to all the relevant people back at the gallery. 'And, yes, Detective, they all know this whole thing is strictly embargoed until you say so.' The reason she's calling is to tell us about some other calls she's made.

Her first was to wake up the director of the Gardner Museum in Boston. 'Yes, at three am,' she says when I ask. 'We used to work together at MOMA. Besides, this is going to be huge, so we need to coordinate our announcements. Also, good news, JJ ... she's going to send over their chief paintings conservator.'

She mentions his name, and it's one I know. His

work restoring Titian's *The Rape of Europa* in 2020 was groundbreaking, and my boss Simon and I were lucky enough to hook into a live Zoom lecture he gave on it. We had to get up at 4 am, given the time difference, but it was all worth it when Simon got to ask a question.

'They'll need him to sign off on the authentication, which will also dispose of the, er, conflict of interests,' Brandy says with a slight hitch in her voice.

I'm looking at the phone, perplexed, then look at George. The news that their conservator's coming is great but not such an earth-shattering revelation that I needed to sit down for it. 'What conflict?' I ask.

'JJ,' says Brandy, 'the Gardner director says if the works are genuine, their trustees will most likely pay you the reward. It's ten million.'

I knew that number from the museum's website, but never seriously imagined they'd pay it to me. So, it turns out George was right – I did need to be seated.

'That's the conflict right there. Their own expert coming solves that.'

Millions of butterflies are flying around inside my stomach. *Ten* million, to be exact.

Petty's been tapping his phone. 'That's around fifteen million in Aussie dollars,' he says, which makes me sink even deeper into the sofa cushions.

Brandy tells us she's also spoken to the head of the Paris Museum of Modern Art, but I stop paying attention.

George shakes my arm, points to the phone and says, 'Will the Paris people look at a reward for JJ too?' It's a question I could never ask myself.

'Hard to say. They don't have a budget for one,' she says. 'The French police closed the case years ago, after one of the crooks gave sworn evidence at the trial that he panicked, destroyed all five paintings and dumped their remains in a trash bin outside his shop. No one ever expected they'd be found.'

'Until now,' says Petty, sitting up straight and cocky, like it was him who found them.

'I'll be calling the FBI's art squad in the morning,' Brandy says. 'They'll put me in touch with the private collectors who own the other four works.'

'And ... ah ... what about *Six Sunflowers*?' I ask. 'Given its history and all. Is there a conflict there too?' My fingernails are digging deep into the sofa.

'We'll have to work on that,' says Brandy.

After she hangs up, I tell the cops what I meant by 'the history'. When I finish, George turns to me. He takes my hand, which is making me freak out again. 'What I'm about to tell you ... I'm telling you as a friend ... a friend of Hugh's, that is. Not as a cop, okay?'

'Oka-a-y?' What could he possibly say that's more momentous than getting a fifteen-million-dollar reward ... living rent-free for years in a harbourside mansion ... or me pissing my pants tomorrow in front of millions of people in the press conference he's got me into?

'You need some top-level legal advice, JJ. And I want you to get it before *any* of these pictures get taken off the walls.'

'What?' I'm stunned. 'Why?' I ask, worried we're heading back to the whole *you're-under-arrest* thing.

'All this talk, you know, about conflicts of interest, it made me think of something. And I'm no lawyer, mind you, but the paintings ... they've been lost for decades, stolen or allegedly destroyed ... and you found them, kind of. You brought them to light, at least. And they've been gifted to you—'

'By someone who nicked them herself—' says Petty.

'But her motives —' I start to say.

'Sure,' says George, 'but the point is … after all that, what if *you* own them? Or some of them? *Finders, keepers,* and all that.'

79

A week later

It's been a blur … tears while grieving with Kate and Vini … being a deer in the headlights at the presser and, no, Hillary's alternate-nostril breathing didn't help but I didn't piss my pants either … tortuous meetings with lawyers … more tears when Leasing Paul comes over and gets me to officially sign the sublease … freaking out every time I see my name or photo staring back at me from a newspaper or a screen … liaising with gallery colleagues about The Art … the endless and exhausting sleepless nights …

And then there's Caroline, the shrink George put me on to. I wouldn't have thought it possible, but she's kinder and gentler than Maggie Bloom in *A Million Little Things*. She's also George's wife. Talk about conflicts of interest!

My first two sessions with Caroline were great. The whole time I sat on her couch, I felt like she was a warm hug in human form. And her chocolate brownies are to die for. At the end of the second session, she told me George has been referring people to her for years, including some of his workmates. Something about the way she mentioned that made me wonder if Hugh had been one of them, so I blurted out the question.

'I can't say,' she said, 'client confidentiality and all, but you should know that George and Hugh got pretty close.'

I suppose you would get close to a person if, like George told me, they saved your life. I wanted to ask Caroline about it, but didn't. I haven't asked George either. I've got a feeling he won't want to talk about it.

I'm on instructions, from George, to keep away from my Redfern studio apartment for at least another week. One of the TV current affairs programs is calling it the 'Billion-Dollar Bedsit' and reporters are still camped outside. The area outside Lesley's is also crawling with media people. He reckons it'll all die down in a week or so. Fortunately, no one's heard I'm staying at Brandy's.

She had been talking about coming back early, given the circumstances. That would've dumped me right into the talons of the media vultures if the gallery's chairman hadn't canned the idea. 'Vacation downtime is too precious,' is how he framed it in his Christmas video to all the staff. He didn't specifically mention the Covid Christmases when no one could visit relatives and friends, but we all knew what he meant. So, Brandy gets her White Christmas and I'm getting to hide out.

Her being away is partly why we're delaying the authentication process till the second week in January. The other reason is that we have to. The lawyers and insurers are fighting tooth and nail over the question George insisted I ask, *Who has legal title to the art?*

Truth is, I'll be fine with whatever answer they come up with. *Que sera, sera* and all that. On this issue, I'm the Doris Day of not caring.

Which brings me to today, my first morning of semi-normal. I haven't been in any kind of state to face the world until now, not even feeling up to taking Scottie and Winston for a walk. The nightshift cop George posted at Brandy's has been doing it for me after her morning substitute arrived.

But today I'm feeling like I *have* to get out, even if some media people are still lurking over at Lesley's. Through my window, I can see them gabbing, huddling over coffees. I hope they're buying them at Bruce's cafe.

I'm wearing a lightweight hoodie, trying to go incognito. Since yesterday, George has an extra cop outside the Finger Wharf, to tail me wherever I want to go. He's decked out to look like a homeless person, though he's the kind who's got a pistol shoved under the elastic of his tracky dacks.

As Scottie and Winston and I head towards the steps to the park, the dogs keep tumbling over each other and running through my legs, winding the leashes around them and trying to trip me. Ordinarily, I'd be laughing and mock scolding them with a finger shake and a *Settle down!* but that's not today. Laughing isn't coming naturally to me, not yet. Even smiling seems wrong after Hugh …

Barista Bruce is waving at us from across the road. With me well hidden under the hoodie, he must've recognised the dogs. He's holding his fingers up in the air … first one, then two, followed by a shoulder shrug that can only mean *Do I make one Lesley usual or two?*

I don't know how he could have missed all the news. Either that or he's being considerate, pretending nothing's happened, or he's helping me keep my cover. I hold my hand up, to bring my thumb and forefinger into a circle … *no coffees, thank you* … but even thinking about those coffees and chats brings a lump to my throat, so I turn and jerk the leashes in the opposite direction, and we head up the hill for solace.

At Mrs Macquaries Chair, I find it reassuring that the sign's still missing the apostrophe. How some things haven't changed. How not every single thing that's wrong actually matters. The dogs take it in that spirit. They still don't care.

I let them off their leashes, in breach of the rules on another sign, hoping the guy tailing me will stay in character and ignore it, which he does. The dogs bound off, rolling on the grass, chasing each other, smelling each other's bums, scaring the bejesus out of seagulls and turning them into perilous pooping machines that are skydiving my head.

For protection, I go to sit – brood, really – under the dark, spreading crown of a giant fig tree. I perch on one of its massive buttressing roots, which spreads overground like a giant's fingers. The expanse of Sydney Harbour is in front of me.

I know I should be overjoyed to be here. No sounds of gunshots, no sirens – just the dogs, the squawks of the seagulls and the breeze huffing in my ears. I'm not taped to a chair, not blindfolded, no duct tape over my eyes, no gun barrel boring into my temple. I'm numb, not dead.

But Hugh is dead. Lesley is in hiding, in fear of her life. And I'm lost.

The possibility I might be getting some of the Gardner Museum's reward only makes me feel worse, given the shell of guilt that's calcified over me. I know that if a normal person thought she had a fortune coming to her, she'd be dancing on the grass. Instead, I'm huddled under this tree feeling crushed, like I'm a fraud and a hypocrite.

Before all this, I'd have been stunned by the knockout panorama, snapping away on my Sony, posting shots on Instagram and videos on TikTok. Not today. Maybe not ever. I've closed my TikTok account. Instagram too. And Facebook. Not that anyone will notice.

I have night terrors about those Winston posts. How, if it wasn't for them, Hugh would be alive. Vini would still have a dad, and Kate a husband. Claude would still be Lesley, and wouldn't have been tortured. I'd still be a nobody with high hopes that will never be achieved, like becoming famous for snapping *the* shot of Russell Crowe.

Instead, I'm Andy Warhol's fifteen-minutes-famous. But the fifteen minutes is dragging on and on – for well over a week now – and it's not because of anything I've actually done. It's just for being a victim of a rotten accident of fate. The whole world knows my name – but, thankfully, not so much the VvG part – and my face is all over the media. Everyone's seen it, except Barista Bruce, apparently. The most popular media nickname for me is the 'Art Whisperer'.

Redfern neighbours keep telling the reporters camped outside the Billion-Dollar Bedsit what an outgoing, friendly person I am, always doing kind things for them – except I've never met a single one of them. When I used to walk home from Redfern station, I always kept my head down and didn't speak to a soul. I double-locked my door as soon as I got inside my studio where I'd sit alone, eating a microwave dinner or a tub of yoghurt in front of the TV.

Despite all the help and kindness I'm receiving, everything is still overwhelming.

Yes, *some* good has come out of it all. The Art's been found. That's huge. I've got a gorgeous stepbrother who, in time I hope, Kate will let me bond with. I'm getting a promotion at work. I had a quiet sunset drink with Leasing Paul last night on *Seaduction* – in the cockpit at the stern so the journos wouldn't spy us. I didn't stay long. He said he understood, and I think he does. Also, I got to wear my new Rabbitohs cap.

Despite the good, I can't erase the bad, or the glaring, unavoidable fact that all of that bad is down to my ugly pride and stupid ambition. If I'd simply accepted my place in the world, was satisfied with my lot as a boringly dependable art conservator who's biggest gamble in life was holding on to the germy train strap on my daily commute to work, if I'd never pictured myself enjoying a different future, if I'd never posted those images, if I'd never acted out my Veronica Mars fantasy, if I hadn't asked Hugh to help me … if, if, if.

There are so many *fucking* ifs, my brain is exploding.

Christmas is tomorrow. It's supposed to be a joyous day that's all about family. Yet all I've done is tear one apart.

80

Time cleans even the dirtiest water. I don't know who said that, or if anyone did. It just came to me. Or maybe it came from Caroline. Either way, it's true.

I'm not a hundred per cent back to my old self but, as it turns out, that's a blessing. The shell I spent my life hiding inside hasn't slipped off but, with Caroline's gentle prodding, it's opening up to possibilities ... new friendships ... even adventure, an experience that Old Me would only get to enjoy via Netflix.

The siege of speculation and pressure, even from inside the gallery organisation ... *are the works genuine? ... are they fakes? ... why don't you get started on this? ...* is stressful for sure, but isn't fussing me like it would have before, because

I've got so much support. There's Brandy and Simon at work, Goldberg too … and Caroline and George.

And Paul. Since I moved into Lesley's, he's kept popping in to check on this or that. Fuse boxes. Fire alarms. Light bulbs. Wi-fi. Water pressure. AC filters. Window seals. Tile grouting. Mostly after-hours, like he did that time with Lesley … Claude. In Redfern, I'd only ever seen my rental agent once – the time I melted the kitchen laminate.

I was imagining Paul's five-star service was just what residents in swanky buildings could expect. But when we were out on the terrace last night, under a glorious, blazing sunset, something happened. His eyes locked onto mine with a searching intensity that made me feel like if I even breathed, the moment would crumple like tissue paper. He asked if he could kiss me – actually asked – and he would have if Winston hadn't pooped on his shoe.

He's not a gold-digger, though. Caroline, who's become quite the confidante to me, was initially stressing about that – because of the reward I might be getting – until I explained how we were already getting pretty friendly before all of this.

And lately, even Kate has been reaching out. We've had a few coffees, and even she and Bruce have got onto first name terms. Yesterday, she asked me to accompany her and Vini to the playground. The little champ is still wearing a splint. He doesn't really need it, but his kindie friends have signed it so he loves it to bits. When I say 'signed', I mean crayon squiggles and stick figures. He rushed me over to the swing he fell off and told me, 'I didn't fwacture my arm. I only spwained it.'

Yesterday was a good day.

At work, we're constantly under what Brandy's calling *presser pressure*, so it hasn't helped that we've fallen two weeks behind our announced kick-off date for the authentication process. It's partly because of all the carry-on with the lawyers.

At first, the relentless media spotlight was intimidating. But with my friends and colleagues egging me on, helping me to focus on the most thrilling project I'll ever be involved with, while I'm not 'enjoying' the glare of publicity, I'm not hating it. Caroline's given me a few tricks, like imagining I'm an actor playing the 'me' I'd like to be. It seems to be working, because when George came by the gallery a couple of days ago to see Brandy, he stopped by the lab and, in a very fatherly way, told me that the woman he'd first met who spent most of her time cowering in a corner … well, I'm not her anymore.

Brandy, on the other hand, I doubt has ever been a cowerer. Ten days ago, after the lawyers had been tearing each other's eyes out for a month and we were still getting nowhere, she came up with a patch to let us get on with the job. Brandy put her foot down and got us all to sign a one-page 'Status Quo' agreement. It doesn't settle the question of 'who owns what?', but simply says that me delivering the works into the gallery's hands doesn't alter anyone's pre-existing rights, whoever they are and whatever their rights are.

Go Brandy.

*

So today, 30 January, was our launch. Day 1 of our authentication process, and what our head of communications has been tweeting as the 'Art Event of the Century'. Elon Musk even retweeted it!

We livestreamed the whole thing, and it was incredible.

And the livestreaming, it was my brainchild. Ahead of presenting the plan to Brandy, I'd spent a week holed up at Lesley's, typing out an entire script, artwork by artwork. I even dared to channel my inner Annie Leibovitz by including the camera directions.

At first I was reluctant to show the plan to Brandy, thinking she'd laugh at it and that we'd be better off leaving it all to our communications people. That was a bit of Old Me sneaking back into the room, I guess. But Caroline said that if I wouldn't show Brandy, she'd ask George to do it.

When I did, eventually, I fully expected Brandy to say *no* or scratch red lines through it. Instead, she took off her glasses and looked up at me, her eyes wide and face aglow, and gave me the best one-word response to anything I've ever gone out on a limb to propose, 'Perfect.'

*

The puns our comms people served up to the media for Day 1 are everywhere. The headline on the *Daily Telegraph*'s website is as corny as they come: *Sydney Gallery takes art world by 'Storm'*.

But it wasn't just the *Tele*. In the US, the *New York Times* led with: *Rembrandt 'storms' back: Van Gogh heir and Australian art museum make history*.

Yes, my ancestry is out there. And so are my middle names, courtesy of a so-called 'investigative reporter' which, in her case, I think is just another term for snoop.

But New Me doesn't mind. If anything, I might now be learning to like it.

Our aim in pushing for the two big Rembrandts – *Storm* and then *A Lady and Gentleman in Black* – as our Day 1 and Day 2 launch pads was to give the gallery the biggest bangs for our publicity bucks two days running.

The unique characteristics of each of these Rembrandts offered us the chance to give the public instant and hyper-visual gratification. My theory was that if in a single day's session, we could prove the authenticity of *Storm* – Rembrandt's only seascape, and did I say *Rembrandt!* – we'd have the world on the edge of its seat. If we managed the same outcome on Day 2, we might get the ratings of a reality TV show, except it would be about art.

The prep alone took over a week. We had ten staff fully committed to it, plus the film crew. We emptied the gallery's glistening new vault, moving its previous contents back to the old vault, shifted the relevant equipment from our restoration lab, and rested all twenty-three works from Lesley's on floating shelves that we'd magnet-fixed against the steel walls.

Day 1 of the livestream – *Storm Day*, as I'd titled it in the production notes – was so amazing, I get goosebumps just thinking about it.

Because of the time zones, we launched at 7 am Sydney time and, incredibly, did the whole thing in under an hour. Authentications can sometimes take days, or even weeks – but, like I said, *Storm* had some unique characteristics that I was hanging our chances of success on, hence the speed.

By noon, the views ramped up from two million to eleven million, and were still climbing. Only nine of those hits were mine. Six were Goldberg's.

Here are the highlights of the Day 1 recording ...

In silence, the camera pans across the gleaming steel walls and centres on *Storm*. Then it pulls back to reveal Brandy, Ed Gilmartin – the Gardner's chief conservator who's flown in from Boston – and me.

The three of us, Brandy in the middle, are dressed in black so we don't detract from the power of the works or the gravitas of the moment. We're all wearing scrub caps, like medicos wear in an operating theatre, except they're black too, and so are our powder-free nitrile gloves.

As if we'd coordinated it, which we didn't, our faces are tight and grim, and our hands clasped. In my case, Actress Me is suppressing a volcanic force building up inside Real Me – it's both exhilaration that we might get a *yes* and trepidation it could be a *no*.

The camera zooms in on Ed Gilmartin and tracks him as he moves away from us. There's now a barely perceptible heartbeat sound in the background. Like the *Storm* puns we fed to the media, it's corny, but it works.

Without a word, Ed – we're on first name terms already! – goes to a huge pine box with a label slapped over it, *Property of the Isabella Stewart Gardner Museum, Boston.* He pulls off the front panel – we'd already left it unscrewed, to save time – and reveals the large gilded frame that had travelled with him to Australia.

It's the first of the two empty frames he's brought. This one is the actual frame the thieves cut *Storm* out of when it was hanging in the museum. *Storm* is a huge work, and the frame is bigger, of course – almost as tall as Ed. Brandy goes over to him, and they each take a side and lift the frame onto the far right of three low-slung easels at the front of the vault.

The camera pans across to me. I'm standing in front of the *Storm* canvas, which is still framed how it was at Lesley's. Ed joins me, and we lift it off the wall and bring it to sit on the middle easel.

The camera zooms in until the work itself fills the screen, showing the intensity of the drama that Rembrandt intended. The surging, crashing waves are pushing the prow high into the air. The gale is ripping the sails, forcing the mast to lean dangerously to the right, and five desperate men struggle with the rigging. Yet, ahead of them, a golden light emerges out of the gloom, a promise of calm seas. Our eyes are drawn downwards into the darkness, where we see Jesus preaching calm to eight others. One of them, with Rembrandt's face, is throwing up over the side.

A moment later, the camera pulls back to show Brandy handing Ed a postal tube. He slides out its contents, a roll of photographic paper, which he takes over to the final easel. Then he unfurls it, to reveal a high-definition life-sized print of *Storm* that the Gardner produced in the 1970s.

As far as a viewer's concerned, we have two *Storms* sitting beside each other ... the print on the far left, and what we hope is the actual painting next to it. The Gardner's original *Storm* frame sits to their right, hopefully to be reunited with the precious charge that, all those decades ago, was brutally cut out of its frame with knives.

The heartbeat stops and Brandy's face appears in a square in the corner of the screen. 'You're looking at three pieces of a jigsaw that the art world has been desperate to put together since Sunday, the eighteenth of March 1990,' she says. 'In the early hours of that morning, two thieves dressed as police officers overpowered the security guards at the Isabella Stewart Gardner Museum in Boston, and brazenly committed the biggest art heist in modern history. They stole eleven paintings and two bronzes that experts believe are now worth between six hundred million and one billion dollars.

'That brazen crime has remained unsolved, and today, we at the Art Gallery of New South Wales, together with our friends from the Gardner Museum, are hoping we can solve it.'

81

'One of the masterpieces stolen from the Gardner was *Christ in the Storm on the Sea of Galilee*, painted by the Grand Master of the Golden Age, Rembrandt, in 1633. Today, we hope to prove that *this* work, right here in our vault, is that very painting.

'There are many tests that art experts can use to do that,' says Brandy. 'For a work that's been stolen but which was heavily studied and documented beforehand, we'll look for *sameness* ... for two or more matching features, complexities that really aren't possible to replicate. And with *Storm*, we're going to try for three of those tests. They're fairly quick too – some might say they're *short cuts* – but if just one of the three doesn't stack up, then this is a forgery. But if they all do ...

'For the first and second tests, we need to compare the painting to the high-definition print to the left,' and she explains that the Gardner took the photograph around fifteen years before *Storm* was stolen.

The camera zooms in on the print, to a small square of cloud above the head of the man at the prow, the one clinging to the jib.

'These tests we're about to do on *Storm* have not been rehearsed. You at home and we here at the gallery will be seeing the outcome simultaneously, and for the first time.'

This, we know, is a huge risk. Some of the trustees expressly counselled Brandy against it, wanting a dress rehearsal, but we held firm. We did no tests on any of the works after we brought them over from Lesley's. That's the compact we made with the public ... the guarantee we'd discover the truth ... fake or fact and win or lose ... at the same time they did.

I haven't shared with Brandy, or anyone, how I attempted a crude version of this first test back at Lesley's when I was with Hugh. Even if it goes right, which I'm sure it will, the other two could easily go wrong.

'In the cloud ... right here,' says Brandy, indicating with a pointer, 'we can see a network of hairline cracks.' After explaining what *craquelure* is, she continues, 'Every painting's *craquelure* is unique – like the fingerprint of a work. Allowing for further cracking from thirty-odd years of mistreatment by the thieves, if the *craquelure* in the *Storm* painting is markedly different from what we see in this print, we'll know it's a forgery. But if they're the same ...' and she leaves them hanging.

Then she continues, 'In the past, *craquelure* analysis might take an art expert hours – or more – but modern technology offers us many time-savers. We'll see one in just a moment.'

A second camera zeroes in on the exact same cloud spot on the painting. The two squares now sit side by side on-screen. The AV technician uses alpha-compositing, and increases the transparency of the right-hand image, the one from the actual painting. Then she moves it left until it sits *over* its cousin taken from the print. To a non-expert eye, every crack appears to line up.

'Dr Gilmartin,' says Brandy, 'please give us your verdict.'

Wearing a loupe – a pair of magnifying glasses set into eyepieces – he moves in front of a large screen mounted on one of the walls. It's displaying the image-on-image but blown up to almost a metre by a metre. He minutely examines the *craquelure*, millimetre by millimetre.

The vault is silent. No one apart from Ed is moving.

Eventually, he steps back and removes the loupe. He's smiling. 'The *craquelure* appears to be a match.'

Inside the steel walls of the vault, the applause and the hoots are deafening.

Now it's time for the second test. 'Next, we'll be comparing weave abrasion,' says Brandy. 'This is where the surface paint has worn thin and we can visibly detect the canvas's weave showing through.' I didn't do this test at Lesley's, so I'm as much in the dark as anyone.

'There,' says Brandy, pointing again. 'There, in the clouds … coming through the paint … hints of the threads of the canvas.' Again, the image from the painting is floated over the image from the print. 'It's not only the precise location of the threads we're looking for, both vertically and horizontally … what we call the warp and the weft,' says Brandy, 'it's their thickness and their number.'

Ed's got his loupe on. The tension in the vault – for me too this time – is immense.

'Another perfect match.'

'*Yes!*' shrieks Brandy, which was not in the script. 'Now, Dr Gilmartin, to our final test. If the painting passes this one, what does it mean?'

He smiles. 'Let's find out.'

This one is the clincher. The *craquelure* and thread tests are incredibly strong indicators, but with enough time and skill, and money, a forger might get close enough to fool at least some experts. What we're testing for next, however, is impossible to fake. It's the reason Ed brought *Storm*'s original frame with him – the one the Gardner has kept hanging on its wall ever since the thieves slit the canvas out of it.

When the crooks cut out the painting, they sliced the canvas right up to the edges of the frame. What they didn't get, of course, was the surplus canvas, those precious painted centimetres hidden beneath the frame.

Ahead of the show, Ed and I did a bit of prep work. We unscrewed the Gardner's empty frame from the underframe, which carries the slashed – and, until now, never-before-seen – remains of the original canvas. We left the frame in place, though, temporarily clamping it to the underframe. We did the same thing with the gilded frame of Lesley's *Storm*.

Now, on air, we undo the clamps one by one – Ed's working on the Gardner frame and I'm doing Lesley's. Each of us, in unison, lifts our golden frame and places it against a side wall.

The easel with the print is taken away.

Lesley's unframed *Storm* canvas sits on one of the two remaining easels. We've exposed the four outer edges of the canvas … and we can see the frays in the threads where they were slashed but where they've since been glued to a 'new' but unpainted undercanvas. The camera zooms in and pans down one of these ragged fringes.

On the other easel is what the Gardner's empty gilded frame has been hiding all these years … *Storm*'s original underframe with around three centimetres of the painted canvas's outside border still tacked to it, the inside edges as tattered as if the slashing and hacking only happened yesterday.

'Will these two remaining pieces of the puzzle fit together?' says Brandy. 'Will the ragged *outer* edges of this *Storm* painting match up with the frayed *inner* edges of what the thieves left behind?

'If the threads, the brushstrokes and the colours at these corresponding edges do match, there will be no question … no question … that this is the Gardner Museum's missing Rembrandt. If they don't …' and she leaves the sentence hanging.

Ed and I lift the original underframe and gently place it so that the gaping hole in its centre sits on top of Lesley's *Storm* canvas.

This is a huge moment. If what we're about to do shows that Lesley's *Storm* is a fake, it probably means that all her other paintings are fakes too, including *Six Sunflowers*.

While that would obviously be a massive letdown, what it won't be is an embarrassment. We've obviously discussed that possibility and both Brandy and the gallery's chairman were convinced that the risk is worth taking. We'll still have shone a bright spotlight on our museum, bringing it right to the centre of the global art map – for a shorter time than we'd hoped, obviously – and we'll have brought the stolen Gardner works back in the news, which might spur others to try to find them.

I hand Ed one of the two headbands I've taken off a side table. He puts his on. I put mine on. The headbands support what look like night-vision goggles but are high-precision binocular magnifying glasses with inbuilt cameras.

After I step up onto a footstool – Ed doesn't need one – we pull the glasses down over our eyes.

82

We begin scanning the top corners – me at the left one, Ed at the right. We're peering where the edges touch, and slowly, methodically, and pretty much in sync, we begin to work our way down the two sides.

No one before us – except for Rembrandt and his students, and restorers in past centuries – has ever seen these parts of the painting butting together.

So far, the threads and the colours on my side play into each other as they should – as if they were once joined up. The brushstrokes, too, are all made in the same directions, running off as you'd hope, whether into or off the edges.

My heart is racing and, personally, I could call this a *yes* right now, but it's not my call. I keep looking down my side, millimetre by millimetre, thread by thread, until I hear Ed let out a deep, moaning sigh, like he's been holding his breath for a year.

I remove my glasses, and see that he's still wearing his and, with his hands raised to his temples, he's mouthing *Oh. My. God.*

'Have we got a match?' Brandy asks.

Ed removes his glasses, mouth gaping, and he drops to the floor, his head in his hands. I go over and put my hand on his shoulder. I kneel down and whisper, 'I've got a match too.'

I put my ear near his mouth and hear, *I've waited for this forever.* He takes a deep breath and, as he gets to his feet, wipes a tear with the back of his sleeve, not giving a toss that millions of pairs of eyes have seen him crying. 'Bless you, JJ, bless you,' he says as he takes my hand and we turn to camera. On the silent count of three, as scripted, we both punch the air and shout, 'This is our Rembrandt!'

When Brandy speaks, I can hear a quiver in her voice. 'You've heard our experts … This *is* the Gardner's Rembrandt – painted in 1633 and missing since 1990.'

What's supposed to happen next is for the camera to zoom in on our second Rembrandt, *A Lady and Gentleman in Black*, and for Brandy to give the audience a taste of what's coming tomorrow.

We're going to X-ray the painting, hoping to reveal the ghostly image of the affluent couple's young son that, for some unknown reason, Rembrandt painted over, but which the Gardner discovered in the 1970s, when they X-rayed the work.

Instead, Brandy goes off script.

'What we've all just watched is an incredible moment in art history. But behind the art are stories,' she says. 'Behind the art we're specifically investigating in our series, the stories are of war and crime and, very recently, deep personal tragedy.'

I see the camera shift to me. I'd like to shrink myself into a single pixel and disappear, but she's cornered me. I bow my head, so the eighteen million people currently watching can't see my eyes.

'To extract these works from the clutches of violent criminals, the woman you see on-screen, JJ Jego, a talented and committed conservator here at the Art Gallery of New South Wales, literally risked her life … and her father Hugh Jego, a courageous detective, lost his. Without these two brave souls, the world may never have seen this extraordinary work by Rembrandt again.'

83

For the next couple of months, it's like I'm in an alternate universe. It's not my notoriety – I've learned to live with that – it's the continuing privilege of being in the presence of these twenty-three works. From the Gardner, three Rembrandts, a Vermeer, a Manet, five Degas, a Flinck, and two bronzes. From the Paris MAM, a Picasso, Matisse, Braque, Léger and Modigliani. And the four stolen from private collectors: a Francis Bacon, Lucian Freud, Renoir and Turner. And the most thrilling of all – to me, anyway – is the one whose authentication we're holding for last, *Six Sunflowers*.

Spending all this time with these works, examining the brushstrokes and stepping back to visualise each artist working on them, and all the while being recorded, knowing that the world is watching … that feeling is, well, it's transcendent.

It's a sensation Old Me never expected to experience, let alone relish, even in my wildest dreams.

While the specifics of the two big Rembrandts gave us short cuts, for most of the others we've been conducting virtual body scans, together with microsampling, and an array of non-invasive spectroscopic techniques: ultra-violet, infra-red, laser, visible light and X-ray.

As a result, these works are taking much longer to verify. To keep up the interest in our livestream series, we've been putting together daily ten-minute videos of the highlights, which … drum roll … Brandy asked me to narrate.

The first-day hits for each of the highlights have *always* headed towards twenty million. The Picasso one is the most popular so far, at a whopping 48 million.

After the Gardner's conservator flew home to Boston – and, yes, he authenticated all thirteen of their works – I've been the one calling out *It's genuine!* It's an unbelievable rush each time, like taking drugs. Not that I'd know, outside of my hospital stay.

Brandy's grin never leaves her face. Visitor numbers to the gallery are booming. Donations are pouring in from all over the world, including six-figure sums from people she's never heard of. Our annual conservation workshops scheduled for June, July and August – which normally have minuscule attendances – were sold out in under three minutes, and we had to schedule an extra twenty-five sessions to meet the demand.

Keeping *Six* – our working shorthand for *Six Sunflowers* – for last was Brandy's idea. My original plan had us doing it straight after the two Rembrandts, but when she saw the impact our 'show' was having, she decided that building up to it would give us the biggest finish. The suspense has been killing me. Seeing *Six* on the wall of the vault every day and not knowing … it's driving me nuts.

Plus, there's *The Lost Van Gogh – Fact or Fake*, the global publicity campaign the gallery has mounted. As we declare each of the other works to be genuine, the interest in *Six* – a work that isn't even supposed to exist – is electric, and it's radiating out to the five museums with other *Sunflowers*. In Amsterdam, London, Munich, Philadelphia and Tokyo, they've got lines of people snaking from the museums' doors, down the steps, along the streets and around the blocks. I've seen at least fifteen YouTube clips of queue fights. And it's *winter* in all those cities!

Brandy's invited a renowned expert to fly out for the authentication of *Six* – Helga Vos, the head conservator at Amsterdam's Van Gogh Museum. I met her on both my visits there.

Helga's brought with her a huge database of analytical information about the various *Sunflowers* that her museum and the four others have collected. Her kitbag's a VvG conservator's dream … computer analyses of the five other canvases … spectrographic images of the exact colours VvG used on them, like geranium lake – a red – and chrome yellow … an image library of fingerprints found on several VvG works so we can compare them with the one I'd found. They've even got a hair – a red one.

The DNA on that strand might also answer our family's questions, but I've decided not to raise that unless *Six* gets a thumbs up.

The day after Helga flies in from Amsterdam, Brandy calls Simon and me down to the cavernous underground Oil Tank Gallery in our new wing.

Since the livestreams started, Simon, who's originally from the north of England and speaks like Ned Stark in *Game of Thrones*, has been coming to work dressed like the classic Oxford academic, in a tweed jacket with leather elbow patches, corduroy slacks and suede shoes he insists on calling desert boots.

When we get down to the Oil Tank, we see Helga's already there, staring at a huge video of a pink elephant that's eating a croissant while watching *The Block* on an ancient black-and-white TV. The work's called *You're Dreamin'* and, personally, I think the curator who put it there is the one who's dreaming.

Like me, Helga's a small woman – though she looks even smaller in front of the elephant – but our similarities end there. For starters, she would *definitely* hurt a fly. She speaks sparingly, with each word a deadly weapon aimed precisely. With the same commanding posture, intense demeanour and shock of pitch-black hair I remember from Amsterdam, she comes across as a coiled spring of intellect. 'She'll have quite a bite,' Simon whispers to me as we approach her, and he's never met her before.

Brandy comes in, and takes the three of us over to a contemplation space where there's a couch and a low-slung table. She's got a red folder in her hand, which she drops onto the table with a *clunk*. As she signals us all to sit, she holds my gaze. 'JJ, I've asked Helga to deliver the verdict on *Six*.'

I'm floored. I'd thought she'd come here to help and give extra reassurance. 'But, Brandy, this is what I've –

what *we've* – been building up to. No offence to Helga, but are you unhappy with the job I've been doing?'

'No, I'm ecstatic, JJ.'

'But *Six* means the most to me.'

'Which is precisely the point. Your family connection and all.'

'Unproven,' says Helga brusquely.

Brandy coughs, raises an eyebrow at Helga and continues, 'JJ, with our findings on the first twenty-two works alone, your name's already carved into the walls of the Art History Hall of Fame but if *Six* is also genuine—'

'That,' says Helga, softening for some reason, 'will be the most important art find of the past century.'

'Which means,' says Brandy, 'we have to be scrupulous in protecting against bias.'

'I'd *never*—'

'I know that. Our trustees know that—'

'I know it too,' says Helga, surprising me.

'But we have to counter even the suspicion of bias. There's also the legal thing.'

'What legal thing?'

Lily comes over. She's carrying a tray with Brandy's turquoise cast-iron teapot and four porcelain cups so fine you can almost see through them. We're silent while Lily pours. The peppermint fumes are making my eyes water.

'Please don't get upset, JJ.'

'It's the tea,' Simon tells her, holding up his cup. 'Peppermint always does that to JJ.' I can tell he's not completely sure it's the tea – and it isn't.

Brandy flips open the red folder and picks up the letter inside it. 'This is a draft opinion from the gallery's lawyers. It's a draft because they're still waiting for some confirmations from Japan. Here's the thing, JJ. It's not beyond dispute but *Six* may well belong to you.'

'*Holy fuck!*' says Simon, leaping out of his seat and accidentally flinging the tea and Brandy's precious cup to the concrete floor. 'Oh, hell. Sorry!' he cries out, blushing, immediately bending down to pick up the pieces.

'Simon, sit. Forget about it. The cups are from IKEA.'

Right at the start, George told me it was possible *Six* could belong to me, but I thought it was ridiculous. When the legal advice came in about the Gardner works – that the museum still owned them – it was entirely unsurprising to me. I assumed similar logic would apply to all the others, namely that a work's last rightful owner – or their estates – would be entitled to get it back.

'*Six* is different,' says Brandy. 'The enormous passage of time ... 1945 to now ... the statute of limitations in Japan ... the old *possession is nine-tenths of the law* thing, which is apparently a real legal thing in a number of jurisdictions, but with some Latin name. Importantly, there are also arguments that the Yakuza didn't *steal* the painting from Koyata Yamamoto, the owner. One explanation is they were entitled to take it because he owed them money – *allegedly* owed them – and he'd given them some kind of security over it, like a mortgage or something. The second is that when he abandoned his house, he also legally abandoned its contents, including the painting, so whoever took it – in this case, the Yakuza – could keep it. They're both incredibly fraught arguments morally, in my opinion, but that's what the lawyers are saying.'

'If all that's true – which, surely, it's not – wouldn't it mean that it's the Farrellys who own *Six* now?'

'Apparently, they're doing a plea bargain, or whatever it's called, and Scotland Yard say part of that deal is that they're giving up all rights over the artworks.'

Simon says what I'm thinking, 'The lawyers are saying JJ might *actually* own *Six*, a painting worth—'

'Zillions. Correct. Here, JJ, do you want to have a read?' She hands me the letter but I push it back. Ordinary writing is bad enough but a screed full of legal mumbo jumbo … forget it.

'Won't Yamamoto-san's heirs have something to say about this?' I ask. 'I read that there's a granddaughter—'

'The Otsuka Museum,' says Helga. She's turning out to be one of the only other people in the world who knows as much *Sunflowers* minutiae as I do, and maybe more. In response to the quizzical look on Brandy's face, Helga continues, 'After Martin Bailey turned up with *Six*'s orange-frame print, the Otsuka got a ceramic reproduction crafted and unveiled it a year later. The granddaughter was there.'

I look at Helga, then back at Brandy. 'Have the lawyers contacted her?'

Brandy flicks through the letter. 'No.'

'Or the relatives' lawyers?'

'Also no.'

'Then I want them to do that.'

'Of course,' she says. 'Still, the point as of now, JJ, is that they're telling us you seem to be the person who can benefit the most from *Six* being genuine … So, you can't be the one who confirms it—'

'It's a conflict of interest. I get it. So, it's down to Helga,' I say, giving her a weak smile.

'Precisely. You can't be anywhere near it.'

'Really? Me, the person who risked ... you know ... I can't be involved ... at all?'

'You can't even be in the vault. I'm so sorry, JJ.'

I stand. I'm shaking, I can't help it. I manage to step over the broken porcelain and walk out.

I ignore the elephant.

84

Six Sunflowers – 16 March

It's the first time the staff and film crew see *Six* front and centre inside the vault, with absolutely nothing around it. Their mouths are gaping, and at home – Lesley's place – I'm hearing a lot of *Dazzlings!* and *Wows!* At least I've got access to the feed before we go live to the public.

The staff have moved all the other works to our old vault. With the completely black backdrop I suggested, they're presenting *Six* like a lone star twinkling out of an inky night sky. Hundreds of metres of matte black fabric are cloaking the vault's steel walls and concrete floor. Helga is dressed in black too, but it's her sole concession to our aesthetic.

I'd seen *Six* at Lesley's, of course, but the way it's presented now – even though I'm not there physically – speaks to me in an unexpected way.

Most people see the *Sunflowers* works quite superficially, as gorgeously rich and startlingly cheery still lifes of giant flowers, symbols of welcome and friendship. They've been told VvG painted them to brighten up the bedroom he was preparing for Paul Gauguin's stay in the Yellow House in Arles.

While that's true, the *Sunflowers* are more than that. At one level, they're VvG's homage, as a lesser-known artist, to a mentor. It's a pledge that, like the sunflower that follows the path of the sun, VvG will follow Gauguin's lead.

With the spiky petals falling off, and the orange seed heads dying, many see *Six* as a *memento mori*, a work that's meant to remind us our time on this earth is limited, and that, like these flowers, we're all going to die.

But for me, it's like a message from my supposed forebear that's perfect for New Me:

Life is short, so live it to the full.

85

Maghaberry Prison, Belfast

Not so long ago, Britain's chief inspector of prisons called Maghaberry 'the most dangerous prison I've been to'. He said it was a place where 'criminal rule is commonplace'.

A lot has changed since then, but some things have not. The day the cell door first clanked shut behind Niall Farrelly, he quickly found the two burner phones he'd prearranged – one to use and one to trade – and an iPad. They weren't hidden. They didn't need to be. Inside Maghaberry, Niall was royalty.

Next to the phones were two bottles of Bushmills Red Bush, his favourite local whiskey. Beside them, in a box lined with plush blue satin, were two Belfast Crystal whiskey glasses engraved with the logo of his family company. Niall, a man who liked to look after his guests, had a reputation to preserve.

He went over to the bed, fluffed the pillow and smiled when he checked the label. It was ultra-premium Hungarian white goose down, 850 fill power, just as he'd requested.

'Nah, it's all good,' Niall tells Angel while he's resting his head on the pillow. 'The lawyers say me and Nessie are gettin' out in no time. Feckin' illegal search and seizure or some shite like that. Hey, what's all that noise I'm hearin'?'

'Cars,' says Angel, telling Niall he's taken a job – 'temporary,' he adds quickly – in the global security team for the Formula One Grand Prix. He's currently in Saudi Arabia, walking the pits.

Niall sits up and does a Google search on his iPad. 'Hey, Australia's next in the F1 calendar, right?'

'*Oui*, but it's *trop* far *pour moi*. I'm … how you say? … sitting that one out. Instead, I go back to Europe and work the preparation for the Italy event.'

'Change of plans, boyo. A trip to Australia courtesy of the F1 – that's exactly what you'll be doin'. Except, straight after that, you'll be takin' a bit of time off … they tell me it's a beautiful country … and you'll be doin' a wee job for the Farrellys while you're there.'

86

Sydney
16–29 March

To test *Six*, Helga's put together more tools than walk out of a Bunnings on a wet weekend.

But tools are one thing and the artisan wielding them is entirely another.

The verifications for the other twenty-two works have felt like a breeze. We've got the results and the audience numbers to prove it, and thousands of positive comments … *clear as a bell … easy to follow … no bullshit jargon … art made easy … JJ's a breath of fresh air.* (I almost left that last one out of the list I shot across to Brandy and our head of comms, until I remembered that I was New Me.)

Six is going to be different. The first minute of the first hour of Helga's first day on the job tells me she's going to give us an opaque mudslide. She starts off in a monotone, which I kind of expected, but she does get a bit livelier as she gets into the swing of it. That said, in the eight hours she takes to compare *Six*'s style and complexity with the voluminous data about VvG's other *Sunflowers* she's got stored in her head and on her computer – all of it fascinating to people like me – I'm watching the numbers, and the public are turning away in droves.

On Days 2 through 3, she moves on to describing the colours, drawing on extracts from the letters VvG wrote while he was working on the *Sunflowers* paintings. It's great stuff, really it is, but it could have been done in an hour.

While Helga's technically brilliant, no question, her clinical A, B, C approach and clipped explanations are losing us our audience. Hours of watching her purse her lips like she's constantly sucking the bitterest lemon juice up through a straw is dragging our numbers down into the single-digit millions.

Brandy's been pulling her hair out over it. Try as she might – and I know she's tried – she couldn't nudge Helga into speeding it up, or into letting Simon join in so it could be more conversational. Her one concession was to agree to run her authentication through the weekends too. No break days.

Helga spends Days 4, 5 and 6 scanning almost every square inch of *Six* with our various spectrometers, XRF, FTIR – which stands for Fourier Transform Infra-Red – and Raman. These are go-tos in art conservation because X-rays, infra-red and lasers are totally non-invasive and don't damage the work. And their latest software is brilliant, creating visual maps of the elements and compounds they find in the paints and overlaying them on an image of the actual painting.

Mounted on wheels, our XRF spectrometer is the big sister of the portable version I'd taken to use at Lesley's. Basically, it's a gun that shoots X-rays into the paint, creating an array of fluorescent energy 'sparks' for the machine to detect and classify. Each spark is a unique fingerprint of an inorganic element from the periodic table, like zinc, lead or mercury – elements that paint makers used back in the day to make particular colours. The other museums that own *Sunflowers* have done extensive XRF analyses on them, and Helga's brought these with her, to make comparisons.

When the Gardner's Ed Gilmartin and I were doing spectroscopic analysis on *The Concert*, we found what we were looking for quite quickly. For Vermeer's yellows, it was evidence of lead and tin. By VvG's time, 200 years after Vermeer, 'lead-tin yellow' had long gone out of use. So, if Helga doesn't find *chrome* in *Six's* yellows, we'll know it's a fake.

Except she does find it.

Similarly, for his brilliant blues, she's hoping for evidence of cobalt and aluminium. She finds them too. Likewise for the evidence of zinc in VvG's whites.

For the red, Helga's got our XRF looking for bromine as a marker of the geranium lake pigment we know VvG used, and she set our FTIR machine to check for aluminium and lead acetate, which the paint makers back then usually mixed into the pigment as a base.

And, yes, she found all of them.

Sadly, she used Day 7 for a recap that was completely unnecessary because Simon had already done one in the Day 6 highlights video.

During Day 8, though, I see that interest is picking up again. She's showing examples of the way VvG's colours shifted over time, even using her museum's *Unravel Van Gogh* app, the one I'd showed Hugh. She explains, pretty much the same way I did – but taking a lot longer – how and why VvG's yellows have browned, and how his reds and lilacs have faded.

At the end of Day 8, I pluck up the courage to phone her and suggest, 'Why not remove the gold frame tomorrow?'

Of course, I'm desperate to find out if the hint of orange I've previously seen beneath the frame's rebate is VvG's original frame. If it is, that will be huge. 'Even if the orange frame's not there—' I go to say, but she cuts me off.

'You don't think I know what I'm doing, JJ?'

Of course she knows. She knows better than I do.

'So, yes, JJ. If we find a strip of the lilac tablecloth under the frame that is not pale blue like the rest of the tablecloth but is *true* lilac because it's been protected from light, that will be very material.

'But we will get there when I want us to get there, okay?' says Helga. 'This is not a pageant I am putting on for the public, JJ. I have a reputation as a professional.'

After a pause, she adds, 'Short cuts are what you buy in a butcher shop.' Then Helga hangs up on me.

On Days 9 through 11, with the ugly frame still in place and hiding what I'm desperate to see, she focuses on VvG's brushstrokes. It's crucial work – of course it is – but I'm sure she's doing it to spite me.

What should be building to our climax is becoming as dull as *Half Past Dead*, one of the worst movies ever made. And Day 12, as it happens, is a complete bust. There's a technical glitch with the cameras, and it takes the whole day to fix it.

The unplanned free day seems to have made Helga more relaxed because Day 13 is different. Inexplicably, she gives Simon the honour of unscrewing the humungous gold frame. He's methodical but fast. That done, he goes back to the side, out of view, and two beefy technicians come in to lift off the frame.

They've hardly moved it when I hear Simon cry out, '*No!*'

The techos and Helga – and me at home – we all freeze.

She's standing between the artwork and the camera, so I can't see what's bothering Simon. He's now shrieking, '*I don't believe this!*' I see him running back into view. '*Lift it off … lift off the frame!*'

As nicely as possible, he pushes Helga out of the way. '*Move it sideways!*' he tells the techos. As they start shuffling to their left, what comes into view isn't the frameless canvas… it's *Six* with its original orange frame intact.

In an entirely out-of-character way, Simon is grabbing Helga and hugging her – and I'm literally dancing around Lesley's town house. Then, still holding her, he turns to camera and says, 'Van Gogh lovers, this amazing woman Helga Vos has just made more art history. All of us watching … we are the first people in over a century to see *Six* in *this* frame, the way Vincent van Gogh *wanted* us to see it.'

Day 14 is when the orange frame is carefully removed. That, too, is a stunner of a day – the bottom edge of *Six*, the strip of tablecloth that's been hidden from the light, is, indeed, the lilac we've been hoping for.

With everything else we've seen, Helga's as good as proved that this is the genuine *Six*.

But Helga being Helga, we're not done. 'Tomorrow,' she intones, 'we do the final tests. We will turn the work over, and remove the wooden backing, so we can see the verso completely unobstructed.'

She goes on to explain that this will be the clincher. I'm expecting her to say why, but she simply says, 'Until tomorrow.'

But she's right, it will be the clincher. For four reasons. The smells released for one. A century of enclosed air, an accumulation of dust and possibly moths.

Second, I'm hoping she'll find a number – 95 – pencilled somewhere on the back. This is the number that VvG's sister-in-law, Johanna van Gogh-Bonger allocated to *Six* in her inventory of all his works, what we in the art world call the 'Bonger List'.

Third will be the opportunity to do a canvas thread count, to compare the warp and weft with what researchers have found with other *Sunflowers*, since most of the canvases VvG painted when he was in Arles were cut from the same bolt of fabric.

And fourth, there's the wooden extensions of the canvas. Helga already noted the indentation on the front that I showed to Hugh. She did that on Day 4. But what she did that I couldn't, was compare it to a black-and-white photograph of *Six* I'd never seen, one she produced from an obscure catalogue printed in 1928. Tomorrow, when she removes the back board, we'll hopefully see those actual extensions.

Like we've said, tomorrow's the clincher.

87

I wake up on Day 15 with a blinding headache, throbbing head and tingling hands. I turn over to nudge Paul awake – yes, we've got to that point but, with everything else that's been going on, it hasn't really come up before now – and there's an aura of stars with a frightening black hole where the little freckle on his cheek should be. I've never had a migraine, but I'm guessing that's what this is. Either that or a brain tumour.

I had buckets of liquorice tea last night – Paul brought some over and I'd never had it before – so perhaps it's that. Or is it from months of sheer exhaustion? Or a sense of impending doom … the fear, despite all my hopes, that what Helga finds today will prove that Lesley's *Six* is *not* the real deal.

Winston leaps up onto the bed, but the yaps that are normally so cute are like dynamite blasts in an echo chamber. Paul takes him outside, brings me paracetamol, and tells me to stay in bed and keep my eyes shut.

I'm about to argue with him – wanting to tell him that today could be the best, or worst, day of my life and by the way, that it's the anniversary of VvG's birth – but even opening my mouth makes me feel nauseous.

He leaves the room again, this time to call a doctor, and I'm lying on my back, eyes closed, and fuming that this is happening to me on *Six*'s last day, our grand finale.

I'm there in the silent darkness for over an hour, and I'm not getting any better. At 7 am, the usual start time of the livestream, I sit up and try to watch from bed but it's killing me. Even listening to the audio with my eyes closed is impossible.

At 7.15 am, the doctor arrives – he's a mate of Paul's – and his first words are, 'It's not a brain tumour,' even though he hasn't examined me. 'First time anyone gets a migraine,' he says – though, to me, it's like he's shouting – 'they go check with Dr Google and get convinced they're going to die.'

'How do you know for sure it's not?' asks Paul, as angsty about his buddy's cavalier attitude as he knows I must be.

'If this works,' the doctor holds up a syringe, 'we'll know.' He gives me a jab of whatever. Paul asks him what it is, but by the time he answers, I've passed out.

'Are you okay?' It's Paul in a whisper, which is encouraging because for the first time today he doesn't sound like a tornado.

'Uh-huh.' I really am feeling fine. I push myself up onto the pillow, 'Looks like your Dr Know-all was right,' I say. 'Must've been a migraine.'

'You need to phone Brandy.'

'What I need, Paul, is a shower. What time is it?'

'Time to call Brandy.' He hands me my phone. 'Make the call.'

He's got a strange look on his face. I can't tell if it's one of those good-news-and-bad-news situations, or if it's all bad news. 'Helga found a problem, didn't she? It's not *Six*, after all. *Fuck, fuck, fuck!* After the huge build-up we gave *Six*, I'll be the biggest laughing stock in the—'

Paul takes the phone, holds it to my face to unlock it, and taps Brandy in my contacts. 'Here. Speak.'

'Brandy,' I start babbling, 'I'm so, so sorry—'

'JJ, shut the fuck up—'

I've never heard Brandy speak like this. My career's definitely over, I know it. 'I'll resign, Brandy. You don't have to fire—'

'No one's firing anybody. Just listen, okay? When Helga took off *Six*'s wooden backing, she found a sheet of paper stuck to the back. She lifted it off and there's an inscription under it. It's in Vincent's handwriting. It's one hundred per cent his. You know her, she's compared it against about a hundred of his bloody letters. It's dated too – on the day he shot himself.'

'What's it—?'

'JJ, it's a directive to his brother. To give *Six Sunflowers* …' She pauses like she's having a heart attack. 'He directed Theo to give *Six* to your fucking great-great-grandmother! In the note, he even writes Theo about the baby. This is incredible. We've just changed art history. And it's the proof your father always wanted.'

88

1 June

Dinner parties are for other people.
My favourite style of cooking? Not cooking.
My best party trick? Not going.

In Redfern, I didn't have a dinner table so much as a tray. I never got around to inviting even one person over to eat because they'd have to sit on my lap or my bed, and both choices were far too awkward.

It's not so much that I'm anti-social. I'm more pro-solitude.

So, tonight's dinner party is my first ever, and a big move for me, which means I'm breaking both my strict rules, see above. That said, I'm playing it safe. First, by cooking fettuccine alfredo – mac and cheese for adults – and, second, by inviting only my friends. That is, not just my close friends, my only friends. All six-and-a-half of them.

Lesley's dinner table – out of habit, I'm still calling this her place – is big enough for us to spread all around it, with room to stretch out our elbows. Not that we will. Or maybe Goldberg will. Like Old Me, he doesn't get out very often.

I'd been putting off asking everyone over until Kate – yes, Hugh's Kate – got sick of my dithering two weeks ago, drew a circle around today's date on the fridge calendar and said, 'If you don't invite them, I will.' She chose tonight because Vini had already circled tomorrow's date and, inside it, drawn stick figures of a plane and a flower.

Kate and Vini will be looking after Lesley's place while I'm gone. When the Bitcoin bandits put their apartment up for auction – and not even the offer of me paying them out from my reward could stop the sale – I asked them to move in, with me. It was the least I could do, and by then, we were seeing each other at least four times a week. After Kate got her promotion, she needed to work back quite a bit, so I started babysitting those nights. Kate, who is technically my stepmother yet barely older than me, has turned out to be a thousand times wiser and stronger than me. She's not my mother, of course, not even close, but she was obviously good for Hugh, the new Hugh, the Hugh I hardly got to spend any time with. And she's simply been great to me. And then there's Vini. He's the half in my six-and-a-half guests.

So, tonight, Kate and Vini will definitely be here since they're here already. Vini's spent the past hour giggling and squealing, and doing slideys up and down the hallway parquetry with Winston, until five minutes ago when, puffed, he climbed up onto Lesley's wing chair. The dog jumped up after him and plonked down on his lap. Vini's already fighting off sleep, with his head drooping and jerking back up repeatedly as he desperately tries to show Kate and me that he's awake enough to stay up for 'the party'.

My two lifesavers, George and Caroline, are coming.

Simon couldn't make it, but there's Goldberg, of course, and Brandy.

Goldberg's been texting me all day … *Will Brandy know who I am? … Do I call her boss/ma'am/Brandy/Dr Edmunds? … I'll be a square peg in a round hole … What if I just phone in sick? … Do I wear a tie? A suit?*

His last one, at 6.45 pm, was, *I think I'm having a heart attack. Not possible*, I texted back, *you don't have one.*

Brandy also texted this afternoon, asking if 'an old mate' who's back in town could drop by, just for a drink. How could I say no?

And there's Paul, of course.

It's an unusually warm night for early June, so we're having our drinks out on the terrace. It's Negronis all round. I supplied the gin, and Goldberg's brought the Campari and sweet vermouth.

Big news. Brandy's just asked Goldberg for a refill. He pulls me into the kitchen and he's doing one of those happy heel-click jumps. 'She actually *spoke* to me. To *me*, Jego.'

I hear the front door, and a moment later Paul comes into the kitchen – he's got his own key now … we deactivated Lesley's randomiser keypad thingy – and he gives me a kiss. 'Hi, Goldberg,' he says after.

Goldberg hands him a fresh cocktail. 'I take it your office towers are still standing in all their glorious excrescence?' He's not a fan of what passes as modern architecture in much of our city.

Paul smiles and slaps him on the back, 'Remind me not to hire you for our marketing department.' He takes a sip. 'Mmm. This is good. But you might be going a bit heavy on the Campari for … um … you know … your boss out there?' I'd told Paul about Goldberg's texts.

'Oh my God! Too much? Do you really think …?' Goldberg pours himself a small Negroni out of the shaker and takes a sip. 'I don't … It tastes …'

'It's fine,' I tell him. 'Paul's yanking your chain. Let's go back outside.'

Out on the terrace, as Brandy's taking her fresh Negroni from Goldberg, I think I catch her giving Paul a wink. Was it a wink, or did she get something in her eye? Then Paul winks back. That one is definitely a wink.

Old Me would never ask, but New Me does.

Before he can answer, the doorbell rings and before I can say I'll get it, Brandy says she will. 'That'll be my mate.' She hands her drink back to Goldberg and heads inside.

I elbow Paul. 'Hey. Again – what's with all the winking?'

I know him well enough now to realise what's coming and we say it together, 'I could tell you but I'd have to kill you.' He gives my arm an affectionate rub.

'Hey, you over there,' a gravelly voice calls from inside, from behind us. Brandy's friend, no doubt. 'I'm here to meet the new Annie Leibovitz. Hey, Red … is that you?'

What?

I turn around …

… and I lose it.

It's Russell Crowe.

He can call me Red all he likes.

89

Next morning, the sunrise rakes its fingers through my bedroom venetians, brushing golden stripes over Paul's stubble. *That bastard!* Which I mean in the nicest possible way. He didn't give even a hint of Brandy's bombshell last night. They were all in on it, Kate too. Even Goldberg, who normally spills secrets like an overfull Negroni. Well, Vini wasn't in on it, obviously.

Russell fucking Crowe ... in my home ... talking to me ... calling me Red, a name I used to hate when I was at school and now love.

I shake Paul.

'Mmph?' he says as he rubs his eyes. 'What?'

Up on one elbow, I shake him some more. 'Did Russell Crowe really ask me to do a shoot for him on his boat?'

'Nuh. You were dreaming.' He chuckles and rolls over. 'Go back to sleep.'

I can't. Apart from tingling all over with the thrill of Brandy getting me this amazing break, I've got a lot to squeeze into my day.

I've got to pack for my flight tonight, but that won't be hard. Despite needing to 'dress' for the various events in Boston and Paris, I'm only taking carry-on. That's at Brandy's urging. 'Live a little,' she told me. 'Buy your outfits over there.' I've got the feeling this advice was influenced, and not positively, by what I told her I was planning to wear for this afternoon's big event at the gallery.

'What's wrong with Kmart?' I asked her. 'I get all my clothes there.'

'It's wrong if you're the centre of attention,' she said, the *tut-tuts* silent but implicit in her voice. 'All the gallery's trustees are coming, and so are the premier and the state governor.' She handed me her personal credit card. 'Get something amazing.'

I did, but I didn't use her credit card. Paul lent me the money, which I'll pay back to him when I return from overseas. The Gardner's presenting me with a cheque for the reward at an event in Boston.

I decide on a kaftan. It's an off-the-shoulder by Camilla, in royal blue silk with a black animal print, and matching leggings. It's the most expensive ensemble I've ever bought, which isn't hard, since I've never owned an 'ensemble' before.

On George's advice, the same as he's always given, we won't be mentioning Lesley – as I mostly still call her to myself – in any of our speeches, so the kaftan's intended as a quiet homage to her and what she did for me. We've kept her out of everything – the media conferences, the livestreams, the interviews – because George was adamant that total silence about her was the only way to give her a chance of avoiding the Farrellys' retribution.

'The more we keep her in the shadows, the safer she'll be,' George said. 'The Farrellys are finished, but they still have friends out there with long memories and longer arms.'

'Should *I* be worried,' I ask him, 'given my role?'

He gives me a genial cuddle. 'Not when you've got me looking out for you.'

*

It's 4.30 pm. Brandy's ushered me into the anteroom ahead of us mingling with the invited guests who, by the way, include Kate, Vini, George, Caroline, Goldberg and Paul.

Vini's wearing a *Sunflowers* T-shirt, and when I last saw him and Kate, he was hugging a VvG crocheted doll she'd bought in the gallery's gift shop. The shop's groaning with VvG merchandise, and sales have been booming ever since the excitement over *Six*. Tea towels, prints, napkins, mugs, scarves, bracelets. Showing at least some respect, they don't have earrings on offer. But apart from that, you name it and the shop's got it.

The lawyers 'finalised' their opinion on all the artworks three weeks ago and, despite all that extra time, they were still hedging their bets, with so many 'views' that if it was a video, it would've broken YouTube.

Their most annoying view was a *non*-view about the ownership of *Six*. On the one hand, they said, VvG's inscription gave my side of the family a clear line of ownership and Theo's widow had no right to sell it. On the other hand, Koyata Yamamoto's family had a strong competing claim, because when he paid top dollar for it in 1920, he had no notice that there was a flaw in the title. Then, seemingly impossibly, they came up with a third 'hand'. The Yakuza taking possession of it in 1945 might have extinguished Yamamoto's rights, and since they transferred their right to the Farrellys, who, in turn, renounced it in their plea deal, it might again revert to me. It's clear as mud, right?

Somehow, this so-called 'opinion' leaked to the media, and speculation has been everywhere. *Australia–Japan legal fight looms over painting. Will she sell it? … Can she sell it? … Will she keep it? … Can she keep it?*

The most excruciating headline was in Melbourne's *Herald Sun*: *Van Gogh heir Australia's most eligible bachelorette.*

Paul laughed it off. I didn't.

Now Brandy takes my hand and fixes her eyes on mine. 'JJ, this is a huge decision. It's life changing. Are you absolutely sure?'

I've thought of little else lately, so I nod.

'It's not too late to change your mind. Does Kate know?'

'Of course she does.'

'Right, then. Let's go.'

*

In this room, we've created a mini temple to Vincent van Gogh. It's completely black except for muted lighting and *Six*, the single blaze of brilliance. It's 5 pm and we're ready to roll. Brandy introduces me and, after the applause dies down, I step up to the microphone. *Six* and a screen showing the gallery's logo are behind me.

The crowd is hushed, apart from chuckles coming from Vini as he runs around showing people his doll.

I start, aware that the screen behind me is now splitting into three windows. One shows Boston, where a small group is joining us at 3 am their time. Another's got a larger group in Paris, where it's 9 am. And the third has a similarly sized gathering in Tokyo, where it's a more respectable 4 pm.

I don't have any notes since I've been practising my speech for days in front of a mirror, and also for every spare minute I've had with Paul and Kate when they've been at home. Apart from Brandy and the gallery's chair, no one in the audience knows what we'll be announcing.

My eyes scan the crowd, and I begin, 'What do you see when you look at this extraordinary painting?' Paul gives me a thumbs up, and I see his lips are moving in sync with mine like he's my prompt.

'Is it a spray of flowers coming to the end of their days? A domestic still life? An exuberant splash of colour? Thick, luscious brushstrokes? Does it show an artist struggling with life? It's all of that. But what Vincent van Gogh *wanted* us to see, what he was expressing through paint, symbolised both a *gratitude* and a *lust* for life.'

'Long after *Six Sunflowers* left Van Gogh's hands, it travelled the globe … It had a life and, in 1945, it had what the world believed was a death. Yet, eight decades later, we're here to express gratitude to a hero who lost his life so this very painting could come back to life – as we can see it has today. I speak of my father, Hugh Jego.'

Vini squeals with laughter and playfully calls out, 'My papa!'

'There's also another family,' I tell the crowd, 'that all lovers of *Six Sunflowers* must express our collective gratitude to.' The Paris and Boston windows close, and the Tokyo one takes their places.

I turn and bow and, as her face starts to fill the screen, I introduce Koyata Yamamoto's great-great-granddaughter. In perfect English, the young woman explains what happened in 1945.

When she's finished, I pick up the story. 'With our two families' ties to this painting born out of love, deception, war, crime and tragedy, we've decided it should never be hidden again. So, we announce today that we are jointly placing *Six Sunflowers* on permanent loan *here* – to *this* museum, the Art Gallery of New South Wales.'

The applause is wild, and George and Caroline are high-fiving. Goldberg is beaming. Kate is bending down, explaining to Vini.

I hush the crowd with my hands, and Brandy steps up to the mic. 'Thank you, JJ. In gratitude for Hugh Jego's courage and Koyata Yamamoto's judgement in acquiring the painting – and, of course, his great loss – the gallery is dedicating this room *solely* to *Six Sunflowers*. From this day, its name will be ...' she pauses, and presses the remote in her hand, and a black cloth drops from across the top of the wall to reveal, in a stunning Van Gogh yellow font ... *The Hugh Jego and Koyata Yamamoto* Six Sunflowers *Gallery*.

Kate knew this was coming but, even so, is looking up at the signage open-mouthed.

Vini is using his VvG doll's hands to wipe the tears from his mother's eyes.

90

Paris
Ten days later

Whats not to love about tucking into breakfast at a Parisian sidewalk cafe in early summer? The exhaust stink of cars honking into the roundabout just metres away, the wafting tendrils of cigarette smoke from the *grande dame* at the table next to mine who's feeding pieces of her croissant to the tar-black poodle at her feet, the cheesy, hammy aroma of my *croque monsieur*, the fumes from my ginger tea, the pong of the waiter's armpits as he grunts and clatters my order onto the cracked, hand-painted table, and the rickety red-and-cream rattan chair wobbling under my bum. I love it all, every bit.

I feel like teenage me in Hugh's holiday videos when the little red light would come on and I'd give my stock

390

intro … *Here we are in Cessnock … Here we are in Byron … Here we are in Melbourne.* Except this time it's Paris, and there's no video, no Hugh, no Mum.

Thanks to rewatching a few episodes of *Emily in Paris* on the plane, I found this particular cafe and I'm wearing a rakish navy-blue beret I bought when I arrived two days ago. The MAM graciously offered me a minder to show me around Paris, but I've been sticking to Emily as my guide. The last thing I needed after the whirlwind the Gardner created around me in Boston was yet another well-meaning person hovering at my elbow, whispering in my ear, nudging me here, guiding me there. In that one week in Boston, I forced myself to smile more than the *Mona Lisa* has in five centuries.

The MAM's event is this evening and, while I'd planned on staying a few more days to soak in all the sights, I've been cramming in everything so that I can leave for home tomorrow. Truth is, I miss my gang – all of them – but mostly Vini. Him coming into my life was like finding a piece of a jigsaw that I didn't know was missing, and I can't wait to make one of these breakfast treats for him. *Croque monsieur* translates as crunch-mister – I looked it up.

My mouth's half full and my mind's in heaven when the waiter returns and puts a frothy cup of coffee in front of me, as well as a side of iced water with a zest of lemon. This time, it's me who grunts. I hold up my hand as he starts turning back to the kitchen. I'm chewing madly and don't want to spit my food out when I speak to him. 'Stop,' I say, '*s'il vous plaît. Je* didn't order *un café*,' and go to hand the coffee back to him. I decide I'll keep the water.

'*Mademoiselle, c'est votre* usual, *non?*'

'My usual?' I'm still holding the cup, confused.

'*Un verre d'eau glacée avec un zeste de citron et un double espresso dans une grande tasse, pas de lait, avec trois centimètres de mousse.*'

'What?'

He gives me one of those *Really?* stares and then translates. 'A double espresso, big cup, no milk, three centimetres of froth and, on the side, a glass of iced water with lemon zest. Your *amie* … your friend … she ordered it for you.'

Lesley? I mean, Claude? Here? I look around but don't see her anywhere. 'My friend. Where is she?'

'*Là-bas.* Over there.' He tilts his head towards another table but it's empty. 'Ah, that taxi,' he points. 'She is there.'

It's zipping away so fast, I can't see the passenger inside, and I'm too slow to take a snap with the camera I've got on the table.

I think about Claude a lot, mostly because of my guilt that we've never honoured her crucial role in everything we've achieved. If she hadn't abandoned her name, her career, risked her life and endured torture, the Farrellys would still be free, and still be funding their sordid operations with the art she helped us return to the world. She'd made laughing stocks out of the Farrellys in the global underworld, and done it virtually single-handedly. If there was one person they wanted dead, it was her and, according to George, even from inside prison they'd use any and every means they could to track her down.

So, for the entire unveiling event at the MAM, instead of soaking up the joy that's filling the hall, and responding to the backslaps and handshakes and kisses on the cheek, I'm completely preoccupied.

Why is Claude in Paris … is she still seriously ill … is she living here or did she travel here and turn up at breakfast just to let me know she's safe … what's she doing now … what's her new cover story and name … has she made any new friends?

So many questions.

Early on, when Paul and I started dating, he had a question about Claude – the same one Kate did. 'Why did she go to all that trouble? Why didn't she simply call the cops when the Farrellys first dragged her into it all?'

I answered him the same way I'd answered Kate. First, I pulled up on my phone the article about Félix Matthieu's dismembered torso being washed up on the beach at Cannes. 'The only way she could stop people who'd do something like that, and still get to live, was to make them think a rival gang had stolen the art, and to fake her death so they'd never think of looking for her. If it wasn't for my screw-up on TikTok …'

In the cab going back to my hotel, the lights of Paris whizzing by me, I'm still thinking about it all when my phone rings.

I see who it is and my mood lifts instantly. 'George, hi! I'm coming home early. I can't wait to see—'

'JJ, Vini's been taken.'

AUTHOR'S NOTE

Six Sunflowers, to me, is the most breathtaking of the *Sunflowers* that Vincent van Gogh painted in Arles, making its destruction in 1945 even more tragic. I hope my novel creates at least a spark of affection for it in my readers.

Also at the heart of *Framed* is my wish to help keep the story of the Gardner robbery alive, in the hope that someone, somewhere might one day reveal where the artworks truly are and see them returned to public exhibition.

A novel like this takes a lot of research. As well as extensive study into the relevant art, art history and art tech subjects, the crafting of this story has benefited from a huge amount of expert help and guidance from some very generous people, particularly art experts in Australia, the UK, Europe and the US.

That said, none of them should be taken to endorse the premise in *Framed*, and any technical details I've got wrong or any flourishes I've intentionally made for story-telling purposes rest entirely on my shoulders.

My thanks go to:

- The Art Gallery of New South Wales, and in particular paintings conservator, Simon Ives. A well-intentioned knock-off of Simon is JJ's boss in *Framed*. He – the real Simon – not only spent considerable time to educate me and helped rub many rough edges off my story, but he took me into the gallery's inner sanctum to experience for myself the wonder of the scientific gizmos that conservators like JJ use in their day jobs. Also Carolyn Murphy, the head of conservation, and Dr Michael Brand, the gallery's director. The name of Brandy

Edmunds, the gallery's director in *Framed*, is a tribute to Michael Brand and the late and great Edmund Capon. Finally, thanks to David Gonski AC, the president of the gallery's board of trustees, who is referred to in *Framed* as the 'chairman' only because I like the ring of it better.

• The Van Gogh Museum in Amsterdam, especially paintings conservator Oda van Maanen, who has been a most gracious fount of everything Van Gogh. If there was an important detail I needed, about paints and colours, about construction and more, she had it at her fingertips. Also museum director Emilie Gordenker, research associate Joost van der Hoeven for advice on the Bonger List, and Dr Louis van Tilborgh, an expert on thread count among other things, who is also a professor of art history at the University of Amsterdam. And there's more I've got from the Van Gogh Museum:

  – In Chapter 57, JJ explains the colour changes in *Six Sunflowers'* lilacs to Hugh by showing him the museum's fabulous app, *Unravel Van Gogh*. The app's online at: https://unravel.vangogh.com/en/story/37/the-colour-has-to-do-the-job-here

  – *Vincent van Gogh – the Letters*. A magnificent repository of the 902 surviving letters that Vincent van Gogh wrote or received during 1853–1890. The letters plus commentary and other resources are online at: https://vangoghletters.org/vg/

• Martin Bailey, renowned Van Gogh specialist and an investigative reporter for *The Art Newspaper* who, in 2013, not only tracked down the rare, orange-framed print of *Six Sunflowers* that's so meaningful to JJ, but he's written several books on Van Gogh that were a boon for me. Among them is *The Sunflowers are Mine: the Story of Van Gogh's Masterpiece.*

- Art experts – in the US and Italy – who've asked not to be named but who know who they are.
- Angus Mordant, irrepressible freelance photojournalist based in New York City. Without Angus's technical guidance and passion, JJ would've had zero hope of becoming the new Annie Leibovitz. Also photographer Jess Leonard for advice on lenses.
- QBE Insurance Group – where I was deputy chair until recently – for explaining the ins and outs of insurance when fine art is stolen. Thanks especially to Ryan Joseph in London, QBE's illuminating specialist on art insurance. Also Desmond Boughton, managing director of J. Safra Sarasin, London insurance brokers who specialise in fine art. Super yachts, too.
- Julian Radcliffe OBE, chairman of the Art Loss Register, the world's largest private database of lost, stolen and looted art.
- Sarah Dunn, nurse and niece, and once again my go-to for all things hospital-related.
- For help with idiom: Patricia Chandon-Piazza and Eric Grinbaum for French; Liam Devlin for Irish; Bazza McKenzie for Australian.

On page 15, JJ says that the book 'Van Gogh's Ear: The True Story' (Bernadette Murphy, Penguin Random House, 2016) is not the true story. While that's JJ speaking, not me, I have revelled in writing my alternative history.

A novel isn't just the product of an author's imagination. It benefits immeasurably from curation by the publisher, in my case Pantera Press. I'm very grateful to Kathy Hassett and Sarina Rowell for their sharp insight and editorial whizz-bangery, and Pam Dunne for proofreading; though the largely absent semi-colons are all mine. Thanks, too, to Kirsty van der Veer, rights manager Katy McEwen, and Kajal Narayan and Talie Gottlieb for marketing and publicity. Of course, Lucy Barrett and our wonderful sales force. For *Framed*'s cover design, Luke Causby. I love its striking visual impact, even though its dramatic licence gives the purist in me a bit of a flinch.

And, crucially, my huge thanks to the booksellers and readers who continue to support my work.

My gratitude, finally, to my family – Jenny, Ali and Marty – for so much, and, in Ali and Marty's cases, giving permission for Winston Jr and Scottie to play their parts in the story.

Framed also sheds some light on coercive control and psychological abuse. Hugh's early treatment of JJ and her mother has echoes of what I experienced when I was younger. For anyone in Australia in similar circumstances, several services offer help, including:

1800 Respect: 1800 737 732
Kids Helpline: 1800 551 800
MensLine Australia: 1300 789 978
Lifeline: 131 114
Beyond Blue: 1300 22 4636

As Leo Tolstoy perceptively wrote in *Anna Karenina*, 'All happy families are alike; each unhappy family is unhappy in its own way.'

ABOUT THE AUTHOR

John M. Green is the author of *Framed*, *Double Deal*, *The Tao Deception*, *The Trusted*, *Born to Run* and *Nowhere Man*.

He left his day job as a banker two years before the global financial crisis – enough of a lag so no one could accuse him of starting the whole mess! He wrote his first novel about it.

His childhood years roaming the back alleys of Sydney's infamous Kings Cross set the stage for his later careers, in law and finance. He became a partner in two major law firms and then an executive director in a leading investment bank.

His interests straddle writing, the arts, business and philanthropy: he is or has been a director of numerous organisations, listed and unlisted, including cyber-security, financial services, education, engineering, publishing and not-for-profits. He's been a Council Member of the National Library of Australia and a director of two publishing houses. He's also an aficionado of magic and mentalism.

He lives in Sydney with his wife, the sculptor Jenny Green.

'The real deal. John M. Green knows his way around a thriller.'

Michael Connelly

#1 *New York Times* bestselling author

PANTERA
PRESS

SPARKING
IMAGINATION,
CONVERSATION
& CHANGE

Who is marking St Jude's
patients for death?

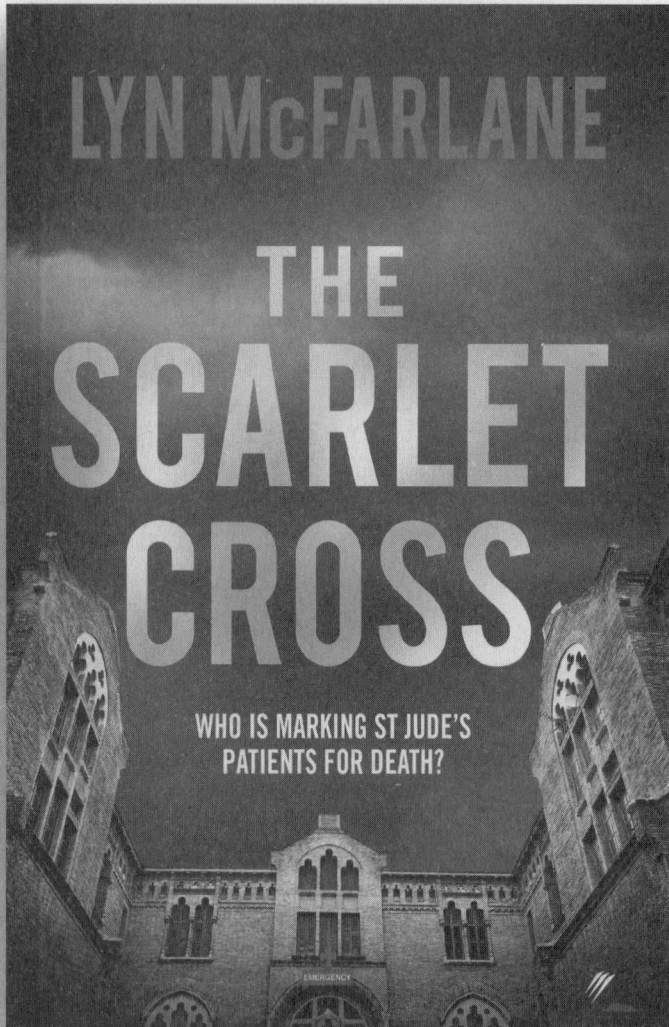

LYN McFARLANE

THE
SCARLET
CROSS

WHO IS MARKING ST JUDE'S
PATIENTS FOR DEATH?

PANTERA
PRESS

SPARKING
IMAGINATION,
CONVERSATION
& CHANGE

Deep down there's something we'd all kill for, isn't there?

THE
FALLBACK
D.L. HICKS

There's nothing more dangerous than a desperate man

PANTERA PRESS

SPARKING IMAGINATION, CONVERSATION & CHANGE